# WARCROSS

# WARCROSS

## MARIE LU

G. P. Putnam's Sons

G. P. Putnam's Sons
an imprint of Penguin Random House LLC
375 Hudson Street
New York, NY 10014

Copyright © 2017 by Xiwei Lu.

Library of Congress Cataloging-in-Publication Data is available upon request.
Printed in the United States of America.
ISBN 9780399547966

7   9   10   8   6

Design by Eileen Savage.
Text set in FreightTextPro.

For Kristin and Jen
Thank you for changing my life
and for being here all these years later

There's not a person in the world who hasn't heard of Hideo Tanaka, the young mastermind who invented Warcross when he was only thirteen. A global survey released today shows that a staggering 90 percent of people ages 12–30 now play on a regular basis, or at least once a week. This year's official Warcross Championships are expected to draw more than 200 million viewers. [ . . . ]

*Correction:*
*An earlier version of this story mistakenly described Hideo Tanaka as a millionaire. He is a billionaire.*

**—THE NEW YORK DIGEST**

# MANHATTAN

New York, New York

# 1

It's too damn cold of a day to be out on a hunt.

I shiver, tug my scarf up higher over my mouth, and wipe a few snowflakes from my lashes. Then I slam my boot down on my electric skateboard. The board is old and used, like everything else I own, its blue paint almost entirely scraped off to reveal cheap silver plastic underneath—but it's not dead yet, and when I push my heel down harder, it finally responds, jerking me forward as I squeeze between two rows of cars. My bright, rainbow-dyed hair whips across my face.

"Hey!" a driver yells as I maneuver past his car. I glance over my shoulder to see him waving a fist at me through his open window. "You almost clipped me!"

I just turn around and ignore him. Usually, I'm a nicer person than this—or, at least, I would have shouted an apology. But this morning, I'd woken up to a yellow paper taped to the door of my apartment, its words printed in the largest font you can imagine.

## 72 HOURS TO PAY OR VACATE

Translation: I'm almost three months behind on my rent. So, unless I can get my hands on $3,450, I'll be homeless and in the streets by the end of the week.

That'd put a damper on anyone's day.

My cheeks sting from the wind. The sky beyond the cut of skyscrapers is gray, turning grayer, and in a few hours this flurry of snow will become a steady fall. Cars jam the streets, a non-stop trail of brake lights and honking from here all the way to Times Square. The occasional scream of a traffic controller's whistle sounds above the chaos. The air is thick with the smell of exhaust, and steam billows from an open vent nearby. People swarm up and down the sidewalks. Students coming home from school are easy to spot, their backpacks and fat headphones dotting the crowds.

Technically, I should be one of them. This should have been my first year of college. But I started skipping classes after Dad died, and I dropped out entirely several years ago. (Okay, fine— technically, I was expelled. But I swear I would've quit anyway. More on that later.)

I look down at my phone again, my mind returning to the hunt. Two days ago, I had gotten the following text message:

New York Police Department ALERT!
Arrest warrant out for Martin Hamer.
Payment $5,000.

The police are so busy these days with the increasing crime in the streets that they don't have time to hunt for petty criminals on their own—petty criminals like Martin Hamer, who's wanted for gambling on Warcross, stealing money, and allegedly selling drugs to fund his bets. So, about once a week, the cops send out a message like this, a promise to pay anyone who can catch the criminal in question.

That's where I come in. I'm a bounty hunter, one of many in Manhattan, and I'm fighting to capture Martin Hamer before another hunter can.

Anyone who's ever fallen on hard times will understand the nearly constant stream of numbers that run through my mind. A month's rent in the worst apartment in New York: $1,150. A month's food: $180. Electricity and internet: $150. Boxes of macaroni, ramen, and Spam left in my pantry: 4. And so on. On top of that, I owe $3,450 in unpaid rent, and $6,000 in credit card debt.

The number of dollars left in my bank account: $13.

Not the normal things a girl my age worries about. I should be freaking out over exams. Turning in papers. Waking up on time.

But I haven't exactly had a normal adolescence.

Five thousand dollars is easily the largest bounty in months. For me, it might as well be all the money in the world. So, for the last two days, I've done nothing but track this guy. I've lost four bounties in a row this month. If I lose this one, too, I'm going to be in real trouble.

*Tourists always clogging up the streets*, I think as a detour forces me down a path right into Times Square, where I get stuck behind a cluster of auto-taxis jammed at a pedestrian walkway. I lean back on my board, pull myself to a halt, and start inching backward. As I go, I glance down at my phone again.

A couple of months ago, I'd succeeded in hacking into the main directory of Warcross players in New York and synced it all up to my phone's maps. It's not hard, not if you remember that everyone in the world is connected in some way to everyone else. It's just time-consuming. You worm your way into one account, then branch out to their friends, then *their* friends, and eventually, you're able to track the location of any player in New York City. Now I've finally managed to place my target's physical location, but my phone's a cracked, beat-up old thing, with an antique battery that's on its last legs. It keeps trying to sleep in order to save energy, and the screen is so dark I can barely see anything.

"Wake up," I mutter, squinting at the pixels.

Finally, the poor phone lets out a pitiful buzz, and the red location marker updates on my map.

I make my way out of the taxi jam and push my heel down on my board. It protests for a moment, but then it speeds me forward, a dot in a sea of moving humanity.

Once I reach Times Square, screens tower above me, surrounding me in a world of neon and sound. Every spring, the official Warcross Championships kick off with a huge ceremony, and two teams of top-ranking players compete in an all-stars opening round of Warcross. This year's opening ceremony happens tonight in Tokyo—so all the screens are Warcross-related today, showing a frenzied rotation of famous players, commercials, and footage of last year's highlights. Frankie Dena's latest, craziest music video plays on the side of one building. She's dressed like her Warcross avatar—in a limited edition suit and webbed glitter cape—and dancing with a bunch of businessmen in bright pink suits. Underneath the screen, a group of excited tourists stop to pose for photos with some guy dressed in fake Warcross gear.

Another screen features five of the superstar players competing in tonight's opening ceremony. Asher Wing. Kento Park. Jena MacNeil. Max Martin. Penn Wachowski. I crane my neck to admire them. Each one is dressed from head to toe in the hottest fashion of the season. They smile down at me, their mouths big enough to swallow the city, and as I look on, they all hold up cans of soda, declaring Coca-Cola their drink of choice during game season. A marquee of text scrolls below them:

## TOP WARCROSS PLAYERS ARRIVE IN TOKYO, POISED FOR WORLD DOMINATION

Then I'm through the intersection and cut onto a smaller road. My target's little red dot on my phone shifts again. It looks like he's turned onto Thirty-Eighth Street.

I squeeze my way through another few blocks of traffic before I finally arrive, pulling over along the curb beside a newsstand. The red location dot now hovers over the building in front of me, right above a café's door. I tug my scarf down and let out a sigh of relief. My breath fogs in the icy air. "Caught you," I whisper, allowing myself a smile as I think of the five-thousand-dollar bounty. I hop off my electric skateboard, pull out its straps, and swing it over my shoulder so that it bumps against my backpack. It's still warm from use, the heat of it seeping through my hoodie, and I arch my back to savor it.

As I pass the newsstand, I glimpse the magazine covers. I have a habit of checking them out, searching for coverage of my favorite person. There's always something. Sure enough, one of the magazines features him prominently: a tall young man lounging in an office, dressed in dark trousers and a crisp collar shirt, sleeves casually rolled up to his elbows, his face obscured by shadows. Below him is the logo for Henka Games, Warcross's parent studio. I stop to read the headline.

## HIDEO TANAKA TURNS 21

*INSIDE THE PRIVATE LIFE OF THE WARCROSS CREATOR*

My heart skips a familiar beat at my idol's name. Too bad there's no time to stop and flip through the magazine. Maybe later. I reluctantly turn away, adjust my backpack and board higher on my shoulders, and pull up my hood to cover my head. The glass windows I pass reflect a distorted vision of myself—face elongated, dark jeans stretched too long, black gloves, beat-up boots, faded red scarf wrapped around my black hoodie. My rainbow-colored hair spills out from underneath my hood. I try to imagine this reflected girl printed on the cover of a magazine.

*Don't be stupid.* I push the ridiculous thought away as I head toward the café's entrance, shifting my thoughts instead to the running checklist of tools in my backpack.

1. Handcuffs
2. Cable launcher
3. Steel-tipped gloves
4. Phone
5. Change of clothes
6. Stun gun
7. Book

On one of my first hunts, my target threw up all over me after I used my stun gun (#6) on him. I started bringing a change of clothes (#5) after that. Two targets have managed to bite me, so after a few tetanus shots, I added the gloves (#3). The cable launcher (#2) is for getting to hard-to-reach places and catching hard-to-reach people. My phone (#4) is my portable hacking assistant. Handcuffs (#1) are because, well, obviously.

And the book (#7) is for whenever the hunt involves a lot of waiting around. Entertainment that won't eat up my batteries is always worth bringing.

Now I step into the café, soak in the warmth, and check my phone again. Customers are lined up along a counter displaying pastries, waiting for one of the four auto-cashiers to open. Decorative bookshelves line the walls. A smattering of students and tourists sit at the tables. When I point my phone's camera at them, I can see their names hovering over their heads, meaning none of them have set themselves on Private. Maybe my target isn't on this floor.

I wander past the shelves, my attention shifting from table to table. Most people never really observe their surroundings; ask anyone what the person sitting nearby was wearing, and chances are good that they can't tell you. But I can. I can recite to you the outfits and demeanor of every person in that coffee line, can tell you exactly how many people are sitting at each table, the precise way someone's shoulders hunch just a little too much, the two people sitting side by side who never say a word, the guy who is careful not to make eye contact with anyone else. I can take in a scene like a photographer might take in a landscape—relax my eyes, analyze the full view all at once, search for the point of interest, and take a mental snapshot to remember the whole thing.

I look for the break in the pattern, the nail that protrudes.

My gaze pauses on a cluster of four boys reading on the couches. I watch them for a while, waiting for signs of conversation or the hint of notes being passed by hand or phone. Nothing. My attention goes to the stairs leading to the second floor. No doubt other hunters are closing in on this target, too—I have to get to him before anyone else does. My steps quicken as I head up.

No one is here, or so it seems. But then I notice the faint sound of two voices at a table in a far corner, tucked behind a pair of bookshelves that make them almost impossible to see from the stairs. I move in closer on silent feet, then peek through the shelves.

A woman is seated at the table, her nose buried in a book. A man stands over her, nervously shuffling his feet. I hold up my phone. Sure enough, both of them are set to Private.

I slip to the side of the wall so that they can't see me, and listen closely.

"I don't have until tomorrow night," the man is saying.

"Sorry," the woman replies. "But there's not much I can do. My boss won't release that kind of money to you without taking extra security measures, not when the police have an arrest warrant for you."

"You *promised* me."

"And I'm *sorry,* sir." The woman's voice is calm and cynical, like she's had to say this countless times before. "It's game season. The authorities are on high alert."

"I have *three hundred thousand notes* with you. Do you have any idea what that's exchanging for?"

"Yes. It's my job to know," the woman answers in the driest voice I've ever heard.

*Three hundred thousand notes.* That's about two hundred thousand dollars, at the current exchange rate. High roller, this one. Gambling on Warcross is illegal in the United States; it's one of the many laws the government has recently passed in a desperate attempt to keep up with technology and cybercrime. If you win a bet on a Warcross match, you win game credits called notes. But here's the thing—you can either take those notes online or to a physical place, where you meet a teller like this lady. You trade your notes to her. She gives you real cash in return, while taking a cut for her boss.

"It's *my* money," the guy is insisting now.

"We have to protect ourselves. Extra security measures take time. You can come back tomorrow night, and we can exchange half of your notes."

"I told you, *I don't have until tomorrow night.* I need to leave the city."

The conversation repeats itself all over again. I hold my breath as I listen. The woman has all but confirmed his identity.

My eyes narrow, and my lips turn up into a hungry little smirk. This, right here, is the moment I live for during a hunt—when the bits and pieces I've exposed converge into a fine point, when I see my target standing physically before me, ripe for the picking. When I've solved the puzzle.

*Got you.*

As their conversation turns more urgent, I tap my phone twice and send out a text message to the police.

> Suspect in physical custody.

I get a reply almost immediately.

> NYPD ALERTED.

I pull the stun gun out of my backpack. It catches for an instant against the edge of the zipper, making the faintest scraping sound.

The conversation halts. Through the bookshelves, both the man and woman jerk their heads toward me like deer in head-lights. The man sees my expression. His face is covered in a sheen of sweat, and his hair is plastered against his forehead. A fraction of a second passes.

I shoot.

He bolts—I miss him by a hair. *Good reflexes.* The woman darts up from her table, too, but I could care less about her. I race after him. He hops down the stairs three at a time, nearly falling in his rush, scattering his phone and a bunch of pens behind him. He sprints for the entrance as I reach the first floor. I burst through the revolving glass door right behind him.

We emerge onto the street. People let out startled shouts as the man shoves them aside—he knocks a camera-clicking tourist flat on her back. In one movement, I swing my electric board to the ground, jump on, and slam my heel down as hard as I can. It makes a high-pitched *whoosh*—I lunge forward, speeding down the sidewalk. The man glances over his shoulder to see me gaining fast on him. He darts left down the street at a full, panicked run.

I veer in his direction at such a sharp angle that the edge of my board protests against the pavement, leaving a long, black line. I aim my stun gun at the man's back and shoot.

He shrieks and falls. Instantly, he tries to stand again, but I catch up to him. He grabs my ankle. I stumble, kicking at him. His eyes are wild, his teeth clenched and jaw tight. Out flashes a blade. I see its glint in the light just in time. I kick him off me and roll away right before he can stab at my leg. My hands get a grip on his jacket. I fire the stun gun once more, this time at close range. It hits true. His body goes rigid, and he collapses on the pavement, trembling.

I jump on him. My knee presses hard into his back as the man sobs on the ground. The sound of police sirens rounds the bend. A circle of people have gathered around us now, their glasses recording away.

"I didn't do anything," the man whimpers over and over again. His voice comes out garbled by how hard I'm pushing him into the ground. "The lady inside—I can give you her name—"

"Shut it," I cut him off as I slide handcuffs onto his wrists.

To my surprise, he does. They don't always listen like that. I don't relent until a police car pulls up, until I see red and blue lights flashing against the wall. Only then do I get up and back away from him, making sure to hold out my hands so that the cops can see them clearly. My skin tingles from the rush of a successful hunt as I watch the two policemen yank the man onto his feet.

*Five thousand dollars!* When was the last time I had even half that much money at once? Never. I'll get to be less desperate for a while—I'll pay off the rent that I owe, which should calm my landlord down for now. Then I'll have $1,550 left. It's a *fortune*. My mind flips through my other bills. Maybe I can eat something other than instant noodles tonight.

I want to do a victory jump in the air. I'll be okay. Until the next hunt.

It takes me a moment to realize that the police are walking away with their new captive without even looking in my direction. My smile falters.

"Hey, Officer!" I shout, hurrying after the closer one. "Are you giving me a ride to the station for my payment, or what? Should I just meet you there?"

The officer gives me a look that doesn't seem to jibe with the fact that I just caught them a criminal. She looks exasperated, and dark circles under her eyes tell me she hasn't gotten much rest. "You weren't first," she says.

I startle, blinking. "What?" I say.

"Another hunter phoned in the alert before you."

For a moment, all I can do is stare at her.

Then I spit out a swear. "What a load of *bull*. You saw the whole thing go down. You all confirmed my alert!" I hold up my phone so the officer can see the text message I received. Sure enough, that's when my phone's battery finally dies.

Not that the proof would've made a difference. The officer doesn't even glance at the phone. "It was just an auto-reply. According to *my* messages, I received the first call-in from another hunter on location. Bounty goes to the first, no exceptions." She offers me a sympathetic shrug.

This is the dumbest technicality I've ever heard. "The hell it does!" I argue. "Who's the other hunter? Sam? Jamie? They're the only other ones canvassing this turf." I throw my hands up. "You know what—you're lying, there *is* no other hunter. You just don't want to pay out." I follow her as she turns away. "I saved you from a dirty job—that's the deal, that's why *any* bounty hunter goes after the people you're too lazy to catch. You owe me this one and you—"

The cop's partner grabs my arm and shoves me so hard that I nearly fall. "Get *back*," he says with a snarl. "Emika Chen, isn't it?" His other hand is wrapped tightly around the grip of his sheathed gun. "Yeah, I remember you."

I'm not about to argue with a loaded weapon. "Fine, *fine*." I force myself to take a step back and raise my hands in the air. "I'm going, okay? Leaving now."

"I know you already got some jail time, kid." He glares at me, his eyes hard and glittering, before joining his partner. "Don't make me give you another strike."

I hear the police radio calling them away to another crime scene. The noise around me muffles, and the image in my mind of the five thousand dollars starts to waver until it finally blurs into something I no longer recognize. In the span of thirty seconds, my victory has been tossed into someone else's hands.

# 2

I ride out of Manhattan in silence. It's getting colder, and the flurries have turned into steady snow, but the sting of the wind against my face suits my mood just fine. Here and there, parties have started to break out in the streets, and people decked out in red-and-blue jerseys count down the time at the top of their lungs. I watch as their celebrations swirl by. In the distance, every side of the Empire State Building is lit up and displaying enormous Warcross images.

Back when I was still living at the foster group home, I could see the Empire State Building if I climbed up onto the roof. I'd sit there and stare for hours as Warcross images rotated on its side, my skinny legs swinging, until dawn came and the sunlight would bathe me in gold. If I stared long enough, I could picture myself displayed up there. Even now, I feel that old twinge of excitement at the sight of the building.

My electric skateboard beeps once, snapping me out of my

reverie. I look down. The battery's been drained to its final bar. I sigh, slow to a stop, and swing my board over my shoulder. Then I dig for some change in my pocket and head into the first subway station I can find.

Twilight has faded to a blue-gray evening by the time I arrive in front of the crumbling Hunts Point, Bronx, apartment complex I call home. This is the other side of the glittering city. Graffiti covers one side of the building. Rusted iron bars cage the first floor windows. Trash is heaped near the main entrance steps—plastic cups, fast-food wrappers, broken beer bottles—all partially hidden underneath a thin dusting of snow. There are no lit-up screens here, no fancy auto-cars driving through the cracked streets. My shoulders droop, and my feet feel like lead. I haven't even eaten dinner yet, but at this point, I can't decide if I want food or sleep more.

Farther down the street, a group of homeless people are settling in, spreading their blankets and pitching their tents in the entryway of a shuttered store. Plastic bags line the insides of their threadbare clothes. I look away, heartsick. Once upon a time they too were kids, maybe had families who loved them. What had brought them to this point? What would I look like, in their place?

Finally, I will myself up the steps through the main entrance and down the hall to my front door. The hall reeks, as always, of cat pee and moldy carpets, and through the thin walls, I can hear neighbors shouting at each other, a TV's volume cranked high, a wailing baby. I relax a little. If I'm lucky enough, I won't bump into my landlord, with his tank and sweats and red face. Maybe I can at least get an uneventful night's sleep before I have to deal with him in the morning.

A new eviction notice has gone up on my door, right where I'd torn the old one off. I stare at it for a second, exhausted, rereading.

## NEW YORK EVICTION NOTICE
## TENANT NAME: EMIKA CHEN
## 72 HOURS TO PAY, OR VACATE

Was it really necessary for him to come back and put up a new sign, as if he wants to make sure everyone else in the building knows? To humiliate me further? I tear the notice off the door, crumple it in my fist, and stand still for a moment, staring at the blank space where the paper once hung. There is a familiar desperation in me, a rising panic that beats loudly in my chest, pounding out each thing I owe. The numbers in my head start over again. Rent, food, bills, debt.

Where am I going to get the money in three days?

"Hey!"

I jump at the voice. Mr. Alsole, my landlord, has emerged from his apartment and is stalking toward me, his frown resembling a fish's, his thin orange hair sticking out in every direction. One look at his bloodshot eyes tells me that he's high on something. Great. Another argument. *I can't deal with another fight today.* I fumble around for my keys, but it's too late—so instead, I straighten my shoulders and lift my chin.

"Hey, Mr. Alsole." I have a way of pronouncing the name like it's *Mr. Asshole.*

He scowls at me. "You been avoidin' me all week."

"Not on purpose," I insist. "I got a gig as a waitress in the mornings now, down at the diner, and—"

"Nobody needs waitresses anymore." He squints at me suspiciously.

"Well, this place does. And it's the only job around. There's nothing else."

"You said you'd pay *today*."

"I know what I said." I take a deep breath. "I can come by later to talk—"

"Did I say later? I want it *now*. And you're gonna need to add another hundred bucks to what you owe."

"*What?*"

"Rent's going up this month. On the whole block. You think this ain't hot property?"

"That's not fair," I say, my temper rising. "You can't do that—you *just* raised it!"

"You know what's not fair, little girl?" Mr. Alsole narrows his eyes at me and folds his arms. The gesture stretches out the freckles on his skin. "The fact that you're living for free in my building."

I hold both hands up. The blood is rushing to my cheeks. I can feel its fire. "I know—I just—"

"What about notes? You got more than five thousand of those?"

"If I did, I'd be giving them to you."

"Then offer something else," he spits. He shoves a sausage-like finger at my skateboard. "I see that again, I'll smash it with a hammer. You sell that thing and give me the money."

"It's only worth fifty bucks!" I take a step forward. "Look, I'll do whatever it takes, I swear, I promise." The words stream out of me in a jumbled mess. "Just give me a few more days."

"Listen, kid." He holds up three fingers, reminding me exactly how many months I owe him. "I'm done with pity checks." Then he looks me up and down. "You're what, eighteen now?"

I stiffen. "Yeah."

He nods down the hall. "Go get a job at the Rockstar Club.

Their girls earn four hundred a night just for dancing on some tables. *You* could probably pull five hundred. And they won't even care about the red on your record."

I narrow my eyes. "You think I haven't checked? I have to be twenty-one."

"I don't care what you do. *Thursday.* Got it?" Mr. Alsole's talking forcefully enough now for his spit to fly onto my face. "And I want this apartment cleared out. Spotless."

"It wasn't spotless in the *first* place!" I shout back. But he's already turned his back and is stalking down the hall.

I let out a slow breath as he slams his door shut. My heart pounds against my ribs. My hands shake.

My thoughts return to the homeless, with their hollow eyes and sloped shoulders, and then to the working girls I've occasionally seen leaving the Rockstar Club, reeking of smoke and sweat and heavy perfume, their makeup smeared. Mr. Alsole's threat is a reminder of where I might end up if I don't get lucky soon. If I don't start making some hard choices.

I'll find a way to work some pity into him. Soften him up. *Just give me one more week, I swear, and I'll get half the money to you. I promise.* I play these words in my head as I shove the key in the lock and open the door.

It's dark inside, even with the neon-blue glow from outside the window. I flip on the lights, toss my keys on the kitchen counter, and throw the crumpled eviction notice in the trash. Then I pause to look around the apartment.

It's a tiny studio, crammed full of belongings. Cracks in the painted plaster run along the walls. One of the bulbs in the room's only ceiling light has burned out, while the second bulb is fading, waiting for someone to replace it before it dies, too. My Warcross glasses are lying on the fold-out dining table. I'd rented them for cheap because they're an older model. Two cardboard boxes of stuff are stacked by the kitchen, two mattresses lie on the ground by the window, and an ancient TV and old, mustard-yellow couch take up the rest of the space.

"Emi?"

A muffled voice comes from underneath a blanket on the couch. My roommate sits up, rubs her face, and runs a hand through her nest of blond hair. *Keira.* She'd fallen asleep with her Warcross glasses on, and a faint crease trails across her cheeks and forehead. She wrinkles her nose at me. "You got some guy with you again?"

I shake my head. "No, just me tonight," I reply. "Did you give Mr. Alsole your half of the money today, like you said you would?"

"Oh." She avoids my stare, swings her legs over the side of the couch, and reaches for a half-eaten bag of chips. "I'll get it to him by this weekend."

"You realize he's throwing us out on Thursday, right?"

"No one told *me.*"

My hand tightens against the back of the dining room chair. She hasn't left the apartment all day, so she never even saw the eviction notice on the door. I take a deep breath, reminding myself that Keira hasn't been able to find any work, either. After almost a year of trying, she's just given up and curled inward, spending her days idling away in Warcross instead.

It's a feeling I know well, but I'm too exhausted tonight to spare much patience for her. I wonder whether the realization of living on the streets will hit her when we finally end up standing on the sidewalk with all of our belongings.

I strip off my scarf and hoodie down to my favorite tank top, go into the kitchen, and start a pot of water to boil. Then I head over to the two mattresses lying against the wall.

Keira and I keep our beds separated with a makeshift divider duct-taped together out of old cardboard boxes. I'd made my side as cozy and neat as I could, decorating the space with trails of golden fairy lights. A map of Manhattan, covered in my scribbles, is pinned on my wall, along with magazine covers featuring Hideo Tanaka, a written list of the current Warcross amateur leaderboards, and a Christmas ornament from when I was a kid. My final possession is one of my dad's old paintings, the only one I have left, propped carefully beside the mattress. The canvas is exploding with color, the paint thick and textured as if still wet. I used to have more of his work, but I had to sell them off every time things got too desperate, chipping away at his memory in order to survive his absence.

I flop on my mattress and it lets out a loud squeak. The ceiling and walls are awash in neon blue from the liquor mart across the street. I lie still, listening to the constant, distant wail of sirens coming from somewhere outside, my eyes fixed on an old water stain on the ceiling.

If Dad were here, he would be fussing about in his fashion professor mode, mixing paints and washing brushes in jars. Perhaps mulling over his spring class syllabus, or his plans for New York Fashion Week.

I turn my head toward the rest of the apartment and pretend that he's here, the healthy, un-sickly version of him, his tall, slender silhouette outlined in light near the doorway, his forest of dyed blue hair shining silver in the darkness, facial scruff neatly trimmed, black-rimmed glasses framing his eyes, dreamer's face on. He would be wearing a black shirt that exposed the colorful tattoos winding up and down his right arm, and his appearance would be impeccable—his shoes polished and trousers perfectly ironed—except for flecks of paint staining his hands and hair.

I smile to myself at the memory of sitting in a chair, swinging my legs and staring at the bandages on my knees while my father put temporary streaks of color into my hair. Tears still stained my cheeks from when I'd run home from school, sobbing, because someone had pushed me down at recess and I'd scraped holes in my favorite jeans. Dad hummed while he worked. When he finished, he held a mirror up to me, and I gasped in delight. *Very Givenchy, very on trend*, he said, tapping my nose lightly. I giggled. *Especially when we tie it up like this. See?* He gathered my hair up into a high tail. *Don't get too used to it—it'll wash out in a few days. Now, let's go get some pizza.*

Dad used to say that my old school's uniform was a pimple on the face of New York. He used to say that I should dress like the world's a better place than it actually is. He would buy flowers every time it rained and fill our home with them. He would forget to wipe his hands during his painting sessions and end up leaving colorful fingerprints all over the place. He poured his meager salary into presents for me and art supplies and charities and clothes and wine. He laughed too often and fell in love too quickly and drank too freely.

Then one afternoon, when I was eleven, he came home, sat down on the couch, and stared blankly into space. He'd just returned from a doctor's appointment. Six months later, he was gone.

Death has a terrible habit of cutting straight through every careful line you've drawn between your present and your future. The line that leads to your dad filling your dorm room with flowers on your graduation day. To him designing your wedding dress. To him coming over for dinner at your future house every Sunday, where his off-key singing would make you laugh so hard you'd cry. I had a hundred thousand of these lines, and in one day they were severed, leaving me with nothing but a stack of his medical bills and gambling debt. Death didn't even give me somewhere to direct my anger. All I could do was search the sky.

After he died, I started copying his look—wild, unnaturally colorful hair (boxes of hair dye being the only thing I'm willing to waste money on) and a sleeve of tattoos (done for free out of pity from Dad's former tattoo artist).

I turn my head slightly and glance at the tattoos winding along my left arm, then run a hand across the images. They start at my wrist and go up my shoulder, bright hues of blue and turquoise, gold and pink—peony flowers (my father's favorite), Escher-style buildings rising out of ocean waves, music notes, and planets against a backdrop of outer space, a reminder of nights when Dad would drive us out to the countryside to see the stars. Finally, they end with a slender line of words that run along my left collarbone, a mantra Dad used to repeat to me, a mantra I recite to myself whenever things get too grim.

*Every locked door has a key.*

Every problem has a solution.

Every problem, that is, except the one that took him. Except the one I'm in now. And the thought is almost enough to make me curl up and close my eyes, to let myself sink back into a familiar dark place.

The sound of boiling water shakes me from my thoughts just in time. *Get up, Emi,* I say to myself.

I drag myself from the bed, head to the kitchen, and hunt for a pack of instant noodles. (Cost of dinner tonight: $1.) My food stash has gone down by a box of macaroni. I glare at Keira, who's still sitting on the couch and glued to the TV (used TV: $75). With a sigh, I rip open the pack of noodles and drop them into the water.

The thud of music and partying comes from elsewhere in the

building. Every local channel is broadcasting something related to the opening ceremony. Keira pauses the TV on one channel showing a reel of last year's highlights. Then it cuts to five game analysts sitting around in the top tier of the Tokyo Dome, in a heated debate over which team would win and why. Below them is a dimmed arena of fifty thousand screaming fans, illuminated by sweeping spotlights of red and blue. Gold confetti rains from the ceiling.

"One thing we can all agree on is that we have never seen a wild-card lineup like this year's!" one analyst says, a finger plugged deep in her ear so she can hear above the noise. "One of them is already a celebrity in his own right."

"Yes!" a second analyst exclaims, while the others nod. A video showing a boy pops up behind them. "DJ Ren first made headlines as one of the hottest names in France's *underground* music scene. Now, Warcross will make him an *aboveground* name!"

As the analysts fall back into arguing about this year's newest players, I swallow a wave of jealousy. Every year, fifty amateur players, or wild cards, are nominated by secret committee to be placed into the team selection process. Luckiest people in the world, as far as I'm concerned. My criminal record automatically disqualifies me from the nominations.

"And let's talk about how much *buzz* the games are getting this year. Do you think we'll break some records?" says the first analyst.

"It looks like we already have," a third replies. "Last year, the final tournament saw a total of three hundred million viewers. Three hundred *million*! Mr. Tanaka must be proud." As he speaks, the backdrop changes again to the logo of Henka Games, followed by a video of Warcross creator Hideo Tanaka.

It's a clip of him dressed in a flawless tuxedo, leaving a charity ball with a young woman on his arm, his coat draped around her shoulders. He's far too graceful for a twenty-one-year-old, and as lights flash around him, I can't help leaning forward a little. Over the past few years, Hideo has transformed from a lanky teenage genius into an elegant young man with piercing eyes. *Polite* is what most say when describing his personality. No one can really be sure of anything else unless they are within his inner circle. But not a week goes by now without him being featured on some tabloid cover, dating this celebrity or that one, putting him at the top of every list they can think of. Youngest. Most Beautiful. Wealthiest. Most Eligible.

"Let's take a look at our audience for tonight's opening game!" the analyst continues. A number pops up and they all burst into applause. *Five hundred and twenty million.* That's just for the opening ceremony. Warcross is officially the biggest event in the world.

I take my pot of noodles over to the couch and eat on autopilot while we watch more footage. There are interviews with squealing fans entering the Tokyo Dome, their faces painted and their hands clutching homemade posters. There are shots of workers double-checking the tech hookups. There are Olympic-style documentaries showing photos and videos of each of tonight's players. After that comes gameplay footage—two teams battling it out in Warcross's endless virtual worlds. The camera pans to cheering crowds, then to the professional players waiting in a private room backstage. Their smiles are wide tonight, their eyes alive with anticipation as they wave at the camera.

I can't help feeling bitter. I could be there, too, be just as good as them, if I had the time and money to play all day. I know it. Instead, I'm here, eating instant noodles out of a pot, wondering how I'm going to survive until the police announce another bounty. What must it be like to have a perfect life? To be a super-star beloved by all? To be able to pay your bills on time and buy whatever you want?

"What are we going to do, Em?" Keira says, breaking our silence. Her voice sounds hollowed out. She asks me this question every time we dip into dangerous territory, as if I were the only one responsible for saving us, but tonight I just keep staring at the TV, unwilling to answer her. Considering that I have exactly thirteen dollars to my name right now, I'm at the most dire point I've ever been.

I lean back, letting ideas run through my head. I'm a good—great—hacker, but I can't get a job. I'm either too young or too criminal. Who wants to hire a convicted identity thief? Who wants you to fix their gadgets when they think you might steal their info? That's what happens when you have four months of juvenile detention on your record that can't be erased, along with a two-year ban on touching any computers. It doesn't stop me from sneaking in some use of my hacked phone and glasses, of course—but it has kept me from applying for any real job I can do well. We were barely even allowed to rent this apartment. All I've found so far is an occasional bounty hunt and a part-time waitress job—a job that'll also vanish the instant the diner buys an auto-mated waitress. Anything else would probably involve me working for a gang or stealing something.

It might come to that.

I take a deep breath. "I don't know. I'll sell Dad's last painting."

"Em . . . ," Keira says, but lets her words trail off. She knows it's a meaningless offer from me, anyway. Even if we sold everything in our apartment, we'd probably only scrape together five hundred dollars. It's not nearly enough to keep Mr. Alsole from kicking us out into the streets.

A familiar nausea settles into my stomach, and I reach up to rub at the tattoo running along my collarbone. *Every locked door has a key.* But what if this one doesn't? What if I can't get out of this? There's no way I'll be able to get my hands on enough money in time. I'm out of options. I fight off the panic, trying to keep my mind from spiraling downward, and force myself to even my breathing. My eyes wander away from the TV and toward the window.

No matter where I am in the city, I always know exactly which direction my old group foster home sits. And if I let myself, I can imagine our apartment fading away into the home's dark, cramped halls and peeling yellow wallpaper. I can see the bigger kids chasing me down the corridor and hitting me until I bleed. I can remember the bites from bedbugs. I can feel the sting on my face from Mrs. Devitt slapping me. I can hear myself crying quietly in my bunk as I imagined my father rescuing me from that place. I can feel the wire of the chain-link fences against my fingers as I climbed over them and ran away.

*Think. You can solve this.* A little voice in my head flares up, stubborn. *This will not be your life. You are not destined to stay here forever. You are not your father.*

On the TV, the lights in the Tokyo Dome finally dim. The cheering rises to a deafening roar.

"And that wraps up our pregame coverage of tonight's Warcross opening ceremony!" one analyst exclaims, his voice hoarse. He and the others hold up V-for-victory signs with their hands. "For those of you watching from home, time to put on your glasses and join us in the *event—of—the—year!*"

Keira has already popped on her glasses. I head to the fold-out table, where my own glasses lie.

Some people still say that Warcross is just a stupid game. Others say it's a revolution. But for me and millions of others, it's the only foolproof way to forget our troubles. I lost my bounty, my landlord is going to come screaming for his money again tomorrow morning, I'm going to drag myself to my waitressing job, and I'm going to be homeless in a couple of days, with nowhere to go . . . but tonight, I can join in with everyone else, put on my glasses, and watch magic happen.

# 3

I still remember the exact moment when Hideo Tanaka changed my life.

I was eleven, and my father had been dead for only a few months. Rain pounded against the window of the bedroom I shared with four others at the foster home. I was lying in bed, unable, yet again, to force myself to get up and head to school. Unfinished homework lay strewn on my blankets, still there from the night before, when I'd fallen asleep staring at the blank pages. I'd dreamed of home, of Dad making us fried eggs and pancakes drowning in syrup, his hair still shining with glitter and glue, his loud, familiar laugh filling the kitchen and drifting outside through our open window. *Bon appètit, mademoiselle!* he'd exclaimed, with his dreamer's face. And I'd screamed in delight as he threw his arms around me and messed up my hair.

Then I'd woken up, and the scene had vanished, leaving me in a strange, dark, quiet house.

I didn't move in bed. I didn't cry. I hadn't cried once since Dad's death, not even at the funeral. Any tears I might have shed were instead replaced with shock when I learned how much debt Dad had accumulated. When I learned that he had been sneaking onto online gambling forums for years. That he hadn't been getting treatment at the hospital because he'd been trying to pay off his debt.

So I spent the morning the way I'd spent every day for the past few months, lost in a haze of silence and stillness. Emotions had long vanished behind a cavity of fog in my chest. I used my every waking moment to stare off into space—at the bedroom wall, at the class whiteboard, at the interior of my locker, at plates of tasteless food. My report cards were a sea of red ink. Constant nausea stole my appetite. My bones jutted sharply at my wrists and elbows. Dark circles rimmed my eyes, something everyone noticed except me.

What did I care, anyway? My father was gone and I was *so tired.* Maybe the fog in my chest could grow, denser and denser, until someday it'd swallow *me,* and I could be gone, too. So I lay curled in a tiny ball, watching the rain lash at the window, the wind tug at the silhouettes of tree branches, wondering how long it would take for the school to notice I wasn't there again.

The clock radio in the room—the *only* thing in the room, other than our beds—was on, a piece of hand-me-down technology donated to the home from a Goodwill center. One of the other girls hadn't bothered turning it off when the alarm sounded. I listened halfheartedly as the news droned on about the state of the economy, the protests in the cities and countryside, the overworked police trying to keep up with crime, the evacuations in Miami and New Orleans.

Then it switched. Some hour-long special began, talking about a boy named Hideo Tanaka. He was fourteen years old then, still brand-new to the spotlight. As the program went on, I started to pay attention.

"Remember the world right before smartphones?" the announcer was saying. "When we were teetering on the brink of a huge shift, when the technology was *almost but not quite* there, and it took one revolutionary device to push us all over the edge? Well, last year, a thirteen-year-old boy named Hideo Tanaka pushed us over a new edge.

"He did it by inventing a thin, wireless pair of glasses with metal arms and retractable earphones. Make no mistake. They're nothing like the goggles we've seen before, the ones that looked like giant bricks strapped to your face. No, these ultra-slim glasses are called the NeuroLink, and you wear them as easily as any pair of regular glasses. We have the latest pair in the studio here"—he paused to put them on—"and we promise, it's the most *sensational* thing we've ever tried."

The NeuroLink. I'd heard it mentioned in the news before. Now I listened as the radio program laid it out for me.

For a long time, in order to create a realistic virtual reality environment, you had to render as detailed a world as possible. This required a lot of money and effort. But no matter how good the effects became, you could still tell—if you looked hard enough—that it wasn't real. There are a thousand little movements on a human face every second, a thousand different quivers of a leaf on a tree, a million tiny things the real world has that the virtual world doesn't. Your mind knows this unconsciously—so something will look *off,* even if you can't quite put your finger on it.

So Hideo Tanaka thought of an easier solution. In order to

create a flawlessly real world, you don't need to draw the most detailed, most realistic 3-D scene ever.

You just need to *fool the audience into thinking it's real*.

And guess what can do that the best? Your own brain.

When you have a dream, no matter how crazy it is, you believe it's real. Like, full-on surround sound, high definition, 360-degree special effects. And none of it is anything you're actually seeing. Your brain is creating an entire reality for you, without needing any piece of technology.

So Hideo created the best brain–computer interface ever built. A pair of sleek glasses. The NeuroLink.

When you wore it, it helped your brain render virtual worlds that looked and sounded *indistinguishable* from reality. Imagine walking around in that world—interacting, playing, talking. Imagine wandering through the most realistic virtual Paris ever, or lounging in a full simulation of Hawaii's beaches. Imagine flying through a fantasy world of dragons and elves. *Anything*.

With the press of a tiny button on its side, the glasses could also switch back and forth like polarized lenses between the virtual world and the real world. And when you looked at the real world through it, you could see virtual things hovering over real-life objects and places. Dragons flying above your street. The names of stores, restaurants, and people.

To demonstrate how cool the glasses were, Hideo made a video game that came with each pair. This game was called Warcross.

Warcross was pretty simple: two teams battled each other, one trying to take the other team's Artifact (a shiny gem) without losing their own. What made it spectacular were the virtual worlds the battles were set in, each one so realistic that putting on your glasses was like dropping you right into that place.

As the radio program went on, I learned that Hideo, born in London and raised in Tokyo, had taught himself how to code when he was eleven. *My age.* Not long afterward, he built his first pair of NeuroLink glasses at his father's computer repair shop, with his neuroscientist mother's input. His parents helped fund a set of one thousand glasses for him, and he started shipping them to people. A thousand orders turned overnight into a hundred thousand. Then, a million, ten million, a hundred million. Investors called with staggering offers. Lawsuits flew over the patents. Critics argued about how the NeuroLink engine would change everyday life, travel, medicine, the military, education. "Link Up" was the name of a popular Frankie Dena pop song, last summer's big hit.

And everyone—*everyone*—played Warcross. Some played it intensely, forming teams and battling for hours. Others played by simply lounging on a virtual beach or enjoying a virtual safari. Still others played by wearing their glasses while walking around the real world, showing off their virtual pet tigers or populating the streets with their favorite celebrities.

However people played, it became a way of life.

My gaze shifted from the radio to the homework pages lying on my blankets. Hideo's story stirred something in my chest, cutting through the fog. How did a boy only three years older than me take the world by storm? I stayed where I was until the program ended and music started to play. I lay there for another long hour. Then, gradually, I uncurled and reached for one of my assignments.

It was from my Introduction to Computer Science class. The first problem on it was to spot the error in a simple, three-line piece of code. I studied it, imagining an eleven-year old Hideo in the same position as me. He wouldn't be lying here, staring off into nothing. He would have solved this problem, and the next, and the next.

The thought conjured an old memory of my father sitting on my bed and showing me the back of a magazine, where two drawings were printed that looked identical. It was asking the reader to figure out the difference between them.

*This is a trick question,* I'd remembered declaring to him with crossed arms. My eyes squinted closely at every corner of both images. *The two drawings are exactly the same.*

Dad just gave me a crooked smile and adjusted his glasses. There was still paint and glue stuck in his hair from when he was experimenting with fabrics earlier in the day. I'd need to help him cut the sticky strands out later. *Look closer,* he'd replied. He'd grabbed the pencil tucked behind his ear and made a sweeping motion across the image. *Think about a painting hanging on a wall. Without using any tools, you can still tell if it's crooked—even by a tiny bit. It just feels off. Right?*

I'd shrugged. *Yeah, I guess so.*

*Humans are surprisingly sensitive like that.* Dad had gestured at the two drawings again with his paint-stained fingers. *You have to learn to look at the* whole *of something, not just the parts. Relax your eyes. Take in the entire image at once.*

I'd listened, sitting back and softening my gaze. That had been when I'd finally spotted the difference, the tiny mark on one of the drawings. *There!* I'd exclaimed, pointing excitedly at it.

Dad had smiled at me. *See?* he'd said. *Every locked door has a key, Emi.*

I stared down at the assignment, my father's words turning over and over in my mind. Then I did as he said—I leaned back and took in the code all at once. Like it was a painting. Like I was searching for the point of interest.

And almost immediately, I saw the error. I reached for my school laptop, opened it, and typed out the corrected code.

It worked. *Hello, World!* said my laptop's program.

To this day, I can't properly describe how I felt in that moment. To see my solution working, *functioning,* on the screen. To realize that, with three little lines of text, I had the power to command a machine to do *exactly* what I wanted.

The gears in my head, creaky from grief, suddenly began to turn again. Begging for another problem. I finished the second one. Then a third. I kept going, faster and faster, until I finished not only that homework sheet but every problem in my textbook. The fog in my chest eased, revealing a warm, beating heart beneath it.

If I could solve these problems, then I could control something. And if I could control something, I could forgive myself for the one problem that I could never have solved, the one person I could never have saved. Everyone has a different way of escaping the dark stillness of their mind. This, I learned, was mine.

I finished my dinner that night for the first time in months. The next day and the day after that and every day since, I channeled every bit of my energy into learning everything about code and Warcross and the NeuroLink that I could get my brains on.

As for Hideo Tanaka . . . from that day on, along with the rest of the world, I was obsessed. I watched him as if I were afraid to blink, incapable of looking away, like he might start another revolution at any moment.

# 4

My glasses are old and used, several generations behind, but they work fine. I put them on and the earphones fit snugly, sealing out the sound of outside traffic and footsteps from upstairs. Our humble apartment—and, with it, all my worries—is replaced by blackness and silence. I exhale, relieved to leave the real world behind for a while. My view soon fills with a neon-blue light, and I find myself standing on the top of a hill, looking down at the city lights of a virtual Tokyo that could pass for the real thing. The only reminder that I'm inside a simulation is a clear box hovering in the center of my vision.

Welcome back, [null]

Level 24 | N 430

Those two lines then vanish. [null], of course, isn't actually my name. In my hacked account, I'm able to wander around as an anonymous player. Other players crossing my path will see me as a randomly generated username.)

When I look behind me, I see my customized room decked out in variations of the Warcross logo. Normally, this room has two doors: play a round, or watch other people play. Today, though, there is a third door, above which some text hovers:

## Warcross Opening Ceremony Game
## Live

In real life, I tap my fingers against the tabletop. As I do, the glasses sense my finger movements, and a virtual keyboard slides out. I search for Keira in the player directory. I find her in no time, connect with her, and a few seconds later, she accepts my invite and appears at my side. Like me (and most other players), she's designed her avatar to look like an idealized version of her real self, adorned with a few cool game items—a gleaming breastplate, a pair of horns—she'd bought.

"Let's head in," she says.

I move forward, then reach my hand out and open the third door. Light washes over me. I squint and my heart gives a familiar leap as the invisible roar of viewers drowns out everything. A soundtrack swells over my earphones. I find myself standing on one of what seems like a million floating islands, staring down into the most beautiful valley I've ever seen.

A wide expanse of lush plains turns into a crystal-blue lagoon, surrounded by towering cliffs and smooth, steep rocks, their tops covered with vegetation. Waterfalls thunder down their sides. When I look closer, I realize that the rocks are actually enormous sculptures, each of them carved to look like past tournament winners. Rays of sun dance through the valley, painting light on the plains even as the floating isles cast patches of shadows; flocks of white birds cry out in formation below us. The towers of a castle on the cliffs peek through the distant mist. Farther, to the horizon, majestic ocean ray–like creatures glide in the air. There, the sky is black, and lightning forks between the clouds. I shiver as if I could sense the electricity in the air.

Even the soundtrack chosen for this level is off-the-charts epic, full of orchestral strings and deep drums, sending my heart soaring.

Above it all, a grand voice echoes across the world. *"Welcome to the Warcross Opening Ceremony Game."*

A soft *ding* sounds, and a transparent bubble pops up in the middle of my view:

### Logged into Opening Ceremony!
### +150 Pts. Daily Score: +150
### Level 24 | ₦580

Then it fades away. My reward for watching the opening game is 150 points, which will go toward my leveling . . . except it won't, since I've hacked this version of Warcross. Too bad. If I played like a normal person, I'd probably be at Level 90 or so by now. But I'm still at Level 24.

"They always do it up, don't they?" Keira's voice makes me blink. She has a look of wonder on her face.

I smile, then take a deep breath and spread my arms out. I leap off my floating isle. And I fly.

My stomach drops as my brain believes I'm actually thousands of feet in the air. I let out a whoop as I soar over the plain, the music egging me on. There are restrictions on the official competing players—some worlds allow players to fly around or swim underwater, while others must obey virtual gravity. But audience members are always free to wander around the landscape however they wish. We're barred from altering it in any way or interfering with the players. The players won't see us, either. They can only hear the roar of our cheers or boos, as well as the referee's calls.

I fly straight through the floating isles like a ghost, angling up to go as high as I can until I can't get any farther from land. Then I turn around and dive back down like a meteor. I finally stop on one of the floating isles, right as the cheers of the audience mix with the voices of the game analysts coming from my earphones, as if I were listening to them on a radio.

"It's time for the annual Opening Ceremony Game!" one of them exclaims. "We've gathered here tonight to watch this all-star performance before the real tournament season begins. At the far end, we have Team Alpha, led by Asher Wing! At the near end, we have Team Beta, led by Penn Wachowski!"

The players finally appear, scattered at opposite ends of the mass of floating islands. I fly away from Keira and head over to see them more closely.

The avatar rule for official, professional Warcross players is that their virtual selves must look like their real selves, without any of the crazy customizations typical users can have, and that each team's members must wear the same color. Team Alpha's color is blue. There's Jena, all blond hair and lanky limbs in her blue, fitted Warcross armor, its dragon scale texture tailored to match the level. She's one of the younger players—only eighteen, same as me—and is from Ireland. As I watch her, she tosses her hair over her shoulders and places her hands on her hips. Her silver armguards gleam in the sun, as do the identical knives strapped to her thighs. The audience screams their approval.

Standing on a floating island nearby is Max. Max, the son of millionaires, is a Harvard grad. His Warcross position is a Fighter, for sheer brawn and power, with the goal of taking others down instead of hunting for the Artifact. At twenty-eight, he's the oldest player in this year's tournaments. His shoulder armor is enormous and hulking, so shiny that it reflects the sky and contrasts sharply against his dark skin.

Then there's Asher, the team's captain, who is the farthest from where I'm floating. Originally known only as the younger brother of Daniel Batu Wing, an actor and stuntman, Asher's now famous in his own right because of Warcross. He has thick brown hair so light that it's almost blond, and his eyes are a playful blue, the same color as the virtual lagoon below him. His deep sapphire armor is finished with steel shoulder plates and leather straps along his arms and waist.

He grins cheekily, crosses his arms against his chest, and calls out a challenge to the other team at the opposite end of the game world, which makes the audience go wild. When I toggle my view to show the audience in the Tokyo Dome, they are shrieking his name and waving glowing batons frantically. MARRY ME, ASHER!!! scream the fan posters. Asher says something through his secure line, words only his teammates can hear. Over his head floats a shimmering blue gem. This is his team's Artifact.

The game announcer has started the official pregame ritual, reading off something about good sportsmanship and honorable gameplay. As she goes on, my attention shifts to Team Beta. They're decked out in red armor, of course—the annual opening game always color-codes the teams red versus blue. Penn, the Beta captain, has a sparkling red Artifact hovering over his head. He and Asher smirk at each other, and the shouts from the audience go up an octave.

Over my earphones, the announcer finishes her speech with

a now-standard reminder of what the objective is, for the benefit of any new audience members who are watching. "Remember,
teams, you have only one goal—take your enemy team's Artifact
before they can take yours!"

The players each raise their right fist. They hit them twice
against their chests, the standard response to acknowledging the
rules. There is a brief pause, as if everything in the level had suddenly frozen.

"Game!" the announcer shouts. The crowd chants along: "Set!
*Fight!*"

The world trembles from the roar of the invisible audience,
and the clouds in the sky start to move rapidly. The storm that
blackens the horizon is sweeping toward us at a frightening
pace, its lightning forking closer with each passing second. As
with every Warcross world, the game gets harder the longer it
goes on.

At the same time, brightly colored marbles appear, hovering
over many of the isles. These items are power-ups—temporary
bursts of super speed, wings to help you fly for short periods,
shields of defense that can stop an enemy attack, and so on. There
are dozens of different power-ups that can potentially appear in a
game, and new ones are added all the time. Low-level power-ups
(like something that helps you jump a little higher) are plentiful. I
see three hovering over isles close to me right now. But high-level
power-ups (like the ability to fly for the entire game) are very rare
and hard to reach. Some power-ups are so valuable that a team
might send one of their players after them for the entire game.

Power-ups can be worth a lot of money in the Warcross com-
munity. In regular games, unused power-ups that you collect can
be stored in your player inventory. You can then sell or trade them

to other players. Valuable power-ups can sell for thousands of notes.

Warcross is so well programmed that I've never tried to steal a power-up—but I recently found a security bug that might let me grab an item from a user's account *right* as she's about to use it.

I find myself looking around us now, wondering how much I could get if I nabbed some of these items for resale. But none of the ones I can see are valuable enough. Fifty notes here, another thirty there. Not worth risking a hack of the biggest opening game ever. Definitely not worth risking another strike on my record.

"Asher is making the first move of the game!" an analyst's voice echoes in my ears. "He's giving Jena some instructions. A power-up grab."

Sure enough, Asher has spotted something before anyone else has. He looks first at Jena, then makes an arm gesture toward a distant marble hovering over a rock jutting high out of the far end of the lagoon. She doesn't hesitate. Immediately she hops off her floating isle and onto another one, making her way toward the rock. Behind her, the isle she was originally standing on now crumbles into pieces.

"Something's caught Asher's eye!" another analyst chimes in. "It takes a lot for him to send away one of his teammates."

At the same time, Asher and his Fighter, Max, lunge forward. The other team is already on the hunt, hurtling toward them. Every time a player leaps from one isle to another, the isle left behind crumbles away. They must all choose their steps wisely. Asher and Max move as one, their attention focused on Penn. They're going to attack him on both sides.

I crane my neck in the direction where the distant object is hovering, in an attempt to see what power-up had caught Asher's eye. My world zooms in. The power-up is a marbled sphere, so red it looks like it was dipped in blood.

"Sudden Death!" an analyst exclaims, right as I gasp.

A rare power-up, indeed. Sudden Death can render a player of your choice frozen for the rest of the game, useless to his or her teammates. I've never seen this power-up in play during a regular Warcross match, and only a handful of times in an official tournament game.

It must be worth at least five thousand—maybe *fifteen* thousand dollars.

Max, for all his size, is faster than Asher. He reaches Penn first, then lunges for the red Artifact over his head. Penn ducks out of the way in time. The isle they're both standing on starts to crack, unable to support them both for long, and Penn makes a leap for the next closest isle. But Max's hand closes around his arm before he can do it—Max lets out a roar and flings Penn backward. Penn goes flying. He manages to seize the edge of an isle before he plummets to the lagoon below. There he dangles, momentarily helpless and dazed. The audience roars as Penn's life bar drops from Max's blow.

### Penn Wachowski | Team Beta
### Life: -35%

Now Asher joins the action. He leaps off his own isle as it crumbles, landing in a perfect crouch on the isle Penn is clinging to. The isle shudders from the impact. He leans down, seizes Penn by his neck before he has recovered from his last hit, and pummels him into the isle's dirt, cracking the ground. A burst of blue light radiates out from Asher in a ring at his attack.

The invisible audience screams, while an analyst shouts, "*Penn's going to go down!* If he doesn't protect his team's Artifact, Asher is going to end this game early—"

Penn frees one hand and unleashes a Lightning power-up on Asher before he can make a fatal blow. A blinding flash of light engulfs Asher for an instant. He throws his hands up in vain, but too late—the power-up has blinded him for five solid seconds. His own life bar drops by 20 percent. Penn lunges for Asher's Artifact. At the last instant, Max saves their Artifact by grabbing it first, so that it now hovers over his head.

The crowd lets out a roar of cheers and boos. I follow suit. But my attention keeps going back to the Sudden Death power-up.

*Don't do it.*

"Sharp effort from Beta! Penn's been working on his defense!" an analyst shouts over the noise. As he speaks, the storm's clouds finally reach us, and the sun disappears overhead. "We lost track of Kento for a while, but it looks like he's now hunting after Jena. Both are going for the Sudden Death power-up!"

Wind blasts us. It makes the floating isles wobble in the air. Fat drops of rain start to fall, making each isle slippery and harder to stand on.

I turn my attention to Jena and Kento, who look like two

small, bright figures fast approaching the power-up hovering over the rock. Then I swoop down from the isles and fly in their direction. Soon, I am hovering near the bloodred Sudden Death, watching as Jena and Kento dash for it.

I focus on the power-up. In theory, if Jena or Kento get their hands on Sudden Death, I might be able to hack into their player accounts. I might be able to steal Sudden Death right out of their account. And then I could sell it.

*Fifteen thousand dollars.*

In spite of myself, my head spins with excitement. Could this work? Hacking into a regular Warcross game has never been done—but an official championship tournament game? Unheard of. I don't even know if I can access their accounts the same way I can in regular Warcross. My hack might not work at all.

If they catch me and I'm arrested, I'll be charged as an adult.

Breaking the law had only quickened my father's death. It certainly hadn't made my life any easier.

I stay where I am, torn, my throat dry.

What if I *do* successfully steal it? It's just a power-up in a game; I'm not hurting anyone. I've never tested this Warcross hack in an arena like this—but what if it works? I could resell it for thousands. I could get that money immediately and give it to Mr. Alsole, pay off my debts. It could save me. And I'd never do it again.

The temptation nips at me, and I wonder if this is how my father felt every time he'd logged online to place *just one more bet.*

Just one bet. *Just this once.*

Jena reaches the power-up first. She only has time to swipe it off the top of the cliff before Kento tackles her.

If I don't make a decision now, it'll be too late.

Instinctively, I move. My fingers tap madly against my tabletop. I bring up a player directory, then hunt for Jena's profile. As I go, Jena kicks Kento off her and then dives in a perfect arc down toward the lagoon. A deafening thunderclap sounds out overhead.

Jena's name finally pops up. I have only a few seconds to act. *Don't do it.* But I'm already moving. A complete inventory of her virtual belongings appears. I scroll until I see the brand-new Sudden Death item in her account, shiny and scarlet.

The only weakness I've ever found in Warcross's security is a tiny glitch when a user is about to use an item. When the item passes from an account into the game and is used, there's a split second when it is vulnerable.

My fingers tremble. Before me, Jena reaches for her new Sudden Death power-up. In her inventory, I see it flash a quick gold. Now's my only chance. I suck in my breath, wait—*don't do it*—and then type a single command just as Jena's item leaves her hand.

A tingle shoots through my body. I freeze. In fact, everyone in the game seems to freeze.

Then I notice that Asher is looking right at me. Like he can *see me.*

I blink. *That's impossible. I'm in the audience.* But Jena is staring at me, too. Their eyes are wide. That's when I realize that the Sudden Death power-up is now officially in my account. I see it in my inventory at the bottom of my vision.

*I did it. My hack worked.*

But, somehow, successfully capturing the power-up has glitched me into the tournament.

A referee's whistle echoes around us. The audience's cheers turn into whispers of shock. I stay where I am, suddenly unsure of what to do. Frantically, I type in another command, trying to go back to being part of the audience again. But it's no use.

Everyone—the players, the announcers, the millions in the audience—can see me.

"Who the hell are *you*?" Asher says to me.

I just stare back, numb.

A flash of red light engulfs the scene, and the omniscient voice echoes all around us. "Time-out," it booms. "System glitch."

Then, my screen goes dark. I'm kicked out of the game and back into my starting room, looking out at a virtual view of Tokyo. The doors in the room are gone now. The Sudden Death power-up is still glowing in my inventory.

But when I reach for it, it vanishes. They've deleted it from my directory.

I rip my glasses off. Then I sit back in my chair, looking wildly around our apartment. My eyes settle on Keira, seated across from me. She's taken off her glasses, too, and is staring at me with the same shocked expression I'd seen on Jena's face.

"Em," Keira whispers. "What did you do?"

"I—" I stutter, then stop. Something about reaching into Jena's account had erased my anonymity. I've been exposed. I stare down at the table. My heart thuds.

Keira leans forward. "I could see you in the game," she says. "Em—Asher *spoke* to you. He could see you. They could *all* see you." She throws her hands up in astonishment. "You glitched the game!"

She has absolutely no idea how much trouble I've just gotten myself into; she thinks this was an honest mistake. Below my rising panic lies an ocean of regret. I don't know what Henka Games does when they catch a hacker, but they'll ban me from the game for sure. I'll go to court for this. "I'm sorry," I reply in a daze. "Maybe they—they won't make a big deal out of it . . ."

My voice trails off. Keira lets out a long breath and leans back in her chair. We don't speak for a while. After being so immersed in Warcross, the silence in the apartment feels overwhelming.

"You're smart, Em," Keira finally says, her eyes meeting mine. "But I have a feeling you're dead wrong on that one."

And as if on cue, my phone rings.

# 5

**We both jump** at the sound. When I peer at the phone, the caller ID says: *Unknown Number.*

"Aren't you going to answer it?" Keira says to me, her eyes as wide as mine now. I just shake my head repeatedly at the phone. I don't move from my spot until, after what seems like an eternity, it finally stops ringing.

Immediately, it rings again. *Unknown Number.*

The hairs rise on the back of my neck. I turn the phone's sound off, then throw it onto the couch so I can't see it. In the silence, I stay hunched in my chair and try not to meet Keira's bewildered stare.

The caller had to be the police. Would they come to arrest me now if I didn't pick up? Would Henka Games sue me? It occurs to me that I've just interrupted a game watched by half a billion people, a game that accepts millions in sponsor money. Would the game studio itself put out a bounty on my head, for other hunters to track me down? In fact, they could be sending out a text alert right now, and all across the city, hunters would be swinging onto their motorcycles or hopping in cabs, eager to catch me. I press my shaking hands tightly together in my lap.

I could run. I had to. I'd grab the first train and make my way out of the city until everything dies down. But I grimace immediately at the impossible thought. If I ran, where would I go? How far could I get with only thirteen dollars? And if—no, *when*—they caught me, it would just make my crime worse. It might be safer for me to stay put right here.

Keira wanders over to the couch. "It's still ringing, Em."

"Then stop looking at it," I shoot back, harsher than I'd meant to sound.

She throws her hands up. "Fine, whatever. Suit yourself." Without another word, she turns away from me and heads for her mattress. I close my eyes, put my head in my hands, and lean against the table. The silence in the room is overwhelming, and even though I can't hear my phone, I can *feel* it, can somehow tell that it's still ringing. At any moment, there'll be a fist pounding on our door.

*Every locked door has a key.* But this time, I've reached the end.

I don't know how long I sit like that at the table, spinning thoughts and plans until they all jumble together or when, in my utter exhaustion, I start to nod off. I don't realize that I've fallen asleep until, somewhere through the darkness, a sound stirs me.

*Ding.*

*Ding.*

*Ding.*

I open one eye groggily. Is that my alarm going off? Sunshine streams in through the blinds of our windows. For an instant, I admire how pretty the bright light looks. In fact, it's the kind of bright light that tells me I'm late for something. A sinking feeling hits my stomach. I'd fallen asleep right at the dining table.

I jerk my head up. My entire body is sore, and my arms are cramped and tingly from being slept on all night. I look around in a daze. What happened last night comes back in a rush. While Keira went to bed, I'd stayed here at the table, my head in my hands, wondering how I could have been stupid enough to reveal myself to five hundred million people. I must have had nightmares last night—even though I can't remember any of them, I'm dead tired, and my heart is pounding furiously.

*The phone calls. The unknown caller ID.* My heart seizes, and my eyes go to my phone, still lying on the couch. I'd slept for a few hours, and no one had come to our door.

Some of my panic from the night before eases, and the shock of standing in the middle of the opening game dulls. Maybe nothing will actually happen. The events even feel like a dream.

*Ding.*

I turn toward the sound again. It came from my phone. Suddenly I remember that it's Wednesday. I'm late for my shift at the diner. That must be my boss texting me, and my text messages still make a sound on my phone. In a heartbeat, my worries shift from my glitch to the danger of losing the only moneymaking gig that I have.

I leap out of my chair. Keira stirs in her corner, partially hidden from view behind the cardboard divider. I rush into the bathroom and jam a toothbrush into my mouth, running a quick comb through my tangle of rainbow hair as I go. I'm wearing the same clothes I wore last night. They'll have to do. No time to change. I curse silently at myself as I finish brushing my teeth. I'm going to get fired for missing my shift. My head bows as I lean against the sink, struggling under the weight of the world.

*Ding.*

*Ding! Ding!*

"Oh, for the love of—" I snap under my breath. When my phone lets out two more *dings,* I give up ignoring it and hurry out of the bathroom. "I'm on my way," I mutter, as if my boss could hear me.

I grab my phone and stare down at the long list of texts.

Eighty-four messages, from a blocked number. They all say the same thing.

> **Ms. Emika Chen, please call 212-555-0156 immediately.**

An uneasy feeling settles in my stomach.

"Em."

I turn to see Keira out of bed and peering through the blinds. Only now do I hear the sound of voices coming from the street below.

"Emi," Keira says. "Come look."

I walk to her on quiet feet. Thin slants of light cut through the blinds, painting yellow stripes against my arms. Keira's lips are folded into a puzzled frown. I pull two blinds apart, and look outside.

A cluster of people jams the steps leading up to our apartment complex. They have huge cameras with them. I see call letters printed on the sides of their microphones—it's the local news stations.

My stomach drops. "What's going on?"

Keira turns to face me, then fumbles in her pockets for her phone. She quickly types something. I hold my breath, listening to the buzz of voices outside.

Keira reads the search results on her phone. The color has drained from her face, and her eyes are wide.

"Emi," she says. "You're everywhere."

I find myself looking at a list of news articles, each one displaying the same photo: a screenshot of *me*, with my rainbow-colored hair, standing inside the Warcross opening game, with Asher turned toward me in shock. Keira scrolls down for me. The articles go on and on, their headlines melding together.

## Audience Member Glitches into Warcross Opening Game

### WARCROSS HACKED!

### *HACKER TEMPORARILY DISRUPTS WARCROSS OPENING*

## Who Is Emika Chen?

My mouth goes dry at the sight of my name. I'm a fool for thinking that my little stunt last night would have attracted anything less than a spotlight. My identity's been blown. Not only blown, but with those blown bits plastered all over the internet like stickers. *It's too late to run.* I stay frozen as Keira continues to search, her expression turning more stunned as she goes.

"They can't possibly be talking about me," I stammer. "They can't. I must still be asleep."

"You're not asleep." Keira holds up her phone again. I read a feed littered with my name. "You're the world's *top* trending topic."

Over by the dining table, my phone dings again. We look at it in unison.

"Keira," I say, "do me a favor and look up a number for me." She follows me to the dining table, where I pick up the phone and scan the endless string of identical texts. "212-555-0156."

Keira types it into a search. A second later, she swallows and looks at me. "It's the number for Henka Games' Manhattan headquarters."

A prickling sensation of dread travels down my spine and along my arms. Henka Games has sent me over eighty text messages. Keira and I look at each other for a moment longer, letting the commotion outside fill the silence in our room. "It's probably their lawyers," I whisper. A rush of light-headedness makes me sway in place. A flurry of thoughts flash by: police sirens; handcuffs; courtrooms; interrogation chambers. Familiar experiences for me. "Keira—they're going to sue me."

"You better call them," Keira replied. "It won't be any better for you if you wait."

She's right. I hesitate for a second before finally grabbing my phone. My hands are shaking so badly that I can barely dial the numbers. Keira crosses her arms, pacing in front of me.

"Put it on speaker," she adds. I do, then hold the phone between us.

I'd expected some general thank-you-for-calling-Henka-Games-for-English-press-1 automated message—the typical greeting from a corporate number. But instead, the phone rings only once before a woman answers.

"Miss Emika Chen?" she says.

I'm so startled by her personal greeting that I fumble all over my answer. "Hi. Here. I mean, me. I mean, that's me." I wince. Why am I even surprised? Obviously, they know my phone number, judging by the text message avalanche—they must've forwarded me straight to a live operator the instant I dialed them. *They've been waiting.*

"Excellent," the woman says. "I have Mr. Hideo Tanaka on the line for you. Please hold."

Keira sucks in her breath and stops pacing. She looks at me with wide eyes. I stare back, paying attention to nothing but the hold music now playing on the phone. I've lost my mind. "Did she just say . . . ?"

We both jump when the music abruptly cuts off. A man's voice comes on the line. It's a voice I'd recognize anywhere, one I've heard in countless documentaries and interviews, one that belongs to the last person I thought I'd ever talk to.

"Miss Chen?" says Hideo Tanaka.

His accent is British. *Attended a British international school,* I remind myself feverishly. *Studied at Oxford.* His voice, easy and refined, carries in it the authority of someone who runs a huge corporation. I can only stand there, phone in hand, staring at Keira as if I could see straight through her.

Keira wheels her arms frantically at me, reminding me that I'm supposed to respond. "Uh," I manage. "Hey."

"A pleasure," Hideo says, and my phone trembles in my grip. Keira takes pity on me and holds it for me. I expect Hideo's next words to have something to do with my hacking incident, so I immediately start to stammer some sort of apology, as if that might help my case.

"Mr. Tanaka, about yesterday—look, I am really, really sorry for what happened—it was a total accident, I swear—I mean, my glasses are pretty old and they glitch a lot"—I wince again—"*I mean*—not that your stuff is badly made or anything—which it's not!—er, that is—"

"Yes. Are you busy right now?"

Am I busy right now? Hideo Tanaka is on the phone, asking me if *I am busy right now*? Keira's eyes look like they're going to pop right out of their sockets. *Don't sound stupid, Emika. Be cool.* "Well," I reply, "I'm actually late for my waitressing shift . . ."

Keira slaps her forehead with the palm of her hand. I hold both hands out at her in a panic.

"I apologize for interrupting your schedule," Hideo says, as if my answer were the most natural thing in the world, "but are you willing to skip work today and come to Tokyo?"

My ears start to ring. "What? Tokyo—Japan?"

"Yes."

I cringe, glad he can't see my face turning red. What did I expect him to say—Tokyo, New Jersey? "Like . . . right now?"

A note of amusement enters his voice. "Yes, like, right now."

"I—um—" My head spins. "I'd love to, but my roommate and I are actually about to get evicted from our apartment tomorrow, so . . ."

"Your debts have been taken care of."

Keira and I exchange a blank look. "I'm sorry—what?" I murmur. "They're . . . taken care of?"

"Yes."

The calculations that run constantly through my head. Rent, bills, debt. $1,150. $3,450. $6,000. *Your debts have been taken care of.* Just like that, they scatter, replaced by nothing except white noise. How can this be? If I went to Mr. Alsole's apartment right now, would he wave us away and tell us that we're good to go?

*Why* would Hideo Tanaka do this? I suddenly feel light-headed, like I might float right out of my body. *Don't faint.* "They can't just be taken care of," I hear myself say. "That's a lot of money."

"I assure you, it was very simple. Miss Chen?"

"Yes. Sorry—yes, I'm still here."

"Great. There is a car waiting outside your apartment, ready to take you to John F. Kennedy International Airport. Pack whatever you like. The car is ready when you are."

"A car? But—wait—when's the flight? What airline? How much time do I have to . . ."

"It's my private jet," he says, unconcerned. "It will take off whenever you are in it."

His private jet.

"Wait, but—all of my stuff. How long will I be there?" My eyes shift back to Keira. She looks pale, still processing the fact that our debts have been erased in the blink of an eye.

"If you'd like any belongings packed up and shipped to Tokyo with you," he replies, "just say the word and it'll be done today. In the meanwhile, you will have everything you need here."

"*Hang on.*" I start to shake my head. Shipping my belongings over? Just how long does he want me to stay there? My brow furrows. "What I *need* is a sec to think. I don't understand." My emotions finally spill out, unleashing a torrent of thoughts. "What's this all about? The car, my debts, the plane—*Tokyo?*" I sputter. "Yesterday, I disrupted the biggest game of the year. Someone should be angry with me. *You* should be. What am I going to Tokyo for?" I take a deep breath. "What do you want from me?"

There's a pause on the other end. Suddenly, I realize that I'm mouthing off to one of the world's most powerful people—to my *idol,* someone I've watched and read about and obsessed over for years, someone who had changed my life. Across from me, Keira watches the phone intently as if she could see what Hideo's expression looks like. I swallow in the silence, afraid for a moment.

"I have a job offer for you," Hideo replies. "Would you like to hear more?"

# 6

Confession: I've been on an airplane a grand total of one time. It was after Mom left, and Dad decided to move us from San Francisco to New York. What I remember of that flight is the following: a tiny TV monitor to watch cartoons on; a little window through which I could see the clouds; a Tetris-like meal tray holding something questionably called chicken; and a mod of the original *Sonic the Hedgehog 2* video game loaded onto my phone, my go-to game whenever I was feeling stressed out.

Somehow, I think my second flight will be very different from my first.

After the call with Hideo ended, the first thing I did was rush down the hall and knock on Mr. Alsole's door. One glance at his dumbstruck face was all I needed to know that I didn't just hallucinate everything.

Our rent is paid through the end of next year.

I pack in a daze. I don't own a suitcase, so I end up stuffing as much clothing into my backpack as it can fit. My thoughts jumble together, every one of them about Hideo. What does he want me for? It must be huge, if it means flying me like this to Tokyo. Hideo has indeed hired a few hackers in the past—to help him work out bugs inside Warcross—but they were way more experienced, and probably with no criminal records. What if he's actually angry with me, and is waiting to dole out punishment once I'm in Japan? It's a ridiculous idea, sure . . . but so is being asked to pack up everything and go to Tokyo. *Asked by Hideo Tanaka.* The thought warms my insides again, and I tingle at the mystery of what this job offer might be.

Keira's eyes trail me as I dart around the apartment. "When are you going to come back?" she asks, even though she'd heard the same conversation that I had.

I cram another T-shirt into my backpack. "Don't know," I reply. "Probably soon." Secretly, I hope I'm wrong.

"How do you know this isn't just some huge prank?" she says. A note of confusion in her voice. "I mean—it *was* broadcast everywhere across the internet."

I pause to look at her. "What do you mean?"

"I mean, what's to stop someone from dialing your number a million times and then playing the biggest hoax of all time on you?"

*That must be it.* It has to be. Some hacker out there thought it would be funny. Somebody broke into my phone's weak security, faked Hideo's voice, set me up—he's probably laughing his head off right now.

But our rent is paid off. What prankster would waste his money like that?

All I can do is shrug. "Well, I'm going to see how far I can push it. Not like I have much to lose."

As I finish with the last of my things, I hurry over to the little menagerie of objects by my bed. My Christmas ornament. Dad's painting. I pick up both, taking extra care with the painting. It's an explosion of blue, green, and gold streaks that, when you step back, somehow look like him holding my hand and walking me through a warm, tree-lined evening in Central Park. I stare at it for a moment longer, then pack it carefully into my bag. I could use a bit of good luck traveling with me.

An hour later, I'm as ready as I'll ever be. I hoist my backpack and skateboard over my shoulders and step out of the apartment, then glance back, my eyes settling on Keira. I have a strange feeling I'm studying a life that I won't be returning to. That this will be the last time I ever see her. And I find myself softening toward her, quietly wishing her well. She'll have a rent-free apartment until the end of next year; maybe that'll help her get back on her feet.

"Hey," I say, feeling unsure of how to say good-bye. "The corner diner is going to need someone now. If you're looking."

"Yeah." She smiles. "Thanks."

"Good luck."

She gives me a single, solemn nod. Like she also knows this may be permanent. "You too," she replies.

Then I close the door behind me and don't look back.

When I push open the building's main entrance doors, an explosion of flashing lights blinds me. I squint and throw a hand over my face. A roar of voices go up. "Miss Chen. Miss Chen! Emika!" I wonder for an instant how the hell these people recognize me, before I remember that, with the rainbow of colors in my hair, it's pretty obvious that I'm the same girl from the published screenshots.

An enormous figure bounds up the steps, pushing journalists

aside in the process. "Allow me, ma'am," he says in a friendly tone as he takes my backpack and board. He holds an arm out in front of me and starts making a path down the steps. When one journalist gets pushy, he shoves him back with a growl. I follow my new bodyguard dutifully, ignoring the questions thrown at me from all sides.

We finally push our way over to a car—the most beautifully sleek auto-car I've ever seen. I bet it's the first time one has ever been spotted on our street. The bodyguard puts my stuff in the trunk. One of the car doors opens automatically, waits for me to shuffle inside, and then closes. The sudden silence, and the separation from the din outside, is a relief. Everything in it looks so luxurious that I feel like I'm ruining it just by sitting here. The clean scent of a new car hangs in the space. Bottles of champagne sit in a molded block of ice. Through the windows, I can see an overlay of virtual markers over the streets and buildings. *Randall Avenue,* reads a string of white letters overlaid across the street we're on. Colorful little text bubbles pop up over each of the buildings. *Green Hills Apartment Complex. Laundr-O-Matic. Chinese Food.* This car has the NeuroLink fully integrated into it.

The car's interior lights up. A voice comes on. "Hello, Miss Chen," it says. I startle.

"Hi," I say back, unsure where I should be looking.

"A preference for the car mood?" the voice continues. "Something serene, perhaps?"

I glance out at the mob of journalists still shouting at the car's shaded windows. "Serene would be nice, Mr. . . . Car."

"Fred," the car says.

"Fred," I reply, trying not to feel weird about talking to a bottle of champagne in an ice block. "Hi."

All of the windows suddenly shift, and the journalists outside are replaced with a view of a stunning landscape—long grasses blowing in the wind, white cliffs out along the horizon, clear ocean and white foam, and a sunset tinting the clouds orange and pink. Even the chaos outside now sounds muffled, covered by calling seagulls and the crash of the virtual ocean.

"I'm George," the bodyguard says as the car starts to drive us forward. "You must have had quite a morning."

"Yeah," I reply. "So . . . do you know why we're heading for the airport?"

"My instructions from Mr. Tanaka were only to escort you safely to the jet."

I go back to staring at the virtual seascape passing us. *Instructions from Hideo.* Maybe it's not an elaborate prank after all.

Half an hour later, the serene views on the windows fade away, and the real world comes back into view. We've arrived at the airport. Instead of pulling into the usual circle where all the other vehicles go, though, ours turns into a small looping road that takes us toward the expanse of tarmac behind the airport. Here, the car pulls into a private garage that is situated next to a small row of jets.

I scoot out of the car's dark interior, then squint in the light. One jet has Henka Games written on its side. It's enormous, nearly the size of a commercial liner—except thin and sleek, with an elegant, sharp-nosed design that distinguishes it from the other jets. The panels along the sides of the plane look strange, almost translucent. The main door is open, and a set of stairs leads down to the tarmac, where a plush red rug lies. This is the plane that Hideo himself uses whenever he travels.

"This way, Miss Chen," George says to me with a slight bow of his head. I'm about to go around to the back of the car to grab my backpack, but he stops me. "You won't need to lift anything on this trip," he adds with a smile. I stand there awkwardly, empty-handed, as George grabs my stuff and leads me in the direction of the jet.

I make my way up the steps. At the top, two flight attendants dressed in impeccable uniforms give me dazzling smiles and a bow of their heads. "Mr. Tanaka welcomes you on board," one of them says to me. I nod back, unsure what to say to that. Is Hideo being kept up-to-date on where I am right now? Does he know I'm boarding his plane at this very moment? My thoughts linger on the flight attendant's words—until I turn to look at the inside of the jet.

Now I understand why the outside panels of the plane looked so translucent. The interior appears lined with glass panels, through which I can see the airport, runway, and sky. On second glance, the panels have the Henka Games logo carved subtly into the surface. Sleek lines of light rim the panels. I've only ever seen the inside of planes crammed with seats—but this one has a full-length leather couch at the far end, an actual bed embedded against each side, a full bathroom and shower, and a set of soft lounge chairs near the front. A glass of champagne and a plate of fresh fruit sit on the table separating the lounge chairs. I'm frozen for a moment, suddenly uneasy in the midst of this extravagance.

George sets my backpack in a back closet of the plane. Then he gives me a tip of his hat and a smile. "Have a lovely trip," he says. "Enjoy the flight." Before I can ask him what he means, he turns away and heads down the stairs to his car.

As the attendants seal the door, one of them invites me to make myself at home. I wander over to one of the lounge chairs, sink cautiously onto the soft leather, and inspect the armrests. Do these glass panels change, like the windows in the car I just rode in? I'm about to ask the attendant approaching me, but I'm interrupted when he hands me a pair of glasses. I recognize it instantly as the current generation of Warcross glasses that are being sold in stores—much more powerful than the old rentals I've been using up until now.

"For your enjoyment," the attendant says, smiling at me. "And for a full flight experience."

"Thanks." I turn the glasses in my hands, admiring the solid-gold metal of the arms. My fingers stop above an elegant logo that says: *Alexander McQueen for Henka Games.* These are the luxury, limited-edition version of the glasses. Dad would have held his breath in delight.

I'm about to put them on when the plane starts to move forward. My eyes go to the glass panels on the sides and top of the aircraft. I can see straight through them to the tarmac, and I can even see the front landing gear. If I stare hard enough, it seems as if the seats were simply floating over the ground, with nothing separating us from the outside. The ground rushes by faster and faster. Above me is clear blue sky and it feels as if we're going to be launched to our certain death.

Then the plane leaves the runway, and my body crushes slightly into the seat. Through the glass panels, the world below us falls away, and just like that—we're airborne.

I don't realize how hard I'm gripping my seat until the flight attendant taps me. I look up to see his relaxed smile. "No need to worry, miss," he says over the hum of the engines. "This is one of the most advanced planes in the world. It's supersonic. From here, we'll travel to Tokyo in less than ten hours." He nods down at my armrest, and when I follow his gaze, I see that my knuckles have turned completely white from my grip. I carefully let out a breath and loosen my fingers.

"Right," I reply.

As we start to level out in altitude, the world disappears altogether into a blanket of clouds. The panels now change to opaque, leaving only two horizontal stripes of glass transparent to the outside.

The flight attendant tells me to put my glasses on. I do as he says. Immediately, I notice several differences between these and my old rental pair. The new glasses are lighter, for one, and fit more comfortably on my face. When I put them on, shading the world around me a tint darker, and plug their earphones into my ears, a female voice comes on.

"Welcome," the voice says. The glasses turn completely black, blocking my surroundings out. "Please look to your left."

When I do as it says, I see a red sphere materialize in the left field of my vision, hovering in the black space. A pleasant *ding* sounds.

"Confirmed. Please look to your right."

The red sphere vanishes. I obey, and when I look to my right, there is a floating blue sphere. Another *ding*.

"Confirmed. Please look up."

The blue sphere disappears, too. I look up and see a floating yellow sphere. *Ding*.

"Confirmed. Please look forward."

In the darkness, a gray sphere appears, followed by a cube, a pyramid, and a cylinder. Again, the *ding* sounds, followed by a brief tingle along my temples.

"Please touch your forefinger and thumb together on both hands."

I obey, and it runs through a quick series of tests for my movements.

"Thank you," the voice says. "You are now calibrated."

These new glasses have such a better system than the old

ones. With this simple calibration, the glasses should now be able to know my brain's preferences and variations enough to sync up everything in Warcross to me. I wonder idly whether my hacks will still work now.

The glasses lighten and turn clear, so that I can see the inside of the plane again. This time, a layer of virtual reality lies over my view, so that the flight attendants' names hover over their heads. As I look on, transparent white text appears in the center of my vision.

**Welcome on board Henka Games Private Jet**
**+1,000 Pts. Daily Score: +1,000**
**Level 24 | ₦1,580**

Then the text fades out, and a virtual video feed appears, displaying a young man sitting at a long table.

He turns to me and smiles. I've seen this man's face enough times in interviews to recognize him right away—Kenn Edon, the creative director of Warcross and Hideo's closest confidant. He sits on the official Warcross Committee, those who choose the teams and worlds that will appear in each year's championship tournaments. Now he leans back, runs a hand through his golden hair, and offers me a smile. "Miss Chen!" he exclaims. I offer a weak wave of my hand in response.

He glances over his shoulder. "She's on. Want a word?"

*He's talking to Hideo,* I realize, and my heart leaps into my throat in panic at the thought that he might see me right now.

Hideo's unmistakable voice answers from somewhere behind Kenn that I can't see. "Not now," he replies. "Give her my best."

My moment of panic turns into a stab of disappointment. I shouldn't be surprised—he must be busy. Kenn turns back to give me an apologetic nod. "You'll have to excuse him," he says. "If he seems a bit distant, I assure you it has little to do with his enthusiasm for you. Nothing can pull him away when he's in the middle of working on something. He wants to thank you for coming here on such short notice."

Kenn sounds like he's used to apologizing for his boss. *What is Hideo working on?* Already, I'm trying to figure out what kind of new virtual reality they have installed in their headquarters. Kenn's not wearing any glasses, for one. The fact that I can hear Hideo reply even though he's not logged in or wearing glasses, or that I can see Kenn talking to me live like this, is definitely new tech. "Believe me," I reply, glancing pointedly around the plane. "I'm not bothered."

Kenn's grin widens. "I can't give you many details yet about why you're coming here. That will be up to Hideo. He's looking forward to meeting you." Another wave of warmth washes over me. "But he has asked me to tell you a couple of things, to prepare you."

I lean forward in my chair. "Yes?"

"We'll have a team ready to take you to your hotel once you arrive." He holds both hands up. "A few of your new fans may be gathered at the airport to greet you. But don't worry. Your safety is our priority."

I blink. I'd seen the list of articles that had popped up this morning, and there had been the crowd of journalists in front of our apartment. But in *Tokyo*, too? "Thanks," I decide to say.

Kenn drums his fingers once on the table. I hear it. "After you arrive, you'll have the night to rest. The following morning, you'll come here to the Henka Games headquarters to meet Hideo. He'll tell you everything you need to know about the draft."

Kenn's last words make me freeze. It's such a crazy thought

that at first I don't know how to react. "Wait," I say. "Hang on. Did you just say . . . the *draft?*"

"The draft to determine this year's players in the official Warcross championships?" He winks, as if he'd been waiting for me to catch on. "Well, well, I guess I did. Congratulations."

# 7

Every year, a month before the official games actually begin, there is the Wardraft—an event watched by pretty much anyone and everyone interested in Warcross. This is where the official Warcross teams select the players who will be on their teams for this year's games. Everyone knows, of course, that the seasoned players will probably be selected again. Players like Asher and Jena, for example. But there are always a handful of wild cards thrown into the draft, amateur players nominated because they are so good at the game. Some of the wild cards then rise to become the regularly chosen players.

This year, *I'll* be a wild card.

It makes no sense. I'm a good Warcross player, but I've never had the time or money to get enough experience or levels to hit the world leaderboards. In fact, I'll be the only wild card in this year's draft who *isn't* internationally ranked. And who has a criminal record.

I try to sleep on the plane. But even though the luxurious, full-length bed feels better than any mattress I've ever been on, I just end up tossing and turning. Finally, I give up and pull out my phone, load up my mod of *Sonic the Hedgehog 2*, and start a new game. The familiar, tinny music of Emerald Hill Zone pops up. As I run down a path I've long ago memorized, I can feel my nerves calming, my heartbeat steadying a bit as I forget about the day and instead worry about when I need to jump-attack a sixteen-bit robot.

*I have a job offer for you.* That's what Hideo had said, an offer he'd tell me more about in person. That doesn't sound like something he'd do for every other wild-card player in the games.

My thoughts go to the stories I've heard about Hideo. Most have never seen him without a proper collar shirt and dress pants, or a formal tuxedo suit. His smiles are rare and reserved. An employee had said in a magazine interview that you were qualified to work at Henka Games only if you could withstand the scrutiny of his piercing stare while giving him a presentation. I've seen live broadcasts of reporters stumbling over their questions in his presence while he waited patiently and politely.

I imagine what our meeting will be like. It's possible he'll take one look at me and send me back to New York without a word.

The time hovering over the ceiling of my bed tells me that it's four a.m. in the middle of the Pacific Ocean. Maybe I'll never be able to sleep again. My thoughts whirl. We'll land in Tokyo in a few hours, and then I'm going to talk to Hideo. *I might play in the official Warcross games.* The thought turns over and over in my head. How is this even possible? Last night, I'd hacked into the Warcross opening ceremony in a desperate attempt to make some fast money. Today, I'm headed to Tokyo on a private jet, on a trip that might change my life forever. What would Dad think?

*Dad.*

I access my account and bring up a scrolling menu, the words a transparent white in my view. I reach out to tap on one hovering menu item.

## Memory Worlds

When I select this, the menu brings up a scrolling subset of options. Each one I look at for longer than a second starts to play a preview of a Memory that I had stored. There are Memories of Keira and me celebrating our first night in the little studio we'd rented, and of me holding out my first check after my first successful bounty hunt. Then there are my Shared Favorites, Memories created by others that anyone can enjoy—like being in Frankie Dena's shoes as she performs at the Super Bowl, or standing in the place of a little boy being swarmed by a pile of puppies, a Memory that has been shared over a billion times.

Finally, I go to my most treasured subset—my oldest Memories, stored in a separate Favorites category. These are old videos that I recorded on a phone before the NeuroLink even came out, videos that I later downloaded into my account. They are of my father. I scroll through them until I settle on one. It's my tenth birthday, and Dad's hands are covering my eyes. Even though it's an old, grainy phone video, it fills my view through my glasses like a giant screen. I feel the same anticipation that I'd felt that day, get the same surge of joy as Dad's hands opened to reveal a painting he'd made of us, walking through a world of colorful paint strokes that looks like Central Park at twilight. I jump up and down, twirl the painting around, and get up on a chair to hold it aloft. My father smiles up at me, then reaches his arms out to help me hop down. It plays until it runs out and automatically goes to the next Memory in my storage. Dad in a black peacoat and bright red scarf, guiding me down the halls of the Museum of Modern Art. Dad teaching me how to paint. Dad and me picking out peonies in the Flower District while rain pours down outside. Dad shouting *Happy New Year!* with me on a rooftop overlooking Times Square.

The Memories play over and over, until I can't tell whether or not they've started again from the beginning, and gradually, I drift off into sleep, surrounded by ghosts.

● ● ● ● ●

IN MY DREAMS, I'm back in high school, revisiting what led to my criminal record.

Annie Pattridge was an awkward, shy girl in my high school, a kid with gentle eyes who kept to herself and ate her lunches in a corner of the school's little library. Sometimes I ran across her in there. I wasn't her friend, exactly, but we were *friendly*—we'd chatted a couple of times about our shared love of Harry Potter and Warcross and *League of Legends* and computers. Other times, I'd see her picking her books off the ground after someone had knocked them out of her arms, or catch her backed up against the lockers while a bunch of kids stuck gum in her hair, or glimpse her stumbling out of the girls' bathroom with a crack in her glasses.

But then, one day, a boy working on a group project with Annie managed to snap a photo of her showering in the privacy of her own home. The next morning, Annie's naked photo had been sent to every student in school, shared on the school's homework forums, and posted online. Then came the taunts. The printouts of the photo, all cruelly drawn on. The death threats.

Annie dropped out a week later.

On the day she did, I got the data of every student (and a few teachers) who'd shared the photo. School admin systems? As much a joke to break as a PC with the password *Password*. From there, I hacked into every single one of their phones. I downloaded all of their personal info—their parents' credit card data, Social Security numbers, phone numbers, all the hateful emails and texts they'd sent anonymously to Annie, and, of course, most incriminating, their private photos. I took extra care to get everything from the boy who had taken the original picture. Then I posted all of it online, titling it: "Trolls in the Dungeon."

Imagine the uproar the next day. Crying students, furious parents, school-wide assembly, snippets in the local papers. Then, the police. Then, me expelled. Then, me sitting in court.

Accessing computer systems without authorization. Intentional release of sensitive data. Reckless conduct. Four months in juvenile hall. Banned from touching a computer for two years. A permanent red mark on my record, age be damned, because of the nature of the crime.

Maybe I was wrong, and maybe someday I'll look back and regret lashing out like that. I'm still not entirely sure why I threw myself into the fire over this specific incident. But sometimes, people kick you to the ground at recess because they think the shape of your eyes is funny. They lunge at you because they see a vulnerable body. Or a different skin color. Or a difficult name. Or a girl. They think that you won't hit back—that you'll just lower your eyes and hide. And sometimes, to protect yourself, to make it go away, you do.

But *sometimes*, you find yourself standing in exactly the right position, wielding exactly the right weapon to hit back. So I hit. I hit fast and hard and furious. I hit with nothing but the language whispered between circuits and wire, the language that can bring people to their knees.

And in spite of everything, I'd do it all over again.

● ● ● ● ●

WHEN WE FINALLY touch down, I'm an exhausted mess. I pull on my crumpled shirt, then grab my backpack holding my few belongings and follow the flight attendant down the ramp. My eyes go to the Japanese text printed over the entrance into the airport's terminals. I can't understand any of it—but I don't have to, because an English translation appears above them in my virtual view. WELCOME TO HANEDA AIRPORT! it says. BAGGAGE CLAIM. INTERNATIONAL CONNECTING FLIGHTS.

A man in a black suit is waiting for me at the bottom of the ramp. Unlike in New York, here I can see his name floating over his head, telling me that his name is Jiro Yamada. He smiles through his shades, bows to me, and then looks behind me as if expecting more suitcases. When he sees none, he takes my backpack and skateboard, then welcomes me.

It takes me a second to register that Jiro is speaking to me in Japanese—and that it doesn't matter, because I can see transparent white text appearing right below his face, English subtitles translating what he's saying. "Welcome, Miss Chen," the text says. "You are precleared through customs. Come."

As I follow him to a waiting car, I scan the tarmac. No journalists waiting for me here. I relax at that. I get into the car—identical to the one that had taken me to the airport in New York—and it rolls me to the exit. Just like before, it puts on a tranquil scene (this time of a cool, quiet forest) to play on the car's windows.

Here's where the crowd is. As we approach the exit gate, a cluster of people rush forward near the ticket booth and flash cameras at us. I only see them through the front window. Even then, I find myself shrinking into my chair.

Jiro lowers his window a sliver to yell at the journalists to move out of the way. When they finally do, the car zooms forward, the tires screeching a little as we swerve onto the street that leads to the freeway.

"Can we take the scenery off the windows?" I ask Jiro. "I've never seen Tokyo before."

Instead of Jiro answering me, the car does. "Of course, Miss Chen," it says.

*Of course, Miss Chen.* I don't think I'll ever get used to that. The windows' forest scene fades away, leaving the glass clear. I stare in awe at the city we're approaching.

I've seen Tokyo on TV, online, and inside Warcross's Tokyo Night level. I've fantasized about being here so much, I've seen it in my dreams.

But now I'm actually *here*. And it's even better than any of that.

Skyscrapers that disappear into the evening clouds. Highways stacked on top of one another, drenched in the red and gold lights of cars racing by. High-speed rails running in the sky and disappearing underground. Commercials playing on screens eighty stories tall. Kaleidoscopes of color and sound, everywhere I look. I don't know what to take in first. As we near the heart of Tokyo, the streets turn crowded, until the sea of people jamming the sidewalks makes Times Square look empty by comparison. I don't realize my mouth is hanging open until Jiro looks back at me and chuckles.

"I see that expression a lot," he says (or rather, my English subtitle tells me he's saying).

I swallow, embarrassed that he caught me gaping, and close my mouth. "Is this downtown Tokyo?"

"Tokyo is too large to have a single downtown district. There are two dozen wards, each with their own characteristics. We're entering Shibuya now." He pauses to smile. "I'd recommend putting on your glasses."

I put the glasses back on, tap their side to put them on clear mode, and when I do, I gasp.

Unlike New York, or the rest of America, Tokyo seems completely redone for virtual reality. Names of buildings hover in neon colors over each of the skyscrapers, and bright, animated advertisements play across entire sides of buildings. Virtual models stand outside clothing shops, each twirling to show off a variety of outfits. I recognize one of the virtual models as a character from the latest *Final Fantasy* game, a girl with bright blue hair, now greeting me by name and showing off her Louis Vuitton purse. A *Buy Now* button hovers right over it, waiting to be tapped.

The sky is filled with virtual flying ships and colorful orbs, some displaying news, others displaying commercials, still others just there seemingly because they look pretty. As we drive, I can see faint, translucent text in the center of my vision telling us how many kilometers we are from the center of the Shibuya district, as well as the current temperature and weather forecast.

The streets are crowded with young people in elaborate getups—giant lace skirts, elaborate umbrellas, ten-inch-tall boots, eyelashes that seem miles long, face masks that glow in the dark. Some of them have their Warcross level floating over their heads, along with hearts and stars and trophies. Others have virtual pets trotting alongside them, bright purple virtual dogs or sparkling silver virtual tigers. Still others wear all kinds of avatar items, virtual cat ears or antlers on their heads, enormous angel wings on their backs, hair and eyes in every color.

"Since it is officially game season now," Jiro explains, "you will see this quite often." He nods toward a person on the street with **Level 80** and ♥ 3,410,383 over her head, smiling as several people give her high fives and congratulate her on her high rank. A virtual pet falcon swoops in circles around her head, its tail blazing with fire. "Here, almost everything you do will earn you points toward your level in the Link. Going to school. Going to work. Cooking dinner. And so on. Your level can earn you rewards in the real world, anything from popularity with your classmates to better service at restaurants, to an edge over others for a job interview."

I nod as I look on in awe. I've heard many parts of the world are tricked out like this. As if on cue, a transparent bubble appears in my center view with a pleasant *ding*.

### First Time in Tokyo!
### +350 Points. Daily Score: +350
### You leveled up!

My level jumps from 24 to 25. I feel a rush of exhilaration at the sight.

Half an hour later, we turn onto a quiet street sloping up a hill and stop in front of a hotel near the top. The name—Crystal Tower Hotel—and address float over the roof. I may have never been to Tokyo before, but even I can tell that this is in an upper-class neighborhood, with perfectly clean sidewalks and neat rows of cherry trees not yet in bloom. The hotel itself is at least twenty stories tall, sleekly designed, with a virtual image of floating koi swimming across its entire side.

Jiro holds my backpack as I scoot out of the car. The edges of the sliding glass doors light up as we approach it, and when we step inside, two attendants bow at us from either side of the entrance. I bow my head awkwardly back.

"Welcome to Tokyo, Miss Chen," the hotel's registration attendee says to me as we reach the front desk. Over her head is her name—**Sakura Morimoto**, followed by **Front Desk** and **Level 39**. She bows her head at me.

"Hi," I reply. "Thanks."

"Mr. Tanaka has requested our best suite for you. Please," she says, holding out an arm toward the elevators. "This way."

We follow her into an elevator, where she pushes the button for the top floor. My heart starts to hammer again. Hideo had personally requested my room. I can't even remember the last time I stayed in a real hotel—it must have been back when Dad had managed to get an invite to New York Fashion Week, and the two of us got to stay in a tiny little boutique hotel because I'd caught the eye of some modeling scout. But it was nothing even close to this.

When we reach the top floor, the attendant guides us to the only door along the hall. She hands me a keycard. "Please enjoy," she says with a smile. Then she swipes the door open and guides me in.

It's a penthouse suite. We walk into a space that is several times larger than anywhere I've ever lived. A basket of fresh fruit and green tea–flavored snacks sits on the glass coffee table. There's a bedroom and a living room with a curved glass window stretching from floor to ceiling that overlooks a glittering Tokyo. From here, with my new glasses on, I can see the virtual names of streets and buildings blinking in and out as I move around the room. Icons—hearts, stars, thumbs-ups—cluster over various parts of the city, emphasizing areas where the most people have bookmarked favorite spots, shops, or meet-ups with friends. I walk toward the windows until my shoes bump up against the glass, then look out at the city in wonder. Warcross's virtual Tokyo is a sight to behold—but this is *real*, and the knowledge of it *being* real makes me light-headed.

A transparent bubble pops up again:

**Checked into Crystal Tower Hotel Penthouse Suite 1**
**+150 Pts. Daily Score: +500**
**Level 25 | N1,580**

"It's even better than I imagined," I say.

The attendant smiles, even though it must be a pretty silly thing for her to hear. "Thank you, Miss Chen," she says with another bow. "If you need anything during your stay, just let me know, and I will see to it."

As she closes the door behind her, I do one more full turn around the room. My stomach growls as if in response, reminding me that I could use a proper meal.

I walk over to the coffee table, where an option called in-room dining is floating over it. I tap the virtual words and I'm suddenly surrounded by dishes hovering in midair. There must be hundreds of options: enormous burgers dripping with melted cheese, plates of spaghetti thick with sauce and meatballs, assorted platters of sushi, steaming bowls of noodle soups in rich broth, crispy fried chicken with rice, fluffy pork buns and pan-fried dumplings, stews thick with meat and vegetables, silky soft dessert mochi with sweet red bean filling . . . the dishes go on and on.

My head spins as I finally settle on fried chicken and dumplings. While I wait, I spend a full ten minutes trying to figure out how to use the toilet and another ten minutes turning the lights on and off just by waving my hands before me. And when my order arrives, everything tastes even better than it looks. I've never had a meal as fancy as this—I can't even remember the last time I ate something that didn't come out of a box.

When I can't eat another bite, I wander to the bed and flop on it with a contented sigh. The bed is ridiculously comfortable, firm enough that I can just sink slowly into it until it feels like I'm lying on a cloud. My mattress back in our tiny studio had been salvaged for free off the sidewalk, a ratty old spring pad that squeaked like hell every time I moved on it. Now, here I am, staying in this vast penthouse suite that Hideo himself had requested for me.

My contented mood wavers, and abruptly I have a sensation of *unbelonging*. A girl like me simply shouldn't be touching these luxury linens, eating this expensive food, sleeping in this room larger than any home I've ever been in. My gaze wanders to the corner of the suite, searching for the mattresses lying on the floor, Keira's figure huddled under a blanket on the couch. She would have looked at me with that wide-eyed stare. *Can you believe this?* she'd say.

I want to reply to her, to someone. But she's not here. Nothing familiar is here, except for myself.

*Tomorrow morning, ten o'clock.* It occurs to me that I don't even have appropriate clothes to wear—no interview suits, no proper slacks or blouses. I'm going to walk into Henka Games tomorrow looking like a kid literally plucked from the streets. This is how I'm going to meet the most famous young man in the world.

What if Hideo realizes he's made a huge mistake?

# 8

A pair of torn jeans, with both of my knees showing through. My favorite old T-shirt with a vintage print of SEGA on it. The same beat-up pair of boots I wear almost every day. A red plaid flannel shirt, faded from too many washes.

Dad would be horrified.

Despite how comfortable the bed is, I'd tossed and turned all night. I'd woken up at the crack of dawn, bleary-eyed and disoriented, my head crowded with thoughts. Now I have bags under my eyes, and my skin has seen better days.

I'd ironed my poor plaid flannel as well as I could, *twice,* but the collar still looks crumpled and worn. I roll the sleeves up neatly to my elbows, then tug the shirt as straight as I can. In the mirror, I try to pretend it's a sharp blazer. The only thing I like this morning is my hair, which seems to be cooperating with me. It's thick and straight, and the rainbow of colors in it shines in the morning light. But I don't have any makeup to cover the dark circles under my eyes—and with exactly thirteen dollars to my name, I'm not about to go out and blow it on face creams and concealer. Both my T-shirt and the flannel look hopelessly old and worn when contrasted with everything bright and new in this penthouse suite. The sole of my left boot is noticeably peeling off. The holes in my jeans look even bigger than I remember.

Game studios aren't exactly known for strict dress codes, but even *they* must have some sort of etiquette for meeting the top bosses.

For meeting *the* top boss in the entire industry.

A pleasant *ding* echoes around the suite, and a light near my bed's headrest alerts me to an incoming call. I tap to accept it, and a moment later, Sakura Morimoto's voice comes on through speakers hidden throughout my room. "Good morning, Miss Chen." Over the speakers, with no virtual overlays, she switches to speaking English. "Your car is waiting outside for you, whenever you are ready."

"I'm ready," I reply, not believing my own words.

"See you soon," she says.

Jiro and the same car from last night are waiting outside. I half expect him to make some sort of remark about my clothes, or at least raise an eyebrow. But instead, he greets me warmly when I approach, then helps me in. We ride along with a scene of sunflowers and sunrise playing on the windows. Jiro's suit is flawlessly sharp, a perfect black outfit with a crisp white shirt that must be some high-end brand. If this is how Hideo's bodyguards look, then what should I be wearing? I keep tugging at my sleeves, trying to magically change my clothes into something nice by straightening them repeatedly.

I imagine Dad's face if he were to see me right now. He'd suck in his breath and wince. *Absolutely not,* he'd say. He'd grab my hand and start dragging me immediately to the nearest boutique, credit card debt be damned.

The thought makes me tug harder on my sleeves. I push the thought away.

The car finally stops before a white gate. I listen curiously as the bodyguard says something to what looks like an automated machine attendant. From the corner of my eye, I notice a small logo on the side of the gate. *Henka Games.* Then the car moves forward, and we continue inside, parking at a spot near the front sidewalk. Jiro comes around to let me out. "Here we are," he says with a smile and a bow.

He leads me through a large set of sliding glass doors. We step into the largest lobby I've ever seen.

Light pours in from a glass ceiling atrium and down to where we stand, in the middle of an open space decorated with towering indoor vines. Water trickles from several fountains along these walls. Stacks of clean white balconies curve along the building's insides. A faint carving of the Henka Games logo covers one of the white walls. Hanging down from the ceiling in drapes are colorful banners of the competing Warcross teams, each one displaying a team's symbol in celebration of the current championship season. I pause for an instant to admire the sight. If I were wearing NeuroLink glasses right now, I bet these banners would be animated.

**Welcome to Henka Games!**
**+2,500 Pts. Daily Score: +2,500**
**You leveled up!**
**Level 26 | N3,180**

"This way," my bodyguard says, guiding me forward.

We walk toward a series of clear glass cylinders, where a smiling woman is waiting for us. She has a gold pin on her perfectly ironed blazer, in honor of the current tournament season, and a clipboard tucked under one arm. Her smile widens at the sight of me, although I notice her eyes flicker briefly to my clothing. She doesn't say anything about it, but I blush.

"Welcome, Miss Chen," she says, bowing her head in a calm gesture. My bodyguard bids me farewell as I'm handed off to her. "Mr. Tanaka is looking forward to meeting you."

I swallow hard as I return the bow. *He won't be, once he gets a look at the mess that I am.* "Me too," I mumble.

"There are a few rules you'll need to follow," she continues. "First: No photos are allowed during this meeting. Second: You will need to sign an agreement stating that you won't publicly discuss what you're told here." She hands me the form on the clipboard.

No photos. No public discussions. Not a surprise. "Okay," I reply, reading the clipboard's paper thoroughly and then signing it at the bottom.

"And third: I must request that you never ask Mr. Tanaka any questions about his family or their private affairs. This is a company-wide policy, and one that Mr. Tanaka is very strict about maintaining."

I look at her. This one is a weirder request than the first two—but I decide to nod anyway. "No family questions. Got it."

The elevator doors open for us. The lady waves me inside, then folds her arms in front of her as we start to head up. I look out at the expanse of the studio, my eyes lingering on the giant team banners as we rise past them. This building is a beautiful work of architecture. Dad would have been impressed.

We keep going until we reach the top floor. A few employees pass us by, each of them sporting Warcross T-shirts and jeans. The sight is reassuring. One of the employees glances my way with a hint of recognition in his eyes. He looks like he wants to stop me, then reddens and decides against it. I realize that everyone working here must have been watching the opening ceremony—and seen me glitch into the game. As I'm thinking this, I catch sight of a few other employees down in the lobby below, their necks craned curiously up in our direction.

She guides us down an open hallway until we reach a smaller lobby, where another set of sliding glass doors stands. The glass is completely clear, so that I can see part of a room beyond it, along with large paintings of Warcross worlds on the walls and a long meeting table. My legs start to feel numb, and fear shoots up my spine. Now that I'm moments away from my meeting, I'm suddenly gripped with the feeling that maybe I don't want to be here after all.

"Wait one moment, please," the lady says as we reach the doors. She presses a finger gently against a pad on the wall, then walks inside as they slide open. From where I am, I see her bow low and ask something in Japanese. All I can understand are *Tanaka-sama* and *Chen-san*.

A quiet voice answers her from somewhere on the far side of the room.

The lady returns and opens the sliding door. "Come in." She nods at me as I pass. "Have a good meeting." Then she's gone, heading back down the hall from where we came.

I find myself standing in the middle of a room with a stunning view of Tokyo. At one end of the room, several people lounge in chairs around a meeting table—two women, one dressed in a blouse and skirt, another in a Warcross tee, blazer, and jeans. A young, golden-haired man sits between them, making gestures in the air with his hands. I recognize him as Kenn, who had spoken to me on the private jet. The women argue back, scrutinizing something about one of the worlds for the Warcross championships.

My eyes wander from them to the last person in the room.

He's sitting on a sleek gray couch right next to the meeting table, his elbows perched on his knees. The other three people are unconsciously turned in his direction, clearly waiting for him to give the final say. He's dressed in a perfectly tailored white collar shirt rolled up to his elbows and with two of the top buttons casually undone, a pair of lean, dark trousers, and deep scarlet oxford shoes. The only game-related item he's wearing is a pair of simple, silver cuff links glinting in the sunlight, both cut in the shape of the Warcross logo. His eyes are very dark and framed by long lashes. His hair is thick and midnight black, except for a curious, thin silver streak on one side.

Hideo Tanaka, in the flesh.

After years of admiring him from afar, I'm not sure what I expected. It somehow startles me to see him without a monitor or a magazine cover obstructing the view, like he's in focus for the first time.

He looks up at me.

"Miss Chen," he says, pushing himself off the couch in one graceful move. Then he approaches me, bows his head once, and stretches out a hand. He's tall, his gestures easy and effortless, his expression serious. The only imperfection on him is his knuckles—they're bruised, newly scarred, and surprising on his otherwise elegant hands, as if he had been in a fight. I catch myself gaping curiously and manage to stop just in time to extend my hand, too. My movements feel like those of a lumbering ox. Even though my clothes aren't that different from everyone else's, I feel dirty and underdressed compared to his flawless style.

"Hi, Mr. Tanaka," I reply, unsure of what else to say.

"Hideo, please." There's that smooth, subtle British accent of his. He encloses his hand around mine and shakes it once, then looks at the others. "Our lead producer for the championships, Miss Leanna Samuels." He lets go of me to hold his hand out toward the woman in the blouse and skirt.

She gives me a smile and adjusts her glasses. "Pleased to meet you, Miss Chen."

Hideo nods at the woman in the tee and blazer. "My second-in-command, Miss Mari Nakamura, our chief operating officer."

Now I recognize her—I've seen her give plenty of Warcross-related announcements. She gives me a little bow of her head. "Nice to meet you, Miss Chen," she says with a grin. I return the bow as well as I can.

"And you've already been introduced to our creative director," Hideo finishes, tilting his head in Kenn's direction. "One of my former Oxford schoolmates."

"Not in person." Kenn hops out of his chair and is in front of me in a couple of strides. He shakes my hand vigorously. Unlike Hideo's, his expression is warm enough to heat a room in winter. "Welcome to Tokyo. You've made quite an impression on us." He glances once at Hideo, and his grin tilts higher. "It's not every day that he flies someone halfway across the world for an interview."

Hideo raises an eyebrow at his friend. "I flew *you* halfway across the world to join the company."

Kenn laughs. "That was years ago. Like I said—not every day." His smile returns to me.

"Thanks," I decide to say, my head whirling from greeting four legendary creators in ten seconds.

The COO, Mari, turns to Hideo and asks him something in Japanese.

"Go ahead without me," Hideo replies in English. His eyes settle on me again. I realize that he hasn't smiled since I walked in. Maybe I really am too underdressed for him. "Miss Chen and I are going to indulge in a chat."

*A chat. A one-on-one.* I feel the heat rising in my cheeks. Hideo doesn't seem to notice, though, and instead nods for me to follow him out of the room. Behind us, the others return to their conversation. Only Kenn meets my gaze as I look over my shoulder at them.

"He doesn't mean to be intimidating," he calls out cheerfully as the doors close.

"So," Hideo says as we head down the hall to the main atrium, "your first time in Japan, isn't it?"

I nod. "It's nice." Why does everything I say suddenly sound stupid?

More and more employees are slowing down to watch us as we pass. "Thank you for coming all this way," he says.

"Thank *you*," I answer. "I've been watching your career ever since the beginning, when you first hit it big. This is a huge honor."

Hideo gives me a half-interested nod, and I realize he must be tired of hearing that from everyone he meets. "I apologize for interrupting your week, but I hope your trip went well enough."

Is he serious? "That's kind of an understatement," I reply. "Thank you, Mr. Tanaka—Hideo—for paying off my debts. You didn't have to do that."

Hideo waves a nonchalant hand. "Don't thank me. Consider

it a small advance payment. Frankly, I'm surprised you were in debt at all. Surely some tech company has noticed your skills by now."

A needle of irritation pricks me at Hideo's easy dismissal of my debt. I guess six thousand dollars—to me, an unconquerable mountain—isn't even worth a second thought when you're a billionaire. "I have a couple of things on my record," I reply, trying to keep the annoyance out of my voice. "My *criminal* record, I mean. They're nothing that serious, but I wasn't allowed to touch a computer for two years." I decide to not mention my father's death and my time in foster care.

To my surprise, Hideo doesn't press me further. "I've employed enough hackers to know a good one when I see one. You would've been discovered sooner or later." He gives me a sidelong look. "And, well, here you are."

He leads us around a corner and toward another set of sliding doors. We enter an empty office. Windows go from ceiling to floor. A bright mural is painted along one corner, a colorful swirl of stylized game levels. Sleek couches are in another corner. The doors slide closed behind us, and we're alone.

Hideo turns to me. "I know you've seen yourself mentioned everywhere online," he says. "But can you guess why you're here?"

*By mistake?* But instead I respond, "On the flight, Mr. Edon said that I was going to be entered into the Wardraft."

Hideo nods. "You are, unless you don't want to be."

"Does that mean you want me to compete in this year's Warcross championships?"

"Yes."

I suck in my breath. Hearing this from Hideo himself, from the creator of Warcross, finally makes it real. "Why?" I say. "I mean, I'm a pretty good player, but I'm not ranked in the international lists or anything. Are you putting me in for the ratings? As some marketing ploy?"

"Do you have any idea what you actually did when you hopped into the opening game?"

"I ruined the biggest game of the year?" I venture a guess.

"You managed to hack through a shield that has almost never been breached."

"Sorry. I'd never tried that hack before."

"I thought you said it was an accident."

I meet his penetrating stare. Now he's taunting me for my stuttering apology during our first phone call. "I'd never *accidentally* tried that hack before," I rephrase.

"I'm not telling you this because I'm upset that you broke in." He lifts an eyebrow at me. "Although I'd prefer that you not do it again. I'm telling you this because I need your help."

Something in his earlier words triggers my interest. "You said that security shield had *almost* never been breached. Who else got in?"

Hideo walks over to the couches, sits down, and leans back. He gestures for me to take a seat across from him. "That's why I need your help."

In a flash, I understand. "You're trying to catch someone. And the best way to do it is for you to enter me in this year's games."

Hideo tilts his head at me. "I heard that you're a bounty hunter."

"Yes," I reply. "I catch Warcross players who owe large gambling debts, and anyone else the police don't have time to get."

"So you must be familiar with the underworld that has popped up since my glasses first came on the market."

I nod. "Of course."

A thriving underworld has always existed underneath the

regular internet. It's the part of the online world you don't see, that no search engine will ever show you. That you cannot even enter unless you know what you're doing. The dark web is where hackers congregate, drugs are trafficked, sex is sold, and assassins are hired. That has only increased with the popularity of Warcross and the NeuroLink glasses. The same underworld exists now in virtual reality, except it's called the Dark World—a dangerous virtual place where I frequently wander, searching for the criminals who like to hang out there.

"And you're comfortable there?" Hideo asks, regarding me.

I bristle at his condescension. "If I weren't, I wouldn't be much use in catching a hacker, now would I?"

Hideo doesn't react to my sarcasm. "You'll be one of several bounty hunters I'm hiring for this job." He reaches toward the coffee table separating us and picks up a small black box resting on top of a stack of game magazines. He holds it out to me. "This is for you. The others will be receiving them, too."

*Other bounty hunters.* Like my past hunts, I'll be competing against others. I hesitate, then take the box from him. It's light as air. I glance at Hideo before opening the box. Inside is a small, plastic container with two round compartments. I twist one of them open.

"Contact lenses," I say, staring down at a clear disc floating in liquid.

"Beta versions. We're releasing them to the public later this week."

I look back up at Hideo in anticipation. "The next generation of NeuroLink glasses?"

His lips tilt up into the smallest hint of a smile, the first I've seen. "Yes."

My eyes turn down again. They look like any contact lenses

would, except that on the rims, in tiny, translucent, repeated lettering, are the words *Henka Games*. All that's needed to identify them as different from a regular pair of lenses. When I shift a little, the lenses glitter in the light, suggesting that their surface is probably coated with a fine web of microscopic circuits. For a second, I forget about my annoyance with Hideo's replies. Instead I feel like I'm back in my group foster home, listening to the radio, hearing about his earthshaking invention for the first time. "How . . . ," I start to say, my fascination coming out as a hoarse croak. "How did you do this? How do you even *power* them? It's not like you can plug them into a wall."

"The human body produces at least one hundred watts of electricity a day," Hideo replies. "The average smartphone only uses two to seven watts to fully charge. These lenses need less than one watt."

I look sharply at him. "Are you saying that it can be charged just by the electricity in my body?"

He nods. "The lenses leave behind a harmless film against the eye surface that is only one atom thick. This film acts as a conduit between the lenses and your body."

"Using the body as a charger," I say. There'd been plenty of movies made about that, and yet here I am, staring down at it right in my hands. "I thought that was just some science fiction myth."

"Everything's science fiction until someone makes it science fact," Hideo says. There's a specific intensity in his gaze now, a glow that brightens his entire expression. I remember seeing it the first time I caught him on TV, and I recognize it now. *This* is the Hideo that draws me in.

He gestures toward a door at the far end of the office. "Give it a try."

I take the lenses and head over to the door, which opens into a private bathroom. There, I wash my hands and hold up one of the lenses. It takes me at least a dozen tries, but finally I manage to put both of them in, blinking away a few tears as I do. They feel ice-cold.

As I return to the couch, I study the room. At first glance, everything seems the same. But then I notice that the brightly colored mural behind Hideo is moving, as if the painting were alive, the colors swirling and shifting in a spectacular display.

My gaze continues to wander. I notice more and more things. Layers of virtual reality, freed from the boundaries of glasses. An old Warcross game plays across another white wall in the room, covering it from top to bottom. The ceiling isn't a ceiling anymore. Instead, I can see a dark blue night and the glittering sheet of the Milky Way. Planets—Mars and Jupiter and Saturn—are magnified and exaggerated in color, hanging orb-like in the sky. Around the room, objects have labels hovering over them. **Potted Ficus** floats above a green plant, along with the words, **Water | +1**, hinting that I would earn a point if I watered it. **Couch** floats above our couches, and **Hideo Tanaka | Level ∞** hovers above Hideo himself. I probably have **Emika Chen | Level 26** hanging over my own head.

A few translucent words appear in the center of my view.

### Play Warcross

Hideo gets up and walks over to sit beside me. Now I notice that he's wearing contacts, too—with mine on, I can see a faint, glittering sheet of colors against his pupils. "Join a session of Warcross with me," he says. A hovering button appears between us. "And I'll show you who I'm after."

I take a deep breath and stare at the button before me for a few seconds. The contacts detect my lingering look, and the real world around us—the office, the couches, the walls—darkens and disappears.

When the world reappears again, we are both standing in a sterile, white space with white walls that stretch to infinity. I recognize it as one of the beginner worlds in Warcross: Paintbrush Level. If you reach out your hands and run them along the white walls, streaks of rainbow paint sweep across the surfaces. I curl my toes slightly and imagine walking—and with those double cues, my avatar moves forward. As we walk, I absently run a hand along one of the walls, watching as the colors streak behind my fingers.

Hideo leads us to a corner of the world, where he finally stops. I relax my toes and stop, too. He looks at me. "This is the first world where we noticed something was off," he says. He runs a hand along the wall, leaving trails of bright green and gold. Then, he digs his fingers against the surface and *pushes*.

The wall opens, obeying his touch.

Behind the wall is a world of dark lines and streaks of light, sequenced into detailed patterns. *The code that runs this world.* This is a glimpse of the API at work in the game. Hideo steps inside the wall, then gestures for me to join him. I hesitate only for a second before leaving the paint-smeared world of white walls and entering the dark mess of lines.

In here, the lines of light cast a faint blue hue against our skin. A jolt of excitement runs through me at the sight, and I scan the columns, analyzing and absorbing as much as I can. Hideo walks a little, then pauses before a segment of code.

My instincts kick in, and my eyes relax, taking in the whole display of code before me. Immediately, I see what the problem is. It's subtle—easily overlooked by someone not experienced with analyzing the NeuroLink's framework—but there it is, a section that looks mangled, the lines tangled in a way that doesn't match the pattern around it, a section out of place with the rest of the organized chaos around us.

Hideo nods approvingly when he realizes that I've noticed it. He steps closer to the tangled part. "Do you see what he did?"

He's not just showing me what had happened. He's testing my skills. "It was rewired," I answer automatically, my eyes darting across the code. "To report data."

Hideo nods, then reaches out to the mangled portion and taps it once. It flickers before snapping back into place, clean and orderly, the way it's supposed to be. "We patched it up. I'm just showing you a memory of how it looked when we first found it. But the person left behind no trace of himself, and he's gotten better at hiding his tracks since then. We've taken to calling him Zero, as that is the default in the access record. It's the only marker he leaves behind." He looks at me. "I'm impressed you caught it."

Does he think *I'm* Zero? I look sharply at him. Has he brought me all the way here, asked me his questions—*Is this your first time in Japan? Do you have any idea what you did?*—just to see if I'm the suspect he's looking for?

I scowl at him. "If you want to know whether or not I'm Zero, you could just ask me."

Hideo gives me a skeptical look. "And would you admit it?"

"I would've appreciated your directness, instead of this roundabout game you're playing with me."

Hideo's stare seems capable of piercing straight through my soul. "You hacked into the opening ceremony game. Should I apologize for suspecting you?"

I open my mouth, then close it. "Fair enough," I admit. "But I didn't do *this*."

He looks coolly away. "I know. I didn't bring you here to force a confession."

I fume in silence.

The world around us suddenly shifts. We've zoomed out of both the code and the Paintbrush Level. Now we're standing on a hovering isle, surrounded by a hundred other floating isles, overlooking a beautiful lagoon. This was the world used in the opening ceremony that I'd hacked into.

Hideo pulls the world as if he were spinning it under his fingers, and it rushes by beneath our feet. I swallow hard. The version that his account is hooked up to is obviously different from mine, giving him in-game abilities that I don't have. It's strange to be inside this game with its own creator and see him play with it as its god. Hideo finally stops us at one portion of the cliffs. He reaches out and pushes. Again, we enter a space of lines and light.

This time, the tangled section is much harder to find. I let my focus turn fuzzy and my subconscious emerge, searching for the break in the pattern. It takes me a few minutes to get my head around it all, but finally, I catch the portion of the code that's off. "Here," I say, pointing. "Same story. Whoever this Zero person is, he set up this level to report stats to him about every single audience member watching the game." The realization sends an ominous shiver through me. I look closer. "Wait—there's more here. He almost disabled the level, didn't he? This spot—he realized that the code was weak here."

When Hideo doesn't reply immediately, I glance away from the code to see him studying me. "What?" I say.

"How did you find that?" he asks.

"Find what? The mangled code?" I shrug. "I just . . . noticed it."

"I don't think you understand." He puts his hands in his pockets. "It took my best engineers a week to do what you just did."

"Then maybe you need better engineers."

I can't seem to control my retorts around Hideo. His chilly demeanor must be rubbing off on me. But he just faces me with a thoughtful look. "And how would you fix this?"

My attention goes to the compromised code. "My father taught me how to take in everything at once," I murmur as I sweep a hand across the text. "You don't have to break down *every* detail. You just need to see the overall pattern to catch the weakness in it." I reach out to grab the code, pull forward an enormous block of it, and swipe it away. Then I replace it with a single, efficient line. The rest clicks into place around it.

"There," I say, resting my hands on my hips. "That's better."

When I look back at him, he's analyzing my change without saying a word. Maybe I've passed his test.

"Decent," he says after a moment.

Decent. *Decent?* My scowl deepens. "Why would someone be interested in collecting this data and messing with the games?"

"Your guess is as good as mine."

"You're worried he's going to sabotage the games again."

"I'm worried he's doing something far worse than that. I refuse to halt the games just to bow to a hacker's threat—but the safety of our audience isn't something I want to compromise." Hideo looks to his side. The world rushes away again, and suddenly we are sitting back in his office. I startle at the sudden shift. These contact lenses are going to take some getting used to. "With your current celebrity status, I thought it best if we hid you in plain sight, put you on one of the teams. It will allow you to be physically closer to the other players."

"Why do you want me close?"

"The nature of the attacks makes me suspect that Zero is one of them."

One of the professional players. Their names rush through my mind. "And what will I and the other hunters be competing for? What's your bounty prize?"

"Each of you will see the prize amount as a pending number in your bank accounts." Hideo leans forward and rests his elbows on his knees. He gives me a pointed look. "If you decide you want to turn this down, that this is more than you want to deal with, I'll have you on a private flight back to New York. You can just treat this as a holiday before returning to your life. I'll pay you a sum for participating, regardless, for catching a major security flaw in the game. Take your time to think it over."

A *sum for participating.* It's as if Hideo were offering me pity money, an easy out if I don't feel up to the challenge of his bounty. I imagine getting on a flight back to New York, returning to my old life while some other hunter catches Zero. A tingle runs through me at the chance to crack this problem, possibly the biggest puzzle I've ever been given the chance to solve. *I'm going to win this time.*

"I've already thought it over," I say. "I'm in."

Hideo nods. "Instructions for the Wardraft will come your way shortly, as well as an invite to an opening game party. Meanwhile, make a list of anything you think you'll need from me. Access codes, accounts, and so on." He stands up. "Hold out your hand."

I eye him warily, then put my hand forward. He takes it, turning it over so that my palm faces up.

He holds his own hand an inch above my palm, until a black rectangle resembling a credit card appears against my skin. Then he presses a finger lightly to my palm and signs his name against it. The feel of his skin moving against mine makes my breath catch.

The virtual credit card flashes blue for a moment, authorizing his signature, and then disappears.

"This is for you to buy whatever you need during your stay," he says. "No limit, no questions asked. Just use your palm whenever you need to make a purchase, and the charge will go directly to this. Cancel it by signing your own name against your palm." His eyes lock on mine. "And keep this discreet. I'd rather not broadcast our hunt to the public."

What I wouldn't have given, during my most difficult weeks, for a card like this. I take my hand back, the feeling of his signature still burning against my palm. "Of course."

Hideo offers me his hand. His expression has turned serious again. "I look forward to our next meeting, then," he says, with absolutely no indication in his tone that this is true. My eyes flicker again to his bruised knuckles before I shake his hand.

The last moments are a blur. Hideo returns to his meeting room without looking back at me. I'm escorted down to the lobby of the studio, where I sign some more papers before heading out to where my car is waiting. As I settle inside, I let out a long breath that I didn't realize I was holding. My heart is still hammering in my chest, my hands shaky from our encounter. Not until we've left the studio behind do I reach into my pocket, grab my phone, and log in to my bank account. This morning, I had thirteen dollars. What sort of money is Hideo tempting me with?

Finally, the account page loads on my screen. I stare at it in stunned silence.

**Pending deposit: $10,000,000.00 USD**

## 9

I have to load the screen a few more times before I can trust the number there. Sure enough, it doesn't change. Ten million.

A ten-million-dollar bounty.

Hideo's insane.

The highest bounty I've ever seen is five hundred thousand dollars. This number is off the charts. There must be more to this job than Hideo is letting on—it can't possibly be as simple as catching a hacker who's just trying to mess up the games, even if the games are the world championships.

What if it's a more dangerous job than I think it is?

I shake my head. Warcross is Hideo's life's work. His main passion. I think back to the glint of intensity that I saw in Hideo's eyes when he showed me the contact lenses. I *do* have a specific set of skills that appeals to him—I hunt criminals, I hack, I'm a Warcross fan who is *very* familiar with the game's inner workings.

Maybe it's been really hard for him to find hunters suitable for this job.

My thoughts return to our meeting. The perfect Hideo I'd pieced together from years of documentaries and articles doesn't seem like the one I'd just met—condescending, unsmiling, cold, the reality of a mythical figure I'd built up in my head. *He doesn't mean to be intimidating,* Kenn had insisted. But Hideo's walls are nevertheless there, making his politeness seem insulting and his intentions vague. Maybe it's all part of being so disgustingly wealthy that he doesn't need to open himself up to anyone.

Or maybe he just doesn't like me very much. I bristle at the thought. Fine. I don't like him all that much, either.

Besides, I don't need to like a client in order to work for him. I certainly don't like the police who I've worked for. All I have to do is my job, keep him updated on my progress, and catch Zero before anyone else does. All I have to do is get the bounty.

*Ten million dollars.* I think of Dad, sitting up late at night after he thought I'd gone to bed, resting his head wearily in his hands, staring at a never-ending stack of overdue bills. I think of him staring blearily at a glowing screen, placing yet another bet with money he didn't have, hoping that this time, *this time,* he'd win it big.

Ten million dollars. *I* could win it big. I'd never have to worry about debt again. I could be safe for life. If I win this bounty, everything changes. *Forever.*

A message *dings* in my view as we pull up to my hotel. It's from Kenn.

> Miss Chen! I don't know what you said to him in there, but . . . well done.

> **Well done? For what?**

**You should know that Hideo has never hired someone that quickly. Ever.**

> **Really? I thought I annoyed him.**

**Everyone thinks that. Don't mind him. Look for a gift at your front door. Hideo had it sent for you the instant you left his office.**

After that meeting, it's hard to believe what Kenn is saying.

> **Thanks.**

**Welcome to the team.**

By the time Jiro drops me off and I make my way up to my suite, the gift—a beautiful box made of black suede—is already sitting on my desk. Next to it is a glossy envelope emblazoned with a gold stamp of the Warcross logo. I stare at it for a long moment, then bend down and open the box.

It's a brand-new, limited-edition electric skateboard, sleek and light, painted in elegant black and white. I test the weight of it in my hands, disbelieving, and then toss it down and hop on it. It responds to me like a dream.

Hideo's bodyguards must have told him about my old, beat-up skateboard. This board is easily worth fifteen thousand dollars. I'd eyed it in catalogues before, fantasized about how it might ride.

I read the card included in the box.

*For you. See you at the Wardraft.*
                                    *H.T.*

One second, he's interrogating me. The next, he's sending gifts. My eyes go from the note to the envelope next to the box. Just a couple of days ago, I'd been standing in front of my apartment, looking in despair at a bright yellow eviction notice. Now I reach out for the envelope, tear it open, and pull out a thick, heavy black note with gold print.

*Miss Emika Chen*
*is officially invited to participate*
*in the Wardraft as a Wild Card*
*on March 3rd*

● ● ● ● ●

I'VE WATCHED THE Wardraft every single year. It always takes place in the Tokyo Dome a week after the all-star opening ceremony, with a packed stadium of fifty thousand screaming fans and all eyes trained on the wild-card players sitting in the stadium's front rows, circling the central arena. One by one, the sixteen official Warcross teams choose their top picks from the wild cards.

Warcross fans know most of the wild cards by heart, because the wild cards tend to be some of the highest-scoring players in the game, those who are constantly on the leaderboards and have millions of followers. Last year, the number one draft pick was Ana Carolina Santos, representing Brazil. The year before that, Poland's Penn Wachowski, who now plays for Team Stormchasers, was picked first. And the year before *that*, it was South Korea's Ki-woon "Kento" Park, who currently is on Team Andromeda.

But I'm used to watching this madness unfold from home, with my glasses on. This time, I'm going to be sitting in the front row of the Tokyo Dome.

My hands shake as I stare at the passing scenery outside. If Times Square had seemed crazy about Warcross, it's nothing compared to Tokyo. Through my contact lenses, the entire main intersection of Shibuya is alight with hovering screens, rotating through each wild card's photo and showing clips from past drafts. Thousands of screaming fans cluster in the streets below. The car drives through a special, blocked-off section where a squadron of police guides us through. As we pass by, people on the sidewalks wave at each of our cars, their faces lit with excitement. They can't see through our tinted windows, but they know that this is the only route taken to escort the players to the dome.

Overhead, my photo appears, covering the entire side of a skyscraper. It's an old picture of me as a high school sophomore, the last year I spent in school before I was expelled. I look grave in it, my hair pin-straight and at least a dozen different bright colors, my skin so pale it looks ashen. Headlines about me are sprinkled everywhere.

## BREAKING NEWS:
### Emika Chen Nominated for Wardraft

---

## From Penniless Glitch to Wild-Card Star!
### *Details in This Week's Issue*

---

### HENKA GAMES STOCK JUMPS
### WITH EMIKA CHEN ADDITION

Seeing my face cover eighty stories is enough to make me nauseous. I force myself to look away from the madness outside and instead press my trembling hands together firmly in my lap.

*Think of the ten million,* I repeat to myself. I glance outside again to see another billboard rotate onto a photo of DJ Ren, who's wearing his giant headphones and hunched over his DJ equipment. Suddenly, it occurs to me that the other two bounty hunters, whoever they are, will probably be watching me at the Wardraft. Investigating me. Are they wild cards, too?

Half an hour later, when we finally pull into the roped-off section of the Tokyo Dome's side entrance, I've almost calmed the butterflies wreaking havoc in my stomach. In a blur, I look on as men in suits open my door, help me out of the car, and usher me down a red carpet that leads into the cool, dark recesses of the stadium's rear. *Think badass thoughts,* I tell myself. My guides lead me into a narrow corridor with a ceiling that gradually slopes higher and higher. The sound of fifty thousand screams grows near. Then, as I enter the main space, the roar turns deafening.

The stadium is bathed in dim blue light. Dozens of colored spotlights sweep back and forth across the space. The aisles are jam-packed with viewers, waving homemade posters of their favorite wild-card players, all gathered here to see us in the flesh. With my contacts on, I can see enormous holographic screens lining the edge of the central arena. On each of these screens, footage plays of the wild cards in action during some of their most popular in-game moves. The players look like they are lunging right out of the screen as giant, three-dimensional figures, and each time they make a good move, the crowd screams at the top of their lungs.

A bubble pops up in my view. My level jumps by two.

The front rows of the stadium are half full of wild-card players. As the guides usher me into a row, I scan the crowd around me and try to match up some of these people with their Warcross personas. My eyes register a few faces. Abeni Lea, representing Kenya. She's ranked in the top fifty worldwide. Then there's Ivo Erikkson, representing Sweden. Hazan Demir, a girl from Turkey. I swallow, wondering if it'd be silly to ask for their autographs.

*Time to work,* I remind myself. Quietly, I make an up-swipe gesture with two fingers and bring up my shields, then hunt for the security that blankets the dome. Hideo gave me a special ID to get past it all, offering me access to the basic information that Henka Games stores about each user, but using the ID will also allow Hideo to track *me* more easily, something that might leave me vulnerable to hacking from Zero or another bounty hunter. So instead, I've edited my access to keep me off the grid. It'll help me work better. If Hideo has a problem with that, he'll just have to take it up with me later.

Soon, numbers and letters appear in random places around the dome, highlighting the areas where the code is generating bits of virtual reality over the actual scene. An overlay of the stadium's blueprint hovers faintly over everything. Most importantly, basic data appears about every person in the arena, in tiny blue digits over each of their heads, so many that the data seems to blur into streaks.

Finally, I get to my seat. Behind us, the stadium lets out another piercing round of shrieks as the giant screens show a montage of Team Phoenix Riders' best plays from last year.

"*Hallo.*" I turn as a girl nudges my side. She has reddish-blond hair tied back in a low, messy tail, and a smattering of freckles across her pale skin. She gives me a lopsided grin. When she speaks again, I see the transparent English translation in my view. "Are you Emika?" Her eyes wander up to my rainbow hair, then down to my arm of tattoos. "The one who broke into the opening ceremony?"

I nod. "Hi."

The girl nods back. "I'm Ziggy Frost, from Bamberg, Germany."

My eyes widen. "Right! I know you! You're one of the best Thieves out there. I've watched so many of your games."

I can tell she's rapidly reading the German translation of my words that's showing up in her view. Then she brightens until I think she might pop. She reaches forward and shoves someone sitting in the row in front of us. "Yuebin!" she exclaims. "Look. I have a fan."

The guy she shoved gives an annoyed grunt and turns around in his seat. He smells faintly of cigarette smoke. "Good for you," he mutters in Chinese as I read my translation of his words. His eyes shift to me. "Hey—aren't you the girl who glitched into the opening game?"

Is this how I'm going to be known forever? The girl who glitched? "Hi," I say, stretching a hand out. "I'm Emika Chen."

"Ah! The American," he replies, shaking my hand once. "You speak Mandarin?"

I shake my head. My dad knew exactly five Chinese phrases, and four of them were swears.

He shrugs at my response. "Ah, well. I'm Yuebin, from Beijing."

I smile. "The top Fighter in the rankings?"

His grin widens. "Yes." He reaches over and nudges Ziggy once. "See? You are not the only one with a fan." Then he looks back at me. "So, you are a wild card now? I mean, congratulations, that is really great—but I don't remember seeing you in the top rankings this year."

"That's because everyone wrote her in at the last minute," Ziggy pipes up. "Hideo himself approved the nomination." Yuebin lets out a whistle. "You must have really impressed him."

So, the rumors about me *have* spread. This is not how I want everyone in Warcross to know me—the girl who glitched into a game out of sheer stupidity, then got into the Wardraft as a wild card because my stunt got me written in. What if Yuebin suspects that I'm in this draft for another reason?

*Don't be so obvious. To him, you're just here to play Warcross,* I remind myself. I force a smile back at Ziggy and shrug. "It probably doesn't matter. I bet I'll be the last one picked."

Ziggy just gives me a good-hearted laugh and pats my shoulder. "What is that saying? Never say never?" she replies. "Besides. Do you remember one year when that player—Leeroy something— actually got drafted into the Stormchasers, even though he always just charged in and messed up his entire team's play? My God, he was terrible." Too late, she realizes she's accidentally insulted me again. "I mean, not that you are as *bad* as Leeroy! My point is that you never know. I mean—well, you know what I mean."

Yuebin gives her a wry look before smiling at me. "You will have to forgive Ziggy," he says. "She never says the right thing at the right time."

"*You're* never the right thing at the right time."

As they forget about me and fall into bickering, I quietly

review what data I can see about each of them. Their full names and addresses, their travel schedules, anything that could help me notice something suspicious about their behavior—I download all of this and store it away for later analysis. But even from a quick glance, neither of their profiles seems odd. No basic shields of any sort to protect their data. Yuebin even has a virus installed on his Link that's slowing it down.

Then again, maybe they're both hiding behind this façade. It's hard to tell without breaking into all of their info—personal emails, private messages, stored Memories—encrypted things even Henka Games isn't allowed to have access to. I need a way in, a weakness, like how I'd stolen the power-up during the opening ceremony game. I need another break in the pattern.

The stadium's main lights dim, and the sweeping lights change color. All of the seats are filled now. The audience's cheers grow louder. I look down the line of seats and follow it around the edge of the central arena, trying to recognize some of the other wild cards and match them up with the top-ranking players I know. Beside me, Ziggy and Yuebin finally stop arguing and sit up straighter in anticipation.

"Ladies and gentlemen!"

The lights now sweep to the center of the arena, where an announcer wearing a Warcross logo T-shirt stands. "Warcross fans around the world!" he says in a booming voice. "Welcome to the Wardraft! We're about to add some wild cards into the mix of your favorite Warcross teams!"

The audience roars with approval. My heart is beating so fast now that it leaves me feeling weak.

"Let's introduce the most important person in here!" he points up at the same time the colorful spotlights shift to focus on a roped-off section of the stadium, a fancy seating area encased inside a glass box. Hovering over the box is a virtual sign that says *Official Seats,* meant to be for Henka Games studio executives. Inside, a young man watches, one hand in his pocket, the other holding a glass. Two bodyguards flank him. Around us, the holograms change to show his face. "The one who made it all possible—Hideo Tanaka!"

The stadium explodes into the loudest cheers I've ever heard, followed by a thunderous chant of "Hih-*day*-oh! Hih-*day*-oh!" that makes the arena tremble. Hideo lifts his glass to toast the crowd, as if this level of insanity were perfectly normal, and then sits back down to watch. I force myself to look away.

"There are sixteen official Warcross teams," the announcer now goes on. "And each team gets a total of *five* official players. We've already chosen the returning veteran players, but every team tonight has at least one open spot—and we have forty wild cards for them to choose from. By the end of the draft, all forty will belong on a team." He waves a hand at our front-row seats. "Let's do a quick introduction!"

The spotlight changes to focus on the first wild-card player, and the music in the stadium shifts to a new song. The player is a boy with brown hair, who blinks at the sudden light on him. "Rob Gennings, representing Canada, Level 82, who plays as a Fighter. He is ranked sixty-sixth in the world." Cheers erupt from the audience. When I look up at the crowds, I can see posters waving enthusiastically, with Rob's name scrawled on them.

Through my own view, I scroll through some basic data on Rob Gennings. *Full name: Robert Allen Gennings. Valedictorian of his high school. Last flight: Vancouver to Tokyo, on Japan Airlines.*

"Next, we have Alexa Romanovsky, representing Russia, a Level 90 player known for her lightning-fast Thief attacks." Another round of cheers. The music shifts to a song that she'd chosen for herself. I study a scrolling list of her info. *Full name: Alexandra Romanovsky. Birthplace: St. Petersburg. A former competitor in the Paralympics.* She was disqualified for picking a fight with a fellow teammate, so she switched her obsession to Warcross after that. She lifts her head high now and nods at the dome's crowd.

The announcer continues down the row at a rapid pace. The spotlight inches around the opposite end of the arena, the music changing with every player. All of these players are well-known and highly ranked. I'm only at Level 28, because usually I'm logged in as an encrypted, anonymous account, and none of my activity or wins get properly recorded.

"Renoir Thomas, from France, is better known as DJ Ren—"

The audience bursts into a deafening round of cheers. I search for him—but the spotlight lands on an empty seat. The music playing for him is one of his own tracks: "Deep Blue Apocalypse," a song with a soul-shaking bass and addictive beat. There's no question that he's the most popular.

"—is currently busy preparing to host the first Warcross party of the year. But rest assured, you'll see him soon!"

The introductions go on. There are a couple of other wild cards dressed up in gray-and-white outfits—Demon Brigade fans, probably hoping their clothes will warm them up to the official team. Others are wearing shirts declaring their favorite professional players. Still others look nervous and out of place, lower-ranking players or players that will probably be drafted last. I fly through the reams of data for each of them, downloading and storing, organizing them into folders. *Be careful of those nervous ones,* I remind myself. It could be a disguise to hide a hacker—

"Emika Chen, Level 28, hails from the United States of America!" the announcer shouts. I jump as the spotlight swings to me, and suddenly everything is blindingly bright. A burst of cheers comes from the stadium. "She plays as an Architect. You may remember seeing her in the opening ceremony game—although you probably didn't expect to! In fact, she was so popular that our viewers wrote her in as a *wild-card* nominee!"

I wave hesitantly. When I do, the cheering turns louder. *Look genuine*, I remind myself. I widen my smile, trying to show some teeth, but from the giant projection of me in the dome, I look like I ate a bad batch of oysters. I wonder if it'd be noticeable if I crawled under my chair right now.

When the announcer finishes introducing the wild cards, the spotlights sweep to the area of the stadium where the official teams are sitting. Screams go up as the announcer introduces each of the teams. My eyes stay fixed on them. I recognize the Demon Brigade's distinct, white-and-gray outfits. Far from them sit the Phoenix Riders already chosen for this year's team, led by Asher Wing, their flaming red hoods and jackets prominent. They utter a bunch of howls and whoops when the announcer says their name. Then come Team Andromeda, in hues of green and gold, and Team Winter Dragons, in ice-colored blue. Team Stormchasers, in black and yellow. Team Titans (purple), Team Cloud Knights (sapphire and silver). Even as I continue downloading information, I find myself distracted as the spotlights sweep over each team, hardly able to believe that I'm in the same space as them.

Finally, the announcer finishes. The stadium turns hushed as an assistant hands him a sealed envelope. "This year, the team who gets first pick of the wild cards is . . ." He pauses while he tears open the envelope in as dramatic a fashion as he can. His microphone picks up the sound, magnifying it until the entire dome sounds like it's tearing apart. He pulls out a silver card, holds it up, and smiles. The holograms shift to show what the card says. "Team Phoenix Riders!"

In the official team section, the Phoenix Riders let out another round of whoops. Sitting in the middle of them, Asher Wing is looking down at our arc of wild-card seats with quiet concentration. My heart is hammering so hard now that I'm afraid it's going to break my ribs.

The announcer waits for a moment as the Phoenix Riders exchange a few words between each other. The silence seems to stretch on forever. I catch myself leaning forward in my seat, eager to hear who they pick. Finally, Asher waves a hand once in front of him and submits his team's pick to the announcer.

The announcer stares at their pick in his view, blinks a few times in surprise, and then waves his own hand once. The selection appears in enormous letters over his head, rotating slowly. Every hologram broadcasts it at the same time.

It's my name.

# 10

*"Emika Chen!"*

A chorus of surprised gasps echoes around the arena. There are people cheering around me, someone's shaking my shoulders, and someone else is shouting enthusiastic words in my face. I just stare in shock. I know Hideo wanted to hide me in plain sight—but I didn't think he would make me the *number one* draft pick. This has to be some sort of mistake.

"This is no mistake!" the announcer calls out, as if answering the thoughts in my head. He turns in a circle with his arms outstretched. "It seems this year's number one draft pick will be an untested, untried, un*ranked* wild card"—he pronounces each word slowly, with huge emphasis—"who nevertheless impressed us all with her disruption of the opening ceremony game!" He rambles on, joking that perhaps Asher Wing of the Phoenix Riders—well-known for unconventional draft picks—has figured out something that the rest of us haven't.

I just find myself staring blankly in the Phoenix Riders' direction. Asher has his eyes trained on me, a smug grin spreading across his face. He's one of the most intuitive captains out of anyone—he would have selected someone he could count on, experienced players who are ranked high. He wouldn't pick me just for the spectacle. Would he? Did Hideo force his hand?

Is *he* Zero?

My gaze shifts up to the private box, where Hideo is still standing, looking straight toward me. Maybe he'd given the Phoenix Riders a command to choose me as the first pick. Maybe it really *is* for ratings. Maybe it's to throw the hacker Zero off my scent, because I'm so publicly exposed. Or maybe it's to throw off the other bounty hunters. Whatever the reason, I find myself wondering when I'll get to talk to him again, to ask him the reasoning behind this.

Someone's shaking my shoulders so hard that I can almost feel my brain sloshing around. It's Ziggy.

"Do you understand how big this is?" she shrieks in my face. I'm unsure of how to respond. "It means you will get used to being followed everywhere for the next few months and being on every news outlet. *Heilige Scheiße!*" She shrieks the phrase so wildly that the translation doesn't even try to interpret it. "Some people have all the luck."

I finally manage to give her a faint smile, then settle in to try to watch the rest of the draft. My thoughts whirl as the announcer pulls a second set of cards and reads them out. The Demon Brigade chooses Ziggy, while the Phoenix Riders nab DJ Ren. The Titans get Alexa Romanovsky. The show continues, but I feel as if the spotlight is still on me. The flashes of light going off in the audience make me dizzy, and I wonder how many people have their glasses trained on my profile, hunting and digging for anything they can find out about me.

"Hey." Yuebin nudges me. "Look, up there." He nods toward the private box. I follow his gaze, ready to see Hideo.

But Hideo is gone now. Only the rest of his company heads are there, chattering among themselves. Hideo's bodyguards have left, too.

"It's like he came here just to see where you would land," Yuebin murmurs, clapping absently as another draft pick happens.

*Just to see me drafted, the way he wanted me to be.* My thudding heart sinks a little, and I feel a strange sense of disappointment without his presence in the arena. I'm about to look back down—but something shifts in the corner of my vision. My eyes dart up to the ceiling.

I freeze.

There, crouched high in the ceiling's maze of beams, is a dark, virtual figure.

I can't see anything else about him except static. The silhouette of his head is turned down, watching the draft take place. No name floats over his head. Everything about his posture looks tense, alert.

Like he's not supposed to be here.

A chill runs down my spine, turning my hands ice-cold. At the same time, my bounty hunter instincts kick in—*screenshot, record a screenshot.* I blink, right as the figure vanishes from sight.

"Hey," I blurt out, looking over at Ziggy, who is cheering on a wild card drafted by the Stormchasers.

"Hmm?" Ziggy replies without looking at me.

"Did you see that?"

"See what?"

But it's too late now. The figure is gone. I scan the ceiling again and again—perhaps the lights have blinded me so much that I can no longer see him—but he's nowhere to be seen now. The lattices of metal and lights are empty.

*He wasn't actually here. He was a part of the virtual reality, a simulation. And only I could see him because of my hack.* Either that, or I just experienced an insane hallucination.

Ziggy frowns, squinting skyward. "See what?" she repeats with a shrug.

"I—" I stop myself, unsure what to say next without sounding crazy. I force a laugh. "Ah, never mind."

Ziggy's attention has already strayed back to the draft. But I keep my eyes on the ceiling, as if he might reappear if I look long enough. *Did I catch him?* As the others applaud another wild card, I bring up a small, secret panel of my screenshot.

Sure enough, there he is. I didn't hallucinate it.

● ● ● ● ●

The remainder of the draft passes in a whirlwind. When it ends and the rest of the stadium starts filing out, guards come to usher the wild cards and the professional teams out through special exits. I walk in numbed silence, even as everyone I pass watches me and as some of the other wild cards occasionally come up to congratulate me. I smile back at them, unsure what to say. In the back of my mind, I still keep thinking about the figure.

*Maybe it was one of the other bounty hunters. Or . . . maybe it was Zero. My target.*

"Miss Chen," one of the ushers calls to me, holding his hand out in my direction and waving. "This way, please."

I follow him automatically. Behind me, Ziggy and Yuebin wave farewell as they hurry off toward another usher who is rounding up the new Demon Brigade and Stormchaser drafts. "*Bye!* See you in a game!" Yuebin calls to me. I wave back.

I'm taken to a waiting car, one of a dozen sleek black vehicles in a line outside a private side exit. A cluster of fans have figured out where to wait, though, and as several of us step outside, they raise their posters and scream at us, holding out pens and booklets. Behind me, Asher Wing emerges from the exit with two handlers at his side. In virtual reality, Asher looks like a standing avatar; in real life, he is paralyzed from the waist down and sits in what must be the world's most expensive wheelchair. Now that I'm close enough to him, I can take in the details of the chair's solid gold rims and customized engraved leather.

I look back at his face, wondering whether I should go up to him and say a proper hello, but stop myself from interrupting as he winks at a blushing fan and scoots his chair back into the crowd for a bunch of photos. The crowd nearly swallows him up before his handlers push everyone off. Then I'm ushered into a car, and my moment passes. I'll have to catch him later, when our team convenes.

The cars take off one at a time, each heading in the same direction down the same road. I know where we're going—I've watched it play out on TV a dozen times. In the heart of Tokyo is the secure neighborhood of Mejiro, where a gated estate of luxury quarters house Warcross teams for the duration of the tournament. It doesn't take us long to get there. As we pull up to the gate, reporters and fans cluster on the sidewalks, flying little drones in the sky to take as much video as they can. Several of the drones hover too close to the gates—when they try to cross over, they hit an invisible shield that disables them, sending them clattering to the ground.

"No cameras, no drones," the guard at the gate repeats over and over in a bored tone.

We enter the campus. Patches of green lawn dot the space, and sprinkled between them are individual buildings surrounded by trees. Through my contacts, a virtual layer of bright colors adorns the buildings, painting each one in the colors of their respective team. Team names and logos hover helpfully over each dormitory, along with a cheery *Welcome!* message that rotates in different languages. Approved delivery drones fly in and out of each dorm, busily dropping off packages.

The car pulls to a stop at a dead end. Someone is waiting for me on the curb as my door swings open.

I find myself looking at Asher's grinning face. I hadn't even noticed that his car was ahead of mine. Over his head floats his name, level, and **Phoenix Riders Captain**. "Hey," he greets, holding a hand out to me. Behind him, clusters of other players are already making their way down the paths toward their buildings. "I'm Asher, repping Los Angeles. Call me Ash."

I shake his hand. "Yeah, I know," I reply, trying not to think about the fact that this is someone I've watched in Warcross games for years. "I'm a fan of your brother's movies. Didn't think I'd get to talk to you today."

His expression flickers cold for an instant at the mention of his brother, but then he's back to normal, giving me a little laugh. "Sorry," he replies. "I wanted to greet you when we were heading to our cars, but you know—fans first."

I smile. "Well, thanks for picking me."

"Wasn't doing it out of charity." Asher shakes his head. "The Phoenix Riders have been struggling for years. We need some good fresh blood. There's nothing generous about wanting the best for my team." His wheelchair turns away, and he tilts his head at me to follow him. "This is where you'll be staying for the next few months," he says as we turn a corner. I look ahead to see a stunning building painted virtually with swirls of red, gold, and white. "I heard Hideo himself approved your nomination into the draft. After the stunt you pulled in the opening ceremony, it's a pretty interesting move."

I smile again, a little more hesitantly this time. "I guess I'm good for the ratings," I reply.

"I guess you are."

*Careful,* I remind myself as I hear the curiosity in Asher's voice. So, Hideo hadn't forced him to draft me. Or, perhaps he knew that the intrigue he'd create over putting me in the draft would be enough to interest any captain. Whatever the real reason, at least Asher doesn't sound like he suspects Hideo's plans, and I intend to keep it that way. The less everyone here knows about what Hideo hired me for, the better chance I'll have at catching our guy.

"And it looks like it's good for *your* ratings, too," I say, shifting the topic. "The Phoenix Riders are trending online over every other team. I bet the Demon Brigade's unhappy about that."

At the mention of a rival team, Asher rests his head back against his wheelchair and taps his right hand against his armrest. He smiles in a way that flashes one of his canines, turning the grin vicious. "The Demon Brigade's always unhappy about something. Glad it's because of us this time."

We reach our building. Asher rolls up the access ramp and spins his chair once in a flourish at the top. He stops at the towering main entrance, a sheer glass door painted with stripes in our team colors, and pulls aside as the panels slide open. "Wild cards first," he says.

I step inside, into an open space three floors high. *Into a dream.*

The sun pours into this central atrium from a pyramid-shaped glass ceiling, flooding the place with light. Directly beneath the glass ceiling is a heated turquoise pool, perfectly square and ready to be jumped into. Brightly colored couches—all red, gold, and white—and thick white rugs dot the living room space. The walls are made out of screens from floor to ceiling. Even as I take in the luxurious interior, I scan the corners of the building, already searching for how the dorm gets online. I'll need to find my way into the system and into everyone's accounts.

Something nudges me hesitantly on my calf. I look down. Standing there, blinking up at me, is a boxy little robot as tall as my knee. Its eyes are bright blue and the shape of half-moons, its body painted a cheerful yellow, and its belly is covered with a clear glass panel, through which I can see a tray of sodas being chilled inside. When it sees me staring, it sticks its belly out, pops open the glass door, and pulls out the soda tray for me.

"His name is Wikki," Asher says. "Our team drone. Go ahead, take a soda."

I don't know what to say to that, really, so I pick a can. "He's still staring at me," I murmur to Asher.

"He wants to see if you like the drink."

I take a sip of the soda. It's delicious, a fizzy strawberry flavor that tickles my insides. I make an exaggerated sound of joy. Wikki seems to take note of this, and over his head, a virtual set of info pops up:

Emika Chen | Strawberry Soda | +1

"He'll record your food and drink preferences throughout your stay," Asher adds.

A robot that tracks everyone's info. I smile at Asher, but not for the reason he thinks. *This is my ticket in.* I make a mental note to figure out how to break into Wikki's system later.

Wikki offers a soda to Asher, too, then pops its belly shut and rolls off to where a boy is sitting on the couches. As I look on, the boy moves his hands in midair as if turning a steering wheel, and every now and then he makes a flinging motion. On the wall is a track winding through candy-colored hills, populated by giant mushrooms. He whips down the path, outpacing other players easily.

"Mario Kart: Link Edition, as you can see," Asher says. "It's a tradition around here."

"A tradition?"

"We play for an hour every night during training to improve our speed reflexes. It gets pretty competitive." Then he claps his hands together loudly and raises his voice so that it fills the dorm. "Riders! Who's here?"

The boy hears Asher first, pauses the game, pops his earphones off, and turns around on the couch to look at his captain. I recognize him right away: the world-famous Roshan Ahmadi, with his brown skin and head of thick, dark curls, representing Great Britain.

"Guess who I've got with me?" Asher says, pointing to my hair.

"You're so subtle, Ash," Roshan replies in a dry British accent that sounds more casual than Hideo's. He nods once at me. "Hello, Emika. I'm Roshan."

"He's returning as our Shield this year," Asher adds. "And he's also the world's top-ranked Mario Kart player, in case you're curious."

"Hey." I take one hand out of my pocket and give him a single wave. "An honor to meet you in person."

Roshan seems pleased by that. He offers me a brief smile. "Likewise, love."

"We've all claimed our rooms already," Asher says, nodding toward the hall that branches away from the main atrium. "Roshan wanted the one with the largest windows. I got the far end, which has some custom upgrades detailed specifically for me. Captain's privileges. Ren's back at the end of the hall. And as for you—"

"Hey!"

A voice calls down at us from one of the floors overhead. I look up to see a girl leaning her elbows over the balcony, loudly chewing gum. Her hair is a jumble of beautiful black curls that frames her round face, and she's dressed in an oversize, white sports jersey that contrasts with her brown skin. On second look, her shirt isn't a sports jersey at all—it's a T-shirt that says QUIDDITCH TRYOUTS in giant sports lettering.

I like her immediately.

"That's Hamilton Jiménez," Asher tells me, loudly enough so that she can hear him. "Or just Hammie. She's our Thief." He winks at her. "And my right-hand girl."

She grins back at him. "Feeling sentimental today, Captain?"

He looks at me. "Fair warning: don't let her talk you into playing chess."

"Don't hate just because you can't win." She blows an enormous bubble and then sucks it back in. Her gaze jumps to me. "Your room's up here. Second floor. I took the larger bedroom, since you're a wild card and I'm not. Hope you don't mind."

I wait to see a fourth player show his face, but the house falls into a moment of silence. "Where's DJ Ren?" I ask.

"Won't see him until later," Asher replies. "Ren's prepping for the party tonight. It's the only free pass he'll get from me, especially since I'm counting on him to be our new Fighter. And let that be a lesson for you, too, Emi. We're here to win."

"Of course," I say.

"Good." He nods, considering me. "Hope you're as good an Architect as I think you are."

Hearing this from him sends a jolt of excitement and anxiety through me. An Architect's job is to manipulate the world of the level in favor of her team. If there's an obstacle, like a bridge, I would collapse it to let us through. If there are floating rocks, I'd push them together to create a bigger platform. An Architect is a designer of the level, dedicated to changing the world on the spot in favor of her team. It's one of the most important jobs on a team. Last year, the Phoenix Riders lost their Architect because he'd been caught gambling away millions on Warcross games. The entire team was punished heavily, too—knocked down to the bottom of the rankings and stripped of their top two players.

"I'll do my best," I say.

"Tomorrow," Asher continues as I follow him into an elevator leading up to the second floor, "we'll catch you and Ren up on how things work in the championship games. I'll walk you both through an official game. Although you"—he pauses to spin around and give me a calculating look—"may already know more than you let on."

I hold my hands up. "It was an accident," I say, feeling like I've repeated this forever. "I didn't know what I was doing."

"You *did* know," Asher counters without hesitation. "In fact, you're a much better Warcross player than your level suggests. Aren't you?" He nods up at the numbers above my head. "After your name went viral, I looked up your Warcross account. I studied the few games that you did play. Those are *not* the skills of an

Architect who is only on Level 28. Why are you so much better than your level suggests?"

"What makes you say that? I just play against other beginners."

"You think I can't see through that?"

He *has* been paying attention to me. It's true—I stream my plays live, when I'm actually linked in under my public Warcross account. But my encrypted, anonymous self is the account I use more often. All the hours I rack up under it don't count into my leveling. Still, I'm not about to tell Asher that.

"I just haven't had the money or time to play as often as I want," I say. "But I'm a pretty fast learner."

Asher doesn't seem to buy this at all, but he lets it slide. "Every other team is going to underestimate you. They'll say I've lost my touch, that I picked you just for the news coverage it'll get the Riders. But we know better than that, don't we? I don't waste my time on players with no potential. You're a weapon in disguise—and I intend to keep it that way until our first game."

It seems I'm becoming the weapon in disguise for more people than I'd like.

We reach the second floor. Asher spins to face me, leans his head against the back of his chair, and exchanges a look with Hammie. She just nods at him, bunches up her curls on her head, and lets them go again. "Hammie will show you the rest," Asher says. "We're heading out in a few hours to the opening party." He starts rolling back toward the elevator. "All the players will be out in force. If you've never seen an opening party before, brace yourself. It's a wild one."

Hammie looks me over the instant Asher leaves. She's the same height as me, but somehow, the jut of her chin makes her look taller than she is. She motions me forward and heads to the door closest to us. "This is your room," she says over her shoulder at me.

I half expect the door to swing open like a regular door, but instead it slides to one side. The room is enormous—even larger than the penthouse hotel suite that I had. One entire glass wall opens up to my own private patio, half of which is taken up by a shimmering blue infinity pool that goes all the way to the edge of the balcony. A waterfall cascades into the pool from somewhere on the roof. The rest of the walls are virtually painted by my lenses with ivory and shimmering gold. When I reach out to touch the colors, they ripple under my fingers, sending waves across my room. At the same time, three small buttons right above my hand hover against the wall. One says *Off*, another says *Switch Scene*, while a third says *Customize*. I decide to turn off the colors for now, then press the first button. The walls are replaced by blank space. I look around. My bed is huge, piled high with furry cushions and blankets, and my rugs match the ones downstairs. A work area dominates the rest of the space—chairs, a clean desk.

Hammie grins at my expression. "And yours is the smallest room," she says.

I turn back to the space. "This place is ridiculous."

"Everything in the dorm is gameified," she explains. "Like the rest of Tokyo. You'll earn three notes every time you customize your walls, and one note for switching the scenery. The room's preprogrammed to your Warcross account. If you're logged in, then the house system knows you're the one who's coming inside."

"How does this work?" I ask.

She walks over and nods at an *On* button hovering near the surface of the desk, but doesn't try to touch it. "You're the only one who can turn on your work area," she says. "Press that."

I touch it. The instant I do, the previously blank desk lights up soft stripes in our team colors, with a welcome message for me over it in white text. A second later, a holographic screen rises up from the desk. It's a standard desktop display—except it's floating in midair. These types of desktops have only recently started shipping in the States, and they're, of course, way out of my price range.

Hammie smiles at my expression. "Swipe the screen toward your walls," she says.

I touch the screen with two fingers, then make a swiping motion toward the wall we're facing. The display on the screen follows my fingers, flying from the screen onto the wall, where it fills up the entire space, fully magnified.

"The downstairs living room has the best work area, of course," Hammie adds. "But this is in all of our rooms. Good for any impromptu team meetings."

If the same system is installed downstairs, then each room's desktop isn't nearly as secure as she thinks it is. I can work my way into the main system, and then I'll be able to get into each of their individual systems, too, regardless of who the work area is tailored for. I smile at the gorgeous, wall-size display. "Thanks."

"I was starting to think no American would ever be the number one pick." Hammie tucks a curl behind her ear. "Nice to have you on the team. Maybe I'll stop teasing Ash and target you for a change." She winks and turns away before I can respond.

I stay where I am until she steps out of my room and the door slides shut behind her. Then I put my hands on my hips and admire the room. My space. In the *Phoenix Riders'* official house. I walk over to where my few belongings have been delivered and placed by my bed, then take out my Christmas ornament and Dad's painting. I prop them carefully up on the shelf. They look small there, too simple for this luxurious room. I imagine Dad standing beside me.

*Well, Emi,* he'd say, pushing his glasses up. *Well, well.*

At the thought of my father, my attention goes to my closet. With a tap of my finger against the door, it slides open, revealing a space as large as the studio where Keira and I lived.

*Holy hell.*

The closet is already filled with an assortment of clothes, every single one of them a high-end brand. I stare in disbelief before I walk inside, running my hands along the hangers. Each item is easily worth thousands—shirts, jeans, dresses, coats, shoes, purses and clutches, belts and jewelry. My hand stops at the shoe rack, where I pick up an exquisite pair of white, red, and green kicks that smell like new leather, the heels decorated with gold studs. Like everything else in the closet, the shoes still have a tag hanging on them, accompanied by a small greeting card.

## GUCCI
### Official Sponsor of
### Warcross Championships VIII

Sponsored gifts. No wonder every professional player always looks like they just stepped off a runway. I slip off my well-worn boots, tuck them carefully in one corner, and then try on the new shoes. They fit like a glove.

An hour flies by while I feverishly try on everything in my closet. There's even a shelf dedicated to face masks in all colors and patterns, an accessory I've seen worn all over Tokyo. I try a few of them on, pulling their straps over each of my ears so that the mask covers my mouth and nose. Might be a good thing to have if I need to go around the city unrecognized.

When I'm done, I stand there, still decked out in lavish items, breathless and uneasy. Each thing in here costs more than my entire debt before Hideo erased it.

*Hideo.*

I shake my head, put everything back, and step out of my closet. There'll be plenty of time later to admire all of this—for now, back to work. Hideo had made sure that I would be drafted onto a team, but now it would be up to me to make sure my team won each round. The longer the Phoenix Riders stay in the championship tournaments, the more time I have to investigate the players.

At this very moment, other hunters are probably hot on Zero's trail, reporting their findings to Hideo while I gape at my new wardrobe. They would have been at the Wardraft, too. What if they also saw the dark silhouette perched in the ceiling's scaffolding? Right now, somebody else might be earning ten million dollars; I might already be doomed to return to New York. And here I am, playing around in my new closet.

I jerk into motion.

First, I bring up my shields and switch to the anonymous, invisible version of my account. Then I sit down on the edge of my bed and pull up the screenshot I'd taken earlier of the dome's scaffolding. The image is a 3-D capture, one that I can rotate from its point of origin. In addition, it's caught all of the data and code running in the dome at the moment of capture.

I squint at the static silhouette in my 3-D screenshot. Zooming in on it only makes it blurrier. I can see the code running the virtual simulations around the dome—but I can't see any code or data on this shape. I type in a few commands and strip away the visuals of the screenshot, so that I'm now immersed inside reams of code. Where his silhouette is, I can only see a patch of static.

I sit back, pondering. He is hidden from me, in every single way—except that I could *see* him. He probably didn't expect that. If this is Zero, then he's not disguising himself as well as he should be. But the Tokyo Dome is on its own network of connections for the Wardraft. The easiest way for this person to have hacked his way up there is if he was already approved to enter the arena, and had already physically cleared security. Someone in the audience, then. Or a player, like Hideo suspects. Or a wild card.

I lean forward again and switch back to the visuals, then zoom in to break down the code that generated the image of him. A stripped-down view of the code pops up. I read through it as I chew absently on the inside of my cheek.

Then I see something that makes me pause. It's just a line. Not even a line—a pair of letters and a zero, lost in the code. A clue.

## WC0

In most of the Warcross code, players are referred to by their Warcross IDs, written as *WPN*. *WP* stands for Warcross Player. *N* is a randomized, scrambled number. So, if I'm looking at code about my own avatar, I'd probably see myself referred to as WP39302824 or something like that.

The *only* time a different ID is used for Warcross players is at the Wardraft. During the draft, players aren't referred to in the code by their regular IDs. They don't use *WP*. Instead, they are *WC*—Wild Cards. My ID in the Wardraft was WC40, because I was the last entry added into the draft.

*WC0*. Whoever the silhouette was, it was someone physically cleared to be there in the Tokyo Dome. A wild card in the Wardraft. Hideo's suspicions were pretty close.

I chew idly on my nail, my eyes narrowed in thought. I need

another moment where every wild card is in the same space at once, and I'll get to be physically close enough to them in order to study their info.

*Tonight's party.* Asher's last words to me echo in my mind. *The players will be out in force.* That will be my chance.

I bring up a virtual menu and tap on the call button for Wikki.

A minute later, the little drone comes rolling into my room, his half-moon eyes turned expectantly toward me. I wave him over, then turn him around so that I can study the panel on the back of his head. At the same time, I bring up his settings.

"Aren't you just the cutest thing," I murmur to him as I carefully remove the covering for the panel. Inside is a maze of circuits. "Wikki, turn off all recording."

The robot obeys, switching off its data gathering. As I fiddle, I realize that it's not made by Henka Games—it's by some other company, with weaker security. Everyone had thought to install protections on everything else, but no one had thought much about the security needed on this little drone that just serves us food and drink, quietly storing information about all our habits as it goes.

An hour later, I've cracked through its shields. It records a lot more data than I thought it did. Not only does it store information about the Phoenix Riders, but it also seems preset to serve the other teams, which means it has optional connections to everyone else's NeuroLink accounts. I smile. *Everyone in the world is connected in some way to everyone else.*

I run a script to overwhelm Wikki's security. While it's working, I worm my way into each of my teammates' accounts. I crack into their emails, their messages, their Memories. From there, I set up my hack to penetrate each of the accounts of the other teams.

It's going to take a while to download everything, but it's running now.

I replace Wikki's panel, double-check to make sure I leave no trace of my presence behind, and then reboot the robot. It turns back on, its eyes blinking, its data gathering set back to normal. I pat it once on the head, then accept another strawberry soda.

"Thanks, Wikki," I say, winking at it. It records my preference, then rolls out of my room again.

I pop open the soda and take a sip. By tomorrow, I should be in.

# 11

By the time the sun sets and we arrive in the heart of Shibuya, the neon lights of Tokyo have already lit up, casting the city in a glittering rainbow of color. Security guards swarm around our limo as we pull up to the nightclub's entrance. The streets are fenced off, so that no cars other than ours can come through, and a red carpet lines the sidewalk.

We are all wearing our lenses. Through them, silver and gold sparks fly on either side of the club's glass doors, while a Warcross logo hovers over the top of the building. The sidewalk's pavement is aglow with a kaleidoscope of bright, swirling colors. The club's name, Sound Museum Vision, hangs over the glass doors as a giant, glowing logo. Even from out here, I can hear pounding music from inside—the deep beats of a DJ Ren track.

The only people allowed inside the club tonight are the official Warcross players, the employees of Henka Games, and a smattering of Warcross fans who were picked by a lottery system to attend. Now they're clustered outside in a haphazard line, waiting for the security to let them in. As our team approaches the entrance, the fans let out a chorus of screams.

The four of us are wearing matching black face masks tonight. Hammie is first, her curls loose, long, and full, her outfit a yellow-and-white dress paired with black heels. Asher comes behind her, looking sleek in a bold red suit, while Roshan is dressed from head to toe in black.

My hands fiddle constantly with the hem of one of my new dresses. It's layered in soft white chiffon, which contrasts nicely with my tattoos and rainbow hair, but it rides up higher than I thought it would. I've never been inside an upscale club like this one, and as we walk past the crowd of fans, I wonder if maybe I should've picked a different outfit. Hideo will be here tonight, after all. The last thing I want to look like in front of him is uncomfortable.

A commotion farther down the fans' line makes me look over my shoulder. Sure enough, Hideo is there, flanked by a bevy of bodyguards. They're giving him some space tonight, though, and when I look closer, I realize that he's kneeling to sign a poster for a little girl. She says something to him excitedly. Even though I can't make the words out, I hear him laugh in return. The sound surprises me—it's genuine and boyish, so unlike his distant demeanor from our meeting. I find myself lingering there for a moment before I finally turn back around and follow my team into the club's main lobby.

The club is underground. As we step out of the elevator, the music suddenly turns deafening, the beat shaking my body through the floor. Hammie sidles up beside me as we go, taking off her face mask and folding it away in her purse. I follow her lead. "Sound Museum Vision's got the best sound system in the city!" she shouts. "All custom-made. They revamped the space a few years ago, too—it's double the size it used to be."

We reach the bottom of the stairs, where another group of security guards lets us in. I step into a yawning cavern of darkness, flashing lights, and a pounding bass that shakes me deep in my chest.

Even without my lenses, this space would be impressive. The ceiling is at least three floors high, and lights of neon blue, green, and gold strobe the room, blinding us with color. A sea of people fills the room, their arms thrown up, their hair tossing wildly. A faint mist hugs the air, giving everything a surreal haze. Enormous screens stretching from floor to ceiling line the walls, as well as the backdrop of the main stage, rotating through an animatic of each Warcross team.

But with my lenses on, the space transforms into something magical. The ceiling looks like a night sky covered by a sheet of stars, with green and red streaks of what look like Northern Lights dancing from one end to the other. Some of the stars move toward us, showering us with sparks, as if stardust is raining over us. Every time a deep bass drops, the ground glows in a symphony of light. Official players on the floor shine in the dark, their outfits lit up in neon, their names, team affiliation, and level hovering over their heads like golden trophies. Around them cluster heavy crowds. Everyone's trying to get a moment of their time on the dance floor.

*Maybe Zero is here, watching,* I remind myself. *Maybe the other bounty hunters, too.*

My eyes dart to the stage itself. The space is enormous, as big as a concert hall, and a live orchestra is sitting in the pit right below. Against the stage's backdrop is a towering screen with an ice-blue dragon's head breaking out through it. Fire appears to shoot out from its mouth in a spectacular display. It takes me another second to remember that the dragon itself is also virtual—it moves as if it were real, twisting and turning its head at every dropped beat, its growl echoing from somewhere deep in the sound system.

Standing in front of the dragon's mouth is a singer with short, artificially blond curls and clothes in neon shades of blue. Frankie Dena! She's singing the chorus to one of her collaborations with DJ Ren: *"Hey Ninja / Gangsta / Dragon Lady / Hey, where you from, no, where you really from, baby / Hey, how 'bout / you cut all that shit out / Yeah!"* Dancers pump their arms to the rhythm.

Then she sees us and pauses.

"The Phoenix Riders are *in the house!*" she shouts. The strobe lights shoot toward us, and suddenly we are drenched in a red glow. Cheers erupt around us, loud enough to shake the floors. Frankie grins and points up to a figure standing high at the top of the dragon wall. "Show your team some love, Ren!"

The figure at the top looks up only briefly from behind a cage of ornate gold bars. He is decked out in his classic DJ attire—a black, well-tailored suit, gold shades, a gold face mask and a state-of-the-art set of headphones with gold metal wings embellishing both sides, as if he were the messenger god Hermes wearing something designed by Hermès. The track shifts in one smooth measure—the sound of electric violins, cellos, and a deep, reverberating beat fills the space. At the same time, the room around us bursts into flames, and the dragon head on the wall morphs into a red-and-gold phoenix. I gasp as the floor seems to move. When I look down, I see bits of it crumbling away to reveal molten lava beneath our feet. The audience screams in delight as each of them remains standing only on islands of rock floating in the lava.

DJ Ren bows his head over his instruments. He raises one arm up high as the music's tempo increases to a fever pitch, until I can hardly bear it. Then he brings a punishing bass down on our heads. The room trembles, and the crowd bursts into a mass of jumping limbs. Music fills me to the brim.

For a moment, I close my eyes and let the beat carry me away. I'm tearing through the streets of New York City on my electric board, my rainbow hair streaming behind me. I'm standing at the top of a wind-whipped skyscraper, arms outstretched. I'm flying through the skies of Warcross, the outer reaches of space. I'm free.

Asher already looks distracted, his attention fixated on the players of the Demon Brigade, who have stepped into the club. Frankie announces their presence, and DJ Ren's wall changes from our phoenix to a horde of skeletal beasts in hooded cloaks riding on horseback, charging through the audience with swords drawn.

"Go talk to the Demons tonight," he mutters to me. "You're our new recruit, so they're going to do everything they can to intimidate you. They want you to go into your first game feeling unsure about yourself."

"They don't scare me."

"I should hope not." Asher blinks at me. "But I want you to look like it. Make them underestimate you. I want them to think they've got you cornered and fearful, and that we made a huge mistake choosing you as the number one pick. Let them feel smug. Then we'll destroy them in the games, and leave them shocked."

Roshan gives Asher a sidelong look. "A little early to be sending our wild card into the line of fire?" he says.

"She can handle it." Asher grins at me. "You've got *line-of-fire* written all over your face."

I decide to smile back, hoping things aren't written so clearly on my face that Asher figures out what I'm really doing here. My attention turns back to the Demons. They're gathered close to the stage where DJ Ren is performing. It's a good-enough excuse for me to go gather data on all of them. "Will do, Captain," I say.

As we begin to cut through the mass of elbows and shoulders, Roshan hands me a drink. "You'll need it," he mutters. "Ash always feels like needling our rivals a little before the games. But if you don't want to talk to the Demons, you don't have to."

Almost everywhere I look, I see official players that I recognize. They're looking back at me, too, noticing me, talking to one another without taking their eyes off me. What are they saying? What do they know? Are any of them bounty hunters, too? For someone used to being off the grid, the attention on me feels a little unnerving. But I just grin back each time.

"Let's go," I say to Roshan. "People are going to be talking about me anyway. I might as well get used to confrontation."

Roshan leans over to me and nods in the direction of the Demon Brigade's Max Martin and Tremaine Blackbourne chatting in a corner. "Well, if we ever play the Demons," he says into my ear in a low voice, "you'll need to deal with that pair. Max is their Fighter, Tremaine's the Architect. And Tremaine is going to gun for you in the game because you're the number one pick. Come on." He puts a hand on my back and leads us forward.

Beside Max, Tremaine looks thin and pale, almost ghostly, in his black-and-white suit. He and Roshan exchange a cold stare as we approach him. Then he raises a skeptical eyebrow at me.

"Hey!" I say to him, planting a wide, naïve smile on my face. "Tremaine Blackbourne, right?" At the same time, I tap my fingers subtly against my leg and start downloading info on both him and Max. "It's so exciting to be in the same space as the teams, isn't it?"

"She's *excited* to be here," Tremaine says to Max while his eyes stay on me. "Guess I would be, too, if I cheated my way into the draft."

*You* wish *you were smart enough to cheat your way in*, I want to spit back—but I take a deep breath and force my reply down.

At my tense expression, Tremaine's smile stretches thinner. "Look at this peach. They bruise so easily, they need a Shield to escort them." His eyes actively avoid Roshan in a way that lets me know that's where his attention really is. "Ash must be losing his edge, picking you first."

Max sizes me up. "Well, maybe Ash just wanted to pick someone who matched his team's pedigree. Isn't that right, Ahmadi?" he says to Roshan. Even as both Demons' stares linger on me, they still don't speak to me directly. Roshan's hand tightens a little against my arm. "Can't even get into a fancy restaurant with a Level 28 rank. She looks like she came from a used clothes bin."

I pretend to lose my balance and stomp down hard on Max's shoe with my heel. Max lets out a yelp. "Oh God—I'm *so* sorry!" I blurt out, pretending to be shocked. "It's impossible to walk in these used heels."

Roshan glances at me in surprise. A small smile hovers on the edge of his lips.

"Look, I know we haven't started off on the best foot . . . literally," I say to Max as he glares at me. "But I thought that maybe we could start over, you know, to show good sportsmanship." I hold my hand out to them, waiting for a handshake.

Tremaine is the first one to burst out laughing. "Wow," he exclaims over the music. "You're as wild card as they get." He makes a point to ignore my outstretched hand. "Look, Princess Peach, this isn't how things work in the championships."

I give him an innocent look of confusion. "Oh? Then how does it work?"

He holds up a finger. "I play you." Another finger goes up. "I beat you. And then, if you ask nicely, I'll sign an autograph for you. That's pretty generous sportsmanship, don't you think?" The fans around them smirk at me, and even over DJ Ren's music, I can hear their snickers. It takes all my self-control to not ball up my fist right now and knock the smile off Tremaine's face. I've gotten in plenty of fights over less.

Instead, I bring up all the info I can on both players. By now, my hack has worked its way into the Demons' accounts. But nothing about the data on these two seems suspicious. I turn my attention to Max Martin's info. His is surprisingly sparse, too. No odd security shields. Nothing useful.

Roshan comes to my aid before the Demons can add anything else. "Save your mouths," he says coolly, his gaze lingering on Tremaine. "They won't help you in the arena."

Tremaine casts me a dismissive glance. I'm glad to see it—they are going to underestimate me. "Big words from the lowest-ranking team." His eyes dart briefly to Roshan. "Go back to your Riders." Then he starts to walk away, and Max follows in his wake.

"Who drove over *their* pets this morning?" I mutter to Roshan, my eyes on Tremaine's back.

"It's just a part of the Demons' strategy. They talk the ugly talk and hope that some of it gets under the skin of their opponents, that it sticks there. Sometimes it works. Repeat an insult enough times, and anyone will start to believe it."

A faint memory of past tournaments comes back to me, and suddenly I recall seeing Tremaine and Roshan frequently together, laughing and smiling. "Hey," I say. "Tremaine used to be a Phoenix Rider, didn't he? Weren't you friends?"

Roshan's expression darkens. "You could say that."

"What happened?"

"Tremaine wants to win. Always," he replies. "Simple as that. So when the Demon Brigade became the hot new team, he wanted out of the Riders." He shrugs. "It's just as well. They suit his personality better, anyway."

And then I remember that Roshan and Tremaine were both wild cards in the same year. Roshan had been the number one pick. I want to ask him about it, but the look on his face tells me that he's eager to change the subject. Maybe they had been more than friends. So I just nod and let it drop.

Hammie waving to us from the other side of the dance floor catches our attention. She's pointing to a cluster of people gathered around someone. It takes me a second to realize that it's Hideo, with the sleeves of his tuxedo shirt rolled up to his elbows and his blazer slung over one shoulder. Kenn walks beside him, greeting fans and players alike with his huge, animated grin. Hideo is more reserved, his expression as serious as I remember it, even as he gives polite greetings of his own.

Hammie pushes her way over to us and grabs us each by the arm. "Let's go say hi."

We end up jumbled in the back behind a group of Cloud Knight players and Team Andromeda, while ahead of us, Max and Tremaine shake Hideo's hand in turn. Tremaine is saying something rapidly to him, while Hideo nods patiently without smiling.

I bite my lip, tugging self-consciously at my dress and cursing my decision to wear this thing.

Then Hideo's gaze lands on me. My breath hitches. He bids a

brief farewell to Tremaine and heads toward us. A moment later, he's here, and Roshan is stepping forward to greet him.

Hammie slaps my wrist. "Stop fussing," she says, glancing pointedly down at my dress.

"I'm not fussing," I mumble, but then Hideo's before me, and my hands freeze at my sides.

"Miss Chen," he says. His eyes linger on my face. "Congratulations."

*Were you responsible for my number one draft pick status?* I want to ask, but instead I smile at him and shake his hand politely. "Believe me, I was as shocked as anyone else," I reply. Behind him, Tremaine and Max stare at us. If Tremaine could stab me with his eyes, he would be doing it right now.

"Every draft has at least one surprise," Hideo replies.

"Are you saying you didn't expect me to be drafted so quickly?"

A ghost of a smile appears on Hideo's lips. "Were you? I hadn't noticed." He leans closer to me. "You look lovely tonight," he continues in a low voice, so that no one else hears. Then he's already nodding farewell, passing us by with his entourage, bodyguards, and a trailing, screaming mass of fans.

"*Damn*," Hammie says in my ear, her eyes still fixed on Hideo. "He looks even better in person than he does in the news."

Roshan is looking straight at me. "Did he just *tease* you for being first pick?"

"I don't think he likes me very much."

"It's enough to put you in the tabloids," Hammie says. "You know that, right? Hideo doesn't talk like that to his players. It's all business." She elbows me hard enough to make me grunt.

"It's not a big deal."

Hammie laughs once, sending her curls bouncing. "I don't

even care. The way Tremaine was seething in the background will fuel me for the rest of the championships."

As several fans line up for autographs from her and Roshan, I glance to where Hideo had disappeared into the crowd. He'd been watching me carefully during the Wardraft. I think back to him standing in his private box as the announcement of my number one draft pick status rang out. *He doesn't talk like that to his players.* How does he talk, then? Hadn't he exchanged words with everyone he met tonight? In the crowd, I catch one final glimpse of his figure as his bodyguards usher him down a hallway.

A name appears in my vision, and I look up instinctively. I'd made my way close enough to where DJ Ren is still standing up behind his mountain of instruments, spinning a fast-tempo beat, the gold wings of his headphones reflecting the neon strobe lights. I'd almost forgotten that he's also an official player in the game— but now I'm close enough to him to pull his data.

I reach out discreetly and bring up DJ Ren's info. Immediately, I halt.

His private information is walled behind a mass of shields— not just one, but dozens. Anything I've managed to download from him is encrypted. Whatever the reason, Ren is no amateur at dealing with his security, and he knows how to protect himself in ways far beyond the average player. In *too* many ways. I stare up at him, thinking. *The figure I'd seen in the Tokyo Dome is one of the official wild cards.*

And there's only one wild card who was absent from his seat during the Wardraft.

# 12

The next morning, I hear Asher's voice drifting up from the atrium as I step out of my room, yawning, my hair tangled in a messy bun. As I go, I run right into Hammie. She grunts in a half-asleep voice.

"Downstairs," she mutters.

"What's going on?"

"Matchups are in," she replies, then stumbles off in the general direction of her bathroom.

Matchups. Today we find out which teams are playing each other. The thought quickly wakes me up. I brush my teeth, splash some water on my face, and put in a new pair of my Warcross contacts. Then I head down to the atrium. Asher's already there, talking in a low voice to Roshan on the couches. Dark circles ring our captain's eyes this morning, but otherwise he looks alert and ready. I glance down at the coffee table. The magazine on the top of the stack features a photo of Hideo at a banquet, seated beside a completely smitten blond woman who is whispering something intimately into his ear. HAS PRINCESS ADELE FOUND HER PRINCE? screams the caption.

Hammie files in moments later, followed shortly by DJ Ren. Ren looks the most frazzled out of us all, with his short brown hair sticking out in every direction and his eyes hidden behind a pair of white sunglasses. His winged gold headphones are still on his head, one side in place and the other shifted slightly off his ear, so that he can hear what's going on. He sits down on the farthest couch from me, leans back, and waves a lazy greeting to everyone. *The only one who wasn't in his place during the Wardraft.* Maybe because he was hiding somewhere, perched virtually in the rafters to spy on everything.

*Maybe he's actually Zero.*

No. Zero should be better at hiding himself than this. And surely Zero isn't tacky enough to wear sunglasses indoors.

Hammie reaches an arm out in front of Ren's face and snaps her fingers twice. "Hey," she says. "Rock star. You're not at the club anymore."

Ren just bats her away. "I'm sensitive to light in the morning," he says in French, while I read his translation.

Roshan raises one brow at that, while Hammie rolls her eyes. "Yeah, I'm allergic to mornings, too, wild card," she replies.

As Hammie talks, I quietly begin to sort through my teammates' data. It looks like Roshan sent a bunch of emails last night, while Hammie's amount of notes has gone down by a significant amount since the night before, indicating she had made some huge purchase. I turn to Ren. Just like yesterday, he has a wall of shields on over his data, set up so that anyone trying to break in would automatically be redirected to a shield instead of to his data. I start to run a program to bypass them.

Roshan sighs. "Ash, tell him to take his headphones off," he says in his patient manner.

Asher crosses his arms. "Lose 'em, wild card. I'm not in the mood for it this morning."

Ren lounges for a moment longer. Finally, he pulls his headphones down and loops them around his neck, then reaches up to take off his sunglasses. His eyes are such a light brown that they look gold.

When we're ready, Asher says, "Wikki, turn on the announcement."

Our team drone blinks in one corner, and when it does, a live broadcast appears across one of the atrium walls. Hideo is standing before a podium and facing a barrage of flashing lights.

"Matchups are in," Asher says, confirming what Hammie had told me. "And we're going to play the first round of the championships."

Hideo had wasted no time making sure I will be in the first game. "Who are we playing?" I say.

Asher brings up a pair of virtual images for us to see. It's our team crest—our red-and-gold phoenix—hovering in midair next to a black-and-silver image of hooded skeletal figures on horseback. Above our crests are the words:

### Round One
### PHOENIX RIDERS vs DEMON BRIGADE

Hammie lets out a whoop, and Asher claps loudly. "We lost to them last year," Asher says, looking between me and Ren, "and then we got punished in our rankings. Everyone's going to think that the Demons will slaughter us. But we're gonna prove them wrong, aren't we?" He grins his canine grin. "Now we just have to predict what the first level will be like."

"Whenever the committee pairs us with the Demons," Hammie says, "it's usually in a level that involves speed. Like Eight-Bit World, from two years ago." She nudges Asher. "You remember Eight-Bit World, right?"

Asher grunts. "Ugh. So many stairs."

"Or space," Hammie adds. "They have a knack for handling 3-D space. So if our level involves being in midair a lot, they might have an advantage. But we train for speed. The Demons like to train for strength and defense."

"In fact, every single one of their teammates trains to defend— not just their Fighter and Shield," Asher finishes. "You watch any game where they do coordinated eight-dives, especially when double-armed, and you'll see how they switch off roles as smooth as glass."

"Dragonfire World, for instance," Hammie says. Everyone nods except me. "Just think about how they eight-dive in formation by the cliffs. I hate their guts, but their guts can also be a work of art."

I have absolutely no idea what they're talking about.

But a chorus of agreement answers Hammie, and more high-level worlds are brought up in rapid succession. More chatter about nicknamed moves that I've never heard of. I stay quiet, trying to take as much of it in as I can, but for the first time since the Wardraft, it occurs to me how out of place I am in this championship. Ren is a wild card, but also a seasoned player who has unlocked and played all of these high-level worlds. I've played none of them. I'm here for the hunt, sure, but I'm also here for the game—and right now, I feel like Hideo has entered me to set me up for certain humiliation.

"It doesn't mean there aren't drawbacks, of course," Asher says, turning his eyes to me. "The Demons are competent at everything and incredible at nothing. You concentrate on being a great Architect, Emi, and you'll win us the game. We'll make sure you're up there in no time."

I smile at him, grateful that he's looped me back in to the conversation. "Any advice for me that's specific to playing the Demons?"

"Plenty. They're going to target you early. Whatever the level turns out to be, you'd better be able to cut out in front of them and get to clear ground."

I think of Tremaine's sneer and Max's insults, then of Roshan's first warning to me. "Will do," I reply.

Asher looks at Ren. "I've never seen any Fighter attack as fast as you, but Max Martin's offense is incredibly strong. You have your work cut out for you."

Ren salutes him with two fingers at his temple. "Yes, Captain."

Across from me, Roshan is the only one who looks solemn at the matchup announcement. Asher glances at him warily, then nods once. "Got any advice for Emi on how to deal with Tremaine in a game?" he asks.

"Ash," Hammie warns.

Roshan shoots him a glare. "He was *your* Rider before he became a Demon. *You* tell her."

Asher just shrugs. "Not my fault that you hooked up with him," he says. "You know Tremaine better than any of us. So keep your personal grievances out of it and help our wild card out, yeah?"

Roshan stares at Asher for another long moment. Then he

sighs and looks at me. "Tremaine is an Architect who has trained in every position. He's the best of the Demons at switching roles, and he's actually a very good Thief and Fighter. So sometimes, in games, his teammates will toss him their own power-ups or weapons, so that he can use them even though he's technically the Architect. When you fight him, remember that he can wear many faces, and that he's fluid enough to pull an uncharacteristic move on you. I'll show you in training."

Asher looks satisfied enough at this, and when Roshan leans back and crosses his arms, he leaves him alone.

"What are the other matchups?" asks Ren.

Asher continues to scroll the midair display to the left. Our two crests swipe out of view and are replaced by two more.

WINTER DRAGONS vs TITANS

He keeps scrolling. ROYAL BASTARDS vs STORMCHASERS. CASTLE RAIDERS vs WINDWALKERS. GYRFALCONS vs PHANTOMS. CLOUD KNIGHTS vs SORCERERS. ZOMBIE VIKINGS vs SHARP-SHOOTERS. It keeps going until we've reached the last of the eight matchups: ANDROMEDA vs BLOODHOUNDS.

My attention has gone back to where Hideo is still standing in front of a podium, flanked on one side by Kenn and on the other by Mari, answering a series of questions. "Can you put on what he's saying?" I ask Asher.

He turns up the sound on the live feed. The rumble of a noisy conference room fills the atrium. Hideo looks into the crowd at a reporter shouting a question to him above the din. "Mr. Tanaka," the reporter says, "you are also releasing the newest Warcross glasses—lenses, excuse me—to the public today?"

Hideo nods. "Yes. They are being shipped around the world as we speak."

"Mr. Tanaka," another reporter chimes in, "we've already

seen footage of long lines and heard rumors of shipments being stolen off trucks. Are you concerned that Henka Games will see its profits decrease because you are giving these new lenses away for free?"

Hideo gives the reporter a cool look. "The benefits of alternate reality deserve to be given to all. The bulk of our profit comes from the worlds themselves, not the hardware."

The reporters start talking over each other again. Hideo turns his head toward another question. "Mr. Tanaka," this one says, "any reason for your interest in Emika Chen?"

My teammates look at me in unison, right as my face bursts into shades of red. I clear my throat and cough. On the screen, though, Hideo doesn't bat an eye. "Please specify?" he replies.

The reporter, eager to get a reaction, barrels on. "Unranked wild card?" he asks. "Number one draft pick? The Phoenix Riders— her team—playing in the first game of the season?"

I can feel my teammates' eyes boring holes into me. Only Asher lets out an annoyed snort and mutters, "*Her* team? *I'm* the captain!"

Hideo's expression remains perfectly calm, even disinterested. *Nothing new,* I remind myself forcefully. *Reporters question his every interaction with a girl.* He's being paired with the princess of Norway on our coffee table's magazine, for crying out loud. The only reaction of any kind that I see, in fact, comes not from Hideo but from Kenn, who's hiding the faintest of smiles on his face. "I do not control the draft picks," Hideo replies. "And the order of the games was chosen by a committee months in advance." Then he looks away to call on another reporter.

Hammie whistles at the screen. "How about *that,* Emi?" she says to me with an eyebrow raised. "Now the tabloids are going to be pairing you with Hideo on their covers next week."

The thought sends my heart racing. It's only the first morning of our first training day, but already my wild-card and bounty-hunter roles are butting heads. If I don't end up giving myself away after a week, it'll be a miracle.

Finally, Hideo steps off the podium, and the broadcast ends. Asher asks Wikki to turn off the feed. Then he looks at all of us. "Well," he says, "we've got one month to get two wild cards up to speed."

I glance at the program I'm running to bypass Ren's shields. Sure enough, I'm almost in.

"Lenses on?" Asher asks. We nod in unison. "All right, then, Riders. Training time starts now."

# 13

Asher leans forward, then presses something on his own display in midair. All of us see a Warcross menu pop up in our view. *If Asher can show us all the same thing, then we are linked on the same network during training.* Ren had been walled behind his shields during the party, but maybe now, if we're all linked on the same network, I can find a way to get into some of Ren's data. Of *everyone's* personal data.

As I ponder this, Asher taps the option that says **Training Grounds**. The world around us fades into black, as if I'd closed my eyes. I blink several times. Then, a new world materializes around us.

This is a Warcross world I've never seen before. It must be exclusive to the professional teams. It looks like a whitewashed world, like it's a virtual world only half finished, its surfaces unpainted and without texture. We are standing in the middle of a white sidewalk, next to a white street crowded with white cars, with white columned buildings towering all around us. When I look farther down the street, I can see a glimpse of a whitewashed jungle, the trees and their trunks the color of ivory, the grass white as it grows at the edge of the city streets. The only color in this world comes from the sky above us, which is bright blue.

For a moment, I allow myself to forget about my hunt. I'm standing inside a level that few will ever get to see, with some of the most famous players in the world.

"Welcome to the training grounds," Asher says beside me. He, like the rest of us, is now dressed in a standard, formfitting suit of red body armor that starkly contrasts with the world around us. It makes it incredibly easy for us to spot each other. "This is a white-washed simulation containing miniature worlds all condensed into one." He nods down the street toward the jungle. "There are forests here, along with the city block we're currently in. A few blocks east, the city ends and an ocean starts. To the west, there are narrow stairways that lead into the sky. The potholes in the city streets will drop you into an underground network of caves. There are examples here of most of the obstacles we might encounter in this year's levels."

I look more closely at each of our outfits. Even though we're all wearing red body armor, there are subtle differences between the suits. Ren's Fighter suit is streamlined, full of smooth plates reinforced by an outer set of warrior armor. His armguards are spiked. Hammie's Thief suit is full of pockets, nooks, and crannies, where she can stash items away. Asher looks like the captain that he is, while Roshan, our Shield, has armguards larger than any of ours, his belt equipped with potions and elixirs he can use to protect the rest of us.

Then there's mine, the Architect's armor. Around my waist is a utility belt, equipped with a myriad of tools I'm all too familiar with. Hammer. Screwdriver. A box of nails. Two rolls of duct tape. A small chain saw. A coil of rope. Tools are tucked along the tops of my boots, too—sticks of dynamite, lock picks—and an assortment of knives are strapped to my right thigh.

"Hammie," Asher says. "You're with me." He nods in my direction. "Emika, Ren, and Roshan. You're a team. Roshan will be your captain." He taps something in midair, and a glittering gem appears over Roshan's head. "Remember—your goal is always to aim for the gem. However you accomplish that is up to you. Let's work out our weaknesses." He glances between our two teams. Then he pushes something in midair.

Jewel-toned power-ups appear all around us, their bright colors electric against the white. Some are on display in store windows. Others are at the tops of the streetlights, while a bunch hang above the buildings.

My eyes follow the power-ups as they dot the training level, noting the easy grabs and the hard ones. I've only ever played beginners or practiced alone in worlds accessible to everyone. What will it be like to have an official team scrutinizing my plays?

"Power-ups in the championship tournaments are different from the ones in regular games," Asher says to me and Ren. "Every year, the Warcross Committee will vote in a dozen new power-ups exclusive only to the championships, and then retire them at the end of the game season. Today, I want us to practice going after these power-ups."

He pushes another button in midair. All of the power-ups vanish—except for one, perched over the edge of a bridge that links two buildings. It's fuzzy, covered with bright blue fur striped with bits of gold and silver, and buzzing slightly.

"Specifically, I want us to be going after *that* one," Asher adds.

"What does it do?" Ren asks.

"Morph," Asher replies. "It gives the user the power to change one thing into something else."

As Ren nods, his attention turned on the power-up, I watch him and quietly tap my fingers against my leg. A little progress bar blinks in the corner of my vision while I run one of my hacks on him. After a few minutes, the only data that I'm able to access is his full name—Renoir Thomas—alongside his photo. I frown a little. My hack manages to access some of his more public information and even a few of his messages—but everything else is still secured behind a wall of shields that I've never seen before.

"Emi," Roshan says, snapping me out of my thoughts. "Step up."

I do as he says.

"This power-up was put into this year's championships for the Architects, since you'll probably use it best. I want you to retrieve it for your temporary captain, Roshan." Asher looks to his side. "You'll be facing off against Hamilton, who will do everything in her power to get it for me first."

Roshan steps over to her and murmurs something in her ear. He's probably telling her to pull some of Tremaine's signature moves, I think, recalling what Roshan had said moments earlier. Hammie nods a few times, her gaze flickering to me as she listens. When Roshan's done, she offers me a dark grin. I try to smile casually in return.

A timer, glowing scarlet, appears over the power-up. Asher taps his wrist. "Phoenix Riders are known for speed," he adds. "So I time every single one of our training sessions, no matter how small or trivial it might seem. Got that, wild card?"

I nod. "Got it."

"You both have five minutes." He looks up. "Go!"

A surge of adrenaline hits me. I don't think; I just bolt. Hammie does the same. She rushes toward the building itself, but I decide to run across the street. As Hammie starts to scale the side of the building, grabbing one brick after another and winding her way around the walls, I sprint toward one of the tall streetlights lining the block across from the building. I pull one of the sticks of dynamite from my boot. Then I plant it at the base of the pole, careful to position it so that the explosion will break the pole in the right direction. I ignite the dynamite. Then I take several steps away so that I'm safe from the blast zone.

*Bam!*

The ground rumbles as the base of the streetlight explodes. The pole careens sharply forward, toppling at an angle against the wall of the building.

"Nice!" Roshan shouts in approval.

I'm too focused to glance toward them. All my energy now hones in on my task. I hop onto the pole, then take a deep breath and start sprinting up it toward the building. The time I've lost from setting up the dynamite is now made up as I rapidly get higher and higher, until I reach the wall of the building. Hammie is still climbing, a good dozen feet below where I am. Two stories above us, the power-up hovers along the bridge.

I press my hands against the wall, then reach for the rope at my waist. If I can fling it and loop it around one of the spotlights along the bridge, I can pull myself up fast enough to get there first.

Suddenly, something tugs sharply against my waist. I nearly lose my balance and fall off. I look down.

The loop of rope at my waist is gone. Below me, Hammie shoots me a grin as she holds it up. *How did she get it so quickly? How did she know I'd use it?*

"You're not the only one with tools, wild card," she calls up at me. She flashes her stun gun at me, its edges gleaming in the light, and then flings my rope up to the protruding corner of the next story up. She pulls herself higher.

Hammie had shot my rope straight off my waist and caught it. No time to fume at her. I turn my attention back to my task and lunge upward along the wall, grabbing for each brick. The two of us climb at a feverish pace.

Hammie's faster than I am. She quickly outpaces me, and seconds later, I'm behind her by at least six feet. I force myself to climb faster.

Right as Hammie reaches the edge of the bridge, colors flash around us. Other spheres and cubes suddenly appear, scattered over the bridge and against the walls. Asher must have turned the rest of the power-ups back on. My eyes dart to a power-up within reach.

It's a bright yellow sphere, hovering against the wall where I am. *Speed Burst.* I seize it, then give it a squeeze in my hand.

The sphere vanishes, covering me in a neon-yellow glow. The world around me seems to slow, and Hammie along with it. I surge upward, climbing twice as fast as I had been only moments earlier.

I pass Hammie and jump onto the bridge right as my power-up runs out. The world snaps back to its regular pace.

The timer above the Morph power-up continues to count down. Thirty seconds left.

Instead of inching along the bridge as fast as I can, I give up several precious seconds and set a quick trap for Hammie. I yank my hammer from my belt and smash each of the hand- and foot-holds I'm using as I make my way along the bridge's edge. Hammie won't be able to use them to follow right behind me. Then I turn back around and keep going. I'm so close to the power-up now.

When I look behind me, Hammie is gone again.

I blink. *What?*

"Up here," her voice calls from above.

I peer up to see her hovering right over me, as if she knew exactly what I would do to slow her down. She was able to reach a power-up—Wings (temporary flight), from the orange glow around her. She grins, then dives for the Morph power-up.

I launch off the edge of the bridge and lunge at her. My hands grab for her legs. I throw her off balance before she can reach the Morph power-up. She lets out a startled, angry yell. For an instant, with her power of flight still working, we tumble in place as she tries to shake me off. Then, to my shock, she comes at me with her fists up.

I barely manage to dodge her first blow. Her second hits me in my chin, and I lose my grip on her. To my surprise again, she doesn't release me. A normal Thief would—but instead, Hammie tightens her grip and continues fighting me in midair.

"Watch her hands!" Roshan shouts out, right as I see something glint in Hammie's fist. It's a dagger. *A dagger?* Thieves aren't supposed to have daggers. In a flash, I realize that this must have been planned by Roshan. Tremaine probably plays like this, switching easily from one role to another. So Roshan must have given her the dagger to test me on how I'd react in a situation like this.

Hammie strikes out at me with blinding speed.

Most players wouldn't have been able to dodge it. But my reflexes have been honed on the streets as a bounty hunter. The memory of me running through New York, catching the gambler, flashes back to me. He had attacked me with a knife, a *real* knife. As Hammie's virtual knife comes at me, I find myself moving on pure instinct—I release her completely with a shove, fall a little, and then shoot out my hands at the last second to grab her ankles.

Her eyes widen. Then her flight power-up runs out.

I use her last bit of momentum in midair to swing myself up. As she starts to fall, I let go of her. The momentum is *just* enough. I reach up as high as I can. My fingertips brush against the Morph power-up. It's in my hand. A tingle rushes up my arm at the acquisition. I let out a shout of triumph.

Then I tumble back down toward the ground. I land hard on my back, knocking my avatar out of commission for several long seconds. There I lie, gasping and laughing. When my avatar recovers, I roll over and check my inventory, eager to see the Morph power-up in my account.

It's not there.

Hammie strides over to me as I manage to sit up. She holds out the Morph power-up in her hand and smiles. "Took it from you right as you landed on the ground," she says.

"How—?" I hesitate, shaking my head. She'd done it so quickly that I hadn't even felt her snatch it from my hands as I'd lain on the ground. I glance over to where Asher and the others are walking toward us. "But—didn't I win the exercise? I got it first."

"You've got a lot of strengths, Emi," Asher says. Hammie offers me a hand and pulls me to my feet. "Very resourceful. The way you play as an Architect—those aren't the plays of an amateur player. Fast on your feet. Accurate. You're much more talented than your Level 28 would suggest. Just like I thought." He nods at Hammie. "But you've got some classic wild-card weaknesses. One." He holds up a finger. "You get tunnel vision. Hammie is a world-class Thief. She's probably faster and nimbler than any Thief you've ever played against. I had to help you out by turning the other power-ups on."

I rest a hand on my hip and look at Hammie. "How did you always know what I'd do next?"

She taps her temple once. "Don't let me talk you into playing chess," she quips, repeating Asher's warning he'd given me when I'd first met her.

"Hammie can structure out your moves a dozen steps ahead," Asher explains. "Like any master chess player. She can sort your potential paths in her head and, judging by your body language, figure out what you're the most likely to do, all while she's on the move. Don't say I didn't warn you."

"I didn't know you'd throw yourself at me during those final moments, though," Hammie adds. "That's the fun of playing a wild card, isn't it? You never know what kind of player you'll get."

A dozen steps ahead. She had probably guessed my moves from the instant we began, maybe the moment I started running toward the streetlight. I sigh. "Well? What other classic weaknesses do I have?"

Asher holds up two fingers now. "You didn't listen to my instructions."

"I got the Morph power-up."

"Your instructions were to retrieve the Morph power-up *for me*," Roshan interrupts me. "Your team captain. The exercise didn't end when you grabbed the power-up first. It ends when you hand it over to me. This isn't a solo game, Emika, and you can't play as if you alone want to win." As he says this, Hammie walks over to Asher and tosses the power-up to him. He catches it without looking.

"Nicely done," Asher says.

She beams. "Thanks, Captain."

I'm glad I'm inside Warcross, so that the others can't tell that my cheeks are turning red from embarrassment. Hackers and bounty hunters aren't exactly known for being great team players.

I don't do well with instructions. But I swallow these thoughts and nod at Roshan. "Sorry," I say.

He shakes his head. "Don't sweat it, love. Thieves aren't supposed to have daggers in their possession—Fighters are. But this is how Tremaine can act during a game, and you just successfully fought him off. I don't think I've ever seen someone react that quickly to a surprise attack. A brilliant first exercise, really, especially from a wild card."

"Yeah." Hammie nods at me, too. "Not bad. You put up a hell of a fight, Emi. You're just going to have to fight a little bit harder to beat me." She winks. "Don't worry—you're still better than Roshan was when he was a wild card."

Roshan gives her an exasperated look that makes her laugh. And in spite of myself, I smile, too.

"Next!" Asher says. "Roshan and Ren. Get up there." The power-ups reset, and this time the Morph power-up is inside one of the buildings. I look on as the others move away. My attention stays focused on Ren. The progress bar in the bottom of my vision has finished and my program is now running on my other teammates, but with the pitiful number of Ren's encrypted files I've managed to grab, I might as well not have run my hack on him at all.

●●●●●

THE SUN HAS already begun to set by the time we finish training. The instant I head back to my room and close my door, I bring up all of my downloaded info on the players and display it on my wall. A long list of data appears—birth date, home address, phone number, credit card information, calendar. I scroll through it, searching.

Hammie's info appears first, detailing some of the plane tickets she'd recently purchased and hotels she'd booked. I catch a glimpse of bits of Memories she's stored away. In one, she's laughing with people who look like her mom and sister as they try to pose for a good shot in front of the Grand Canyon. In another, she's at a chess tournament, staring down at the board. It's speed chess—each player's taking a fraction of a second to make a move. I pause in spite of myself, awed as her fingers fly across the board. I'm barely able to track her moves, let alone keep up with why she's making them. In sixty seconds flat, she checkmates her opponent's king. A roar comes from the audience, and her opponent shakes her hand grudgingly.

In her final Memory, she's looking on behind a barricade as a man in uniform walks to a waiting helicopter. Nothing unusual; lots of people record Memories of greeting loved ones or sending them off. The man glances over his shoulder at her and waves. She waves back, recording in his direction long after the helicopter has taken off.

I switch to Asher. There's nothing incriminating or interesting in any of his data either, other than a few texts about flight arrival and departure times. His most recent Memory, aside from the draft and the party, is of him at the airport's private jet strip, waiting beside an older boy in sunglasses who I recognize immediately as his brother Daniel. Bodyguards stand near them both, but Daniel carries bags labeled with Asher's name instead of letting the handlers do it. The brothers don't utter a word to each other. And when the time comes for Daniel to finally hand over Asher's bags to an attendant, Asher heads for the jet's stairs without saying good-bye.

I try to shrug off the familiar note of guilt I always feel when combing through others' private data. *It's your job,* I remind myself. No room for feeling bad. Still, I delete the Memories of both Hammie and Asher from my records so that I can't watch them again.

A few of Roshan's messages are to his parents, one is to his sister, and one is a delivery receipt for some sort of gift. There are no recorded Memories, but to my surprise, the gift receipt tells me that it was sent from Tremaine, with a single line written on the card. *Did you get my letter? T.* I search the rest of his data, but there's no indication of the letter in question, or that Roshan has responded to Tremaine's gift yet. Nothing terribly suspicious, but I flag the data anyway for future reference.

Finally, I arrive at what little I have of Ren's information. Most of it is of no consequence—plans for setting up equipment for the opening-night party; mail from fans. There's one Memory of him, recorded at a party from last year, where he's kissing a girl backstage as someone onstage is announcing his name. I clear my throat and turn my eyes away. Thankfully, the Memory shifts to Ren heading to his instruments in the center of the stage.

Everything else in Ren's files is encrypted, including a few emails I'd managed to retrieve from his trash. I swipe through each one. No matter what I run on them, each one looks like a cube of gibberish floating in my view, locked tight behind a shield.

That's when I finally run across something that makes me pause.

It's a deleted email hidden behind his menagerie of shields, hovering in my view as a locked cube. I turn it in midair. When I do, I notice a tiny, recurring marker at the edge of each side of the cube.

"Well, well," I whisper, sitting up taller. Any feelings of guilt I'd had now fly right out of my head. "What's this?"

The marker is a red dot, barely noticeable, part of the message's encryption. And right beside it, in the tiniest letters, is the inscription *WC0*.

So Ren *was* the silhouette in the Wardraft. Based on the red dot, this message was sent to him from inside the Dark World.

I sit back on my bed and furrow my brow. This means that not only was Ren the one I'd been tracking at the Wardraft, not only was he inside the Dark World recently, but he is talking to others there.

And no one goes into the Dark World unless they're doing something illegal.

# 14

The first time I'd set foot in the Dark World was during my first bounty hunt.

I was sixteen, and on my own. The boss of a local New York street gang had put out a $2,500 bounty on one of his members, and I'd seen it as a brief mention in some online forum.

I'd read about other young people like me trying their luck in the competitive bounty hunter world. They seemed to have no special skill that I didn't have, and it looked like a way—if you were good—to make a comfortable income. The best bounty hunters could rake in six figures a year.

I had another reason to go after this bounty. My father owed $2,000 in gambling debt. After he died, I'd made a promise to myself to not fall into working for anyone in the criminal world—but in order to do that, I had to free myself from this debt. Otherwise, the people Dad owed the money to would come looking for me the instant I turned eighteen.

So I did as much research as I could about how to get into the Dark World. I honestly thought that by following a few online guides, I would somehow be able to waltz into this den of crime unscathed.

The Dark World operates by no rule except one: Stay anonymous. Your safety is only as good as your disguise. I learned this the hard way after I made my way into the world, found my target, and tracked him down in real life. Only then did I realize that I'd accidentally exposed a part of my identity while in the Dark World. In no time, my personal information—age, history, location—was broadcast to the entire Dark World, and my equipment was compromised.

I got the money, paid off my father's gambling debt. But over the next few months, I completely gutted my laptop and phone, stayed off-line and out of sight, kept the lowest profile I could. Even then, I'd get weird phone calls in the middle of the night, strange letters delivered in the mail. The occasional threat left on my physical doorstep. Eventually, I had to move.

I never worked for a gang again. It would be months more before I gathered the courage to return online.

That's the thing about the Dark World: You can prepare for it all you want, but the only way to truly understand it is to head in.

● ● ● ● ●

"MISS CHEN," HIDEO says as our call connects. "Good to hear from you."

It's the next morning, before training begins again in earnest, and Hideo's virtual image is in my room, leaning forward in his office chair and resting his elbows on his desk. The single streak of silver in his hair catches some of the light filtering in from his windows. Beside him, Kenn is standing close to the desk with his hands in his pockets in a way that tells me I'd interrupted a conversation they were having. He glances at me over his shoulder. Two bodyguards stand at attention behind them.

"Calling so soon with an update?" Kenn remarks. He glances back at Hideo. "Maybe you really did find your perfect bounty hunter."

I try to feel professional in my bare feet and shredded black jeans. "You must've been busy since the opening ceremony party," I say to Hideo. My eyes dart briefly to Kenn. "Am I interrupting some business?"

"You are the business," Kenn replies. "We were just talking about you."

"Oh." I clear my throat. "Good things, I hope."

Kenn grins. "I'd say so." He pushes away from Hideo's desk without explaining his words further. "I'll leave you both to it, then. Have fun."

Hideo exchanges a glance with Kenn. "We'll pick up again in a bit."

Kenn steps out of sight. Hideo watches him go, then gestures briefly at the door with one hand. Without a word, his two bodyguards bow their heads and head out of the room, leaving Hideo alone.

When they're gone, he turns back to me. "I hope life has been pleasant since you took all the attention at the Wardraft."

"I just figured that you'd instructed the Phoenix Riders to draft me first."

"I didn't tell anyone to make you the number one pick. Asher Wing did that on his own. You're quite the commodity."

So, Hideo hadn't been involved in that, after all. "Well," I say, "the Wardraft was interesting in more ways than one. Look what I found." I bring up my screenshot from the Wardraft and hover it between us. It rotates slowly, giving us a full view of the dome. The unmistakable shadow of the figure's silhouette is perched prominently in the dome's tangle of metal. Over his head is the word [null]. "On the day of the Wardraft, I saw someone watching from the Tokyo Dome's rafters."

This catches Hideo's interest. He studies the screenshot, his eyes narrowing on the dark silhouette perched in the dome's maze of beams. "How do you know it's a he?"

"Oh, I know better than that. It's Ren."

Hideo's stare darts from the screenshot over to me. "Renoir Thomas?"

I nod. "DJ Ren. A marker in the screenshot's code pointed to him. Since then, I've hooked up all of the official players to my Warcross profile." I pull up everyone's accounts. "I may need to go through some of their Memories, see who else might be involved."

Hideo's gaze goes to the digital map I've created that shows where each of the Warcross players currently are. Most are in their dorms. A group of Andromedans are out in the city, while Asher has left the Riders' dorm. Ren is still sitting in his room.

"You're more dangerous than I thought," Hideo muses, admiring my handiwork.

I offer him a smile. "I promise I'll be nice to you."

This time, I manage to coax a laugh from him. "Should I be even more concerned?" he says to me.

I let his question linger, and bring up Ren's email. "I've been running a hack on Ren's info," I reply, pulling the email forward to hover between us as a dark, encrypted cube of data. "Found this yesterday, although I can't seem to unlock it."

Hideo scans the file once. Like me, his eyes go immediately to the red marker on the edge of the cube. "This was sent from the Dark World," he says.

I nod. "And wrapped in a shield I don't recognize."

Hideo brings his hands slightly apart, then rotates the cube once. "I do," he mutters. He expands his hands again. The cube grows larger, and as it does, he pulls one side of it so that I can see its surface in detail. I narrow my eyes at it. The surface is coated with an elaborate, winding series of endlessly repeating patterns.

"It's called a fractal shield," he explains. "A new variation on onion shields we've seen lately, except that the fractal shield's layers loop endlessly, multiplying each time you burrow through a top layer. The more you try to break it open, the more secure it becomes. Your hacks will run in place forever without getting anywhere."

No wonder I couldn't break my way through it. "I've never seen this before."

"I wouldn't expect you to. This is mutated from security we developed inside Henka Games."

I lean forward, my gaze running over the surface of the cube. "Can you break it?"

Hideo puts his hands against two surfaces of the cube. When he removes his hands, a copy of the top of the fractal shield floats above the cube. "An infinite shield requires an infinite key," he says. "Something that multiplies at the same rate and type as the shield itself."

"Every locked door has a key," I murmur.

At my words, Hideo meets my gaze. He smiles.

He types several commands that are invisible to me, then runs it through a Henka Games program. A key forms in his hands, blacked out and ever-shifting, its own surface coated with the same endless patterns. I look on as he takes the key and presses it back against the cube.

The surface of the cube suddenly stills. The infinitely repeating fractals that cover it vanish. Then, in a flash, the cube disappears—replaced by a message.

It only says one thing.

**1300PD**

My gaze hitches on it at the same time Hideo's does.

"Pirate's Den," we say in unison.

To a normal person, 1300PD would be meaningless. But to me, it's a scheduled event. The 1300 is 1:00 p.m., written according to a twenty-four-hour clock—and PD stands for "Pirate's Den," an abbreviation I know well. It's a notorious gathering place in the Dark World.

The event is tagged for March twentieth.

"Well," I say. "Guess I know where I'm going this week."

Hideo considers the message for a moment longer before giving me a questioning look. "You're headed in alone?"

"*You* crack the fractal shields." I lean back on my bed and cross my arms. "It's *my* job to walk with the criminals, Mr. Tanaka."

At that, he smiles a little. "Hideo, please."

I tilt my head at him. "You insist on calling me Miss Chen in public. It's only fair."

He lifts an eyebrow. "I try not to give the tabloids more gossip than they can handle. They're particularly aggressive at this time of year."

"Oh? And what gossip is that? That we're on a first-name basis? Scandalous. It seems like the tabloids are already making up their own gossip about me, anyway."

"Would you prefer I call you Emika?"

"I would," I reply.

"Well." He nods. "Emika, then."

*Emika.* Hearing him say my first name sends a pleasant shiver down my spine. "I'll keep you updated," I decide to say, shifting to signal an end to our call. "Should be enlightening."

"Wait. Before you go."

I pause. "Yes?"

"Tell me about your arrest from a couple of years ago."

*He's been doing research on my record.* I clear my throat, suddenly angry that he's brought it up. I haven't talked about my arrest in years. "It's old news," I mutter as I begin to launch into a summary of what had happened to Annie, how I'd hacked into the school's directory.

Hideo shakes his head, stopping me. "I already know what you did. Tell me about how the police knew it was *you*."

I hesitate.

"You're far too skilled for them," Hideo continues. He studies me intently, his expression the same as it had been when he'd tested me during our first meeting. "They didn't actually catch you, did they?"

I meet his gaze. "I confessed."

Hideo stays silent.

"They thought Annie did it," I go on. The memory of sirens, of me walking into the principal's office where the cops were gathered, of Annie's cuffed wrists, her tear-streaked face looking up at me in shock, comes back to me now. "They were going to arrest her. So I turned myself in."

"You turned yourself in." There is a note of fascination in his voice. "And did you know what you would be sacrificing in doing that?"

I shrug. "Didn't have time to dwell on it. Just seemed like the right thing to do."

Hideo is quiet. His attention is now completely locked on me. "I suppose chivalry isn't dead," he finally says.

I don't quite know how to respond. All I can do is return his look, feel another wall around him fall away, see the glint in his eyes change. Whatever he thought of what I said, it's made him let down his guard.

Then the moment's over. He straightens in his chair and breaks his eye contact with me. "Until next time, Emika," he says.

I murmur my own farewell and end the call. His virtual self disappears from my room, leaving me alone again. Slowly, I exhale and let my shoulders sag. Hideo hadn't mentioned anything about the other bounty hunters, which means I'm probably ahead of them on this job. So far, so good.

It takes me a moment to realize that I'd forgotten to turn off my hack when I was having my conversation with Hideo. That meant that I was crawling *his* profile for data, too. Hideo has his own protective shields up on his info, but even so, I'd managed to grab one unencrypted file from his account, one newly created earlier today. Now sitting in my downloads, blinking at me. I peer at it long enough that it opens, thinking that I want to look inside.

My room fades away. I find myself standing in some sort of gym, equipped with large punching bags, racks of weights, mats, and long mirrors. This is one of Hideo's Memory files. *I shouldn't be poking around in his data.* Right away, I start exiting, but the Memory plays before I can.

Hideo is punching a bag in a furious rhythm, each impact shuddering in my view. Kickboxing? I pan around the Memory's world—then stop when I see the reflection in the mirrors.

He's shirtless, and his chest and back are slick with sweat, his muscles wound tight. His damp hair shudders with each hit he makes. His hands are wrapped in white bandages, and as he continues his ferocious assault on the punching bag, I can see glimpses of blood staining the bandages over his knuckles. The scars I always see. *How hard has he been hitting that bag?* But what shocks me is his expression. His eyes are black and fierce, a look so full of focused anger that I physically pull away.

I think back to the intensity I'd seen on his face during our first meeting, when he was talking about his newest creation, about his passions. I can see a similar light in his eyes here in the way he throws his punches—but this is a darker intensity. One of deep fury.

Hideo's bodyguards wait patiently at the edges of the room, and standing right next to him is someone who must be his trainer, decked out head to toe in padded gear. "Enough," he says now, and in response, Hideo pauses to turn on him. If I didn't know better, I'd say that the look the trainer gives me—to *Hideo*—is wary, even a little afraid.

The trainer starts to circle, and Hideo does the same. His movements are fluid and precise, deadly. His hair falls across his face, obscuring his eyes momentarily from view. The trainer twirls a long wooden stick in one hand, drags it along the ground, and then hoists it. He comes at Hideo, swinging the stick at him with blinding speed. My view blurs. Hideo dodges the blow easily. He sidesteps again, then a third time—on the fourth strike, Hideo lunges. He brings one arm up, fist clenched, as the stick comes down on it. The stick snaps with a loud *crack* against his forearm. Hideo darts forward. His fist strikes the trainer's arm pads so powerfully that the trainer winces at the impact. Hideo doesn't let up. He rains blows on the man's arm pads in a blur of motion—the final punch lands so hard that the trainer stumbles backward and falls.

Hideo stands there for a moment, breathing heavily, his expression hard. As if he were seeing someone else lying there. Then, the fury in his eyes fades, and for a moment, he looks like himself again. He offers the trainer his hand and pulls him back up to his feet. The session ends.

I watch in stunned silence as Hideo bids farewell to his trainer, then heads out of the room's double doors with his bodyguards flanking him, his hands still wrapped in bloodied bandages. Then the Memory ends, and I find myself in my own room again, jolted back into a peaceful scene. I finally exhale, realizing I'd been holding my breath.

So that's how Hideo gets his bruised knuckles. Why does he train like a demon possessed? Why does he strike as if he wants to kill? I shiver at the memory of his expression, of those vicious, dark eyes, absent of any hint of the playful, polite, charismatic version of himself that I thought I knew. I shake my head. Best if I didn't mention watching this Memory to anyone. Aside from his own bodyguards, Hideo probably didn't intend for anyone to see that.

The shifting light in my bedroom starts to reflect from the pool outside my balcony, and the glow startles me back into reality. I'm here for a job, not to spy on Hideo's private training sessions.

I exit from my account and remind myself to focus my thoughts on Ren instead. In the back of my mind, though, Hideo's conversation with me plays on repeat. And when I finally leave my bedroom to join my teammates in our training for the day, it's the memory of his dark eyes that lingers, the mystery behind his bloodied knuckles and furious gaze.

# 15

Three days pass in a blur of training activity. The Phoenix Riders run drills of every possible combination. I'm paired with Hammie, then with Ren, then with Asher and Roshan. I'm paired with two of them. I'm paired against them. Our environments change from jungle to city to towering cliffs. We practice in levels from past championships and everything in between.

Asher trains us with an intensity I haven't seen before. I struggle to keep up. Every new world I play is a world everyone else has already played, every new maneuver a familiar one to the rest of my team. Just when I think I'm getting the hang of something, Asher will halve the time required of us to do certain missions or perform certain moves. Just when I start getting used to a world, Asher moves us on to the next one.

I end my days exhausted, slumped against the couches with my teammates, my mind crowded with new information as Asher reviews with us what the next day will be. My dreams are filled with our drills.

While Hideo had made sure I would end up on a team, he can't help the Phoenix Riders win. If we lose, my teammates will disband for the season, and it'll be that much harder to follow Ren around. Hideo is counting on me to fulfill this end of the bargain. If I don't, I might end up forfeiting the bounty to some other hunter who *can* stay in the Championships.

"You're new to this." Roshan tries to reassure me one night as we pile against one another on the couches. Wikki is making his rounds to each of us, handing us plates of piping-hot dinner. "It *should* take you time to wrap your head around everything."

On my other side, Hammie digs a fork into her food. "One of these days, Roshan, your bleeding heart is going to bleed all over us." Her eyes flicker to me before she brings her loaded fork to her lips. "We can't afford for her to go easy on herself."

"She shouldn't have been in the draft," Ren interjects.

Hammie scowls at him. "Easy, wild card."

"I'm just saying." Ren holds up his knife and fork in defense. "I didn't DJ international events on my first try. It's not healthy." He looks at me. "Don't force her into situations she's not ready for. You might kill her."

I look away from him, but not before his words send my sixth sense tingling. *Does he suspect me? Is he watching?*

Roshan nods in reluctant agreement at Ren. "We can't afford for her to burn out. There *is* such a thing. But you already know that, Hams."

"That was only because I was a Titan that year, and Oliver was a pitiful captain compared to Ash."

"I appreciate the flattery," Asher says as he pops a fry into his mouth, then looks at me. "You've been missing your cues in training, Emi."

"She hasn't slept through the night all week," Roshan interjects. "I can see it on her face."

"I'm fine," I mutter, trying to rub away the dark circles under my eyes. I need to get away. If my teammates start poking around too much, they'll find it's more than just our exercises causing my sleepless nights.

Asher clears his throat from where he's seated, and the others settle down. He nods at us all. "No training tomorrow. Sleep in, eat a late breakfast. We'll start up again the day after that."

I give Roshan a gentle nudge of gratitude, while Hammie shoots Asher a sullen look. I'm reminded of the relentless way she played speed chess in her Memory. "You know who isn't taking tomorrow off?" she says. "The Demon Brigade."

"You know what's useless to me? A mentally exhausted Architect. Emika's been making mistakes all day." Asher nods at where Ren is eating quietly beside him. "Ren has a call with his recording studio tomorrow, anyway. Day off will do us good."

I watch Ren in silence as we finish dinner and drift off to our rooms. I've been analyzing him each day, looking for an additional sign, some further clue. Each night I comb through his data with the new key Hideo had given me. Nothing. He's heading into the Dark World tomorrow, and I still have no answers as to why. And for all I know, he's watching me, too.

"Em," Hammie calls to me as I head to my door. I turn around to see her hurrying toward me, a package tucked under her arm. She holds it out to me. "Wear this around your head when you sleep. It knocks me out pretty fast."

I squeeze the soft fabric. "Thanks," I say.

She shrugs once. "I don't mean to keep pushing you." She shoves her hands into her pockets. "You can tell me, you know, if you're having trouble with something. I'll train one-on-one with you."

I can see her chess mind sorting through the pieces of my words, not quite believing my excuses, looking a dozen steps ahead for what I might do next. She senses something's bothering me. "I know," I reply, giving her a smile. "Maybe tomorrow."

"It's a plan." She smiles back and I feel a twinge of guilt. I've never been a part of a group like this—a tight-knit group of friends that do everything together. We could be closer, if I let her in.

Instead, I just bid her good night. She does the same, but I can see the doubt in her eyes as she turns away and heads to her own room. I watch her go before sliding my door shut behind me.

That night, as I'm taking a late swim in my balcony's pool in an attempt to clear my head, I get a message from Hideo.

*You're frustrated.*

I pause in my laps, blink warm water out of my eyes, and tap on Hideo's hovering text in my vision before I can think it through.

My chat request is sent, and a moment later, Hideo accepts it, appearing at the edge of the pool as a virtual image. He's in a room dimly lit by warm light, pulling his tie loose. Without it, he looks more his age, impossibly young and less authoritative. To my annoyance, my heart tugs sharply at the sight of him. His knuckles don't look bruised tonight. I guess he hasn't been boxing in the past few days.

I lift my arms out of the water and fold them on top of the pool's tiled edge. Droplets of water on my tattooed skin catch the moonlight. "How can you tell?" I reply.

"I haven't heard from you in days."

I'm in no mood to share my training insecurities with him. "What if I'm just saving up info for the next time I report to you?" I say instead. "I haven't even gone into the Dark World yet."

Hideo turns away for a moment as he puts away his cuff links. "And is that why I haven't heard from you?" he says over his shoulder.

"Is this your way of telling me I should be making faster progress?"

He looks back at me, his expression partly hidden in shadows. "It's my way of asking if I can help you out."

"I thought I was the one helping *you* out."

He pauses again, but in the dim light, his head turns slightly toward me to reveal the hint of a smile on his lips. His eyes hold mine for a moment. I'm glad for the darkness that hides my reddening cheeks. "I know you're exhausted," he finally says.

I look away and brush beads of water from my arm. "No pity needed."

"None given. I wouldn't have put you there if you couldn't handle it."

Always with his knowing attitude. "If you want to help me out," I say as I sink back into the water, "you could always offer some moral support."

"Moral support." He turns to face me, his smile turning playful. "And what kind of moral support would you like?"

"I don't know. Some encouraging words?"

Hideo raises an eyebrow at me in amusement. "Very well." He takes a step closer to me. "I'm checking in because I miss hearing from you," he says. "Does that help?"

I pause with my mouth open, my momentary bravado disappearing. Before I can reply, he bids me good night and disconnects our chat. Hideo's image vanishes, replaced with empty air, but not before I get one last glimpse at his face, his eyes still on me.

● ● ● ● ●

THAT NIGHT, I dream that Hideo and I are back at Sound Museum Vision, except we're not in the middle of the dance floor. Instead, we're upstairs, tucked in some dark corner of the balcony overlooking the space, and he has me pushed against the wall. He's kissing me hard.

I startle awake from the dream, flustered and irritated with myself.

His words are still ringing in my thoughts when the day comes for Ren to go into the Dark World. As the others get ready to grab lunch, I lock my door and log in to Warcross.

Instead of heading into the usual game, I bring up a hovering keyboard and type in a series of extra commands, my fingers tapping against the floor. The room flickers, and suddenly it goes dark, leaving me suspended in complete blackness.

I hold my breath. I visit the Dark World often enough, but no matter how many times I go, I'll never get used to the suffocating black that descends over my eyes before I can enter.

Finally, horizontal red lines appear in my vision, lines that— when I zoom in—turn into code. It fills my vision, page after page, until it finally hits the bottom and gives me a blinking cursor. I type in a few more commands, and a new ream of code fills my view.

Then, suddenly, the dark red code vanishes, and I'm standing in the middle of a gritty city's streets, my typical [null] name hanging over my head. Other darkened figures bustle past, none of them paying any attention to me. I stand underneath a series of endless, glowing neon signs running along the buildings over-head. They illuminate me in different colors.

I smile. I'm past the shields that protect the surface level of Warcross and have dived into the sprawling, encrypted, anony-mous underground world of virtual reality that has sprung up right under the Warcross platform. It's a second home, this place where everyone speaks *my* language, and where those who might otherwise be powerless in real life can now be incredibly powerful.

Most people who frequent the Dark World don't even bother with a name for it. If you're here, you're "down under," and any-one who knows what they're doing should know that you're not talking about Australia. The world I walk through now makes no logical sense, at least not in the usual way. Narrow, dilapidated buildings stand right in the middle of the street, while some doors leading into buildings hang upside down, as if impossible to get into. The main street intersects with other streets in midair that lead from windowsill to windowsill, connecting the impossible. Like one giant Escher painting. When I look skyward, a series of dark trains run parallel to one another, disappearing into both horizons. They look weird, stretched out, as if distorted through some sort of circus mirror. Water drips nearby, running into the gutters and pooling in potholes.

I glance up at the neon signs. If you look closely at them, you'll notice that they aren't really signs at all, but lists of names highlighted in neon. If you're stupid enough to visit the Dark World without knowing how to protect your identity, then in no time, you'll see your real name and your personal info—Social Security numbers, home addresses, private phone numbers—listed up there on those signs. That's what the names are: a running list of all the users who dared to come down here unprepared, broadcast to the rest of the Dark World and leaving them at the mercy of those who walked these streets.

That's where *I'd* been listed, the first time I went down here.

I pass a sign for the main street. *Silk Road,* it says. Underneath the lists are rows of shops with their own neon signs. Some of them sell illegal goods—drugs, mostly. Others have a little red lantern hanging outside their door, offering virtual sex. Still others have a video icon over their doors, signaling live virtual voyeurism. I look away and hurry on. I may be hidden behind a black suit and a randomized face, but just because I frequent this world doesn't mean I'm ever comfortable with it.

Now I bring up a search, then tap **Pirate's Den** when the result scrolls by. The world blurs around me, and an instant later, I'm standing at a part of the street where the buildings give way to a pier. A pirate ship looms along the shore, lit up with strings of lanterns that dangle in intervals to the top of its masts, the lights reflecting against the water in a sheet of glitter.

The Pirate's Den is one of the more popular hangouts down here. The ship's bow displays an ornate wooden carving in the semblance of a backward copyright symbol. *Information wants to be free,* I mouth the Den's slogan silently. A scarlet banner hangs over the gangplank leading up to its main deck, where a steady stream of anonymous avatars are now walking.

Today, the banner advertises betting on a Warcross game happening inside. These are matches with haphazard rules run by gangsters, the matches where I find and catch the gamblers who get in trouble with the law. *Darkcross games,* everyone jokingly calls them. I can only imagine how many indebted Warcross gamblers are going to come out of this one.

*Ren's probably here for this,* I add to myself as I head up the gangplank.

On board the ship, the speakers are playing an electronic track pirated from an unreleased Frankie Dena album. A glass cylinder looms in the center of the deck, upon which a list of names and numbers constantly updates and loops. The names on this list are famous ones—prime ministers, presidents, pop stars—and beside each name is an amount of notes offered. The assassination lottery. People pitch in money to whichever person they'd like to see killed. Whenever one of these pots rises high enough, some assassin in the Dark World is bound to be motivated to assassinate that person and win the pot.

It happens rarely, of course. But the Pirate's Den has existed in one form or another almost as long as the internet's been around, and every decade or so, there's an assassination that actually goes through. In fact, Ronald Tiller, a universally hated diplomat acquitted of a rape charge, had died several years ago in a mysterious car explosion. I'd seen his name at the top of the assassination lottery list a week before it happened.

I glance up to a balcony that overlooks the cylinder of names. There are a couple of avatars sitting there, watching. One of them is leaning forward with his elbows on his knees, observing the list silently. Potential assassins, waiting for the right amounts of money. I shiver and look away.

On the other walls are lists of statistics about each official Warcross team. The stats on the Phoenix Riders and Demon Brigade take up one entire wall. Beneath it runs a scrolling list of betting odds against the two teams. The favor is overwhelmingly on the Demon Brigade's side.

Groups of unnamed avatars cluster here and there, deep in their own conversations. Many of them are hulking in appearance, even monstrous—bulging arms and long claws, black pools in the place of eyes. Some Dark World folks really like to look the part.

I search for Ren. He could be any of these avatars, disguised just like we are.

I check the time. *Almost one.* I crane my neck, scanning the crowd as I tap out commands, searching for any sign of Ren's signature in here. Nothing.

Then—

The gold dot reappears on my map. As I make my way through the crowd, I suddenly see an alert telling me that Ren is in the room. Sure enough, when I check his data, I see the *WC0* marker pop up in his info. My heart starts to beat faster. He's the silhouette I'd seen in the arena. *What—or who—is he here for?*

I glance around as the crowd quiets, an expectant hush in the air.

Suddenly, the assassination list on the glass cylinder temporarily disappears. It's replaced with the following:

#### OBSIDIAN KINGS vs WHITE SHARKS

The Dark World has its own set of famous teams, too—except these players stay anonymous and play very, very dirty. Regular Warcross teams are sponsored by wealthy patrons; Dark World teams are owned by gangsters. When you win, you win money for the gang that owns you. When you lose, the audience casts bets for you to go onto the assassination lottery. Lose enough times, and you just might see yourself listed at the top of the lottery. And then even your own sponsor might be the one to assassinate you.

Everyone who is looking at the cylinder now sees a *Join* button hovering in the center of their vision. I press it. A field pops up to ask me how many notes I want to bet. I look around the room, staring at the numbers that hover over each of the other gamblers:

₦1,000. ₦5,000. ₦10,000. I even see a few who have cast bets of well over ₦100,000.

I cast a bet of ₦100. No need to stand out here.

The world around us changes, and suddenly we are no longer standing on the deck of the Pirate's Den, but on top of a skyscraper, illuminated by a bloodred sky. Neon-white players pop up in the world, glowing alongside power-ups. The view of the Pirate's Den minimizes to a smaller screen in the corner of my vision, one that will appear over the center of my view whenever I glance down at it. Now I use it, searching for Ren's gold dot.

There he is, standing just a few feet away from me. Over his head is a light green number of notes: **100**. I raise an eyebrow. Not a very high bidder, either. That's strange. Usually, when I track someone down under, the gambler tends to blow eye-popping numbers of notes.

But Ren is risking his reputation as a professional player just to gamble a handful of notes here in an illegal game. Doesn't add up. He's not here for the game. He's dallying around, probably just keeping a low profile while he waits. I'm willing to bet he's here to make contact with someone.

The announcer comes on, introduces the ten players, and then starts the match. Unlike regular games, this game has two numbers displayed at the bottom of my view. Each number is the total notes bet on each team. I can hear the roar of the audience as the players dart into motion. Two opposing players reach each other and both swing their arms back to attack. As they do, one of them suddenly glitches out of sight. He glitches back in behind the other player, and before the second player can react, the first one kicks him off the building's roof. The crowd cheers. I just stay quiet, watching. In a real game, a move like that would have been banned immediately. But here, with no official Henka Games employees overseeing it, anything goes.

As the game continues, the notes bet on each team changes in my view in a live display. Obsidian Kings, who started out with more bets than the White Sharks, are now falling behind. As their Architect is taken down by an Icicle power-up (temporary paralysis), the Sharks go up even higher.

I sigh. Nothing unusual has happened, other than Ren's unusually low bet. What if I'm just wasting my time in here, and Ren is a giant red herring?

That's when I notice a new gambler enter the Pirate's Den.

I would have missed him, were it not for my hack. Most people around me don't seem to notice his presence—except for a few. Like Ren, who turns to stare at him, too.

In the midst of all these hulking avatars, the newcomer is inconspicuous, a lean shadow. His face is hidden completely behind a dark, opaque helmet, and he wears a fitted suit of black body armor. Lean muscles ripple as he moves, outlined by the Den's neon lights. And even though I have no info on him at all, nothing to tell me who this person might be, a chill runs through me from head to toe, some sixth sense of certainty. This is who Ren has been waiting to see. This is who Ren is meeting.

It's Zero.

# 16

*You don't know* that for sure, I remind myself. *It could be anyone.* But everything about him—his sense of command, a confidence that betrays how often he comes here, the fact that there is nothing, *nothing* I can read about him—makes my heartbeat quicken.

I shouldn't feel this surprised to see him here. But still—bumping into Zero face-to-face makes me forget myself for a moment. I barely react quickly enough to move out of his way as he cuts through the crowd.

Abruptly, Zero pauses. His head turns in my direction—but more specifically, he sees *me.*

*I'm not supposed to be able to see him,* I realize. That's why no one else in the crowd seems to notice. In fact, he is probably supposed to be invisible to everyone except the people who already knew he was coming, those who he knows are his supporters. Zero had noticed me trying to get out of his way. He knows I can see him.

Can he tell who *I* am? What if he's staring at me through his own hack, downloading all of my info? Questions fly through my mind. If I exit now, it'll be obvious that I saw him.

*Ignore him. Just stand still and look at the game. He isn't here.*

Zero stares quietly at me, then steps closer. His black helmet is completely opaque, so that all I see in it is the reflection of my generic avatar. Even though everyone in here is encrypted, Zero has absolutely no info at *all*. Not a fake identity, not a randomized username, nothing. He is a black hole. He paces around me in a slow, deliberate circle, studying me, silent as a predator, his steps echoing in the den. I stand as still as I can, holding my breath, careful to stay calm. In real life, I am typing furiously, pulling back what I'm doing and guarding myself. No doubt that his real-life person is doing the same thing right now. Even though I should be encrypted and off the grid, I feel like his stare is stripping me bare. My heart beats steadily in my chest. I'd dealt with gangsters before. If I could keep my cool around them, I remind myself, then this should be nothing.

A girl standing very close beside him jots something down on a clipboard. She has a short blue bob haircut and wears a black blazer with jeans, but her eyes are what startle me. They are completely white. At first I think she's one of the other gamblers. But when she and Zero both turn their heads simultaneously, I realize that she is a proxy, a security shield behind which Zero can completely hide his identity. If someone does manage to record this session in the Pirate's Den, and they somehow notice Zero, the only info they'll get is this girl's, whose data will lead to nothing.

What did she jot down on her clipboard? Info about us?

Zero stares at me for another beat. Then, miraculously, he turns his attention away. His proxy does the same. My hands are clenched so hard that I can feel my nails cutting into my palms.

As I look on, Zero casts a bet of 34.05 notes on the Obsidian Kings. I frown. What a strange number to bet. I wait in silence, until exactly one minute passes. Then, Zero casts another bet, this time in favor of the White Sharks. 118.25 notes.

Now he's betting on the opposite team? What the hell is he doing?

Another gambler across the den now also casts a bet of 34.05 notes. A minute later, he then casts a bet of 118.25 notes in favor of the White Sharks. The exact same pair of bets that Zero cast. Zero's proxy jots something down on her clipboard.

He's not betting at all. He's communicating with the other gambler.

*Of course he is. Record the numbers,* I tell myself. I look on as Zero waits another few minutes before casting a new bet. This time, it's 55.75 notes for the Obsidian Kings, and 37.62 notes for the Sharks.

Sure enough—across the den, a different gambler now casts the same bets in order. Again, the proxy jots this down.

I watch in perplexed silence as this continues, on and on, as everyone around me continues to cheer on the game. No one else seems bothered by these bets—they have no reason to be, really, because only the big bets are bolded and significantly change the tallies on either side. Why would anyone care about these strange, small sums?

Then, Zero casts a pair of bets—and Ren is the responding gambler.

Finally, when the match ends, Zero stands up with his proxy and steps away from the glass cylinder without a word. Beside him, his proxy nods once at the crowd, and the ones who had responded in code now nod back once. Overhead, the electronic track momentarily shifts to a different melody, as if it had hit a glitch. *Go out with a bang*, the singer on this new track croons. *Yeah / let's go out with a bang.* Then the track hops back to its usual beat. The Obsidian Kings end up winning, and the tally over the White Sharks disappears, divided and paid proportionally among the winning gamblers. I look down at my list of recorded numbers that Zero had bet.

Fifty pairs of numbers. All of them are small bets. They range as high as 153, and as low as 0. As I stare at them, a possibility comes to me. It's such a strange thought that at first I dismiss it. But the more I stare at the numbers, the more they seem to fit.

They're locations. Longitudes and latitudes.

What if they're locations of *cities*? My mind feels feverish with dread, the coming together of something big, of finally stumbling upon significant clues. Why, exactly, is Zero assigning a bunch of locations to others? What is he planning?

In a daze, I initiate a log out to leave the Dark World. Right as I do, I glimpse Zero across the room one last time.

He's staring straight at me.

# 17

I don't know if he recognized me. He might not have been paying attention to me at all, and his glance might have just been coincidental. But the memory of his head turned in my direction sends a shudder through me as I now find myself back in my room, staring out at the balcony again. I let out a slow breath. The serenity of the real world feels jarring after my jaunt in the Dark World.

*What if Zero is on to me?*

I pull up a map to hover transparently before me, along with the list of coordinates I'd just jotted down in the Pirate's Den. Then I turn my attention to the longitudes and latitudes on the map's sides.

"Thirty-one point two," I mutter out loud, running my finger along the projection. "One hundred twenty-one point five."

My finger stops right over Shanghai.

I do another set of numbers. "Thirty-four point zero five. One hundred eighteen point twenty-five."

Los Angeles.

40.71, 74.01. New York City.

55.75, 37.62. Moscow.

And so on. I compare each set of numbers, sometimes adding a negative in front of a number whenever it ends up in the middle of nowhere or in the ocean. Sure enough, *every* set of coordinates matches up with a major city. In fact, Zero had listed out the top fifty largest cities in the world, each one repeated back to him by someone else in the crowd at the Pirate's Den.

Whatever Zero's doing, it is a global operation. And somehow, I have an ominous feeling that his endgame involves much more than just messing up some Warcross tournaments.

*What if lives are at stake?*

A knock on my door jolts me from my thoughts. "Yes?" I call out.

No answer. I stay where I am for a moment, then get up and walk to my door. I push the button that slides the door open.

It's Ren, leaning against the side of the entryway, his headphones looped around his neck. A smile appears on his face that doesn't reach his eyes. "Heard you skipped lunch," he says. He tilts his head at me. "Headache?"

My blood freezes. Still, I remind myself to be calm—so I narrow my eyes at him and put my hands on my hips. "Heard you skipped to make music," I reply.

He shrugs. "I have a contract with my studio to fulfill, Warcross or no. The others told me to come up here and get you. They're starting a round of games downstairs, if you want to join." He nods toward the stairs.

*What were you doing in the Dark World, Ren?* I think to myself as I study his face. *What does your connection to Zero mean? What are you planning?*

"Not tonight," I lie, nodding toward my bed. "I have an appointment to get a license for my new board."

Ren looks at me for a beat that's just a hint too long. Then he pushes away from my door and turns toward the stairs. "Busy little wild card," he says in French, his words translating in my view.

*Busy little wild card.* I wonder, for a moment, whether he suspects me of following him. As he heads down the stairs and disappears from view, I close my door and place a quiet call to Hideo. When he picks up, a virtual version of him appears in my view.

"Emika," he says. It sends a thrill through me of both excitement and urgency.

"Hey," I whisper. "Can we meet?"

● ● ● ● ● ●

BY THE TIME I emerge from my room, Asher, Roshan, and Hammie are gathered on the couches, shoving pizza into their mouths while they play Mario Kart. Ren lounges nearby in a soft chair, watching them play. Their karts zoom along a rainbow-colored road that tunnels through the center of a galaxy.

"Oh yeah!" Hammie shouts as her kart edges into first place. "This one's mine, boys."

"Calling it too soon, Hams," Roshan shoots back. "That's your final warning."

"Don't go this easy on me, then."

"I don't throw games."

My gaze darts to Ren. He looks calm and unfazed, his gold-winged headphones looped around his neck. He notices me now and gives me a lazy smile, as if he'd always been here, instead of gambling in the Dark World just an hour ago.

Hammie shrieks. "No!" A blue shell comes whizzing out of

nowhere and hits her kart right as she's about to cross the finish line. As she struggles to get her kart moving again, the other karts zoom past her. Her rank goes from first to eighth as she finally drags herself across the line.

Asher bursts out laughing as Hammie shoots up from her seat and throws her hands up. She glares at Roshan, who gives her his gentle smile. "Sorry, love. Like I said, I don't throw games."

"Sorry, my ass!" she exclaims. "I want revenge."

"Man, Roshan," Asher replies, clapping him on the back. "Angel in real life, demon in a kart."

Ren glances at me. "Hey, Emika," he says. "You want in? I'm joining the next round."

*Why were you in the Pirate's Den, Ren? What were you doing with Zero? Are you a danger to everyone in this room?* But outwardly, I smile and hoist my electric board on my shoulder. "I was going to go try my new board in the city."

Beside Ren, Hammie groans. "Come *on*, Em," she says.

"I just want some fresh air tonight," I reply. I give her an apologetic look. "Like I said. Tomorrow, I promise."

As I turn to leave, Asher calls out to me. "Hey, wild card." I turn back around to see him giving me a serious look. "Last time you get to skip out on your team. Got it?"

I nod without saying a word. Asher then turns away, but before I can head out, I see Ren giving me a brief smile. "Have fun," he calls out to me before turning away, too.

I steal away down the back hall, step out the door, then tug my shoes on and head toward a black sedan that is idling in the driveway. I'll have to switch up how often I see Hideo at night like this. These are the sedans used by team players for transportation around the city—but still, best not to arouse suspicions. Asher will expect me to hang around for team-bonding time, especially in the weeks leading up to the first official game.

By the time I reach the Henka Games headquarters, night has completely fallen, and the heart of Tokyo has turned back into a wonderland of neon lights. The headquarters themselves even look different, and with my lenses on, the walls are covered in swirls of color and artistic renditions of the company's logo. As the car pulls up to the front of the building, I'm greeted by two of Hideo's bodyguards, both dressed in dark suits. They bow their heads at me in unison.

"This way, Miss Chen," one says.

I give them an awkward bow in return, then follow them into the building. We walk in silence until we reach Hideo's office.

Hideo is leaning over a table, his head down in concentration, his dark hair tussled. He's dressed in his usual collar shirt and dark trousers, although the shirt is black this time, with pencil-thin gray stripes. My eyes go down to his shoes. They are blue-and-gray oxfords today, embellished with black lines. His cuff links are purposefully mismatched, one a crescent moon and the other a star. How does he always look this polished? *Dad would be impressed.*

He looks up when we enter. I remember that I'm supposed to bow my head in greeting and give him a quick bob.

"Emika," he says, straightening. His serious expression softens at the sight of me. "Good evening." He exchanges a brief glance with each of the bodyguards. One of them opens his mouth to protest, but when Hideo tilts his head once toward the door, the man sighs and guides both of them out of the room.

"They've been with me since I was fifteen," Hideo says as he steps around the table toward me. "You'll have to forgive them if they're occasionally overprotective."

"Maybe they think I'm a danger to you."

He smiles as he reaches me. "And are you?"

"I try to restrain myself," I answer, returning his smile. "For now, I'm just here to tell you what I found."

"I'm assuming you discovered something interesting in the Dark World?"

"*Interesting* doesn't even begin to cover it." I glance around the office. "I hope you're ready to settle in. I've got a bunch of information for you."

"Good, because I was thinking we try something different with our meeting tonight." His gaze lingers on me for a beat longer. "Have you eaten yet?"

Is he asking me to dinner? "No," I say, trying to stay casual.

He takes a dark gray peacoat off the back of a chair and pulls it on. Then he tilts his head once toward the door. "Join me."

# 18

We end up in Shibuya, right in front of a skyscraper with the name *Rossella Osteria* floating at the top of it. We take an elevator to the roof of the building, where a set of tall glass doors slides open for us. I walk into a space that makes my jaw drop. A segment of the floor is made of glass, *real* glass, not a virtual simulation, and through it swims a stream of gold and scarlet koi fish. Vases of flowers adorn marble pedestals around the edges of the restaurant. The entire place is empty.

The host hurries over to greet Hideo. "Tanaka-*sama!*" he exclaims in Japanese, bowing his head low. In his nervous gestures, I can see myself when I first met Hideo, falling all over myself under Hideo's serious stare. "A thousand apologies—we didn't know you had scheduled anyone to come with you tonight."

He sneaks an anxious glance at me. Suddenly I realize that he must think I'm Hideo's date. Maybe I am. I shift awkwardly on my feet.

Hideo nods at him. "No apologies needed," he replies in Japanese, then glances at me. "This is Miss Emika Chen, my colleague." He holds his hand out for me to walk in front of him. "Please."

I follow the host, perplexed and hyperaware that Hideo is behind me, until we reach an outside patio framed by ornate pillars and lit by trails of fairy lights. Heat lamps glow in regularly spaced intervals, their flames adding a golden warmth to our skin, and the lights of the city shimmer down below. As we take a seat, the waiter hands us menus and hurriedly takes his leave, so that we—and the bodyguards—are the only people remaining out here.

"Why is this restaurant completely empty?" I ask.

Hideo doesn't bother touching the menu. "I own it," he replies. "Once a month, it's reserved for me and any potential business meetings I might have. I thought you might prefer some Western food, at any rate."

My stomach growls loudly in reply, and I cough in an attempt to hide the sound. I wouldn't be surprised if Hideo owned half of Tokyo. "Italian's great," I say.

We order our food, and before long, the plates arrive, filling the air with the rich aroma of basil and tomato. As we eat, I bring up my account and send Hideo an invite to join me. "I followed Ren into the Pirate's Den," I say.

"And? What did you see?"

"And he was with this guy." I put down my fork and bring up a Memory of what I'd seen in the Den—the figure in dark armor, accompanied by his proxy, placing bets on the illegal Warcross game.

Hideo leans forward at the sight. "Is this Zero?"

I nod, tapping the table twice. "I'm almost certain it was him.

He was hidden behind an armored avatar and this proxy, and he was giving out a lot of information to what seemed to be his followers in the Pirate's Den. *Dozens* of followers. This is no lone operation."

"What kind of information was he giving out?"

"Coordinates of cities. Look." I pull up the list of numbers I'd recorded, explaining the system of small bets that Zero had been using to pass them along to his followers. Then I bring up a virtual map to hover between us, scattering the coordinates across it. My finger stops at the coordinates 35.68, 139.68. "And this—Tokyo—was the city that Ren answered for. Maybe everyone else also responded based on whatever city they're physically located in."

Hideo's eyes narrow as he analyzes the locations. "These cities are where the largest dome events happen for the championships." He glances at me. "Any clues as to how many meetings he has already conducted before this?"

I shake my head. "No. But he seems like he's got a large group. I need another encounter with Zero to get a better sense of what all this means, but the chances of me getting more information from him like that before the games start are slim."

Hideo shakes his head once. "You won't need to. We'll bring him to us. The first official game happens on April fifth. We already know he and his followers will be watching it, and that Ren will be the one assigned to the dome event in Tokyo. It's likely he will be in direct, encrypted communication with Zero during this game."

"You want me to hack his system during our game?"

"Yes. We'll plant something on you in the first official game. Force Ren to interact with you in the middle of it, and it will disable the shields that protect him. It will expose any data between him and Zero."

It sounds like a solid plan. "What are you going to plant on me?"

Hideo smiles a little. His hand brushes my wrist, turning it over, and his thumb presses carefully against my pulse. A tingle runs through me at his warm touch. Then he moves his hand away from mine and makes a brief gesture in the air. My data appears between us, the text glowing a faint blue. I look on in fascination as he weaves my data into what we already have of Ren's, an algorithm right before my eyes, fashioning it into the equivalent of a noose.

"What is it?" I ask.

"A snare. Grab his wrist at any point during the game. It will cut through his security and expose his data for you." Then he takes my hand again and wraps the trap around my wrist like a bracelet, the web of data glittering against my skin for a moment before turning invisible. Something about the gesture feels nostalgic, and suddenly I can see my father hunched over the dining room table, humming cheerfully to himself as he measures strips of fabric against his wrist, a half-empty wine bottle nearby, the floor around him cluttered with sequins and reams of cloth.

I pull my hand away and into my lap, feeling momentarily vulnerable. "Will do," I say.

Hideo's expression wavers. He studies me. "Are you all right?"

"I'm fine." I shake my head, annoyed with myself for being so obvious. *Just a memory, that's all.* And I'm about to say this to him in order to brush it away—but then I look up, meet his eyes, and this time, I feel my own walls lowering. "I was remembering my father," I say instead, gesturing at my wrist. "He used to measure out short lengths of fabric by wrapping them around his wrist."

Hideo must have caught the shift in my tone. "Used to?" he says softly.

I look down, concentrating on the table. "It's been a while since he died."

Hideo is quiet for a long moment. There's a familiarity in his look, a beat of silence shared by everyone who has ever experienced loss. One of his hands tightens and loosens. I watch the bruises on his knuckles shift. "Your father was an artist," he finally says.

I nod. "Dad used to shake his head and wonder where the hell I got my love for numbers from."

"And your mother? What does she do?"

My mother. A faded memory flashes through my mind of Dad holding my tiny, chubby hand, the two of us looking on helplessly as she laced up her boots and adjusted her silk scarf. While Dad spoke to her in a low, sad voice, I stared up in awe at the silver handle of her suitcase, the perfection of her nails, the silky blackness of her hair. I can still feel her smooth, cool hand against my cheek, patting it once, twice, then pulling away without any reluctance. *She's so beautiful,* I remember thinking. The door closed behind her without a sound. Not long afterward, Dad's gambling habit started.

"She left," I reply.

I can tell that Hideo is piecing something together about me. "I'm sorry," he says gently.

I look down, annoyed at the ache in my chest. "After Dad passed away, I preoccupied myself at my foster group home by digging obsessively into your API. It helped me, you know . . . forget."

There it is again, that brief moment of understanding on Hideo's face, of old grief and dark history. "And are you able to forget?" he says after a while.

I search his gaze. "Do your bruised knuckles give you release?" I answer in a soft voice.

Hideo looks out toward the city. He doesn't comment on why I asked him about the bruises, or how long I've been wondering about them. "I think we know the answer to both those questions," he murmurs. And I find myself overwhelmed by another slew of thoughts crowding my mind, guesses of what might have happened to Hideo in his past.

We settle into a comfortable silence as we admire the shimmering lights of the city. The sky has turned fully dark now, the stars erased from view by the neon streets of Tokyo below. My eyes turn upward, instinctively, as I search for any hint of constellations. No use. We're too far inside the city to see anything more than one or two dots in the sky.

It takes me a moment to notice that Hideo has leaned back in his chair and is watching me again, a small smile hovering on the edges of his lips. The darkness of his eyes shifts in the low light, catching hints of fairy light as well as the warmth from the heat lamps.

"You search the sky," he says.

I turn my eyes down and laugh. "It's just a habit. I've only seen the sky full of stars when Dad used to take me on road trips through the countryside. I've looked for the constellations ever since then."

Hideo glances up, then moves his fingers in a single, subtle motion. A clear box appears, asking me to accept a shared view. I do. The virtual overlays in my view adjust—and suddenly, the *true* night sky appears overhead, a sheet of spring constellations against countless numbers of stars, silver and gold and sapphire and scarlet, so bright that the Milky Way band itself is visible. In this moment, it seems entirely possible that starlight could rain down upon us, dusting us in glitter.

"One of the first things I put on my personal, augmented

reality view was an unobstructed night sky," Hideo says. He looks at me. "Do you like it?"

I nod without saying a word, my breath still caught in my throat.

Hideo smiles at me, *truly* smiles, in a way that brightens his eyes. His gaze wanders across my face. He is so close now that, if he wanted, he could lean forward and kiss me—and I find myself leaning toward him, too, hoping that he'll close the gap between us.

"Tanaka-san."

One of Hideo's bodyguards approaches us, bowing his head respectfully. "A call for you," he says.

Hideo's eyes linger on me for a final moment. Then he moves away, and his presence is replaced with cool air. I nearly slump in my chair from disappointment. Hideo turns away from me and glances up. When he sees the bodyguard's expression, he nods. "Excuse me," he says to me, then stands and walks back inside the restaurant.

I sigh. A cold breeze blows by, making me shiver, and I turn my eyes back to the sky, where the sheet of stars still hangs in my view. I imagine him creating this, his face turned skyward, too, longing to see the stars.

Maybe we both need the cold air to clear our heads.

I work for him. He's my client. This is a bounty hunt, just like every other hunt I've ever done. When I finish—when I *win*—I'll be on my way back to New York and never have to take on another hunt again. And yet, here I am, sharing something about my mother that I haven't thought about in years. I think back to the look in his eyes. Who had he lost from his life?

I'm starting to think I won't see Hideo again tonight when something warm is draped around my shoulders. It's Hideo's gray peacoat. I look up to see him pass me by. "You looked cold," he says as he sits down again.

I slide his coat down over my shoulders. "Thank you," I reply.

He gives me an apologetic shake of his head. I hope he says something to acknowledge the spark that had danced between us, but instead, he says, "I'm afraid I have to leave soon. My guards will escort you out of a hidden exit, for your privacy."

"Oh, of course," I reply, trying to hide my disappointment behind something that I hope sounds upbeat.

"When can I see you again?"

I look sharply at him. A swarm of butterflies stirs in my stomach, and my heart starts hammering again. "Well," I start to say, "aside from what we already discussed, I'm not sure I'll have much more to report until after—"

Hideo shakes his head once. "No reports. Just your company."

*Just my company.* His gaze is calm, but I notice the way he's turned toward me, the light in his eyes. "After the first game," I hear the words stumble out of me.

Hideo smiles, and this time, it is a secret smile. "I look forward to it."

# 19

The morning of our first official game begins with Asher ramming his wheelchair repeatedly against my door. I startle awake, squinting and muttering, barely able to process his words.

"Level's in!" he's shouting as he moves on to ram Hammie's door. "Get up! Up!"

*Level's in.* My eyes fly open, and I bolt upright in bed. *Today is the first day.*

I fumble around in my blankets until I find my phone, then do a quick scan of my messages. There's only one new message, and it's from Hideo.

Best of luck today. You'll hardly need it.

I can't tell if the flurry in my stomach is from the anxiety of my first game or from his words. In the last couple of weeks since our dinner, I've talked to Hideo almost every day. Most of our exchanges are innocent, strictly business, but sometimes—when our chats happen late at night—I feel the tug that reminds me of the moment during our dinner when he'd leaned close.

> See you in the dome. And thanks—believe me, I could use the luck.

I don't think I believe you at all, Miss Chen.

> Now you're making fun of me, Mr. Tanaka.

Ah. Is that what you're calling this?

> What should I call it instead?

Moral support, perhaps?

I smile.

> Your moral support is going to distract me in the arena.

Then I apologize in advance.

I shake my head.

> You're such a flatterer.

I'm no such thing.
See you in the dome, Emika.

That's all he says. I wait for another message, but when none comes, I shake off my thoughts and swing my legs over the side of my bed. I hurriedly throw some clothes on, run a toothbrush along my teeth, bundle my rainbow hair up into a messy bun, and put in my NeuroLink lenses. For a moment, I stare at my reflection. My pulse beats loud in my ears. I imagine Keira back in New York City, watching me in the game as she's curled up on the couch. I picture Mr. Alsole doing the same, his eyes squinting with disbelief.

Time to go. I let out a shaky breath, turn away from the mirror, and rush out.

Everyone else is already in the atrium, clustered around Asher as he brings up the morning transmission for us. Hammie nods at me as I join them. Nearby, Wikki hurries from one of us to the next, serving each person their favorite breakfast. Hammie's is a waffle piled high with syrup, fruit, and whipped cream, while mine is a breakfast taco with an enormous dollop of guacamole. Ren, in typical fashion, is fussing over a platter of egg whites and boiled spinach, while Roshan just nurses a cup of spiced chai and grimaces at the plate that Wikki offers him.

"Not today," he complains.

Wikki blinks at him with the most sorrowful look a drone can muster. "Would you like to reconsider? Scrambled eggs with goat cheese is your fav—"

The mention makes Roshan turn green. "Not today," he repeats, patting Wikki once on the head. "Nothing personal."

"Eat," Asher says to him over his own plate of scrambled eggs. "You need *something* today if you want your brain to be functional."

I try to follow his advice, but I only manage three bites of my breakfast taco before I push my plate away, full from my crowd of thoughts.

Hammie waves around a forkful of waffle and nods at the image displayed in midair before us. "Our first game looks like it's going to be a fast one," she says.

The first level that Hideo's committee has created for our game looks like a world of glittering ice and towering glaciers. As I look on, the landscape rotates for us in midair, showing us a glimpse of what it will be like. Below it is listed a series of rules.

Roshan reads them out for us with a concentrated frown. "This will be a racing level," he says, picking a piece of date out of his eggs and popping it in his mouth. "Everyone will be moving forward at all times, on individual hoverboards. If a player gets knocked off her board, she will be resurrected one full pace behind the others, at the lowest possible altitude to the ground."

I take in the full landscape as it rotates, committing the terrain to my memory.

Asher leans back against his headrest and regards us. His eyes settle first on Ren. "Time to test your Fighter skills," he says. "You're next to me, wild card." Then he looks at me. "Ems," he adds, nodding at the rotating map. "You're starting on my other side. Hammie, stay a little ahead of her. Grab as many power-ups as you can and pass them to her. Roshan, take care of the wild cards and make sure they don't fall behind if they're killed early on. Let's go win this."

I look at Ren. He gives Asher a single nod, as if he were here only for the victory, as if he hadn't just visited the Dark World to help bring down the entire game. My hand rubs unconsciously at my wrist, where Hideo had wrapped the invisible noose.

Two of us can play at this.

TODAY, THE TOKYO Dome is completely covered with the colors and symbols that represent us and the Demon Brigade. Through our lenses, we can see the image of a scarlet phoenix hovering high above the arena, alongside a horde of black-and-silver-hooded demons. Staring in the direction of the dome brings up a bunch of both teams' statistics in midair. The Demons have won two championships. We've only won once, but we won it by beating *them*. I let myself think back on the insults that Tremaine and Max had thrown my way. Today should be an interesting match.

The inside of the arena looks even more spectacular. During the Wardraft, the lower arena was taken up by circles of wild cards sitting and waiting for their assignments. Today, all of that is gone, replaced by a smooth floor currently displaying a rotation of a red-and-gold phoenix soaring in front of the sun, and then fading into a demon horde full of grinning skulls and dark hoods. Ten glass booths are arranged in a circle on this floor, five for us, five for the Demons. In official games, the players step inside these booths to ensure that everything is exactly fair for both teams: equal temperature differences; air pressure; Link calibrations; connection to Warcross; and so on. It also prevents players from eavesdropping on commands given by their opponents.

The stadium is completely packed. An omniscient voice is already calling out each of our names as we enter the arena, the voice deep and reverberating, and as it does, each name rotates in flames in the arena's center. The cheers send tremors through me as we file into the center of the arena and wait to be led to our booths. On the opposite end, the Demons arrive, too. "Ireland's Jena MacNeil, the youngest captain in the official games!" they call out. "England's Tremaine Blackbourne, her Architect! Max

Martin of the USA, the Demons' Fighter!" They go down the line. Darren Kinney, Shield. Ziggy Frost, Thief. She meets my eyes briefly, as if apologetic, but then straightens and gives me a determined nod. I stare back calmly. We may have been friendly at the Wardraft, but right now, we're rivals.

My attention turns to Tremaine. He's glaring at me, so I decide to give him a dazzling smile in return.

The stadium voice announces my name. I'm deafened by the chorus of screams that come up from the audience. There are banners with my name on them, waving frantically in the packed seats. EMIKA CHEN! Some of them say. TEAM USA! TEAM PHOENIX RIDERS! I blink at them, bewildered to see the display. Somewhere at the top of the arena, the voices of the game's analysts argue back and forth about today's game.

"By all accounts," one says, his voice deafening in the arena, "we should see the Demon Brigade slaughter the Phoenix Riders, currently the lowest-ranking team in the championships."

"But Asher Wing is one of the most talented captains in the games," another pipes up. "He has kept his wild-card choices surprising and mysterious. Why did he pick them? We'll have to see. But don't count the Phoenix Riders out yet!"

I step into my booth and let it seal me in. Suddenly, the world turns quiet, and the audience's roar and analysts' voices lower to a muffled din.

"Welcome, Emika Chen," says a voice inside the booth. A red sphere appears and hovers before me. "Please look forward."

This is the same calibration that I'd done when I first boarded Hideo's private jet. They are making sure that each player's calibrations are in sync. I do what the voice says as it runs me through the full calibration. When it's finished, I look through the glass on either side and see each of my teammates in their own booths. The pounding of my heart fills my ears.

Out in the center of the floor, the lights dim. The announcer's voice comes on in my earphones. "Ladies and gentlemen," he exclaims, "let's—get—*started*!"

The arena around us fades out, and we are transported into an alternate world.

Cold sunlight makes me squint. I hold up a virtual hand to shield my eyes. Then, gradually, the glow fades, and I find myself suspended in midair, overlooking a vast expanse of blue ice and snow-covered glaciers, all shifting and cracking under their own weight. The snow glitters under an alien sun in a million points of light. The sky is a sheet of purple and pink and gold, and giant planets are suspended against it, their rings curving past the horizon. Enormous ice monuments tower in the landscape, erupting from the glacier at random intervals. The monuments look carved from the wind, hunched and holed and weathered, translucent, and stretch as far as the eye can see. Even the music playing around us *sounds* cold—synthetic bells, echoes, a background wind, and a deep, thudding, rhythmic beat.

But what really catches my attention are the towering cliffs of blue ice on either side of us, forming our path. Frozen inside this blue ice are enormous beasts. A polar bear as large as a skyscraper. A white wolf with a missing eye, its jaws frozen into a snarl. A snake-like dragon. A saber-toothed tiger. A woolly mammoth. I shiver in awe at the size of them. They look as if they could explode from the ice at any moment.

My stomach dips as I dare to look down. I'm outfitted in bright red Architect gear, my boots and thick hood trimmed with scarlet fur, and I'm standing on what looks like a hovering board strapped to my boots. Blue flames shoot from two cylinders attached to its base. To my left, Asher and Ren are both dressed in similar red snow gear, each of them also hovering in midair on boards. *This is going to be a race.*

To my right, our opponents appear.

The Demon Brigade is dressed in bright silver. Jena gives Asher a smirk, then a mock salute. Asher just crosses his arms and ignores her. Max Martin's gaze sweeps coldly across us all. But Tremaine is the one with his full attention focused on me, his ice-blue eyes unreadable. He will be aiming for me, and I remember how I'd trained for him with the others, how Roshan had warned me of his adaptable nature. Nearby, Roshan's jaw is set tight. The two refuse to look at each other.

"Welcome to the first official game of the championships!" we hear through our headphones. "Today, the Demon Brigade faces off against the Phoenix Riders in the White World, a landscape of speed, stealth, and quick thinking. There will be no time to hesitate!"

Our team Artifact appears over Asher's head, a glittering red diamond. A silver diamond appears over Jena's head. Dozens of colorful power-ups pop up around the level, suspended in the air and over the monuments and down on the ground. I look over them, searching for any within my range that might be worth a grab.

"Emi." Asher's voice comes on in my ears, fed into our personal team loop. "The monument closest to you. See the Lightning power-up? Get your hands on it."

I catch sight of a white-blue marble suspended in the center of a gaping hole in the first ice structure. In my mind, I bring up the 3-D rotating landscape we'd been shown before the game, as clear and detailed as if it were still hovering before me. I allow myself a brief smile. "Got it," I reply.

"And what an interesting choice for Captain Asher!" the analysts are now saying. "Flanked on either side by not just one, but *two* wild cards in the Phoenix Riders' first match of the season. Emika Chen and Renoir Thomas must have impressed him during their training."

"Good luck," Ren says as the announcer reads out the familiar rules of gameplay. I know it's directed at me, and as usual, I can't quite tell if he's saying it earnestly or maliciously. I give him a tight smile.

"Same to you," I reply. Silently, I remind myself to look for the first chance to seize him.

We all tap our chests twice with our fists as the announcer finishes. The world stills. All I can hear is silence.

Then, the starting call blares.

"Game! Set! *Fight!*"

The world around us comes to life. Blasts of wind send snow flying high into the sky. The flaming exhausts on my hoverboard turn ninety degrees—I'm shot forward like a bullet from a gun. Instantly, my boarding instincts kick in—while the others around me wobble unsteadily, I crouch down in position, perfectly balanced. Asher glances at me in surprise. Snow rushes into my face, obscuring my vision. I blink it away.

Already, my board is speeding up. The white landscape rushes past me, and the ice monuments loom close. Beside me are Asher and Ren. Asher has started to pull ahead of us. I gingerly test my hoverboard, then realize that a button exists on the board beneath each of my heels. When I push my front heel down, I speed up. When I push my back heel down, I brake. I'll have to be careful—if I brake too hard, I'll stall in midair and go tumbling.

Beside me, Ren breaks away and heads off in Asher's wake. I grit my teeth, then decide not to follow after him for now. Ren had heard Asher's instructions to me. If I'm too obvious about trailing him instead of listening to our captain, he'll know I'm up to something else.

The diamond shines brightly over Asher's head. In the center of my vision hovers a transparent, circular map, showing ten dots for where each player happens to be. I nearly lose my balance as another blast of wind hits us. The first ice monument rushes toward me.

"Now, Emi!" Asher snaps in our comms.

I look at the Lightning power-up hovering in the middle of the giant hole in the structure. Then I shift my weight to my back leg. My hoverboard zooms upward. I hunch down until I'm as low on the board as I can go—the change speeds me up, and I rocket toward the marble.

I snatch it out of the air as I zip through the hole.

My memory of the 3-D landscape flashes in my mind. I see the way the structure looks on all sides, the crevices nearest it, and the way the terrain tilts. In a split second, I make a calculation of how this ice structure might topple if I mess with it right now. *Do it,* I tell myself. I whip out a stick of dynamite from my belt and slap it onto the side of the structure as I pass through. Then I rush downward.

"Get out of the way!" I say through our secure feed.

Behind me, an explosion shakes the level. Snow and shards of ice fly past me. I cringe and duck down low on my hoverboard. The structure I'd blown groans, the sound echoing across the landscape, and I glance over my shoulder to see it toppling forward toward all of us. The other Phoenix Riders scatter, thanks to my warning. I dart sharply sideways, too, so suddenly that I almost topple out of control. At the same time, I aim the Lightning power-up straight at where the Demons are clustered. I throw it.

Lightning strikes all of them except for their captain, Jena, lighting up the space in a flash of brilliant gold. For a single, precious second, the Demons all freeze.

Jena only gets a chance to glance up at the giant, falling shadow before shouting a warning to her teammates. *"Move! Move!"*

But the Lightning attack has thrown off the Demons. Their players scatter left and right as the structure collapses in an explosion of cracking ice. They barely make it—all except for Darren Kinney, their Shield. The falling pillar clips him hard on his shoulder, and he goes spinning wildly out of control, disappearing into the cloud of white. His life bar shrinks to 0 percent.

**Darren Kinney | Team Demon Brigade**
**Life: -100% | STRIKE OUT!**

||||||||||||||||||||||||||||

**EMIKA CHEN strikes out DARREN KINNEY!**

He regenerates a good fifty yards behind me, with a new life bar.

*"First strike!"* the announcer screams in disbelief as the audience goes insane with cheering. "Goes to *Emika Chen!"*

Hammie whoops joyously over our comms, while Ren lets out a curse and Roshan sounds bewildered. Asher's voice finally comes on. "Next time—*warn me*," he shouts, even as his tone is one of admiration.

I'm trying to concentrate on the dizzying landscape that rushes past us. Jena's Artifact hovers glittering and silver over her head. "You're welcome!" I shout back. All around us come the screams and cheers from our invisible audience.

"I don't believe it!" an analyst yells. "Another early move

from a wild card in the first game of the season, and what a move it is! She couldn't have picked a more accurate way of toppling that structure toward the Demons. We've been underestimating Emika Chen. This is going to be a fun one, folks!"

Suddenly, one of the Demons sidles up to me, then spins around on his board so that he's facing me. It's Tremaine. My smile vanishes as he lunges for me, slashing me hard in the chest with the blade embedded on his armguard. My vision blurs scarlet.

### Emika Chen | Team Phoenix Riders
### Life: -40%

My hoverboard wobbles as I dart backward, and I nearly lose my balance. Tremaine lunges again. He's so fast that his limbs seem to blur. If he knocks me off my board, I'll go tumbling into oblivion and regenerate behind everyone. I'll be useless for a long time. My hands scramble for the hammer at my belt.

Out of nowhere, Roshan appears on my other side right as Tremaine throws another strike at me. Roshan narrows his eyes and brings his forearms up in a bracing cross. The move activates his armguards—an enormous, glowing blue shield bursts outward from them in a circle, arcing protectively in front of us both. Tremaine's attack hits the shield instead, sending sparks flying everywhere.

"Babysitting your new Architect?" he taunts Roshan.

"Don't be so jealous," Roshan says. He uncrosses his arms, letting the shield down for an instant, and lunges at Tremaine with his own fist. A smaller blue shield glows around his moving arm. It hits Tremaine hard enough to make him reel backward, dropping his life bar by 15 percent. The three of us maneuver down into a valley of snow-covered stone, then weave up to avoid a sharp outcropping of rock. I veer sharply out of the way as Roshan continues to fight with Tremaine—but Tremaine veers with me, determined to knock me down. My recollection of the landscape flies through my head. I use what I remember in order to avoid crashing against a cliff.

The analyst is talking so fast now that he can barely catch his breath. "And the Demons send their Architect after Emika! Roshan comes to her aid! If Tremaine catches Emika at this outcropping—she *avoids it*! Barely! It's as if she knows this terrain! Roshan shows us why he's one of the best Shields in the games! He's not letting their Architect fall, folks, not if he can help it!"

Power-ups zip past us. I eye them until I find what I'm looking for—a Speed Burst. It's glowing bright yellow and hurtling near me. I take a mighty swerve toward it. My hand reaches out. I barely manage to grab it.

I use it right away. The world around me slows as I dash forward.

The light in this level is changing; the ice monuments are lit with golden rays and dragging long shadows across the glaciers. The cliffs of blue ice lining our path take on a darker, more ominous color, and the frozen beasts inside them start to look alive. From the corner of my vision, they seem to stir. It takes me a moment to realize that the sun is setting. If this keeps up, we are going to need some power-ups that light our way. I look forward, searching for Ren. Asher has handed off our Artifact to Hammie, who zips ahead of us all. Now Asher and Ren team up as they swerve toward Jena, who is sandwiched on both sides by Tremaine and Ziggy.

"It looks like we're heading for our first showdown between the captains!" the announcer shouts.

Jena sees Asher's move. She ducks low on her hoverboard and dives. Her teammates dive with her. They tumble until they look like they're going to crash into the ground—and then suddenly pull up, so that they're skimming right above the glacier. Asher and Ren dive down, too. Plumes of snow whip up as they zoom by.

I turn my board higher, trying to protect myself from all the flying snow. Ahead of me, Hammie whips her own board up sharply enough to veer herself off to the right. Her movements are so quick that I can barely keep track of her. She snags another power-up, a bright blue one, and then does a dizzying spin on her board to grab a third. Another Speed Burst. She tosses it back to me as she inches her way over to Tremaine.

I look back down at the crew skimming along the glacier's surface. There are enough formations between here and the horizon for me to trap them in, if I can do it right. Tremaine is probably thinking the same thing. I point my hoverboard down and follow them, low against the ground.

"Emi," Asher says into my secure comms. "Archway ahead. Blow it up."

"Got it."

"Ren and I will veer off at the last second, go around behind Jena. When she and her team try to avoid the rubble in front of them, we'll catch them from the back and take her Artifact."

I nod, even though I know Asher can't see me. "I'll knock it out before they can say—"

My words die as an enormous shape explodes out of the ice cliffs lining our path.

It looks like a prehistoric polar bear, except as tall as a skyscraper—and its jaws are open wide, revealing a row of sharp teeth, each one as long as the nearest towering ice structure. Its eyes glow scarlet. It lets out an earthshaking roar, then lunges toward the closest player.

The closest player is me.

My limbs go into autodrive. I slam my back foot down on the gas. At the same time, I swivel my hoverboard so sharply to my left that I spin 180 degrees. My board shoots me back in the direction I came. The bear's mouth yawns on either side of me—its jaws start to close. *Just a little farther.* I shoot out of the beast's mouth at the same time its jaws close, and the accompanying blast of wind sends me tumbling forward. The bear's front paws land heavily, shaking the world.

Through the dust, Roshan appears and hurtles toward me— as if he were going to ram right into me. I throw my arms up instinctively. Then I veer sideways in a desperate attempt to save myself.

We narrowly avoid a collision. As he passes me, he grabs my arm and zooms upward as the bear lunges up for us again. Before I can protest, he puts all his strength into flinging me high—and I find myself sailing up toward the arch that still looms ahead. Below me, the bear's jaws snap shut on Roshan.

### Roshan Ahmadi | Team Phoenix Riders
### Life: -100% | STRIKE OUT!

Nearby, another enormous beast explodes out of the ice cliffs. A one-eyed white wolf. Players scatter left and right as it swings its head around, jaws chomping. It catches Ziggy. She vanishes in its mouth, regenerating fifty yards away along with Roshan. Ren wobbles on his board and spins out of control as he tries to avoid the wolf's gaping mouth.

This is my chance to get him. I turn my board in a sharp arc, then hurtle toward Ren. He sees me coming a split second before I ram hard into him, sending both us careening away from the wolf. I grab for his wrist until my hand finally closes around it.

The noose activates. I see it glow gold in my view, then disappear. A blue glow flashes around Ren before vanishing. An instant later, a file from him pops into my view. I grin. *Broke through.*

"Get off me," Ren snaps, trying to yank himself free. His move sends us both tumbling off our boards and into the white land below. Everything goes bright in my view—and an instant later, I've regenerated a pace behind the others.

"And both Rider wild cards are struck out by a rookie mistake!" the analyst shouts. Ren shoots me a dirty look from where he's regenerated several yards away from me. Asher scolds me over our line. But I don't care. I've laid Hideo's trap. My focus turns away from Ren and back to the game.

I hunt madly for a sight of my teammates on my map. Finally, I glimpse Asher and Hammie hovering near the center to the archway, flying in tight circles as they are trapped in by two other beasts. Some Demons are heading their way, too.

I yank out my dynamite and zoom toward the top of the archway. As I reach it, I slap a stick of dynamite to the top of the ice structure. Then I pivot down and dart away right as it goes off. Another earth-shattering explosion—the impact shakes my board violently, and snow flies all around me, making me squint. I'm down to my last dynamite.

Behind me, through the dust, Ren materializes with Asher and Hammie on his tail. Our Artifact still hovers over Hammie's head. I call to her, then toss her my hammer from my utility belt. Her hand shoots out and she catches it without even turning around, then winks at me in thanks over her shoulder. As she hurtles away from the nearest beast, she throws the hammer at its eye as hard as she can. It hits true, making the beast flinch away with a roar.

The Demons are above us, looking down. They have the advantage now, and they know it—even from here, I can tell that Jena has a grin on her face. She still has their Artifact, and it hovers over her head, silver and shining. Her lips move as she gives instructions to her team.

"Hams," Asher says through our comms as we all continue to hurtle through the darkening landscape. "Give me the Artifact. Turn off your hoverboard's lights." His eyes are locked on Jena. "And get *hers*."

Hammie winks at Asher as she transfers our Artifact to him. In the twilight, both our Artifact and our opponent's glow with a noticeable blue halo. "Yes, sir."

"Roshan, back her up. Ren, cut them off. And Emi—"

But I never get to hear what Asher wants me to do. An explosion goes off right above a monument near us, rocketing us all apart. Tremaine had thrown a stick of dynamite near us. A blur of light streaks past us and rams right into Ren, sending both of them tumbling. It's Max. Ren lets out an angry snarl and flings the other Fighter off him. At the same time, Hammie hurtles out of sight, her hoverboard nothing more than her engine's bright red sparks of fire propelling her forward. I don't have time to think about where she's going—because in the next instant, Jena comes rocketing down toward us with Darren and Ziggy at her sides. She's headed straight for Asher. Asher bares his teeth and laughs, then rushes up to greet her.

My eyes flicker to the glacier's ice below us. Along the cliffs, a white dragon is stirring to life, its movements cracking the ice that encases it. I narrow my eyes. If I can just gain control of that dragon . . . My hands go to the length of rope dangling at my waist, and as Asher and Ren attack the Demons, I dart toward the surface and slow my board down near the dragon.

As I dive, I notice lights following closely behind me— somebody's hoverboard is skimming the ground in the darkness. *It's Tremaine.* And he's closing on me fast. I only have time to look up once before he barrels into me. We both tumble straight into the glacier's surface. The impact knocks us clear off our boards.

The world around me tumbles, and all I can see is flying snow and evening sky. Then everything blinks out—the next instant, both Tremaine and I have struck out and regenerated a full pace behind the others.

Tremaine turns a murderous look on me. My Speed Burst power-up from Hammie is still in my inventory—and now I use it. It disappears from my hand in a flash of light. The world rushes forward, and I can almost feel the blast of wind against my skin. Right as I yank out my own length of rope, the dragon finally breaks free from the ice. Its gaping mouth roars to the surface.

I fling my rope, aiming to lasso the tip of its nose. One try. Then another. On my third, I manage to swing the loop across the creature's snout. The dragon pivots its head in my direction, then lets out a furious shriek. A column of fire bursts from its open jaws. I use the momentum from the rope to swing onto its head. My rope becomes a makeshift harness. Below me, Asher and Max are locked in battle.

"Move back!" I say into my comms. Asher's eyes flicker briefly at me. It's all the warning he needs.

I yank the dragon's head down as Asher suddenly breaks free and darts away. The creature shrieks in rage, then lunges at Jena, the nearest player—all she can do is throw her hands up before the creature swallows her in one bite.

## Jena MacNeil | Team Demon Brigade
### Life: -100% | STRIKE OUT!

The audience bursts into excited chaos. I can barely even hear the announcer's voice over it all.

A pace behind us, Jena blinks back into existence. Asher is already waiting for her. In a flash, he pounces right as Jena materializes. Before she can get a handle on what's happening, Asher's hand closes on the Artifact hovering over her head.

Game over.

The world is engulfed in scarlet and gold as an enormous phoenix bursts into flames across the entire sky.

The audience explodes in wild cheers. "*I don't believe it!*" the analysts are yelling over the chaos, their voices cracking from excitement. "It's *all* over! Jena MacNeil and the unstoppable Demon Brigade—taken down by the Phoenix Riders in the most stunning upset we've ever seen! *Oh my God!* The Phoenix Riders *win!*"

Asher throws his head back, lets out a piercing whoop, and raises his fist in the air.

And that's when I see the black figure again. He's standing on top of the ice monument, clad in the same fitted black armor I'd seen on him in the Dark World. *Zero.*

A chill rushes through me. Why can I see him? Why is he here?

The world around us pauses. The dragon I'm struggling to

control suddenly stops in midair, frozen, and then fades from view. The landscape darkens into blackness. I blink as the Tokyo Dome itself comes back into view, as well as fifty thousand spectators screaming wildly at the top of their lungs. To either side of me, my teammates come out of their booths.

"That was the most *badass* move I've ever seen!" Roshan exclaims, reaching me first and clapping me hard on my back. I open my mouth to thank him for protecting me, but Hammie hurls herself at me, smothering me and Roshan in a hug. I'm drowned out by the rest of our team piling on top of us. They crush me in, tangled and laughing. Blood roars in my ears. On the other side of the arena, the Demons are shouting at one another, and Tremaine is stalking away from Jena without so much as looking up at the audience.

My first official win in a championship game. But all I can think about is that *Zero was there*. I saw him. I search for Ren. He is smiling and laughing, too, but his expressions are off, forced. The smile doesn't touch his eyes. He glances over his shoulder, as if he'd seen something the others didn't. Then the tension breaks, and he goes back to grinning and hugging the others. *He'd also seen the figure.*

As I continue to cheer, I bring up the file that I'd managed to grab through Ren's broken shields. There's little there, as if I had pulled away before I could properly seize the data from him. But it did manage to grab something, possibly something Zero was communicating to Ren. The name of a program.

```
proj_ice_HT1.0
```

What? I frown at it, my thoughts racing, trying to make sense of the name. *proj_ice. Project Ice?* Does it have something to do with this White World level? *HT. HT?* *Hideo Tanaka*. Project Ice Hideo Tanaka. It could be a file connecting Hideo with this opening game level. Right? Or—

Then, my heart skips in terror as I connect another meaning to the word *Ice*. *Oh my God*.

Zero wants to assassinate Hideo.

And at that moment, every light in the stadium goes out.

# 20

The stadium plunges into darkness. Startled shouts come from the audience. Over the chaos, the announcers try to maintain some semblance of order. "Everyone stay in your seats," one says, still cheerful. "It looks like we have a temporary malfunction, but it will soon be fixed."

I stare through the pitch black at a red error message flashing in my view.

### Incorrect User Access

The file that had activated now flashes once, then blinks out of existence as it self-destructs. I'm left staring at an empty shell, the only part that's left of what the in-game object had retrieved. The file had been meant to destroy itself if the wrong user ever got her hands on it. Was the reason why Zero chose to keep messing with levels in Warcross because he has been passing information to his followers this way? And if that was true—who else in the games works for Zero?

But none of that matters at this very instance. While Hideo and I were racing to unlock data from Ren, Zero had been busy, too—glitching the arena itself. He had cut the power.

*The security doors up in the balcony seats don't work right now.*

The realization hits me so hard that I can barely breathe. I place a call immediately to Hideo. "Get out of there," I say in a rush the instant the call goes through. "Your life's in danger. *Right now.* Get—"

I don't even finish my sentence before I see a spark of light up in the balcony seats. It flashes once—twice—and then the blackness returns. People in the audience glance toward it, puzzled, but I know what it must have been.

Gunshots.

"Hideo? Hideo!" I say as I try to reconnect my call, but it doesn't go through. I curse as I fumble my way through the darkness. The security teams have taken out flashlights, and thin rays of light float around the arena, cutting through the black. The NeuroLink's connection also seems to have gone down, making it so that no one can bring up a virtual grid in their view to see where they're going. I recall the stadium's layout from my own memory—and before anyone can come up to me and stop me, I dart away from my station and hurry through the darkness, relying on what I remember to navigate through the space. People protest as I bump past them. It seems like an eternity before I finally find my way to the stairs. I hop blindly up two at a time. As I go, I try to message Hideo.

No response.

As I reach the second landing, red emergency lights flood the arena. Even though they're technically dim, I squint against them after the pitch blackness. Security cams blink on overhead. The NeuroLink comes back online, my profile rebooting in the corner of my view.

The announcers' voices ring out reassuringly as they try to organize the audience. "Watch your steps, folks!" The audience doesn't seem to realize that there was a gunman in here.

I reach the security box at the same time as I see Hideo's bodyguards clustered around the area. My eyes hunt frantically for Hideo's familiar face.

I nearly collapse in relief as I see Hideo crouched down in the security box room, surrounded by his bodyguards and colleagues. He looks unharmed. Beside him, Kenn is speaking rapidly to several of the guards in a low, angry voice.

"What the hell happened?" I say as I hurry over. "Where's the shooter?"

Kenn recognizes me and gives me a grim look. "The security cams up here were looping old footage. Security's swarming to try to catch the shooter."

I turn my attention to what Hideo is doing. One of his bodyguards is on the ground, clutching his shoulder and grimacing. Blood stains his hands. I recognize him as one of Hideo's faithful, ever-present shadows that I've seen go everywhere with him. Hideo's face is clouded with concern, his eyes opaque with that deep, dark fury I'd seen before in his Memory. He's saying something quietly to the hurt guard, who shakes his head and struggles to push himself to a sitting position. Beside him, one of the other bodyguards shakes his head as he listens to something on an earpiece.

"The police outside couldn't keep up with him, sir," he says.

Hideo doesn't look away from the injured man. "Keep searching." His voice is frighteningly quiet.

The bodyguard shifts. "They're saying they lost him in the empty parking structure—"

"Then tear it apart until you find him," Hideo snaps.

The bodyguard doesn't hesitate this time. When Hideo glances up at him with a raised eyebrow, the man bows his head quickly. "Yes, sir." He heads out with two of the others.

"You shouldn't be here," Kenn says to Hideo in a low voice. "For the last time—I'll handle things in the arena. Go home."

"I can handle this just fine."

"You *do* realize someone just tried to kill you, right?" Kenn snaps back. "This isn't just some bug in the game—this is your *life* we're talking about here."

"And I'm no less alive now than I was before the attack." Hideo gives his friend a firm stare. "I will *be fine.* We'll talk tomorrow."

This sounds like an old argument that Kenn has never succeeded in winning, and it occurs to me that this probably isn't the first time Hideo's life has been threatened. Kenn makes an irritated sound and throws up his hands. "It's not like you used to listen to me at uni, either."

Hideo straightens when he sees me. "If it hadn't been for your call moments earlier," he says, "I would be the one lying on the ground."

A chill runs through me. In a single moment, my job has transformed from a thrilling chase to something much more ominous. I thought I'd been getting closer, making progress—instead, I'd stumbled upon something even worse. Had any of the other bounty hunters seen what just happened? I look back to the blood on the bodyguard's shoulder. There's a faint, metallic scent in the air. Hints of my old panic, the familiar desperation to *solve* this problem, rise in my stomach. *Everything has a solution. Why can't I find this one?*

Hideo helps his injured bodyguard stand and talks to him in a low voice as another of his men drapes a black blazer over the bleeding shoulder, covering it from view. Whatever Hideo had murmured was too quiet for my translator to pick up, but it does make the injured man give him a grateful look. "Keep this under wraps," Hideo says, eyeing us all. "The attack failed. We're tracking the suspect. No need to panic the crowds."

"Hideo—" I start to say, but stop at the look on his face.

"Go to your team," he says gently. "Continue your celebrations. We'll talk later tonight."

"And you're going someplace safe?"

He nods as the bodyguards take over for their hurt friend, then watches as they lead him to a set of private stairs. All I can do is stare. Hideo's shoulders are straight, and his posture is calm— but his eyes are tense, far away from here. His hands clench and unclench at his sides. Even if he doesn't show it blatantly, I can sense that he's shaken.

Kenn finds my gaze and holds it for a moment. *Talk to him*, he seems to say. I can sense the silent plea from him, a friend who knows Hideo well enough to know how difficult he can be.

"Hideo," I say softly. "You need to get out of here. Out of Tokyo. Someplace where you can keep a low profile."

The lights in the stadium finally turn on, illuminating the space with blinding brightness. I blink away stars. Down below, the crowd murmurs in halfhearted confusion as they continue making their way toward the exits, but it is quickly replaced by cheering again as they celebrate the game. No one knows what just happened. Through the speakers, the security is reassuring the crowd, saying, "A transistor sparked in the upper levels of the dome, but everything is under control now. Please mind your steps and follow the exit signs." As the people funnel out, Hideo turns to look at me. His eyes are still that dark color, and the look in them is furious, cold, determined.

"I'm not going anywhere," he says. Then he turns away with his bodyguards.

# 21

If I thought the amount of publicity I'd gotten so far was overwhelming, it was nothing compared to after our first win. We'd barely made it out of the Tokyo Dome when the first enormous broadcasts appear on the sides of the buildings surrounding the arena, the headlines in giant, screaming letters.

## ASHER WING, FIRST PICK EMIKA CHEN LEAD PHOENIX RIDERS TO STUNNING UPSET WIN

A recap of me plays over and over beneath each of these headlines, my rainbow hair flying in the wind, my figure crouched on the head of a towering creature, lassoing its head, forcing it down toward Jena. Above the dome, the two crests—the phoenix and the hooded demons—suspended over the building have now morphed into only our phoenix, its flaming wings spread as wide as the dome, its head arching up to the sky in triumph.

My level has skyrocketed from 28 to 49.

But all I can think about is that Hideo could have died tonight. And that no one knows. My thoughts continue to churn, looping back over and over on Kenn's words. *He will listen to you. Please.* What is Hideo saying about me that makes Kenn think this?

A mob of reporters descends on our bodyguards as we flee the arena toward our waiting cars, and suddenly I can't see anything but a field of flashing lights and microphones.

"No training tonight!" Asher exclaims as we finally reach our waiting limousine and all climb in. The others cheer as he gives the car an instruction to take us into Shibuya instead of back to our dorms. Behind our car, a team of bodyguards climbs into a second car and follows us. Reporters in vans linger in traffic nearby, tailing us. My mind stays on Ren, and instead of looking up and grinning at the reporters outside the window, like Asher's doing, I keep my eye on where Ren's clapping Roshan on the shoulder.

A message blinks on in my view. It's Kenn.

> Can you get away tonight?
> To go to Hideo?

> He's not even listening to you.

> He never listens to me, not when he's got
> an idea planted in his mind. But I'm not
> his bounty hunter, and more specifically,
> I'm not you.

> Why would he listen to me?

I can almost feel Kenn's frustration as he answers.

> I can count on one hand the number of people he fully trusts. But he talks to you frequently. He takes you to dinner, unannounced.

> I'm not his bodyguard. I can't force him to protect himself.

> You're his hunter. He has hired you to tell him what he needs to know. You have a right to insist on his safety. He won't shut his door on you.

I glance up from our conversation as my teammates roar with laughter about something. Tonight's our celebration night, and they'll expect me to be just as excited about our win. If I leave too soon, they'll be poking and prying in no time, and Ren will suspect something's up.

"Hey," Hammie says to me, and I look up to see her curious expression, her cheeks still flushed from victory. "You okay?"

It's strange to me that no one else in the stadium knows what happened, that they must really think the two sparks of light in the balcony seating were blown transistors instead of gunfire. I must be wearing all of my anxiety on my face right now. I give her a brilliant smile that I hope looks convincing, and then shake my head. "I'm fantastic. Just still in shock."

Hammie grins and pumps a fist in the air. It nearly hits the limo's ceiling. "Karaoke, baby!" she shouts, and the others all shout along with her. I do as well, cheering as loudly as I can in order to drown out the storm of thoughts brewing in my head. I do it so forcefully that I almost believe it.

Soon, we've settled in a karaoke bar in the heart of the Roppongi district, with men in black suits guarding every entrance and exit. The halls are lined with floor-to-ceiling mirrors, reflecting the light of chandeliers adorning the ceilings, while the doorways to each private karaoke room are painted in glittering gold. Outside each doorway stand virtual figures of smiling supermodels, congratulating each of us by name as we walk past. I stare down the hallway, memorizing a path out, before we enter our own private room.

In here, the music has already been turned up to deafening levels. Ren laughs as he scrolls through the song list with Roshan. Every time they rotate onto a new track, our room transforms to match it—"My Heart Will Go On" changes the room into the bow of the *Titanic*, while "Thriller" surrounds us with dancing, leather-clad zombies on a dark street. Roshan, usually reserved, can't help laughing as Ren says something in French while mimicking the "Thriller" shuffle.

I watch Ren from the corner of my eyes as I sit sandwiched between Hammie and Asher. Had no one else noticed his expression as the game ended? Even now, there is something tense about his posture, as if things tonight hadn't gone as well for him as they had for the rest of our team.

"To Roshan!" Hammie yells, startling me from my thoughts. "Most Valuable Kicking-Tremaine's-Ass Player!"

Roshan sobers a little at the mention of Tremaine, but he hides it behind a smile. "To Hams," he calls back. "Thief of a Thousand Power-Ups."

"To Emika!" Asher exclaims. His cheeks are flushed, pushed up by a huge grin. He shakes his head. "Girl, you put the *wild* in wild card."

"To Emika!"

"To Emika!"

The cheers flow fast. *I need to sneak out,* I think as I laugh along. It might be my overactive imagination, but Ren's smile seems tighter than everyone else's, his happiness for me strained.

It doesn't take long for the chaos in the room to reach a peak. Asher leans heavily against Hammie, repeatedly telling her that he loves her. She's whispering into his ear in return. The karaoke microphone squeals in protest as Ren yells an off-key note into it. Roshan winces at the sound. As everyone bursts into another storm of laughter, I grab my phone and text Hideo.

> Where are you now?

A few seconds pass with no response. Maybe Kenn put too much faith in me, or too little faith in Hideo's stubbornness. I bite my lip, then send a second message.

> I have more info for you. Best to talk in person. It's an emergency.

Info from his hunter—it's the only thing I can think of to say that might get him to see me.

More time drags on. Just when I'm starting to think Kenn has gotten it all wrong about me, an encrypted message appears. I confirm my identity to unlock it, and in return, an address pops up in my view. Hideo's address. I almost sag in relief. Then I store the location in my GPS and delete the message.

Beside me, Asher raises his voice. "Anyone want to play a shots game? We need the waiter to come back."

I hop to my feet. "I'll go find him!" I say, then make a bee-line for the door. Perfect. By the time the waiter gets to them, they'll be so busy having fun that none of them will notice I've left. Plenty of time for me to come up with a good excuse. I exit the room and hurry down the hall. As I go, I bring up my map with Hideo's current location.

His gold dot pops up somewhere in the northern area of the city. I hurry down a side corridor. Moments later, the hall leads me out into the narrow back alley behind the building and near its garbage bins.

A cold drizzle has dampened the sidewalk, and as I step out-side, I'm hit with a blast of chilly night air. Neon lights reflect against the wetness, painting the ground a menagerie of smeared gold, green, and blue. The city block's number—16—hovers in bright yellow letters over the pavement, while a gold dotted line leads from where I stand to the corner of the block, where it turns right and disappears from view. A cheerful **Start!** message and an estimated arrival time hover in the center of my vision, waiting for me to follow the map. Thirty minutes.

I shiver, draw my hoodie tightly up so that it covers all of my hair, and pull on a black face mask. I also download a virtual face to disguise myself. Anyone on the street who's logged in to the NeuroLink should now see me as a complete stranger instead of a face they recognize from the news. Better than no disguise. Then I throw my electric skateboard down and jump on it. It shoots me forward as I follow the gold line.

Half an hour later, I emerge in a quiet, upper-class neighbor-hood on a hill overlooking the city. The travel time shifts in my view as I go, counting down the minutes that it will take for me to arrive. The drizzle has turned into a steady rain now, soaking through my hoodie and drenching my hair. I try to stop myself from trembling.

Finally, I'm here. The gold dotted line stops in front of the gates of a warm, well-lit estate with a curved wall and carved lions outside its doorway. I don't know how much security Hideo usually has at his residences—but tonight, at least five cars are sitting here, and two bodyguards are at the front gate, waiting to greet me. Others look like they're scattered around the estate.

One of them approaches me now, then tells me to hold out my arms. I turn off my virtual face and do as he says. He pats me down thoroughly, pausing to inspect my board. When he's satisfied, he holds out an umbrella for me as I hurry to the entrance.

"It's okay, I don't need the umbrella anymore," I tell the man. When he eyes me sideways, as if he never gets this order, I gesture to my soaking clothes. "Seriously."

He reluctantly puts it down, and we walk in silence for a moment before reaching the front entrance. Inside the house, I hear a dog barking.

Hideo answers the door. His bodyguard blinks in surprise, as if this is not something Hideo does often. He's still dressed in his clothes from earlier, but one sleeve of his shirt is pushed up to his elbows, while he's undoing the cuff link on his other sleeve. His collar is flipped up, the top buttons open, and his black tie is draped loosely over his shoulders. His hair is damp with a few drops of rain, the silver streak shining white. He looks concerned and bewildered, a sudden, startling reminder to me of just how young he is. It's so easy to forget.

"You're soaking wet," he says.

"And you're alive," I reply. "That's good."

The bodyguard leaves us alone. Hideo opens the door wide

and ushers me inside. Beside him trots a fat orange-and-white dog with short legs and enormous fox ears. It stops in front of me, wags its stubby tail, and looks up at me with a panting smile. I pet it vigorously, then remove my wet shoes near the doorway and step inside.

The home is impeccably clean, with soaring ceilings and beautiful, modern furniture. Soft music plays from some sort of built-in sound system. To my surprise, I see no virtual letters, colors, or numbers anywhere in the house. Everything is real. How much does a house as gorgeous as this cost in a city as expensive as Tokyo?

"You're trembling," he says now.

I shrug it off. "Just get me out of these clothes." Then I realize what I've said, and heat rushes to my cheeks. "I mean, well, not that—"

The edges of Hideo's lips twitch with a smile, a brief respite from his grave look, and he nods for me to follow him. "I'll bring some dry clothes for you."

"I got a glimpse of a single file from Ren," I tell Hideo as we head down the hall. Then I mention its name. "It's obvious that Zero wanted to, well . . . try an assassination today. How's your bodyguard doing?"

"He'll live. There have been worse attacks than today."

Worse attacks. "Any word on the culprit?"

Hideo shakes his head as he pushes his second sleeve up to his elbow. He's weary, his dark mood still not lifted. "Kenn says the power had been thoroughly cut. In all the confusion, whomever it was managed to get away and blend in with the crowds. We'll be studying every nook and cranny of the dome for evidence, but I won't lie. They were ready."

The culprit is still out there. I try to swallow my fear. "Just because nothing happened today doesn't mean Zero's not waiting in the wings to act. It could be one part of his grand plan." I take a deep breath. "They're going to try again. They could have been trying even before this. And there will be plenty of times when you won't be as guarded as you were in the dome."

Hideo's lips tighten slightly, but it's the only response he gives about his safety. He stops for a moment to look at me. "Did it report any data back about you?"

I hesitate. I hadn't thought about the possibility of Zero grabbing info of *me* from the object—and the idea sends a shiver through me, even as I warm at Hideo's obvious concern. "Shouldn't be possible," I reply. "I'm fine. Besides, it's not me that we should be worried about. The more pieces of this that I find, the more ominous it sounds."

"My security detail is used to being careful. After your warning, we did a full sweep of my home. They'll be watchful."

"That's not what I mean. Hideo, you almost *died* tonight. You realize that, don't you?"

"I'm well protected here. There are eight bodyguards on my premises alone." He nods toward the rest of the house. "It sounds like you're edging closer and closer to finishing this, at any rate."

"I don't understand how you can be so calm about this," I say, my frustration rising. No wonder Kenn sounded so exasperated. "You need to get out of Tokyo. It isn't safe for you here. Every moment you stay puts you in danger."

Hideo casts a serious look my way. "I'm not going to be chased out of my city by a vague threat," he replies. For the first time since I've known him, a note of anger creeps into his voice. "This isn't the first time someone has targeted me, and it won't be the last."

I'm about to raise my voice, but then I sneeze. The cool air in the house is seeping straight into my soaked clothes, and I realize that my teeth are chattering.

Hideo tightens his lips. "We'll continue this after you warm up. Come with me."

We reach a spacious bedroom, its glass walls leading out into a serene Zen garden adorned with golden dangling lights. A large bathroom suite branches off from one side of the room.

"Take your time," Hideo says, nodding toward the suite. "When you're ready, we'll talk further. Would you like tea?"

*A nice cup of tea after your assassination attempt. Sure.* I nod, too cold to argue. "I'd love some."

Hideo closes the bedroom door and leaves me alone. I let out a long, slow breath. So far, I'm not doing a very good job of convincing him of the real danger he's in. I sigh and strip off my hoodie, jeans, and undergarments, laying all the clothes out carefully along the bathtub to dry. My reflection in the mirror catches my eye; my makeup from the tournament earlier now looks smeared and smoky, dampened by the rain, and my hair hangs in wet strands of color. No wonder Hideo isn't listening to my advice—I look half crazy. My gaze wanders from myself to the rest of the bathroom. The shower is enormous, with a rain showerhead installed right into the ceiling. I turn the faucet and let the hot water steam for a bit, then step inside.

The shower washes away some of my jumbled thoughts, and by the time I step out, I feel a little calmer about being here. I towel myself off and weave my wet hair into two messy side braids, then step out of the bathroom.

A set of clean clothes has already been laid out for me. A creamy white sweater. A pair of loose pajama pants. I pull the sweater on; it smells just like Hideo, and is so large on me that it hangs down almost to my knees. The collar slides sideways, baring one of my shoulders. I don't even try to wear the pajama pants. They're far too long.

I walk over to the bedroom door, open it, and emerge halfway out into the hallway to tell him I need something shorter.

But he's already here, holding a teacup in one hand and ready to knock on the door with his other. "Emi—" he starts to say when he sees me. We both freeze.

Hideo blinks. His eyes dart to the loose, white sweater I'm wearing, then quickly away. "I wanted to ask if you had a tea preference," he says.

My shoulder and legs suddenly feel very exposed, and the flush on my cheeks now turns to magma-level red. I start to stumble some words out.

"Sorry, I—I was going to ask if you, um, had smaller pants." Another bad line. "I mean—not that you have small pants that would *fit* me"—digging a deeper hole for myself—"I mean, the pajama pants keep falling off—" I'm a very good digger. I wince, then shake my head and stop talking, letting my hands wheel in circles as if they can convey my meaning.

Hideo laughs a little. Unless my imagination is messing with me, a slight flush colors his cheeks, too.

I snap out of my reverie, then slam the door shut right in his face.

There's a pause, followed by Hideo's familiar voice. "Sorry about that," he says. "I'll find something better for you." Then his footsteps echo down the hall.

I walk over to the bed, bury my face in the sheets, and let out a groan.

Moments later, Hideo opens the door a crack and waves a pair of shorts blindly at me. I take them. They're still baggy on me, but at least they stay on.

I venture out into the hall and into the living room, where Hideo is reading by a crackling fireplace. His dog lies at his feet, snoring softly. The windows here lead out to the garden, and the bead-like patter of rain can be heard against the glass. The walls are lined with portraits and with shelves of books—pristine early editions—neatly organized and artfully arranged. Then there are shelves displaying vintage video games and consoles, as well as prototypes of what look like the earliest versions of the NeuroLink glasses. Some of them are as large as bricks, but each one gets progressively smaller and lighter, until I finally see the first edition of the official glasses propped up at the end of the shelves.

Hideo looks up from his book when he hears me approach, then notices me studying his shelves. "My mother took good care of my early NeuroLink prototypes," he says. "She and my father made sure to save them."

His neuroscientist mother and computer repair shop father. "Mint condition," I reply, admiring the prototypes.

"They believe that objects have souls. The more love you put into one, the more beautiful it becomes."

I smile at the affection in his voice. "They must be very proud of what you created."

Hideo just shrugs, but he looks pleased at my words.

"You don't have any augmented reality overlaid in your home," I say as I sit.

Hideo shakes his head. "I like to keep my home real. It's too easy to lose yourself in an illusion," he replies, nodding at his physical book.

I'm very aware of our proximity to each other, as if I could feel the ghost of his presence against my skin.

I take a deep breath. "Do you have any enemies you can think of? Someone who would want to hurt you like this? Maybe a former employee? An old business partner?"

Hideo looks away. After a while, he replies, "There are enough people who dislike Warcross and the NeuroLink. Not everyone appreciates the new. Many fear it."

"It's ironic that Zero fears it so much, then," I reply, "but uses his own knowledge of technology to try to stop you."

"He doesn't sound like someone who bothers with logic."

"And what about Ren? You should disqualify him from the games immediately. It's pretty clear that he's involved with this plan. He might even be involved with potentially harming *you*. What if the file I saw today had been meant for him? What if he had somehow sent a signal from within the game to the person who tried to attack you?"

Hideo pauses for a moment at that, before finally shaking his head. "He's been a reliable source of information, and he might lead to more clues. If I remove him now, it'll be obvious to Zero that we know about him. They might suspect *you*."

I sigh, wishing I could argue with that reasoning. "Why don't you want to leave Tokyo? You could have died today."

Hideo looks at me. His eyes reflect the light of the fire. "And signal to Zero that he's won? No. If his entire plan is just a threat against me, then I'll be relieved."

Our conversation fades into silence. I struggle to figure out something to say, but nothing that comes to mind seems appropriate, so I just end up staying quiet, prolonging the awkwardness. My eyes wander back to the shelves, and then to the portraits on the walls. There are photos of Hideo as a child and a teen—helping out in his father's shop, reading by the window, playing games, posing with a bunch of medals around his neck, smiling for early press photos as he first hit the newswires. Curious. As a child,

Hideo didn't have the silver streak in his hair or the few silver threads sprinkled throughout his dark lashes.

Then my eyes stop on one particular photo. There are *two* boys pictured in it.

"You have a brother?" I say without thinking.

Hideo is silent. Immediately, I remember the warning that I'd gotten right before I first met Hideo. *Mr. Tanaka never answers questions about his family's private affairs. I must request that you do not mention anything in that regard.* I start to apologize, but my words fade as I realize it's something even more than that. Hideo's expression is strange now. He's *afraid.* I've hit an old wound, a yawning abyss thinly scarred over.

After a long moment, Hideo lowers his eyes and looks toward the rain-dotted windows. "I *had* a brother," he replies.

*Mr. Tanaka never answers questions about his family.* But he *had* just now, had opened up to me, however briefly. I can hear how foreign the words sound on his lips, can see the discomfort it brings him just to say them. Does that mean he never invites others to his home, either, where such a vulnerability is hanging right on his wall? I watch him, waiting for him to say more. When he doesn't, I say the only thing I can. "I'm so sorry."

Hideo spares me by leaning toward the table. "You mentioned you wanted tea," he says, sidestepping my words the same way he did on the night I'd met him at his headquarters. His moment of weakness that he'd offered me has already vanished, gone behind the shield.

*This is the piece of his history that haunts him,* I think, recalling the beat of grief we'd shared when I'd mentioned my father. Whatever had happened, he hasn't made peace with it. It might even explain his stubborn refusal to stay safe. I nod in silence, then look on as he pours a cup for me and another for himself. He hands me my cup, and I hold it with both hands, savoring the heat and the clean scent.

"Hideo," I begin softly, trying again. I'm careful to steer clear of whatever mystery shrouds his past. My eyes linger on the faint scars of his knuckles. "I don't want to see you get hurt. You didn't stand with me in the Pirate's Den and feel the ominous presence of that guy. I don't know what he's up to yet, but he's obviously dangerous. You can't play with your life like this."

Hideo smiles a little. "You came all the way here tonight just to persuade me to leave Tokyo, didn't you?"

His teasing makes me blush again, which makes me irritated with myself. I put down my cup and shrug. "Well, I didn't think it was something I could properly discuss with you without being here in person. And I wanted to warn you without somehow being overheard by my teammates."

"Emika," he says. "You don't need to give me a reason for coming over. I appreciate you watching out for me. You saved my life today, you know." Whatever I was going to say next fades away at the look in his eyes. He puts his cup down, too, and leans closer to me. The movement sends a jolt up my spine. "I'm glad you're here."

I search his eyes, trying my best to steady my heartbeat. "You are?"

"Perhaps I've been too subtle."

Up until now, I've largely assumed that all of my interpretations of Hideo's words have been exaggerated on my part, but it's pretty hard to misunderstand *this* statement. *He talks about you often enough,* Kenn had said. I swallow hard, but don't pull away. "About what?" I whisper.

Hideo's lashes are lowered, and there is something sweet and uncertain in his gaze. He hesitates. Then he waves one hand in a subtle gesture, and a transparent screen appears in my view again.

*Link with Hideo?* it asks.

"Let me show you something," he says. "It's a new communication system I've been working on. A secure way for you to contact me."

I look at the hovering window for a moment, then accept it. The edges of my vision flash clear blue. "What does it do?" I ask.

*Send a thought to me, Emika.*

It is Hideo's own voice, soft and warm and deep, echoing inside my mind. A tingle of surprise rushes through me. When I look at him, he hasn't opened his mouth at all, nor has he made any motion to type. It is *telepathy* through the NeuroLink, the next evolution of messaging, an intimate, secret bond linking us together. I startle at the novelty of it, then hesitantly send a thought back to him.

*You're in my mind?*

*Only if you allow it. You are free to disable our Link whenever you desire.*

I can't help smiling, caught between feeling unsettled and excited. It has been almost a decade since Hideo first created something that changed the world, and yet here he is, still doing it, year after year. I shake my head in disbelief.

*This is incredible.*

Hideo smiles, his dark mood lifting for a moment. *I don't think you realize how much I enjoy your company. So I want to let you in on a secret.*

Suddenly, I realize that not only can I hear his words in my mind through our new Link . . . I can *sense* something. I can *feel* a hint of his emotions through the connection. *Oh,* I think back without even realizing it, my breath catching.

I can sense desire in him, a dense, smoldering heat. For *me*.

*I've wanted to kiss you*, Hideo thinks to me, leaning closer, *since the night I saw you in that white dress.*

Since the party at Sound Museum Vision. I'm suddenly very aware of my bare shoulder. The steady undercurrent of his emotions through our Link makes me light-headed, and I wonder if he can sense the same coming from me, the rapid, fluttering beat of my heart, the heat rushing through my veins. He must, because one side of his smile tilts higher.

I suddenly feel bold in this dim light and new bond, this space that has become all too warm. *Well?* I ask him.

*Well.* His gaze falls on my lips. *Perhaps we should do something about that.*

All I can think about is his nearness, his dark eyes, his breath stirring against my skin. There is a spark in his gaze now, that darkening of his eyes, something fiery and hungry, something that *wants*. He hesitates for an agonizing second. Then, his head tilts down toward me. The soft skin of his lips presses against mine, and before I can even register it, he's kissing me.

My eyes flutter closed. He's gentle at first, his emotions restrained and searching, one of his hands coming up to carefully cup my face. I lean into his touch, signaling to him that I want more, fantasizing about what he might do next. *Can you sense what I want?* As if in answer, a low groan of pleasure rumbles deep in his throat. Then he draws closer, pins me against the couch, and kisses me harder. The Link between us magnifies our emotions tenfold, and I fight for air, overwhelmed at the heat of his desire coursing through us—and my own responding passion rushing back to him. I can sense *his* thoughts, glimpses and glimmers of his hands against my skin, running along bare thighs. My entire body tingles. His hand buries in my hair, tilting my head up toward him. Through the fog of my thoughts, I realize that I've wrapped my arms around his neck and pulled him close, until every inch of my body is pressed against him. He feels so warm, the muscles of his arms and chest firm underneath his clothes. The sound of rain against glass continues quietly in the background.

Hideo pulls away for a brief second, his lips hovering right over mine. His breathing is soft and labored, his brows furrowed, the fire still alight in his gaze. His emotions crash against mine, roiling into one, and he is undone in this moment, the reserved, distant, proper version of him stripped away to reveal the part that is unthinking and savage. I am trembling from a storm of sensations, unsure what to focus on, wanting to drink it all in at the same time, struggling for the perfect words.

*Okay*, I end up gasping. *You were definitely too subtle.*

His secret smile returns. "I'll make up for it," he murmurs against my ear, and then he kisses me again. My teeth tug once, teasingly, on his lower lip. Hideo growls in surprise, and he pulls away from my mouth to kiss the line of my jaw. His lips work their way along my neck, sending shivers up and down my back. His warm hand has found its way inside my sweater, running up along my bare back, tracing the valley of my spine. I can feel the calluses at the base of his fingers, rough against my skin. A million thoughts flash through my mind. I arch toward him. Vaguely, I realize that I've slid down along the length of the couch, my head now on the armrest, and Hideo's body is heavy against mine, pushing me down. His lips go from my neck to my collarbone, kissing along the line of my tattoo, to my bare shoulder.

Then, abruptly, a needle of a foreign emotion slices through our raging tempest, a thread of worry from him. To my disappointment, Hideo leaves one last kiss against my skin. He sighs, murmuring a faint swear against my ear, and pulls away. I'm left feeling suddenly cold, still reeling from what just happened. Slowly, I prop myself up on my elbows and stare at him. He helps me up, then lets his hands linger on mine for a moment. The Link between us settles into place, quivering, until it is calm and quiet again.

"I'm getting you into more than you bargained for," he finally says.

I frown at him, my own breath still short. "Well, I'm not complaining." I lean closer to him. "I *will* find Zero. I'm going to finish the job you hired me for."

He looks at me for another moment, then shakes his head and smiles. The careful shield he always keeps around him has fallen away, leaving an inner layer of him exposed. *There's something he wants to tell me*. I can see the war on his face. "I won't keep you any longer tonight," he says. His heart retreats behind the shield again. "Your teammates probably want to celebrate with you." And with that, he reaches up and disconnects our Link. The sudden absence of his subtle undercurrent of emotions and the echo of his voice in my mind makes me feel emptier. A tiny button lingers in the corner of my vision, something I can tap to reconnect us.

I try to nod along so that he can't see the disappointment on my face. "Right," I mutter. "Celebrate. I'd better head back."

He kisses my cheek. "I'll talk to you tomorrow," he says. But even as he pulls away, I know that the space between us has changed permanently.

I nod, as if in a dream, as if I can't stop taking this drug. "Yes."

# 22

In the following days, the other official teams have their first round of games. The Andromedans defeat the Bloodhounds in record time, their world set in a maze of fiery catacombs. The Winter Dragons beat the Titans in a trap-filled jungle. The Stormchasers beat the Royal Bastards in the neon streets of a futuristic spaceport. The Gyrfalcons advance against the Phantoms, the Castle Raiders beat the Windwalkers, the Cloud Knights destroy the Sorcerers, and, much to everyone's surprise, the Zombie Vikings defeat the Sharpshooters.

I watch and analyze each of the games along with my teammates. I train with them as the second round of games begins. We beat the Stormchasers in a blitz of a second round, where Asher and the Stormchasers' captain, Malakai, faced off one-on-one at the top of an isolated tower while the rest of us fought our way up the tower's sides.

Every day, I pore through a bunch of data on the other players.

I look for more signs from Ren as he moves around the dorms. He doesn't make eye contact with me. I wonder if he knows.

At night, I dream I'm in Hideo's bed, tangled in his sheets, my hands running along his bare back, his hands gripping my hips. I dream that someone breaks into his home as we sleep, that I stir beside him to see a faceless figure in dark armor standing over his bed. I picture the news the next morning, broadcasting Hideo's death. I jerk awake, gasping.

● ● ● ● ●

**Good morning, beautiful.**

I wake up to a dark, stormy day outside and Hideo's message on my phone. The light in my room is blue-gray, and my heart is pounding from another night of restless dreams. I read his message several more times before I'm sure that he's alive and well, and then I flop my head back against my pillow and sigh, weak with relief. A small smile lingers at the corners of my lips at his words.

**Morning.**

Then I sit up, pull on my shirt, and head to the bathroom to put in my lenses. When I return, a request is blinking in my view, asking if I want to Link with Hideo. I agree, and a moment later, a virtual Hideo is in my room, still bare-chested and in the middle of pulling on his own shirt. I grin, tempted to tell him to just leave it off. He pours himself a cup of coffee while his dog waddles around his legs in a happy circle. It's pleasantly strange to see Hideo in a way no one else does—boyish, relaxed, wholly vulnerable, hair rumpled and wet from a shower, his sweatpants hanging low on his hips. The pale light coming in through his windows highlights the edges of his hair and face.

He smiles when he sees me. "Before you ask," he says, nodding off to the side where I can't see, "my bodyguard is standing right by the door."

I smile back and shake my head. "Glad you're finally taking your safety seriously." Then I sober. "I don't suppose you've thought more about leaving Tokyo?"

Hideo sips his coffee. "Second rounds start this week. If I'm not there, people will start to ask questions."

I sigh. "Just . . . think about it. Please?"

A bodyguard calls to him. Hideo turns his head slightly. "Mr. Tanaka," reads my translation. "Reporters are ready for your interview."

Hideo gives his bodyguard a subtle nod of his head. "In a moment," he says. He walks toward me until we're separated by inches, and then leans down toward me. If he were standing in my room right now, I could probably feel his breath stir against my neck. "I promise I'll think about it," he murmurs. "But you have to understand how hard it is when you are still here in the city."

My toes curl, and I shiver with pleasure. Through our Link, I can tell that my emotions are reaching him in ripples. *You're hopeless,* I think to him.

*Only in the morning.*

*I remember you being pretty hopeless that night, too.*

He turns his eyes down, and his lashes catch the light. A smile lingers on his lips. *I'd like to kiss you right now.*

*What if I didn't let you?* I tease.

*You wound me, Emika.*

I laugh. *Maybe I want to kiss someone else.*

Jealousy flashes across his face, and his eyes darken to cinder. Even through the physical distance between us, I can sense his emotions through our Link, that deliciously warm desire. *Come over. Tonight.*

My stomach flutters. *But, my teammates . . .*

*I'll make it worth your time.*

The flutters turn into somersaults. "To your home?" I whisper, unable to hide my own smile.

He hesitates. The uncertainty returns to his face, and for a moment, I think he's going to shake his head and change his mind again. After a pause, though, he surprises me with a nod. *Come with me tonight. I'll show you my old home.*

My heartbeat quickens. This is another secret from his past; I can hear it in his voice, feel it through our Link. I find myself nodding. *Okay,* I reply.

We both log out of our Link, and I exhale, then get up and head out of my room.

By the time I make my way downstairs, it's raining hard outside. Hammie and Asher are on the living room couches, engrossed in a quiet debate about how best to mess up the Cloud Knights' defense. Asher's arm is draped over the back of the couch, his hand idly touching Hammie's shoulder, and she doesn't move away. Roshan is playing a game and streaming himself live on his social channels. Ren is nowhere to be seen. The dorms are quiet, save for the pounding of rain against our atrium's glass ceiling.

"Emika."

I nearly jump out of my skin at Ren's voice. My fist goes up instinctively, and I whirl around to see him standing behind me in the hallway, turned as if headed to his room. Then I let out my breath and lower my fist. I should have sensed him there—I'm supposed to be so good at reading a room. "You scared the crap out of me," I blurt out.

He just raises an eyebrow at my reaction, then replies in French. Transparent white text appears in my view as it translates. "Are you always ready to punch people that surprise you?"

All of my suspicions about Ren after tracking him over the past couple of weeks must have made me jumpy when I'm around him. "Just the ones that lurk in dark hallways."

"Do you have a minute?" he says, nodding me over. "I want to ask you something."

"About what?"

Ren stares quietly at me. "About Hideo."

I blink, momentarily stumped for an answer, and my eyes dart quickly to Ren's. He's watching me carefully. What had he noticed in my expression? Had he purposely tried to catch me off guard to see what my reaction would be? Quickly, I compose myself and give him a confused laugh instead. "Why—have I finally shown up on some tabloid?" I say, exaggerating my teasing voice.

Ren grins in return. "Something like that," he replies. His words send a shiver down my spine. "Come on. We can chat in my room."

If I don't go with him, it'll look suspicious. So I find myself following him down the hall that leads to his quarters. *It's nothing,* I tell myself. Besides, it might give me an opportunity to do some hunting that I don't normally get to do: *talk* directly to one of my potential targets.

I've never been down here before, but it's impossible to mistake which room is his—from the hallway, I can hear the muffled, deep, steady sound of a beat, just barely loud enough to be heard.

The door slides open as Ren stands in front of it and reveals a large suite lit with a dim neon-blue glow. He steps inside. I hesitate for a moment before I join him.

Ren's room looks completely different from mine, like he had it customized to his satisfaction. Padded foam squares line the walls, while the center of his room has a table shaped like an arc above which hovers a system of floating screens, some displaying what look like sound meters, others displaying metrics and bars that I can't begin to decipher. A musical keyboard and a panel of sliding buttons are also attached to the arced table. Ren's pair of gold winged headphones are lying on the desk. The room pulses with a deep, rhythmic beat that makes the ground vibrate and my heart beat in time. My eyes wander around his room in awe, even as I hunt for clues. I quietly bring up Ren's hacked profile, and his information lights up in transparent text around him.

"You wanted to talk about Hideo?" I ask.

He nods, then sits down and spins around once in his chair. He loops his gold headphones around his neck. "Yeah. When we first met, you mentioned that you've listened to my music before, right?"

I nod. "I was a fan of your music when you first came on the scene in France."

"Wow." He gives me a smile that I can't quite tell is genuine, and then plays with a few of the bars on his board. "I didn't know you knew about me that early on."

*I didn't know you knew about me that early on.* Immediately, a warning bell goes off in my head. "You kept yourself pretty niche," I answer, carefully now. "Like you didn't want to be discovered yet."

Ren leans back in his chair and props his feet up on the desk.

"All of my early work was in French. I didn't know you spoke my language."

I watch him as he pulls his headphones on, my heart beginning to beat faster. *I didn't know you spoke my language.* Is he talking about French, or is he talking about the language of hacking? "What does this have to do with Hideo?" I ask, trying to bring it back to his original topic. "Is he a fan of yours, too?"

"I've been composing a track for him as a gift, after everything's over," Ren goes on, his voice lighthearted. "To thank him for entering me in the Wardraft. I wanted to get some feedback on it from someone who knows Hideo well and also knows my music. You know, to see if it's something he'd like." And at that, he looks expectantly at me. "You seem pretty friendly with him."

*He knows. Does he know?* I force my smile to stay intact as I give him a shrug. "Do I?" I say, just as lighthearted.

"At least, that's what the tabloids are all whispering about."

"Well," I reply, keeping my eyes level with his. "We all have friends in high places, don't we?"

Ren returns the look for a moment, unrelenting, and then finally glances away. "Here. Have a listen. I could use the help."

Ren had once said in an interview that he doesn't appreciate outside input on his work. Now here he is, offering me his headphones, and I don't know what to make of it. When he gives me an encouraging smile, I reach out and accept the headphones, then slip them on.

It's a deep bass, all alone with a smooth, beautiful violin above it and something that sounds like chimes. A female vocal starts on the track. "*Let's tear through Tokyo from zero to sixty / yeah, like we're running out of time in this city,*" she croons. As I listen, I glance at Ren. A track about Tokyo.

Then, I hear a line that sends a jolt through me. *"Let's go out with a bang / yeah, it's time to go out with a bang."*

It's the same track that had played for a second in the Pirate's Den.

*He's setting me up.* I look quickly at Ren and notice him watching my face with a thoughtful expression. He composed the track that had played during the Darkcross game—and now he's making me listen to it to see if I find it familiar. Judging from the way he's looking at me right now, he can tell that I've heard this song before. And that means he knows I must have been there at the Pirate's Den at the same time he was.

*He knows I'm following him. He knows I'm watching Zero.*

Ren takes his headphones back. His eyes never leave me. "Do you think Hideo will like it?"

His words are ominous to me now, and I fight to look unaffected. "It's good. Maybe he'll even add it to the tournaments next year."

"Maybe he'll even add it to the final tournament *this* year," Ren says, giving me a smile. He leans forward, rests his elbows on his knees, and traps me with an unblinking stare. "We have to go out with a bang, right?"

I smile and nod along with his statement, but it sounds like a thinly veiled threat. My heart beats faster. *Let's go out with a bang.* Now Ren has repeated the same line from the Pirate's Den—and even though it could *still* mean nothing at all, my mind jumps to a different conclusion. Whatever it is that Zero's group is trying to do—involving so many international cities, involving Hideo's life—it's going to happen on the day of the final tournament.

And now he knows I'm involved.

# 23

A couple of hours later, as I meet Hideo in a private car, I still haven't shaken off my conversation with Ren. *He could've been speaking literally.* But that music track was no accident. He knows I was in the Dark World tracking him—or, at the very least, he knows I was also there in the Pirate's Den during the same time.

If Hideo notices my troubled thoughts, he doesn't mention it. He seems distracted, too. Even without our Links connected, I sense a certain unease in him, something that turns his eyes distant, the same thing that made him break away from me that night at his home. I debate telling him about my conversation with Ren, but then decide against it. It's too vague. I need to dig deeper.

It's a slow drive through the rain. A couple of hours later, we arrive in the wooded outskirts of Tokyo, where the city gives way to gently rolling hills and narrow streets of neat, three-story buildings, their elegantly curved roofs painted black and red. Pines line both sides of the road. A single pedestrian wanders down the sidewalk, and a gardener is carefully trimming a nearby hedge—but aside from the faint *clip-clip-clip* sound of his shears, it's quiet. The car finally pulls up to a house at the end of a street, where round bushes and rocks adorn the front path. Pots of flowers line the pathway in neat rows. The porch light is on, even though it's still late afternoon.

Hideo rings the doorbell. Someone's voice comes from the other side, muffled and female. A moment later, the door opens to reveal a woman dressed in a tidy sweater, pants, and slippers. She blinks up at us through glasses that magnify her eyes. Then her face crinkles in delight at the sight of Hideo—she utters a small laugh, calls out to someone over her shoulder in Japanese, and then holds her arms out at him.

Hideo bows, lower than I've seen him bow to anyone. "*Okaa-san,*" he says, before wrapping her in a warm hug. He gives me a sheepish smile as she stretches up to pat both his cheeks like he's a small boy. "This is my mother."

His mother! A warm feeling overwhelms me, bringing with it a flutter of emotions. I blush and follow Hideo's example, bowing as low as I can. Hideo nods at me. "*Okaa-san,*" he says to his mother. "*Kochira wa Emika-san desu.*"

"This is Emika," my translation reads.

I murmur a bashful hello and bob my head respectfully. She smiles warmly at me, pats my cheeks, too, and exclaims something about my hair. Then she ushers us both inside, away from the world.

We remove our shoes by the door and put on slippers that Hideo's mother offers us. Inside, the home is sunny, cozy, and absolutely immaculate, lined with framed photos and green potted plants, clay pots, and odd, metallic sculptures. A bamboo mat and rug cover the living room's floor, cushioning a low table with a teapot and teacups. An open sliding door reveals a lush Zen garden. Now I see why Hideo designed his house in Tokyo the way he did; it must remind him of *here*, his true home. I'm about to comment on how lovely their home is when an automated voice comes on over speakers somewhere in the ceiling.

"Welcome home, Hideo-san," the voice says. In the kitchen, the stove turns on under a teakettle without anyone touching it.

His father comes out to greet us moments later. I look on, fighting down a tide of envy, as the couple fusses over their son with all the enthusiasm of parents who don't get to see their children nearly as often as they would like.

Hideo's mother exclaims something about making us a snack and bustles off, leaving her glasses on the table. Without missing a beat, Hideo picks up the glasses, follows his mother into the kitchen, and gently reminds her to put them on. Then he opens the refrigerator door to see that there aren't any groceries in the fridge to make a snack with, either. Hideo's mother frowns in confusion, telling him that she was sure there was something. Hideo talks to her in a low, affectionate voice, his hands on her shoulders, reassuring her that he will send for groceries right away. His father looks on from the hallway, coughing a little, the sound indicative of something chronic. I shift at the sound. Neither of his parents is old, but they seem frailer than they should be at their age. It stirs unpleasant memories of my own.

When Hideo returns to my side and sees me watching him, he just shrugs. "If I don't remind her, the house system will," he says. "It watches out for them when I'm not here. They refuse to accept a servant." His voice is light, but I've heard him enough times now to detect a deep sadness running underneath it.

"Have your parents always lived here?" I decide to ask.

"Ever since we moved back from London." Hideo points out

the decorations on the side tables. "My mother has been learning how to make clay pots since she retired from her neuroscience work. The metallic sculptures are my father's, welded together with leftover computer parts from his repair shop."

I pause to admire a sculpture. Only now do I see that each piece, although geometric and abstract, seems representative of their personal lives. A couple walking arm in arm. Family scenes. Some of the sculptures depict his parents with *two* boys. I think back to the portrait I'd seen in Hideo's own home. "They're beautiful."

Hideo looks pleased, but I can sense the quiet, dark side of him returning the longer we stand here, as if coming home had given that side of him the fuel it needs to exist. He stares out the window for a moment. Then he nods at me. "So, Emika," he says, giving me a small smile. "Have you tried an *onsen* yet since you've been in Japan?"

"An *onsen*?"

"A hot spring."

"Oh." I clear my throat, my cheeks turning pink. "Not yet."

Hideo nods toward the door. "Want to?"

● ● ● ● ●

As THE SUN starts to set, Hideo takes me to a place overlooking a set of mountains, where a bathhouse sits encircled by cherry trees in full bloom. I watch him carefully. His mood has improved since our arrival, but it hasn't rebounded completely back to his usual self. Now I walk quietly beside him as we approach the entrance to the bathhouse, wondering how I can cheer him up.

"You come here often?" I say as we approach the entrance to the bathhouse.

Hideo nods. "This is my private *onsen*."

The waters of the hot spring are still and calm, a cloud of steam hovering over it. Smooth rocks encircle the edge of the spring, while cherry blossoms drift down from the trees, coming to rest on the water's surface. One side of the spring overlooks a mountain range, where the ridges are just now catching the last rays of the sun. The other side overlooks a river.

By the time I step toward the spring in a robe, Hideo is already in the water. I'm glad for the heat; maybe it can cover some of my blush, which is already threatening to burn up my face as I study his damp hair and bared muscles. I clear my throat, and Hideo looks politely away, giving me time to remove my robe and sink into the hot water. I close my eyes and let out a small moan of relief.

"I'm never leaving," I murmur as Hideo comes to join me.

He brushes damp locks of my hair behind my shoulders, then pushes us to a corner, where his hands grip the edge of the spring on either side of me. My face feels as hot as the water now, and I become keenly aware of our bare skin brushing together.

"What do these mean?" Hideo murmurs, running one of his hands along the length of my tattooed arm. His fingers trace wet lines along my skin.

In a contented daze, I look down and straighten my arm so that we can see the full length of my tattoos. "Well," I whisper, "the flower is a peony, my father's favorite." My fingers drift away from my wrist, and Hideo's fingers follow. "The ocean wave reminds me of California, because I was born in San Francisco."

Hideo's hand stops near my elbow, on an elaborate, geometric sculpture rising out of the waves. "And?"

"An Escher structure," I reply. "I'm a fan."

Hideo smiles. "Good choice."

I smile, too, keenly aware of his warm touch against my arm.

My hand travels higher along my tattoo, pausing briefly on a series of stylized feathers floating up into the sky, then on that sky transitioning into a field of planets, their rings tilted like a vintage vinyl record, which then transform into stripes of sheet music, upon which a melody is written.

"Mozart's 'Queen of the Night' aria," I finish. "Because, well, I fancied myself as one."

"Mmm." Hideo leans in to plant kisses along my neck, and I shiver. "A bounty hunter wandering the Dark World," he murmurs. "Very appropriate."

I close my eyes, my lips parted, and soak in the warmth of his arms wrapped around me, his kisses trailing along my damp skin. The rough scars of his knuckles brush past my waist as his hands pull me close. There is a shyness in his eyes now that makes him look so young, an expression that tugs my heart closer to him. I can't remember when we start kissing or when we stop, or when he leans against me, made weak, whispering my name. We seem to exist in a fog of heat and dusk, and I don't know where the time goes, but it seems that night falls in the blink of an eye, and soon the evening has swallowed us. We're quiet now, leaning our heads against the stones lining the spring and watching the hanging lanterns illuminate the water with gold. Overhead, stars are winking one by one into existence—*real* stars, not a virtual simulation. It's barely after dusk, but already I can see more stars than I've ever seen in my life, blanketing the sky in a sheet of light.

Hideo has his face turned up to the stars, too. "Sasuke was playing in the park," he finally says, his words quiet in the empty space. I shift my head against the stones to hear him better. He seems thoughtful now, his mind somewhere far from here.

This is why we came here. This is the secret that weighs on

him. I turn my head slightly toward him, waiting for him to continue. He seems to struggle in silence, wondering whether letting me into his world will be a huge mistake.

"What happened?" I whisper.

He sighs, closes his eyes for a moment, and then makes a subtle motion with one hand. A screen appears between us. Hideo is sharing one of his Memories with me.

I accept it without a word. In the next instant, the *onsen* and nightfall and view around us vanish, and both Hideo and I find ourselves standing at the edge of a park, surrounded by a golden, autumn afternoon, where the sun outlines the trees in a haze of light. A few auto-cars are parked along the sidewalk. Red and orange leaves drift lazily to the ground, dotting the green grass with warm color. A short distance from us, two young boys are heading into the park. I immediately recognize one of them as a young Hideo; the other must be his brother.

"You hadn't invented the NeuroLink yet when this happened, did you?" I say as we watch the boys enter the park. "How did you create this Memory?"

"I remember every last detail about that day," Hideo replies. "I was nine. Sasuke was seven." He nods at the image of the brothers. "The park's layout, the placement of every tree, the golden leaves, the temperature, the angle of the light . . . I remember it all as if it had happened only minutes ago. So I reconstructed this moment for myself as a Memory, in its entirety, adding new details to it every year."

We now follow the point of view of young Hideo as he walks calmly, leaves crunching under his boots, his coat's collar pulled up high against the chilly day. He's yanking a bright blue scarf out of his backpack. Running a few feet in front of him is Sasuke—clearly the younger of the two—all grins and laughs, his boots crunching in the leaves as he sprints forward. When the boys speak, it is in Japanese.

"*Yukkuri, Sasuke-kun!*" the young Hideo shouts at his brother, waving the blue scarf in the air. I read the English translations in my view as he continues. "Slow down, Sasuke! Put on your scarf. Mom's going to kill me if you don't wear it."

Sasuke ignores him. He's carrying a basket full of plastic eggs, all colored blue. "Okay, this time you're red," he calls back at Hideo over his shoulder. "I'm blue. If I snatch all of yours before the sun hits that tree over there"—he pauses to point—"I get to have your favorite model car."

Hideo rolls his eyes and lets out an annoyed sigh as they reached the park's central clearing. "But it's part of a *set!*" he argues, even though he doesn't say no. He finally catches up to his brother. Despite Sasuke's protests, Hideo forces him to stand still while he wraps the blue scarf around his brother's neck and tugs his collar up higher. "We can't stay out for long. Dad needs our help at the shop before dinner, and Mom needs to be at the lab until late."

Sasuke pouts like a little brother would. "Fine," he mutters.

The boys separate and head off to opposite ends of the park. As they go, Hideo pulls out a bag of plastic red eggs from his backpack. They both start tossing them all over the place, each one taking great pains to hide them properly from the other.

A blue egg comes tumbling into view, and Hideo looks up to see Sasuke wearing a goofy grin. "Threw it too hard!" he shouts. "Can you toss it back?"

Hideo grabs the egg and flings it back at his brother. The egg flies far past the clearing and disappears into the thick of the park's trees, where they line the banks of a tiny stream overgrown with bamboo. He laughs as Sasuke's grin changes into an exasperated frown. "Wait for me, Hideo," he calls over his shoulder, and then he stomps off into the trees to fetch the egg. Hideo turns his back and keeps setting out the other eggs. A few minutes later, he glances over his shoulder.

"Are you done yet?" he calls out.

No answer.

Hideo stands up straight and stretches, savoring the warm glow of the afternoon sun. "Sasuke!" he calls again at the thicket of trees. The only sounds that answer him are the faint trickle of the stream's water and the hush of golden leaves drifting in the air. The breeze whispers through the swaying bamboo stalks.

A few seconds pass before Hideo lets out a sigh and starts trudging over to his brother's end of the park. "Come on. We don't have all day," he says. "Sasuke! Hurry up!" I look on as we follow him through the trees and into the overgrown grasses, slowing occasionally whenever the foliage turns too thick.

"Sasuke?" Hideo calls again. His voice sounds different now—the exasperation gone, replaced with a twinge of confusion. He stops in the middle of the trees, looking all around him as if unable to believe that there was another person who had just been here. Long minutes drag by as he does an exhaustive hunt of the small thicket. He calls again. Now there is a note of concern. Then, fear. No sign of another boy. It's as if he had simply ceased to exist.

"Sasuke?" Hideo's voice becomes urgent, frantic. His steps quicken into a run. He hurries out of the thicket and back into the clearing, hoping that his brother had somehow wandered back there without hearing him. But the rest of the park stays empty, the boys' blue and red plastic eggs still scattered all over the grass, waiting for the game to start.

Hideo halts in the middle of the clearing. The Memory turns

panicked now, the world blurring around us as Hideo spins in place, looking one way, then the other, then running to another section of the park. The view shakes wildly as he goes. His breaths come in short gasps, sending clouds of mist up in the chilly air. When I catch a glimpse of his face reflected against the metal of a parked car, his eyes are wide and dark, the pupils dilated with terror. "Sasuke! *Sasuke!*" Each shout sounds more like a scream than the last. Hideo calls and calls until his voice begins to crack.

He stops abruptly, gasping for air, and clutches his head with his hands. "Calm down. Sasuke went home," he whispers. He nods to himself, believing it. "He went home early without telling me. That's where he is." Without another hesitation, he starts running home, scanning the sidewalks wildly, looking for the back of a small boy wearing a bright blue scarf. "Please, please," I realize he's whispering to himself as he goes. The word trails out in a repeated line, thin as a ghost.

He doesn't stop running until he reaches his home, a house I now recognize. He pounds on the door until his father opens it, his face bewildered. "Hideo—what are you doing here?" He cranes his neck and looks behind Hideo at the sidewalk. "Where's your brother?"

At the question, Hideo seems to waver in place, and I can see that, in this instant, he knows his brother never came home, he *knows* something terrible has happened. Behind him, the sun has already started to set, washing the landscape from gold into pink.

All I can think is that it is far too beautiful of a day.

The Memory ends. I'm startled as the *onsen* reappears around me and Hideo, the peaceful fog of hot water and the glisten of early lamplight on the rocks. I look at him. He doesn't say anything; he doesn't look at me. He doesn't even seem to be here anymore, for the look on his face is distant and grim. Afraid. After a pause, he brings up another Memory. It is the same sequence we just watched—except he has altered the park's landscape, shifting the stream a little this way, a little that. He brings up a third Memory. Same sequence, but with the brothers in slightly different positions.

"I can't tell you how many times I've gone over this scene in my head," he finally says to me in a soft voice. He flips to another, and yet another, each with subtle details changed. This time, the scene shows Hideo turning around a few seconds sooner and calling Sasuke back before he can go into the trees. Another one shows Hideo steering Sasuke out of the park and back home before they can start playing their game. Yet another shows Hideo going with Sasuke to retrieve the plastic egg instead of leaving him to do it himself. My heart cracks a little with each new variation. This is his endless hell. "I can remember every single detail about that day . . . except the details that matter. Where he went. When I stopped hearing his footsteps in the leaves. Who took him. I think about what might have happened if I'd done this. Or that. If things had shifted even a little." He shakes his head. His jaw is so tight that I'm afraid he might break it. "I don't know. So I keep building."

He's torturing himself. I watch with a lump in my throat as he brings up another constructed Memory—this time of the same night, with flashlights dancing through the park. His mother's and father's voices are high and frantic, breaking. Then the scene switches to a young Hideo on his knees before his parents, sobbing, begging forgiveness, hysterical, inconsolable, even as they try to make him get up. The scene switches yet again to Hideo lying in bed, curled up, silent, listening to the faint crying of his mother coming from his parents' bedroom. It switches to him waking every morning and looking in the mirror . . . and seeing a thin, silver streak grow steadily into his black hair. I wince. The trauma was what had slashed him in white. And even though I am not him, I understand, and even without the Link connecting our emotions right now, I can feel the vicious, unending shame that clouds his heart.

I try to imagine my father disappearing one day and never coming back, what it must be like to grieve with no closure at all, to live with an open-ended mystery twisting a knife forever in my heart. I think of the porch light at the entrance of his parents' home, turned on even in the afternoon. I imagine that pain and, even in my imagination, I can feel my heart bleed.

A long moment passes after the Memories end, filled with nothing but the sound of water rippling against the rock. When Hideo speaks again, his voice is low, weighed down with a haunting, all-consuming guilt. "They never talked about Sasuke again after his disappearance. They blamed themselves, put the shame on their own shoulders, and bore it silently. Our neighbors and the police stopped talking about Sasuke, too, out of respect for my parents. They can't look at photos of him; I could only save what I had. He exists now solely in their sculptures. My mother aged overnight. She used to remember *everything*; she led her neurology team. Now she misplaces things and forgets what she was doing. My father developed a cough that never went away. He gets sick frequently." Hideo's eyes follow the path of the Gemini constellation, the stars that form the shape of twins. "As for me . . . well, Sasuke loved games. We played every day, made up all kinds of games together. He was cleverer than me—had aced every exam he ever took, tested effortlessly into every elite academy you could think of."

I understand now. "You invented the NeuroLink because of

your brother. Warcross was inspired by that game Sasuke played in the park. You created Warcross for him."

He pauses, and the water ripples as he turns to me. "*Everything* I do is for him."

I brush his arm with my hand. Nothing I say can possibly be right in this moment, so instead, I say nothing at all. I only listen.

"I don't talk about him, Emika," Hideo says after another silence. He looks away again. "I haven't talked about him in years."

This is Hideo stripped of his fortune and fame and genius. This is him as a boy, waiting every day for his brother to come back, falling asleep every night to the same nightmare, trapped forever wondering if he had only done *one thing, anything,* differently. It is hard to describe loss to someone who has never experienced it, impossible to explain all the ways it changes you. But for those who have, not a single word is needed.

Hideo pushes away from the edge of the spring and nods toward the steps leading back up to the bathhouse. He offers me his hand. I take it, my eyes flickering as always to the scars on his knuckles. "It's getting late," he says gently.

# 24

We have dinner that night with Hideo's parents. I look on at how carefully Hideo fries meat, chops vegetables, and sets rice in the steamer. While he does, his mother fusses over my complexion. "This tiny child," she scolds gently, beaming up at me. "Hideo, why haven't you been feeding her? Make sure you give her a big bowl. It will add some pink to her cheeks."

"*Okaa-san*," he says with a sigh. "Please."

She shrugs. "I am telling you, she needs nutrition if her mind is to perform at its best. You remember what I told you about how neurons use the energy delivered by your blood?" I exchange a wry smile with Hideo as she launches into an explanation about blood.

Hideo is the one who sets the table, who lays the food out for us, and who pours everyone tea. Dinner is so delicious that I wish it could last forever—juicy, tender cuts of chicken fried to perfection; gleaming rice topped with a fried egg; lightly pickled vegetables for garnish; soft mochi cakes made of sticky rice flour for dessert, each stuffed with strawberry and sweet red bean; soothing cups of hot green tea. As we eat, Hideo's parents speak Japanese to each other in low voices, sneaking occasional smiles at me as if they think their movements are too stealthy for me to notice.

I nudge Hideo sitting beside me. "What are they saying?" I whisper.

"Nothing," he replies, even though I see a faint blush on his cheeks. "I don't usually have time to cook, that's all. So they're commenting on it."

I grin. "But you cooked dinner for me?"

The smile I get in return from the creator of Warcross is, of all things, *bashful*. "Well," he says, "I wanted to do something for you, for a change." He looks expectantly at me. "Do you like it?"

Suede gift boxes holding fifteen-thousand-dollar electric skateboards. Flights on private jets. Closets full of expensive clothes. Dinners at restaurants he owns. And yet, none of that has made my heart skip like this earnest, hopeful look on his face as he waits to hear if I enjoyed the food he made for me.

I lean my shoulder into him as I hold my bowl. "Decent," I reply. He blinks in surprise, then seems to remember what he'd once said to me during our first meeting. A laugh escapes him.

"I'll take it," he says, leaning back.

Still. Even as he talks easily with both his mother and father, I can't help thinking about his words from earlier, that Sasuke is a topic never discussed with them, that their grief and shame run so deep that they can't even bear to have their second son's portrait in the house. No wonder I never heard about this in all the documentaries I watched about Hideo. No wonder he has such a strict company policy of not talking about his family.

"They don't want to move," Hideo tells me on our ride back into Tokyo. "I've tried convincing them a thousand times, but they don't want to leave our old home. So I do my best to keep them safe here."

"Safe?" I ask.

"There are bodyguards watching their home at all times."

Of course there would be. I hadn't even noticed them, but now I think about the random passerby on the sidewalk, the gardener working on the hedge.

By the time his car pulls up in the back of the Phoenix Riders' dorm, it's nearly midnight. I stare at the overlays on the tinted windows, currently showing an empty car interior so that no one will be able to see us both inside.

"I'll see you soon," I whisper to him, reluctant to leave.

He draws closer, touches my chin with one hand, and guides me into a kiss. I close my eyes and lean into it.

Finally, too soon, he pulls away. "Good night," he murmurs.

I have to force myself not to look back as I get out of the car and head toward the dorm. But even long after his car has pulled away and left me alone, his presence lingers. There was a new expression in his eyes tonight, the kind open only to a few . . . but there are still secrets behind it. I wonder what it will take to uncover another of them.

● ● ● ● ●

THE REST OF the week flies by. On Friday morning, the familiar sound of Asher ramming his wheelchair into my door stirs me out of my restless sleep in my dorm room. "Game three!" he shouts, the excitement obvious in his voice as it fades down the hall. "Let's go! We're gonna knock out the Cloud Knights in record time!"

I rub a hand across my face. I feel groggy today, my mind

stifled and my heart still pounding from another round of night-mares, and my limbs are weighed down as I drag myself out of bed. While I dress, a message pops into my view from Hideo.

Good luck today. I'll be
watching from the balconies.

I shake my head. Now he's just thumbing his nose at his attackers.

I thought you were going to
stay away from the upper decks.

We've redone the security cams, rewired
the stadium, and security detail has been
doubled. They'd be fools to attack in the
same place again. I'll be fine.

I already know there's nothing I can do to talk him out of it.

Well, be careful, ok?
Keep your eyes peeled.

My eyes will be on you, I'm afraid.

A nagging worry lingers in my mind, but his words still pull a smile out of me. I head downstairs.

The other Phoenix Riders chat animatedly on our way to the stadium this morning. I feel strangely disconnected from it all. Ren doesn't seem to act any differently toward me, but his non-chalance bothers me even more. Maybe I should have told Hideo about him after all. Maybe he would have been disqualified from today's game. I narrow my eyes as I watch Ren crack a joke with Asher. No. Hell if he's going to force me out of my element. I'm going to keep using him to get to the bottom of this.

The stadium feels like a blur today, and as we enter the arena and go to our individual terminals, I feel like I'm walking in a fog. The announcer sounds far away, and the cheers from the audience turn into a mess of background noise. I keep my head turned up to the balcony seats. Sure enough, Hideo is there, surrounded by bodyguards.

Then the world goes dark, and I find myself transported into another realm.

"Welcome to the Lost City Level!"

The echo of the announcer's voice fades away as the virtual world materializes around us. Dim light filters down from the ocean's surface far above. I find myself floating above a spectacular, ruined city surrounded on all sides by walls of colorful coral. Stone pillars tower up toward the surface. Piles of rock are everywhere, looking like once-grand theaters and bathhouses. Turquoise light shines from within some of their crevices, forming glowing lines that seem to point out pathways to take. The ruins stretch as far as I can see, dappled sunlight dancing against their surfaces, and drifting over them are a field of shining, jewel-like power-ups. The only thing keeping us from feeling completely immersed is the sound of the crowd's cheers all around us.

I look to either side. My teammates are all here, dressed in outfits of bright white with flippers on our feet and fins on our arms. I look down at my hands. They are equipped with buttons in my palms. When I experiment with pressing them, my avatar jerks forward a bit. This will be how we get around.

Far on the other side of the ruins appear our rivals. The Cloud Knights. They are dressed in outfits of bright yellow, standing out against the blue tint of this place. All of our eyes are turned toward them—all except Ren's. I glance at him to see him staring down at the ruins already, as if searching for something. My jaw tightens. *Follow him.*

"Game! Set! *Fight!*"

The game starts. Asher barks orders at us through our comms, and we split immediately. On the other side of the ruins, the Cloud Knights dive down for the ruins, no doubt ready to lose themselves inside the maze of crumbled structures. We dive, too. I clench my fists down on the buttons on my palms, and I jerk forward through the water in a blur of motion, slicing a trail behind me. A bar appears in the center of my view, showing how much oxygen I have left.

As we get to the point where we start splitting up, my teammates reappear as tiny dots on a small map in my view. But the only person I'm paying attention to is Ren. He swims away from the others and toward a series of collapsed columns that form a cave. Considering what had happened after our first round, I change course from where Asher tells me to go and instead trail after Ren.

"Emi," Asher calls through our comms. He sighs. "Can you follow my lead for once? I said go *center*, toward that collapsed amphitheater."

"I see a better route," I lie, continuing in my direction. "Don't worry."

Asher makes a sound as if to argue, but then he stops, as if he'd remembered my successful moves from our last game. "Your only solo move," he says. "Hear me?"

"Yes, Captain."

He flickers out. The light grows dim around us, with only faint rays of blue and silver dancing against the stone formations. I keep my gaze on Ren. He's moving at a good pace in front of me and has just rounded a corner. Where is he going?

"And it looks like the Cloud Knights have secured the first rare power-up of the game!" the announcer's voice comes on all around us. "The silver-and-gold Invisibility!"

*I should be concentrating on the game right now.* But I find myself continuing on my hunt. My oxygen level starts to deplete. **Warning: 25% left** flashes in my view. Up ahead, I see a spot between the rocks where bubbles of air are coming out in a steady stream—but if I stop now, I might never catch up to Ren. So I skip it, then propel myself onward. I'm so close.

Then—suddenly—everything around me shifts. The underwater ruins vanish.

I'm no longer floating in an ocean, but standing in a cavern encircling me, trapping me in. Dim, scarlet light illuminates the space. The sounds of the audience's cheers abruptly go silent. I blink. What had happened? In real life, I reach up to adjust my earphones. Did they glitch? It's as if I'd suddenly been taken out of the game. I can't even see my teammates on a map anymore.

"Hello?" I say, shifting around. My voice echoes.

If my game has glitched, then I should take off my lenses right now and alert the authorities. The game would be paused as they fix it. But instead I continue looking around, my heart beating faster now. No. This is not an accident. The red hue of this space looks too similar to the Dark World.

When I blink again, a tall figure is standing in front of me. He's clad in the fitted black armor I've become so used to seeing now, and his face is completely hidden behind a dark, opaque helmet. His head is turned directly toward me. For a moment, we just stare at each other in silence.

Zero's proxy. Or his follower.

Or, maybe, himself.

I find my voice. "You're who Hideo is after," I say, taking a step forward.

"And you're the one who's been trailing me. Hideo's little lackey." His voice sounds deep and distorted in this cavern.

This is really him. He knows who I am. He knows what I'm doing. Instantly, I think of the moment when I'd seen him appear in the last game. Had he set that to test whether or not I could see him? And now he has sabotaged this game in order to speak directly to me.

"My teammates will see that I'm trapped," I say to him. My words come out forceful and frustrated as memories of Hideo's near-assassination flash back at me. "You can't keep disrupting every world."

Zero walks closer to me, his muscles shifting underneath the black armor, until we are separated by a mere foot. He stares down at me. "Here's what your teammates currently see."

A window pops up in the center of my view, and I see the underwater ruins. I see myself, ignoring Asher's repeated commands and idling in an area away from the others, collecting simple power-ups. I see myself getting trapped in an obvious airless pocket.

"Right now, as far as they're concerned, you've managed to seal yourself in an underwater cave in the ruins. And you're running out of air fast."

"Why are you here?" I say. "What do you want?"

"I'm here to give you a fair offer," he replies. His voice echoes around me.

"A fair *offer*?"

"How else should I say it? A deal. A proposal. A suggestion. Take your pick."

My temper flares. "I've been causing problems for you, haven't I? You were forced to speak to me directly? What's this—are you angry that someone has finally managed to get close to bringing you in?"

"Do I sound angry?" My words make him laugh once. It's a low, quiet sound. "You're too good to be working for him. How much does Hideo pay you to keep you so loyally at his side? To come when he whistles? Or is something else drawing you to him?"

"Your charm overwhelms me," I say in my driest voice.

"And what if I overwhelm his number?"

I narrow my eyes. "Are you honestly offering to hire me?"

"Everyone has a price. Name yours."

"No."

Zero shakes his head at me. "Choose carefully."

"I *am* careful."

"Are you?" He looks down at me so that I can see my own avatar's face reflected in his helmet. "Because, as far as I can tell, you've been living a risky life in New York City. Because you've been risky in choosing your . . . *relationships*."

A shiver runs through me. Has he been researching my past? Has he been watching me? Does he know about Hideo and me? "And *you* are messing with the wrong person," I say through gritted teeth.

"I was giving you a compliment."

"This is your idea of a compliment?"

"I'm not known for making offers, Emika. Interpret that however you'd like."

My hands clench into fists. "Well, you can take that generous offer," I say in a low voice as I move toward him, "and shove it up your virtual ass."

He leans close to me. "Everyone always thinks they're so brave."

And when I look down, I notice with horror that the arm of my suit, originally bright white like my teammates', is turning black. Plates of dark armor clip into place around my wrist, then cover my forearms, then creep up to my shoulders. They line my chest and neck, my waist and legs. I choke out a gasp and step away from him, as if this will stop it. But in this moment, I no longer look like an Architect. I look like his hunter, dressed entirely in black.

"Get away from me," I snarl. "Before I kill you."

"It is you," he replies, "who came to me."

His words just make me angrier. "I'm going to give you one more chance to turn yourself in. It'll make life easier for everyone."

He just watches me, his silent calm unnerving. Finally, he starts to turn away. "You're going to regret this," he says. Then, before I can shout anything else at him, he vanishes. So does the scarlet cavern.

Suddenly, I'm thrust back into the game. The roar of the audience abruptly returns, followed by the announcer's shocked voice and the jumble of my teammates' voices all ringing in my ears. I look frantically down, expecting to see myself still encased in black armor that resembles Zero's—but it's gone, as if it were all a hallucination. My white game suit is intact again.

"Emi? Ems!" Asher shouts. "What the *hell* are you doing?"

"Forget her—" comes Hammie's voice, frantic. "She's out. I'm going for the Artifact *now*!"

I realize I am floating, frozen, trapped inside a set of ruins with only a small eyehole through which I can see the rest of the game unfolding. Asher is trying in vain to fend off three

Cloud Knights. He's going to lose his Artifact. I try to ram myself through my underwater cage, but I can't—and then I realize it's because I have no more oxygen left. My reserves are red. That's what Hammie had meant. I'm dead, struck out of the round until I can regenerate. What had happened?

"I don't believe it!" the announcer is shouting now. "After their incredible first win, the Phoenix Riders may be disqualified early this year if they don't do something soon—"

Hammie appears at the last second, flickering into view like a phantom in the water. She lunges for the Cloud Knights' Artifact before they can register her presence, right at the same time as the Knights lunge for Asher's. Both teams seize the other's Artifact at almost the exact same time. The crowd screams.

A few seconds pass before the final score appears in our views.

"The Phoenix Riders manage to hang on to victory by a *millisecond*!" the announcer shouts.

As the world vanishes around me and the real world—the arena and the screaming crowds—comes back into view, I see Asher roll out of his station in a furious mood. His face is twisted in anger. He's glaring at me. So are my other teammates. I look up at the enormous holograms in the stadium that are replaying segments of the game, only to see myself, ignoring the others and sabotaging their moves. Boos are mixed in with the cheers in the crowd. Some are shouting for a replay, that we hadn't won this round at all.

"What the *hell* happened?" Asher demands as he approaches me. "That was the most embarrassing, shameful display I've ever seen from a pro player. You tried to throw that game on purpose."

What can I say? Zero's figure is still hovering in my mind, ominous and silent. "I'm sorry," I start to say, "I—"

Asher turns his head in disgust. "We'll talk back at the

dorms." From the corner of my eye, I see Roshan shake his head at me in confusion, while Hammie looks away in disappointment. We had won, but it didn't look like it at all. My gaze goes to Ren, who's watching me. The edge of his lips tilts ever so slightly. My jaw tightens. *He knows.*

Suddenly, the holograms in the arena change. The crowd goes still for a moment. *I* go still. My teammates all pause in unison.

Then, everyone bursts into gasps and shouts. As they do, I can only find enough strength to stare in stunned silence at the grainy screenshot that is now publicly broadcast to everyone in the arena, and probably to everyone watching this game. Everyone in the *world*. I don't know who had taken it, or how. But somehow, I know Zero is involved. This is the beginning of his attack on me.

The holograms display a giant photo of me stepping out of Hideo's home at night, of him leaning in to kiss me, of his hand still holding on to mine. It's unmistakable.

The news is out.

# 25

### *PHOENIX RIDER SNAGS*
### *HEARTTHROB BILLIONAIRE!*

———

## HIDEO TANAKA PLAYS HIS WILD CARD

———

### WILD CARD GETS BILLIONAIRE BOYFRIEND

———

### EXCLUSIVE: 1ST LEAKED PHOTOS
### OF HIDEO AND EMIKA

When we arrive at the dorms, I go straight to my room without saying a word to anyone. I'm too afraid to look at my phone. I've already turned off my messages. Even so, it was impossible not to catch a glimpse of the headlines screaming by on marquees near the Tokyo Dome, broadcasting the news to the public. Now I curl up on my bed, my heart pounding from the onslaught. From how grainy the shot looked, it must have been taken with some insanely high-powered camera lens, from some remote hill.

After a few moments, I hesitantly turn on my messages

and enable ones from Hideo. A message from him pops up immediately.

> Stay inside. I'm sending extra
> security to the team quarters.

I'm about to respond when a knock sounds at my door. Hammie's voice drifts through to me.

"Are you staying in there forever?" she demands. "Or are you going to offer us any kind of explanation?"

I hang back for a while on my bed, my head down, gathering my strength. Then I sigh and stand up. "I'm coming," I reply as I walk to the door. When I open it, I find myself staring into Hammie's narrowed eyes. She brings up a tabloid cover to hover between us. This one has published the grainy photo of Hideo and me, along with the headline: LOVE OR CHEATING?

"Downstairs," she says, waving her fingers once and erasing the cover from view. She turns away toward the stairs before I can respond. I hesitate, then follow her.

Down in the atrium, Roshan is activating blackout shields on the floor-to-ceiling windows in an attempt to keep journalists out—but I can still hear the photographers clicking madly away, the flashes of their cameras reflecting off the glass. Before the windows go completely dark, I catch a glimpse of the main courtyard leading out to the security gate. A mob of paparazzi have crowded there, some of them pushing past the security. Two guards chase down a reporter and cameraman sprinting toward our dorms. It's a feeding frenzy.

Roshan temporarily looks away from the outside crowds to focus on me. His usually gentle expression has been replaced with one of suspicion. Asher regards me with a scowl. I sit down on the couches with Hammie, trying to avoid Ren's stare—but even then, I can feel his smugness directed at me.

"When were you going to tell us?" Roshan finally begins.

"I . . ." I shake my head. "It's complicated."

"Is it?" Hammie replies, glancing in disdain at the darkened windows. "All those times you didn't want to hang out with the rest of us, was it because you were off seeing Hideo Tanaka? We're supposed to be a team, Emi. But obviously you didn't think we could handle your fancy relationship."

I scowl at her. "What's going on between Hideo and me has nothing to do with how I feel about you and the team."

Asher shoots me a hard look. "It has everything to do with us. We just got into the final championship round, but now people think we won unfairly—they think Hideo's favoritism for you made the judges hand the win over to the Phoenix Riders."

"No, it was clear that we won," Roshan interjects. He's watching me, telling me silently to defend myself. "And it must be hard to talk about such a high-profile relationship. Right? We're listening, Em, but you have to give us something."

*If only you knew the half of it.* "How was I supposed to bring everything up? This was something in my personal life. I didn't think I had to bring it into our team practices."

"Except you did," Hammie says. "You were always ready to skip out on time with us or leave early from training. And what was that pitiful display today?"

Asher nods at Hammie's words as he continues looking at me. "You ignored everything I said. You told me you knew better. I gave you the benefit of the doubt because I had faith in you, because you've proven yourself before, but—" He pauses in frustration. "I am your *captain.* I chose you as the number one draft pick. I've worked hard to build a team of this caliber. Even if we go on to win the championships this year, who's going to believe that we earned it? I can already see the headlines. *Phoenix Riders cheat their way to the top.*"

"Oh, come on," I reply, my voice rising now in frustration. "It's just a game. I—"

"It's *just* a *game?*" Hammie interrupts. Everyone around me tenses, and I know I've said the wrong thing. It is precisely the thing I have always hated hearing from others. I start to correct myself, but she leans forward and glares at me. "Then why are you even here? Why are you even competing in Warcross if it's so beneath you? Weren't you living in New York's gutters before you came here?"

"You know I didn't mean it like that."

"Then you should get out of the habit of saying things you don't mean. I'm damn good at Warcross. *Being* good at Warcross allowed me to buy my ma her own house, send my sis to a good university." She pauses to stretch her hands out at the dorm. "That's why everyone loves Warcross, isn't it? Why we're all obsessed with the NeuroLink—why *you* use it? Because it makes things possible?"

"It's not what I meant," I repeat. "There's too much that you don't understand. When there's a lot more at stake than a championship, then, yes—it *is* just a game."

I hadn't planned my outburst correctly, and I regret some of it right away. Hammie looks incredulous. Then, skeptical. Nearby, Ren regards me curiously. He's daring me to say more.

"Wait," Roshan says, making a twirling motion with one finger. "So, this isn't just a fling. What do you mean, when there's a lot more at stake?"

I take a deep breath. Everything is on the tip of my tongue

now, ready to tumble out—but I stop just short of saying too much. Ren is still here, sitting with us. Zero has threatened me. It's not worth putting the others at risk. I mutter a curse under my breath and stand up. "I'm sorry."

Hammie leans her elbows on her knees. "There's more you're keeping from us. And I can't understand why."

"What aren't you telling us, Em?" Asher asks, his voice very quiet now.

"I have my reasons."

Something sympathetic flickers in Roshan's gaze. The edge of Ren's lip quirks up again, so subtle that no one else notices, and his eyes harden at me. I stare levelly back, refusing to give him the satisfaction of intimidating me. Then I turn around and head back to my room. Asher calls my name, but I don't respond.

*Careful, Emika.*

The voice echoes in my ears. I freeze in my steps.

There, through my virtual view, is Zero, standing at the end of the hallway leading up to the second floor, his silhouette encased in dark armor and his opaque helmet turned toward me. My mouth turns dry at the sight of him.

*I warned you,* he says.

"What are you doing here?" I say in a hoarse croak.

Behind me, I hear Hammie's voice as she walks toward me. "Emi," she says, "who are you talking to?"

He just stares calmly at me. *Check your Memories.*

My Memory Worlds.

Suddenly, my heart seizes. I type a quick command and bring up a window to search for my Memory Worlds, all the carefully compartmentalized pieces of my father that I spend so much time revisiting. *No. Please.* When they come up, I freeze.

The files are blank. The option **New Memory World** hovers over them.

I tremble. Impossible. I put up all sorts of security shells on them, buried them deep in my accounts so that nothing could ever happen to them, secured them in the cloud, cloned them multiple times out of an abundance of caution. I search frantically for my cloned versions now. But they are gone, too. Dad, humming cheerfully at our dining table as he cuts fabrics. Dad, crafting handmade Christmas ornaments with me. Dad, showing me how he mixes paints. Dad, sharing roasted peanuts with me in Central Park; wandering the halls of museums; celebrating my birthday.

Zero has deleted them all.

I'm stunned, reeling from the wound.

*Stay out of my way, and I might return them to you. Continue, and this will only be the beginning.*

My fingers curl tightly into fists at my side. My anger sharpens like a blade toward the armored silhouette before me. It takes me a second to realize that tears are blurring my vision. Behind me, Hammie finally approaches. "Emi, what's going on with you?" she says.

Zero's head tilts ever so slightly. Like he's mocking me. *Too late.*

And just then, an explosion rips through our dorm.

# 26

A faulty gas line. That's the public explanation given for the blast.

I don't get a better sense of what happened until I see it broadcast on the small TV in my hospital room. From the outside, it looks horrendous—one moment, the Phoenix Riders' dorm still standing; the next, a deafening explosion and an orange ball of fire erupting from the roof of our atrium. Windows shatter, spraying glass everywhere. As the fire billows out of control, pouring black smoke into the air, nearby dorms' lights turn on and the players from the other teams come running over. Some are screaming. Others stand with their hands on their heads, at a loss for words. But most come rushing to our windows, shouting our names. Even Tremaine—bullying, obnoxious Tremaine—is there, helping Roshan pull Asher out through a window.

Then the fire trucks come, along with the ambulances.

Flashing lights fill up the TV screen. There's a news announcer talking in front of our dorm, then interviewing Hammie, who looks awake and dazed as she clutches a blanket around herself. Asher suffered some cuts and bruises from broken glass, as did Roshan, but miraculously, all of us came out of it alive.

It doesn't mean we're not all shaken up, though.

"Miss Chen," a nurse says as she peeks in through my door, bobbing her head once. "You have a visitor."

I sit up with my arms wrapped around my legs, then nod quietly at her. My limbs feel numb. "Okay," I reply. She leaves, and a moment later, returns with two others.

It's Roshan, clutching a box, followed by Hammie. They look like they haven't slept in days. I open my mouth to greet them, but Hammie just shakes her head and reaches out to pull me into a hug. I wince—my arm still burns from the scratches I'd gotten, while my back aches from when the blast had tossed me off my feet. "Ow," I groan, but the hug feels nicer than the pain, and I lean into her.

"Ash sends his love," she says against my shoulder. "His brother and parents are with him in his hospital room."

"I'm sorry," I whisper to her, tears welling in my eyes. The blast has thrown me all off. "I'm so sorry. Ham—"

"You don't remember anything, do you?" she says, pulling away a bit to look at me. "You half carried me to the back door before you collapsed. Stop apologizing."

The explosion, the fire, the smoke, the faintest recollection of me shouting Hammie's name as we lean against each other. I shake my head repeatedly.

Roshan holds out the box with a grim face. "We salvaged what we could," he says.

When I open the box, I see broken shards of my Christmas ornament, along with burned scraps of what must be my father's painting. I run one hand across the remains. The lump in my throat grows until I can't swallow it anymore.

I wipe my eyes with one hand. "Thank you," I reply as I place the box carefully beside me.

Roshan leans close. "Based on what little we know, Ren's being questioned by the police right now. I don't buy the gas leak story."

"But you know more about this than we do, don't you, Emi?" Hammie adds, searching my gaze. "You have to tell us what's going on. We deserve to know."

*Your lives were threatened, too.* But still, I hesitate. If I tell them everything, it might only endanger them more. They might fall on Zero's radar. They never asked to be involved in any of this, never entered the championships to hunt down a criminal, were never getting paid to put themselves at risk.

Hammie studies me like I'm a chessboard. "You remind me of myself from several years ago," she says. "I always offered help— but I refused to accept any. My mother scolded me about that. Do you know what she told me? When you refuse to ask for help, it tells others that they also shouldn't ask for help from you. That you look down on them for needing your help. That you like feeling superior to them. It's an insult, Emi, to your friends and peers. So don't be like that. Let us in."

Hammie's words strike me clean in the chest. Even though I've lied with the best before, I know that both of them can see the truth on my face—that I'm involved in something beyond my capabilities.

Something that could have killed them.

I'm used to working alone. Even if I told them everything,

what good would that really do? Am I really going to drag them into this hunt with me?

But this is no ordinary hunt, and Hideo is no ordinary client. If our lives are all in danger, then we have bigger problems to deal with than whether or not I put my faith in my teammates.

The mention of my name on the TV makes us turn toward the screen in unison. The news anchor is talking beside a photo of me, taken when I was celebrating our first win with the other Riders.

"—that this morning, Hideo Tanaka announced that he is officially pulling two players from the Phoenix Riders, currently one of the top-ranked Warcross teams: their Fighter, Renoir Thomas, and Architect, Emika Chen. No word yet on the reasons behind either decision, although speculation—"

*Pulled from the team.* All the air rushes out of my lungs.

Roshan and Hammie whirl to face me. "Pulled?" Hammie whispers sharply.

Roshan is quieter, searching my gaze. He seems ready to say something, then decides against it.

I only hesitate one more time. Then I pull Roshan and Hammie in for another hug. "Tonight," I whisper in their ears. "I promise. I can't talk about it out loud right now." Then I break away and say, "The fact that you've brought me this box is help enough."

Roshan frowns, but Hammie gives me an imperceptible nod. She tries to smile. "Will do," she replies. It sounds like the right answer to what I said, but I know it also means she understood what I meant.

"Miss Chen," the nurse says as she steps back in. "You have another visitor."

Roshan and Hammie exchange another pointed look with me.

Then they get up and head out of the room. A moment later, the nurse opens the door wider to usher in my new visitor.

Hideo comes striding in, his face a mask of anger and worry. His eyes lock on mine, and some of his expression dissolves into relief.

"You're awake," he says as he sits down on the side of my bed.

"You can't," I reply, pointing at the TV. My mind is still spinning. "Pulled? Really? Why didn't you tell me?"

"Would you have me keep you both in and risk everyone's lives?" Hideo replies. "We didn't know how long it would take for you to wake up. I had to make a decision." His eyes are dark with fury, although it seems to be directed inward; his expression reminds me of how he looked as he spoke about his brother.

"What about not caving to intimidation?"

"That was before Zero threatened you and other players."

"How will taking me out of the tournaments stop whatever Zero's planning to do during the final game?"

"It won't." Hideo's jaw tightens. "But I'd rather not see you involved in it. The whole reason for entering you in the games was for you to have better access to information, but I think you may have collected everything you possibly can from being an official team member." He sighs. "It's my fault. I should have taken you off the team a long time ago."

The thought of abandoning my team and sabotaging their chances at a win . . . I close my eyes and lower my head. *Breathe.* "I heard Ren's talking to the police."

"He's in custody, yes, and being interrogated."

I start shaking my head. "You're not going to get anything out of him that way. His arrest will only alert Zero that you're on to him, and he'll move his operations further underground.

Hideo, *come on*. The next time I go to a game sponsored in the Dark World, I'll have no—"

"You won't be," Hideo interrupts. His eyes search mine, dark and resolute. "I'm letting you off the job."

I blink. "You're firing me?"

"I'm still paying you the bounty," he replies. Why does he sound so distant? His tension makes him cold, even hostile.

My head is spinning. *But—every locked door has a key.* I haven't found the key yet—I can't leave now. "It's not about the bounty," I say.

"You've earned it. The money is sitting in your account now."

*The ten million.* I start shaking my head in disgust. "You have to *stop doing that.* Why do you always think you can just throw money at people and get them to do what you want?"

"Because it was the whole reason why you came here in the first place," Hideo says, his tone clipped. "I'm giving you what you wanted."

"What the hell do *you* know about what I wanted?" My voice rises. I can feel the burn of my cheeks. Flashes of my father appear in my thoughts—then, myself curled in a ball on my foster-home bed, struggling to find a reason to live. *All of my Memory Worlds are now gone, deleted, taken by Zero.* I can't look back on my memories of my father if I wanted to. "You think I'm just here for the money? You think you can fix everything by writing a check?"

Hideo's eyes seem to shutter. "Then we understand each other less than I thought."

"Or maybe you're not understanding *me*." I narrow my eyes at him. "I saw Zero standing in our dorms before the bomb went off. Listen—he didn't show up there to threaten me just on a whim, or just because he now knows who I am. We tracked down Ren and have proof that he's connected to Zero's mission. You even have him in custody now. That means Zero feels *threatened*. He thinks we're closing in, and that's why he's lashing out. Planting a bomb means that he's risking alerting the authorities in an attempt to keep me off his trail. We've backed him into a corner. *All* of the momentum is on our side."

"And that means he's at his most unpredictable," Hideo finishes. "This is someone we still know nothing about, and I am not going to see another bomb go off just because I want you to catch him for us."

"Just because you take me off the job doesn't mean he won't attack again."

"I know. That's why I've cancelled every dome event."

"Every dome event? Around the world?"

"I will not have people physically gathering by the thousands in stadiums across the world, not if it poses a risk for them. They can enjoy the rest of the tournaments from the comfort of their homes."

*No, I can't give up now.* My old, familiar panic is rising up again, the terror of seeing the wall go up between the problem and the solution. Of standing helplessly by while danger circles someone I love. There's something missing here, as if a new development had suddenly changed Hideo's mind about everything. "You always knew this job involved some risks. Why are you pulling me out now? You're too afraid of seeing me hurt?"

"I'm too afraid of involving you in something far bigger than yourself, that you didn't even choose."

"This is what I *do*," I insist. "And I *know* what I'm *doing*."

"I'm not questioning your talent," Hideo responds, sounding annoyed now. He looks like he wants to say something more, but stops short and just shakes his head. "Right now, all I want to do is minimize any risks, to make sure no one will be harmed." He looks at me. "You've already done your job, Emika. You gave us enough information to know when his operations will happen, and you tracked down someone involved with his plans. It's enough for us to keep the audience safe. I've dismissed the other hunters, too. Let the police take it from here."

"But you still haven't *caught* Zero. That's not called finishing my job. So if you have a better explanation than that, I'd like to hear it."

"I've already given it to you."

"*No, you haven't.*"

"You want a better explanation?"

"Yes," I reply, my voice rising. "I think I deserve one."

Anger flashes hot in Hideo's eyes now. "I'm telling you to *leave*, Emika."

"I don't take orders from an ex-boss," I snap.

Hideo narrows his eyes. Suddenly, he leans forward, puts his hand on the back of my neck, and pulls me forward. He kisses me hard. My slew of words comes to a screeching stop. A knife cuts through my rising anger.

He pulls away, his breath short. I'm too startled to do anything except gasp for air. He leans his forehead against mine, then closes his eyes. "Leave." His voice is raspy, desperate, angry. "*Please.*"

"What aren't you telling me?" I murmur.

"I cannot, in good conscience, keep you on this job." His voice turns quieter. "If you don't believe any of my other reasons, at least believe this one."

Before all this, I used to sit on my bed and flip through article after article about Hideo, wondering what it might be like to meet him someday, to become as successful as him, to work with him and talk with him and *be* like him. But now Hideo is before me, exposing some fragile, inner working of his heart, and I'm sitting here and staring back, flustered and confused.

*Something is missing. Something he's not telling me.* Had Zero threatened him in some way, too? Had he threatened *me* in front of Hideo and prompted Hideo to pull me out of everything? I shake my head and hug my knees tighter. My mind spins.

He studies me for a moment. "You and your teammates will be moved somewhere safe. I'll see you after the tournaments are over." Then he stands up and leaves my bedside.

# 27

That night, I sleep poorly. The hospital bed doesn't fold quite right, and no matter what I do, I can't get comfortable on it. When I finally do drift off, old memories seep into my dreams, scenes from when I was eight years old, when my life was back in New York City.

I came home from school one day with my yearbook clutched in my arms. "Dad, it's here!" I shouted as I shut the door behind me. The school had let my third-grade class decorate the book's front cover that year, and I'd spent the entire past week painstakingly drawing in the elaborate swirls on the cover's corners.

It took me a second to realize that our home was in complete disarray—strips of watercolor paper everywhere, cut-up clothes in small piles on the floor, paintbrushes and buckets strewn across the dining room table. In one corner of the room was a haphazard dress Dad was working on, pinned to a bust in a dozen places. I threw down my backpack at the front door and looked on as Dad bustled past me, holding a few pins between his lips.

"Dad?" I said. When he didn't answer, I raised my voice. "Dad!"

"You're late." He flashed me a quick scowl as he settled back into his rhythm of work. "Help me get the snow peas out of the freezer to defrost."

"Sorry—I was finishing up my homework in the library. But look!" I held up the yearbook with a grin. "They're here."

I'd thought for sure that his eyes would jump immediately to the swirls on the cover, that he'd break into his familiar smile and hurry over to have a closer look. *Oh, Emi,* he'd say. *Look at your line work!*

Instead, he ignored me as he started pinning up another section of the dress. He was humming to himself, some melody I knew but couldn't quite place, and his hands trembled slightly as he worked. Was I in trouble? I ran through a list of possible things I could've done wrong, but came up empty.

"What are you making for dinner?" I asked, trying to coax him into a conversation as I placed the yearbook down on the kitchen counter. He didn't respond. I gathered up his paintbrushes scattered on the dining table and dropped them back into the brush jar with a clatter then wiped the table clean with a damp cloth. His laptop was open on the table, and I caught a glimpse of a site with numbers in bold red, along with images of dice and cards and a symbol I didn't yet know was a gang's sign.

It read, -$3,290.

"Dad?" I asked. "What's this?"

"It's nothing," he replied without turning around.

I didn't understand yet that it was a gambling site belonging to a criminal ring, but I did know what a minus sign in front of red numbers meant. I sighed loudly. "*Dad.* You said you're not supposed to be spending money like that."

"I know what I said."

"You said you'd stop."

"Emika."

I didn't catch the warning in his voice. "You promised," I insisted, louder now. "Now you're not going to have money again. *You said—*"

"*Stop* talking."

His voice cracked like a whip. I froze, my words withering on my tongue, my face turned up in shock at my father's expression. His eyes had finally found mine, and the light in them shone feverish with fury, red from crying. In a flash, I knew what had happened. There was only one thing that could turn my father from a gentle, lighthearted man into someone angry and cruel.

*He'd heard from my mother.*

Already, the furious light had started to ebb from his face. "I didn't mean that," he said, shaking his head as if confused. "Emi—"

But my own anger had risen now. Before Dad could say anything else, I took a step away and tightened my lips. "She messaged you, didn't she? What'd she say to you this time? That she misses you?"

"*Emika.*" He reached for my arm, but I'd already twisted away and was hurrying toward my room. A high-pitched ringing echoed in my ears. The last thing I saw before I slammed my door was the sight of my father standing there before his half creation, alone, shoulders sloped, his figure turned in my direction. Then I crawled onto my bed and began to cry.

Hours passed. Later that night, my door creaked open an inch and I saw my father peek in, holding a plate piled high with pizza. "May I?" he said quietly.

I glared at him from under my blankets as he came in and shut the door behind him. Dark circles rimmed his eyes. For the first time, I realized how exhausted he looked, that he must not have slept well for days. He sat down on the edge of my bed and held the plate out at me. I wanted to be stubborn, to stay mad, but my stomach growled at the smell of tomato and melted cheese, and I dragged myself into a sitting position and reached for a slice.

"Your yearbook looks stunning, Emi," he said after I'd wolfed down a slice. He gave me a weary smile. "I can tell how hard you worked on it."

I shrugged, still not ready to let him off the hook, and grabbed a second slice of pizza. "So what happened to you today?" I grumbled.

He stayed silent for a long moment.

"What did she want this time?" I asked. But I already knew. Every six months or so, my mother would contact him because she missed him, only to disappear again. She never mentioned me. Not once.

When I asked again, Dad finally took out his phone. He held it out to me without saying anything. I peered down at it.

My mother had sent him a photo of her hand. On her finger was a large diamond ring, cut into a brilliant square.

I looked back up at my father's tired eyes.

*She was so beautiful.* But beauty can make people forgive a thousand cruelties.

We sat for a while without saying a word. Then I touched Dad's hand quietly with my own. He looked down, away from me, ashamed to meet my eyes. "I'm sorry, Emi," he said in a small voice. "I'm so sorry. I'm a fool."

I just shook my head. And when I wrapped my arms around his neck, he held me tight, trying to piece back together the lives she'd left behind.

●●●●●

I STIR FROM my dream, my hands clenched into fists. The time on my phone reads 3:34 a.m., and the TV in my room is still on, cycling through the news.

I lie still in the silence. It takes a long time before I finally relax my hands and let myself sink back against the bed. I watch the news without paying much attention to it. The reporter has already started discussing the Wardraft runners-up wild cards who will replace me and Ren.

"—Brennar Lyons, Level 72, a wild card from Scotland who will now represent the Phoenix Riders as their new Architect. And Jackie Nguyen, a Fighter—"

The reporter's voice fades into indecipherable noise as my thoughts turn to my teammates. What are they thinking now? The public explanation for Ren leaving was that he had been caught gambling. The explanation for me was that I'd received death threats for news about my relationship with Hideo going public.

*Hideo.* His declaration replays in my mind, as surely and sharply as if I had recorded it as a Memory.

My eyes wander to the box Roshan and Hammie had given me before they left, and I reach for it again, opening it to run my fingers against the broken ornament shards and scraps of canvas. My heart rate still feels elevated; my chest, still pained.

I punch my fist down against the bed. Zero is going to get

away with everything. My thoughts run through all that we'd managed to uncover so far. Coordinates of all the major cities where Warcross tournaments were going to be held. Disrupted patches inside each Warcross world in the championships. A file that had self-destructed; an assassination attempt. And a soundtrack Ren had created, potentially to be played during the final Warcross game.

So many pieces. I repeat them in my head until the news cycle on the TV has finished and starts all over again.

Then, a new message appears in my view.

My thoughts scatter for a moment, and I glance at the note to read it. How did this message get through? It's not from someone I've approved. In fact, there's no tag on it at all. I hesitate—and then I reach out to tap it.

**For you, from one hunter to another.**

That's all it says. I let out a breath I didn't know I was holding. *From another hunter?* Somehow, one of the other bounty hunters had found a way to hack through my own shields. They know who I am.

My head jerks up to the security cam in one corner of my room's ceiling, wondering if they are hacking it to watch me, and then my attention goes back to the message. It has an *Accept Invite?* button attached to it. I sit up straighter. Then, with trembling fingers, I decide to accept.

A virtual figure materializes a few feet away, his hands and arms hidden behind armguards and gloves. His blue eyes are stunningly bright. A jolt hits me as I see his face.

It's Tremaine.

He raises an eyebrow when he sees my shocked expression.

"Hello, Peach," he says, a sneer spreading on his face. "What an honor."

"I—" I start, then stutter to a halt. "You're one of Hideo's other hunters?"

He offers me a mock bow. "I looked just as surprised when I found out about *you*."

"How did you get a message through my shields?"

"You're not the only one with a few tricks up your sleeve."

"Why are you contacting me? Why are you showing your face?"

"Relax, Emika. I found something that you might be interested in." Before I can ask him what it is, he reaches up and makes a swiping motion with his hand. A file materializes between us, hovering in the air like a glowing blue cube.

"You have the other piece of this file," he says.

I frown at the glowing cube for a second before I realize that I'm looking at another piece of *proj_ice_HT1.0*. The same file that I grabbed from Ren before Hideo's attempted assassination. "How do I know you're not just trying to give me a virus?"

He actually looks offended at my question. "You don't think I could find a subtler way of doing that? I'm trying to help you, you idiot."

I scowl, my teeth clenching. "Why? We're supposed to be rivals."

He smiles again, touches two fingers casually to his brow, and salutes me. "Not if Hideo already dropped both of us from the job. I've received a compensation payment already, so there's not much incentive for me to stay on this hunt. I have bigger hired jobs to concentrate on right now." He tilts his head at me. "But I bet *you're* still keen on protecting Hideo, aren't you?"

I blush, annoyed.

He nods at the hovering file. "Thought I might as well pass along what I've collected. A gift from one hunter to another. That way, if you find Zero, you'll know who's responsible for your win."

I shake my head, still unwilling to touch the file. "I don't trust you."

"And I don't like you either. But we don't have time for that right now, do we?"

We eye each other for another beat before I finally reach out and accept the file. For a moment, I expect something in my view to go horribly wrong, like I've just downloaded a virus. But nothing happens. The file seems clean.

Maybe he's being genuine, after all.

I look back at Tremaine. "You helped Roshan get Ash out of our building."

At that, his expression wavers. I wonder if his change of heart had anything to do with that moment—if he, as another hunter, also understands what had really happened.

Tremaine shrugs and turns away. "Just tell Roshan I stopped by," he mutters. Before I can say anything else to him, he vanishes, leaving me alone again in the room, staring numbly at the spot where his virtual form had just been.

How is this possible? I think back to the opening ceremony party, when I'd confronted him and Max Martin, when he'd sneered at me. His data had looked perfectly normal, disguised to be indistinguishable from an average player's—I hadn't even seen any shields installed to protect his info. He had probably set up an entire, elaborate system of false info to throw off anyone who tried to get to him. He'd likely been studying me, too. He'd been right in front of me, and I'd missed him entirely. *You tricky bastard*, I think.

. I squint at the file, trying to make sense of it. It's clearly garbled, just like the piece that I have.

My eyes dart back to the contents in my box.

My Christmas ornament and Dad's painting had been destroyed, but just because they were destroyed doesn't mean some traces of them, however small and broken, weren't left behind. And if there are enough pieces, you can see what the original object was supposed to be.

I bring up a main menu and tap my fingers rapidly against my thighs. A scrolling list appears. I sift through it backward until I finally reach the day of our first Warcross tournament.

Then I pause.

proj_ice_HT1.0.

I tap on it. Sure enough, an error message pops up, telling me that the file no longer exists. But this time, I run a hack that forces the file to open, regardless. The hospital room around me disappears, and I am immersed in a field of mangled ghost code.

It is all nonsense, partially corrupted—just like the file Tremaine had sent. I pull up what he sent me, and then I run both files together, splicing them into one. Suddenly, there is just enough info for the file to open.

It is a Memory.

I am standing in someone else's recorded Memory, inside a massive, dimly lit space. A train station? Wherever it is, it's a real, physical location. Cobwebs adorn the air between archways, while thin shafts of light slice through the darkness to dot the floor below. People are gathered here in a loose circle, but they remain silent, their faces hidden in shadows. Others appear as virtual figures, as if they'd logged in from distant places to be here.

"The track's done," someone says. I startle, realizing that the words are coming from the person I'm watching this through. It's Ren's voice. *This is one of Ren's Memories.*

One of the figures in the darkness nods so slightly that I barely notice it. "Hooked up?" he says. His words come out as a whisper, but from the way the tunnel's archways curve at the ceiling, I can hear his words as clearly as if he stood right beside me.

My point of view—Ren—nods. "It'll play the instant the championship final's world loads."

"Show me."

The authority in the mystery figure's voice makes me freeze. This is Zero, in real life, flesh and blood.

Ren obliges. A second later, music is piping through my earphones, the familiar beat of his track. When it hits the chorus, he pauses it, then brings up a ream of glowing code for everyone to see. "This will start the countdown on the rigged Artifacts," he says.

I suck my breath in sharply. Rigged Artifacts? The teams in the finals will have rigged Artifacts?

Rigged to do what?

"Good," Zero says. He looks around the room at each person in turn. As he does, they each bring up a hovering copy of an assignment, syncing with one another and checking their progress. In my view, Ren brings up a copy of it, too. My eyes widen as I read it. This is what I've been looking for.

It details what Zero is going to do.

During the final game, Zero is going to switch out the Artifacts and replace them with rigged ones. Corrupted ones. Ones containing a virus on them that will sweep through to every active NeuroLink user.

It's why Zero had been gathering so much data inside each of the Warcross worlds. Why he was assigning locations to his followers. They're making sure the virus will trigger in each location, that no security shields can stop them.

My breaths come short and quick now, my eyes darting frantically across the text. What will the virus do? Destroy the NeuroLink? What does he *want* from destroying it? What will it do to people who are logged on during the final tournament? *The final tournament.* It's no coincidence that he chose this time to unleash a virus. The maximum number of NeuroLink users will be online around the world at the height of this final game.

Why would Zero, someone clearly skilled in technology, want to destroy this technology?

In the Memory, Ren speaks up again. "One more you should check," he's saying. "Emika Chen. The other wild card."

Zero turns to him. "You've found something?"

"She's connected to Hideo outside of the tournament, in more ways than one. She's sniffing out your trail. If she finds something significant and alerts him to it, he'll find a way to stop all this."

A chill sweeps through me at his words. Ren had found me first; he had alerted Zero to me, possibly even at the same time that I'd alerted Hideo to *him*.

"I'll look into her." Zero's voice is calm. "We'll be watching their comings and goings, and if she tries to alert him, I will know. We can always make this a double assassination."

The Memory ends. It fades around me until I'm back in my hospital room. I sit there with my heart pounding, head whirling, feeling more alone than ever.

A *double assassination.* This meeting must have happened

before the first attempt on Hideo's life—I'd shared information with him, and in return, they'd tried to kill him. Then Zero had appeared to me, warning me to stay out of it, offering for me to join him instead. *The house bombing.* Zero has no qualms about coming after me, too.

Instinctively, I reach to connect with Hideo.

I should send all of this to him right now—tell him everything about Zero's planned virus, the rigged Artifacts. But if I contact him, Zero might know. And if he sees Hideo do something about the final game to stop this plan, then Zero will definitely know that I've been communicating with Hideo. He might change their plan, and then everything I've already discovered will be useless.

I have to stop this without tipping off Zero, without Hideo's involvement. And that means I have to find my way into the final game and stop Zero from planting those rigged Artifacts.

I let out a long, shaky breath.

Maybe I *am* in over my head. And a small, scared part of my mind reminds me that, if I just *stop* right now, just leave like Hideo had insisted I do, Zero might return my Memories to me.

But I can't stand the thought of leaving. If I do, what will happen? My gaze now returns to the box sitting at my side. All I can concentrate on are the shattered remains of my precious things. All I can linger on is the thought of Zero hidden behind his insufferable mask, frustratingly opaque, telling me what to do. My temper stirs, and my fists tighten.

Hideo wants me off the official games and the hunt. Zero has warned me to stay away. But I've never been good at following instructions. I'm a bounty hunter. And if my bounty's still out there somewhere, I have to finish this.

I get out of bed, walk to the corner of the room underneath

the security cam, reach up, and yank its wires out. It goes dark. Then I call Roshan and Hammie. When they answer, my voice comes out as a hush.

"Ready to hear the truth?" I say.

"Ready," Roshan replies.

"Good. Because I could really use some help."

# 28

Common sense would tell me that this is absolutely the worst possible time to log back in to the Dark World. I almost died in an explosion, I'm no longer on the job, and a hacker and his crew are after me, turning me from the hunter into the bounty, ready to take me out the instant I show some sign of continuing on their trail. There might even be assassins after me by now—I'm probably on the assassination lottery list in the Pirate's Den.

But I'm out of time.

Now my virtual boots slosh through puddles in the Silk Road's potholes as I pass street after street of neon-red signs, all listing the names and info of people who have been exposed in the Dark World. There is more traffic in this section of the Silk Road, a jumble of anonymous users crowding into alleys and in front of doorways, creating the sense of a night market. Wayward strings of lightbulbs hang overhead, beyond which I can see the mirrored, upside-down version of the city hanging down toward us from the sky.

I glance warily at the stalls I pass. Some sell virtual Warcross items laid neatly out on tables, everything from gold rings to glittering capes, leather boots and platinum armor, healing elixirs and treasure chests. Others sell illegal, real-world items. One offers outlawed guns and bullets, promising overnight delivery for cases of thirty and up. Another sells drugs—the stall is set up as professionally as any online shopping site, where you add grams of cocaine and meth to your shopping cart, get the packages delivered to your doorstep two days later, and leave customer reviews for the vendor without ever endangering your identity. A third stall hawks diet pills not approved by health departments, while another offers discounts to watch a famous Dark World girl's R-rated livestream. I grimace and look away. There are stalls for stolen artwork, poached ivory, currency exchange between virtual notes and bitcoins and Japanese yen, and, of course, gambling on both Warcross and Darkcross games.

I see bets being cast right now for the final tournament—and the amounts are astronomical. A number hovers over each stall, telling me how many people are currently considering purchases at that vendor. The number over the betting stall says 10,254. Ten thousand people making bets at this one little gambling stall alone. I can only imagine how many bets people are casting right now in larger gambling shops like the Pirate's Den. It's another reminder of how many people will be on the NeuroLink during the final game, and it makes me move faster.

I stop at a currency stall to exchange a huge chunk of my money for notes. Even now, converting this much money physically hurts—what I wouldn't have given just a few months ago to hang on to this much for the rest of my life. But I trade it anyway, looking on as the numbers in my view change from one type to another. Then I continue on. Finally, I reach the intersection of the Silk Road and Big Top Alley. When I look down the alley, I see the vendor I'm looking for: the Emerald Emporium, home to expensive, valuable, and very, very rare power-ups.

The outside looks like an enormous circus tent, painted with broad black-and-gold stripes that glitter under the strings of lights. The flaps of the tent's entrance curve to both sides, revealing a yawning, pitch-black hole into which a velvet carpet extends. An immediate, instinctive fear hits the back of my stomach at the sight. Dad and I had once gone hiking in the woods at midnight, and when we had to walk through the black space of a gnarled tree trunk, I'd nearly had a panic attack. Everything in darkness looks like fragments of monsters. The entrance to this circus triggers the same sort of fear—stepping into the black unknown, beyond which is something dangerous. In fact, this intimidating entrance is all part of the vendor's security shell, to deter window-shoppers. If you're too scared to enter, then you're probably too scared to make purchases.

A pair of twins on stilts stand on either side of the entrance. They lean down toward me as I approach, their faces painted white and their eyes completely black. "Password," they say in unison, their frowns identical. At the same time, a transparent, hovering box appears in the center of my vision.

I type in the password for today, a string of thirty-five jumbled letters, numbers, and symbols. The twins consider for a moment—and then move aside, silently holding out their long arms for me to enter the Emporium. I take a deep breath and step forward.

Inside is completely black. I continue walking, counting my

steps out carefully. When I finish taking ten steps, I stop and turn to my right. I take eight more. Stop, turn left. Fifteen steps. I continue walking in a long, elaborate combination like this until I finally take twenty steps forward and stop completely. For users who don't know how to get past this second security shell, they'll get trapped entirely in the darkness. It'll then take them weeks to reclaim their lost avatar and account.

I reach out and knock. To my relief, a *rap-rap-rap* sounds out as I do so, as if I were knocking on wood. A gate slides up, and I enter the enormous belly of a circus, the space lit up with hundreds of dangling bulbs.

Shelves and pedestals are everywhere, displaying glass jars inside which are power-ups of all kinds—scarlet gems and white marbles, rainbow-hued balls of fuzz and blue-striped cubes, black-and-white-checkered spheres, and clear, soap-like bubbles. Some of these power-ups have only been seen once in games, never to be offered again, while others are prototypes, still in development at Henka Games but yet somehow now in the hands of hackers who are selling them here. Over each one hovers its name in gold letters, along with its starting bid price. **Sudden Death: ₦46,550. Alien Attack: ₦150,000.**

Clusters of anonymous avatars gather in front of the rare ones, chattering excitedly. Security bots glide around the floor, looking like ladies with mechanical jaws and long-nosed masks and black parasols. I study their movements. There is always a pattern to the way they move, however randomly. A shopping cart icon floats in my view now, as well as a field that I can type an amount into. I look around, admiring each of the glass jars on display, before I finally find one on a pedestal, inside which is a marble that looks like a frozen crystal ball, its surface adorned with beautiful feathers of frost.

Team Freeze: N 201,000. This will, according to the accompanying description above it, immobilize the entire enemy team for five full seconds.

The people gathered around this glass jar all have auction paddles, and I realize that an auction is happening for it right now. I join in, accepting a paddle from a nearby security-bot lady. There are five bots patrolling this auction now, two of them drifting over from an auction that had finished moments earlier. Standing next to the glass jar is a little girl, the auctioneer, wearing a top hat nearly as tall as herself. "Two hundred and fifty-one thousand notes!" she says at a loud, rapid clip. "Do I hear two fifty-two?" Someone raises their paddle. "Two fifty-two! Do I hear two fifty-three?"

The bidding goes on and on, until it narrows down to a battle between two users. I watch them carefully. The highest bid is now 295,000 notes, and the second user is hesitating on raising the bid to 300,000. The little girl continues to shout out the number, waiting for someone to take it. No one does. The highest-bidding avatar straightens, puffing his chest out in excitement.

"No one for three hundred thousand?" the little girl says, looking around. "Two ninety-five going once, going twice—"

I raise my paddle and call out, "Four hundred."

All eyes whirl to me in shock. Murmurs ripple through the crowd. The little girl points at me and smiles. "Four hundred!" she exclaims. "Now we're flying! Do I hear four hundred and one?" She looks around the tent, but no one budges. The other avatar glares at me with a look of murder, but I'm careful not to stare back.

"Sold!" The little girl claps in my direction. My shopping cart icon suddenly updates, the number 1 now showing, and my number of notes drops by 400,000. At the same time, the Team Freeze power-up vanishes from the glass jar on the pedestal, and the other avatars start to wander off, muttering. The losing bidder lingers, though, his eyes still on me—as are the eyes of the security bots.

I thank the auctioneer, then go to look at the rest of the jars. I can still afford to spend another million notes, and I need to gather as much help as I can get.

I join a second auction happening for a power-up that looks like a round, growling, fuzzy black creature with two large paws. Artifact King. If your enemy's Artifact is within your line of sight, then using this power-up will automatically teleport that Artifact straight into your hands, instantly winning your team the game.

This time, the starting bid is 500,000 notes.

Again, the auctioneer calls out the rapidly rising bids. Again, it boils down to a few active bidders. I'm one of them. The bid rises to 720,000 as I face off against one other opponent, and yet still, he won't back down. Finally, in frustration, I throw down an amount that I know is much more than the power-up is worth.

"*Sold*—for eight eighty!" the auctioneer exclaims. 880,000 notes.

I wince at the dent this makes in my funds, then check my backpack to make sure both items are properly stored. In real life, I run a scan to see if anyone is trying to break into my inventory. Rich users will sometimes come in here and clear out several big items. Other users will then lie in wait until the rich user has turned his back, then hack into his inventory and steal those power-ups. A couple of avatars have already turned their attention to me after my two purchases, and their interest makes the hairs rise on the back of my neck.

I have less than 200,000 notes left, which won't buy me anything big enough to be worth using in the final game. So instead I look around, wondering who I might be able to target in order to steal myself one more valuable power-up. Finally, I settle on an auction happening for an item that makes me light up. I've never even heard of this one before—leading me to believe it has to be a prototype or even an illegal, user-created item.

Play God: ₦751,000. 14 Bids.

This power-up gives you the temporary power to manipulate anything and everything in a Warcross level. Perfect.

The auction is almost done, having narrowed to two users, but this time I stand by as an onlooker, watching behind the security bots as the price continues to climb. Eventually, it tapers off, stuck on nearly a million notes as one of the users hesitates.

"Do I hear a million?" the auctioneer shouts. "An even million? No?" He counts down—and when it looks like no one else will take it, he points out the winner. "*Sold*, for nine ninety!"

The winning bidder is a tall man wearing a plaid coat. As he pockets the power-up and turns away, I edge my way closer without drawing the attention of the security bots. In real life, I'm typing furiously, trying to find a moment when the man is alone and vulnerable. The security bots continue their randomized rotations; some of the assets being used to guard this auction now drift off to patrol another one that has just started.

At last, I see my window—a gap where two security bots have turned away and left a narrow, clear path to the man. I head toward him, increasing my pace as I draw closer. Then, right as he's about to turn around, I lunge forward and grab for his suitcase.

An ordinary avatar wouldn't have nearly the strength to do such a thing. But I've built up years of code on my avatar, programming myself for just this kind of grab. So when my hand closes on his suitcase's handle, I twist hard—and the suitcase comes away in my grasp.

The man's no fool, though. No one who spends a million notes on a power-up can be. Instantly, two other avatars near us whirl on me. He has hidden security of his own here. I twirl barely out of their reach before I make a beeline for the exit. If I can get back inside the black tunnel, where the security bots can't go, I can make it out of here with my items intact.

One of the avatars whips out a dagger and lunges, ready to tear through me. I sidestep, but the second avatar catches me by the leg and yanks me off balance. The world topples around me, and I'm suddenly staring at the room from the floor. I kick out—at the same time, I type frantically. But nothing I can do right now will increase my security beyond what it already is; there's simply no time. Around us, the security bots have noticed the scuffle and gather instantaneously near the entrance, sealing the tent in. Others rush to me, the mechanical women's eyes flashing, their black parasols spinning like razor-sharp blades. Their hands clamp down on my arms. I kick out as the man bends down to grab the suitcase's handle. His two helpers seize my backpack.

Suddenly, one of the security bots holding me slashes out at the man with the edge of her parasol. I yelp as it slices clean through his arm. They are pixels, of course—but the man still falls backward, his left hand now cut off from the rest of the space, useless. I look at the bot in surprise, but it ignores me and attacks the other two avatars before turning on the other bots.

"*Go, Em!*" it shouts at me.

My heart leaps. It's not a bot at all. It's Roshan's voice.

I scramble to my feet and hurtle toward the exit. Another bot covers my escape—it's Hammie. Then, a third. *Asher!* Their protection throws off the attacks from the others, which don't seem ready to counterattack several of their own. I slip between two security bots that have rushed into the fray but are still unsure how to handle the hijacked bots. Then I'm at the entrance, and the sounds of everything behind me fade away.

I follow the number of steps and turns out of the entrance, and then burst through the front tent flaps to find myself deposited back in the narrow alley. The twins standing at the entrance don't pay attention to me. Hastily, I bring up a dialog and log myself out of the Dark World. Everything around me turns black—and an instant later, I'm back in my virtual personal room.

I still have the suitcase. I still have my backpack. My items are here.

I set to work unlocking the suitcase. I can't hang on to it for much longer without attracting more suspicion. After several attempts, the suitcase finally pops open. Inside is the Play God power-up, blue and beautiful, its swirling clouds smudging underneath my fingertips.

I stare, heart pounding. I carefully stash each of my three new power-ups into my inventory, locked up behind multiple shells. Then I wait in my virtual room, sending out pings and invites every few seconds to the accounts of my teammates.

For a while, no one appears. Had it locked them out of everything? Were they caught?

Roshan materializes, followed by Hammie. Then, at last, Asher. They no longer look like security bots—they've thrown off the shell now. I break into a smile. I've never worked with anyone else on a hunt before—but now, with my teammates on my side, it seems that much easier.

Asher speaks first. "Well?" He peers at me with a raised eyebrow. "I hope you got something useful after all that trouble."

I nod, then bring up my inventory to show them what I have.

Asher's eyes widen, while Roshan mutters a swear. "Tremaine had better be telling the truth about the file he sent you," he says.

"Truth or not," Hammie adds, "the final will be an interesting one with these in the mix."

"If these won't help us beat Zero," I say, "then nothing will."

# 29

With all the scandals happening, the final between Team Phoenix Riders and Team Andromeda is already poised to be the most widely watched game in Warcross history. The news is reporting nothing today except for footage and reels about the games, each station frantically trying to outdo the next, channels in every language and country. It feels like the entire world has paused to tune in. Across Tokyo, shops and restaurants close as if it's a national holiday. People who can't log in easily at home now crowd into internet cafés and bars, their lenses on. The city is lit up with icons, the symbols clustering in the areas where the most people have gathered.

I step away from the window of my hotel room and go back to sit on the couch. I'm holed up in one of Tokyo's dozen downtowns, registered under a false name at this hotel. As far as I know, Hideo thinks I've headed back to New York. Since our conversation in the hospital, he has only sent me one message.

*Stay away, Emika. Please believe me.*

Now I stare at a transparent clock displayed near the center of my vision, counting down the time. Just a few short weeks ago, I'd accidentally glitched myself into the opening ceremony game for this year's tournaments. Now, there are only five minutes until the final game starts. Five minutes before I need to glitch myself into the game—only this time, I'm doing it on purpose. I double-check everything, making sure I've turned on my recording function. I'm storing today's game as a new Memory World in my account. If things go wrong in the game today because of Zero, at least I'll have a recording to study.

That is, if his virus doesn't hit me first.

Finally, words hover over my view.

## Warcross Championships VIII
### Final
### PHOENIX RIDERS vs ANDROMEDA

I take a deep breath. "Here we go," I murmur. Then I reach out, tap the words with a finger, and the world around me goes dark.

I hear the whistle of the wind before I see anything. Then, the world fades into view and I'm standing on a ledge, looking down into a perfectly circular lake surrounded on all sides by sheer metal walls hundreds of feet high. When I look behind me, I realize that there is nothing but open ocean on the other side of the walls.

In the center of the circular lake, ten steel bridges—none of them connected—extend out to the walls like a star. They each lead to a tall, metal hangar door embedded in the wall, spaced out evenly. Security bots stand on either side of each enormous door. As I watch, power-ups materialize over the steel walls and along the edge of the lake's waters, the colorful marbles lining the bridges both over and under. I double-check the power-ups in my own inventory. All there.

*Let's tear through Tokyo from zero to sixty / yeah, like we're running out of time in this city.*

The intro music playing all around us makes the hairs rise on the back of my neck. Ren's new track, to activate the rigged Artifacts.

*Let's go out with a bang / yeah, it's time to go out with a bang.*

It takes me a while to notice the roar of the audience's cheers thundering all around the landscape. The ever-present announcer voices come on, as excited as ever.

"Ladies and gentlemen," they declare. "Welcome to the Silver Circle!"

Down below, the players finally flicker into view. Each one appears standing on a bridge, near the center of the lake where they do not connect. The Andromedans are unmistakable in scarlet-red suits—their captain, Shahira, has her scarf pinned tightly back and her team's scarlet-ruby Artifact hanging over her head, while their Fighter, Ivo Erikkson, has his hair slicked back and a scowl on. My heart sits in my throat as my gaze turns to my teammates. Their suits are blue, a stark contrast against the steel walls around them. Asher (bearing the Riders' blue diamond Artifact over his head), Hammie, Roshan. Then, the two new additions. Jackie Nguyen, to replace Ren. And my replacement—Brennar Lyons, their new Architect.

**Ready?** It's Asher, contacting me through an encrypted channel I set up for him. His message shows up as transparent white text in the bottom of my view.

I nod, even though I'm not sure I am. **I hope so,** I reply. I bring up my inventory of precious power-ups.

**When I get in, pass me your Artifact.**

**Will do.**

Then I focus on Brennar and comb through his data. If I'm going to glitch myself into his place, I'd better make sure I can do it on my first try. What will happen today, if the Phoenix Riders don't win the game? What will happen if Zero triggers his plans?

The announcers are introducing the players now. I strip down Brennar's data, then make a frustrated sound. **I can't glitch in until the game gets going,** I say to Asher. **He's not activated yet.**

**I'll be watching,** he replies. **I'll warn you if I see anything.**

I take a deep breath and look back down at the scene. Each of the players stands at the edge of their bridge, looking down at the water below them, then glaring at one another. No one can reach the other—everyone is separated by a good fifty feet of space in the central gap. I can see Asher's lips moving, giving each of the Riders their instructions. My attention shifts to the enormous metal doors lining the inside of the circular steel wall. Red lights start to flash at the top of each door. What's kept inside? And where is Zero? My skin prickles in real life knowing that Zero is watching this game right now, perhaps watching it in the same way that I am. Waiting to disrupt it.

"Game! Set! Fight!" the announcer shouts. The invisible audience lets out a thunderous cheer.

At the same time, an earsplitting alarm goes off, echoing all across the world. It comes from the flashing red lights at the top of each of the ten steel doors. The players whirl around. Hammie is the first to start running toward her door along her bridge. I bring myself lower for a better view, until I'm hovering over the bridges.

The doors shudder in unison, then begin to pull up, the sound grating with their weight. Hammie's run turns into a sprint. She shouts something back at the other Riders. The Andromedans are making their way down their respective bridges, too, and as the doors rise farther, I get a glimpse of what's inside.

Metal legs, thick as buildings. Circular chrome joints, steel sinews. Then, as the doors rise higher, a barrel-like chest, each one different in design, with powerful arms hanging on either side. At the top, transparent glass lining the metal heads. My jaw drops as my gaze travels up. Ten mecha robots, each waiting to be boarded.

The waters in the lake and out in the open ocean churn furiously now, turning choppier as a storm approaches from the horizon, black and threatening. I double-tap on the area of my view where I can see Brennar running toward his mech. The world zooms in around me, and suddenly I'm directly above him, looking on as he approaches the steel door. He begins to climb the ladder along the side of the robot.

On the next bridge over, Hammie has reached the top of her mech and is now standing on its head. She searches for the entrance, finds it, pries something open—and hops in, disappearing from view. Seconds later, the inside of the mech's eyes light up, bathing the metal around them with a green glow. A whirring sound starts—like some kind of turbo jet engine—and rises to a fever pitch. Her mech stirs to life, the joints moving as fluidly as if Hammie *were* the robot. It lifts one leg. Then another. The bridge trembles from each step.

Asher reaches his mech second. As he enters the robot, his Artifact also vanishes from view. I let out a breath in disappointment. The same will probably happen with Shahira—meaning that if I want to use my Artifact King power-up to steal her Artifact,

I'll have to first get her out of the mech. Shahira hops into her robot a breath behind Asher, and then Franco, the Andromedans' Architect, follows suit. I look down at Brennar. He's almost there, but there's no question that he's slower than the others, having been yanked into the final tournament with no time at all to train. Even so—he wasn't chosen as a wild card for nothing. He reaches the top of his mech, hops in, and starts the robot. Its eyes power up, glowing bright blue.

I bring up a grid over Brennar and his mech, and data about them pours into a green, rotating block of code over my view. I have to time this correctly. If I do it wrong, I might glitch myself into the scene outside of Brennar altogether, and I could be exposed to the entire audience. Zero would know instantly where I am and what I'm doing. And once I'm in as an actual player, I'll have to move fast. In real life, Brennar will know right away when he's no longer able to control his avatar. He'll alert the security, and they will pause the game. They'll find me and shut me out.

"Shahira is moving to strike!" the announcer exclaims, and my attention whirls momentarily to where Shahira's mech is now running down the bridge toward the central gap. As she reaches the end of the bridge, her mech crouches down like a leopard ready to spring. Then, it gives a mighty leap into the air—and blade-like wings extend from either side of it, unfurling in a magnificent display. She launches into the air with a single swoop. As she goes, she grabs a speed power-up, and in a burst of temporary power, she leaps across the gap and onto the bridge where Asher's mech now stands. The bridge shakes from her impact, and the sound reverberates across the virtual space.

I type faster. I have to get into this game. As Brennar's mech steps forward, I bring up a lattice-like image of him inside it. Then I fly down as close as I can get to his mech. I hover right in front of the robot's eyes. Through them, I can see the outline of Brennar inside. *Ready*, I mouth to myself.

Then I type a command. For a split second, Brennar sees me hovering outside of his mech. He blinks in shock at the sight.

The world rushes around me, and when I open my eyes, I am *inside* the cockpit of the mech. More important, I'm inside of Brennar's body, with complete control over his avatar.

**Hey, Captain,** I say to Asher.

**Welcome back,** he replies. And a second later, he turns to face Hammie's mech, ready to pass her our Team's Artifact. She's ready for him, already anticipating his move. In a few strides, she's at his side, clasping her mech's metal hand with his. A flash of light illuminates them both for an instant, and then every player is alerted that our Artifact is now in Hammie's hands.

She doesn't waste a second. As Shahira barrels down on Asher, Hammie reaches for me. I take her mech's hand. Another flash of light—and our Artifact is now with me. The crowd roars in excitement.

I bring up my deactivation hack, take a deep breath, and run it on the Artifact in my hand. It takes a few seconds. For a moment, I think it won't work.

Then the Artifact sparks with electricity. A ream of garbled code appears in my view. The Artifact turns black. I run an analysis of it again—and smile when it doesn't respond. Deactivated.

Now the countdown starts. I have only a minute or two, at most, before Brennar alerts everyone of what happened to him and then security resets me out of the game. I don't know when, or if, Zero will know what I've done to our Artifact, but there's no time to dwell on it now. I return the deactivated Artifact to Hammie, who passes it back to Asher, and then I turn my attention to the inside of my mech.

The controls inside the mech are beautifully simple—designed for each of us to understand it instantaneously. There are weapons built into the arms and shoulders, and when I move my arms and legs, the robot moves its arms and legs. I search for Shahira. She has engaged Asher in locked combat in the air over the lake, while Franco is heading toward Asher too in an attempt to overwhelm him. Others are turning their attention to me.

I have to get Shahira out of her mech.

Team Freeze, to disable the enemy team. Artifact King, to steal Shahira's Artifact. And Play God, to permanently alter the landscape. I run forward with my mech along my bridge, look over at the scene, and get ready to activate my Freeze power-up.

"To your left!" Asher suddenly shouts at me. "He's shifted toward you—"

I startle and swing my mech's head around just in time to see Ivo Erikkson's flying mech barreling down on me, its jaws open as if to take a bite. All I have time to do is brace for impact.

He hurtles into me. Metal slams against metal as we both go tumbling off the bridge and into the lake. The impact jars me hard; for an instant, all I can see is a blur of water outside my glass view. *Use the power-up*, my instinct says, but I push it down. If I do it now, Shahira will fall into the water and sink, then reset on the bridge. Instead, I aim my arm directly at Ivo's head. Then I slam my fist down on a launch button.

A rocket fires at Ivo's mech, slamming his head backward. He releases me. My mech is suddenly floating free in the water. No time to waste. I reach for my Play God power-up and activate it.

The world suddenly stops, as if paused mid-frame in a movie. In my view, a transparent number now counts down the seconds I have to alter the landscape. My fingers fly. I pull myself out of the water and settle on a bridge—then yank the bridges together so that they close the gap in the center. Metal screeches as the bridges pop free from their columns. My gaze settles on where Shahira and Asher are still locked together in midair. I clap my hands together, then push them apart. Shahira's mech goes flying off Asher's, freeing him. At the same time, I bring her closer to me, forcing her mech to land on the now-connected bridge between us.

All around us, the audience's gasp echoes. The announcer's voice comes on, confused. "A power-up has been activated—we're not sure where Brennar got this from, but he has used an item that has never appeared in a game since the genesis of the tournaments! We are standing by for more info—"

The security knows something is wrong now. *Hideo* knows. And that means Zero probably knows, too. The timer runs out on my power-up. The world moves again. Shahira's mech crouches, shaking its head for a moment as it tries to reorient itself. I immediately activate my second power-up. Team Freeze.

Her mech freezes in its motions. All around us, the Andromedans freeze, too. Through Brennar's comm, Asher's voice comes on. "Go!" he shouts.

But I have no time to explain. I jump up from my seat inside my mech and grab hold of the cover over my head. I push it up. Rain lashes me, dotting my view, and I realize that the storm on the horizon has now reached us, one thing I hadn't changed during my control of the surroundings. I haul myself out of my mech. The other Phoenix Riders are circled around me, the backs of their mechs turned to protect me.

I crouch on top of my mech and turn my attention to Shahira's frozen one. Through its eyes, I can see her staring back at me, eyes wide, unable to move. I hop down onto the shoulder of my mech and break into a run along its extended arm. Overhead, the announcer's voice echoes above the storm. "Brennar has broken from the pack and used a second power-up! We are trying to figure out—"

They are going to stop the game at any moment now. I'm surprised they haven't stopped it already. What is Hideo doing? *Just concentrate.* I reach my mech's hand and take a flying leap onto Shahira's mech arm. The rain has turned the metal into a slippery slope—and I almost slide off during my landing. My arms grapple for support. I manage to scramble to my feet and continue sprinting up her arm. I climb up the side of the mech's head. As the audience breaks into a rumble of confusion and bewilderment, I yank open the hangar right as the Team Freeze runs out.

I look down through the opening at Shahira, who has just unfrozen enough to turn her head up at me. Her Artifact shines right over her head, scarlet red. I take out my third power-up. Artifact King.

I move to activate it.

But I can't. I blink, shocked. My limbs are frozen, head to toe, and I stand there with my power-up in my hand, unable to budge an inch. Below me, Shahira narrows her eyes and jumps up to pull herself out of the mech. She comes to stand in front of me. I realize through a haze that she has used a power-up on me, too, something that has rendered me frozen.

"I warned you, Emika," she says.

And, even though the words are in Shahira's voice, *I know.* I know that it is not her who is really talking to me.

It is Zero, inhabiting her body.

I struggle in vain as Shahira approaches me, her gait now having the same predatory grace as Zero's. Her ruby Artifact shines brightly above her head. *So close.* She circles me once, just as Zero had done in the Pirate's Den, and then she reaches out and takes my power-up.

*No!* I want to shout, but I can't. Shahira holds out the power-up to me as if we were clinking glasses. "Two can play at this," she says. She turns her back and starts running toward Asher's mech.

*Why isn't Hideo stopping the game?* Surely by now everyone can see that the game has gone wrong. As the audience roars with a cacophony of confusion, cheers, boos, and incredulous shouts, the power-up finally wears off on me. I stumble forward, gasping, then start sprinting after Shahira. Whatever happens, *I can't let her use the power-up on Asher.* I can't let her reactivate our Artifact. I have to deactivate hers. My hands grapple for the rope at my waist.

"Hey!"

All of our heads turn to see Hammie's mech hurtling toward us. She brings her legs down hard into the water, sending waves pummeling over the bridges. The hangar on her mech's head flies open, and out shoots Hammie in a blur of motion, suspended in the rain in a flying leap. She holds up a bright-green power-up she'd grabbed earlier. Then she flings it at Shahira.

An explosion lights up the end of my mech's arm, just shy of where Shahira is running. She skids to a halt, but the blast still throws Shahira off her feet and sends her flying through the air. On our other side, Franco's mech comes charging through the water, bent against the strengthening winds. "Hammie!" I shout, but it's too late. Franco grabs Hammie with one mech arm, closes the fist, and throws her. She goes flying through the air, landing with a splash in the churning open ocean beyond the wall. With his other hand, Franco catches Shahira and saves her from her fall.

Asher's mech is moving fast now, fist raised at Franco. I stop running for a second to duck down. I see Asher soar high over me, his mech's eye a distant scarlet dot high in the sky. He smashes hard into Franco's side—the impact knocks me to my knees. Water slams into me as the waves from Asher's landing pour over the ruined arm of my mech. I wipe water from my eyes and look up. Franco strikes back against Asher, each blow a deafening crunch of metal. In the midst of everything, I find Shahira. She is racing up Franco's arm toward Asher's mech. I run in her direction.

"Need a lift?" Roshan's voice comes on in my comms. I turn just long enough to see his fist come from nowhere, scooping me up and closing around me. His mech is flying, his metal blade wings beating so hard that they form a whirlpool in the lake's water. I soar through the air to where Franco and Asher are locked in a death grip.

Nearby, Ivo's mech comes hurtling toward us, aiming straight for Roshan. We're almost there. "Let me go!" I call to Roshan, banging my fist against the inside of his palm.

He does as I say and drops me. I fall toward Asher's shoulders. At the same time, Shahira reaches his opposite shoulder. We both climb. Rain lashes against me, threatening to hurl me into the water. I hang on as tightly as I can and try to climb faster. Franco lands another hit hard against Asher's chest, sending me careening wildly to one side, hanging on by only my arm. I force myself to swing back. *Keep going.*

I reach the top of the mech's head right as Shahira gets to her feet. She runs toward the head's cover. If she gets it open and sees Asher's Artifact, she can use the power-up on him, and we'll lose. I clench my jaw and force myself onto my feet. Then I sprint toward her. Everything seems to happen in slow motion.

Shahira pulls the head's cover open.

She raises her hand to use the power-up.

I reach her, throwing myself at her with every ounce of strength I have.

My hands close on the power-up. I yank it out of her—Zero's—grasp right as she is about to use it. *Do it, now.* I turn my view's focus on Shahira's Artifact. Before she can stop me, I aim the power-up at her and throw. Her eyes widen.

The power-up bursts into a ball of black smoke, engulfing both of us. Through the darkness, Shahira's ruby Artifact appears in my hand. My fingers close around it at the same time I run my deactivation hack. It sparks wildly, streaks of electricity whipping out from it in every direction. Then, a split second later, it turns black.

Mine. Game over.

The audience explodes into chaotic noise all around us. The sound is deafening, drowning out anything and everything. "It's *all* done!" the announcer's voice shouts over the noise, mired in confusion. "But hang on, folks, what happened in the arena today? This is an *unprecedented* hack of the final tournament! We are standing by for more—"

*It's all done.* I clench the Artifact like my life depends on it. *That's it. Is that it?* A choked laugh breaks out of me, and all the energy rushes out of my chest. Asher's voice has come on through my earpiece, and he's shouting something ecstatically, but I can't understand what he's saying. I can't concentrate on anything except the fact that the game is over.

Then, something strange happens.

A jolt of electricity sparks through me. Like a static shock. I jump. A unified gasp ripples through the audience, too, as if everyone had felt it at the exact same time. Numbers and data flicker over each of the players, in and out, then gone.

*What was that?* I stand there, blinking for an instant, unsure of what just happened. A feeling of dread hits me.

In front of me, Shahira's avatar vanishes, replaced by Zero, his dark armor and opaque helmet black under the stormy sky. He stares at me. "You triggered it," he says. His voice is low, furious.

"Triggered what? You're done!" I shout at him. "And so is your plan."

Something about my words seems to surprise Zero. "You don't know."

*Don't know? Know what?*

He straightens. "My plan," he says, "was to stop *Hideo*."

# 30

*What?*

I shake my head, not understanding. But before I can reply, Zero vanishes as the Silver Circle world around us freezes and fades into black. When I blink again, I'm back in my hotel room, and the games are done. I sit for a moment, startled by the silence. It's all over so suddenly. I'd done it—and even though I still haven't figured out who Zero is, I know that I've stopped his plans, whatever they happened to be.

*You don't know. My plan was to stop* Hideo.

What the hell is that supposed to mean? What don't I know? Something tugs at the back of my mind, a nagging little worry.

As if on cue, a message pops up in my view. It's Asher. I accept it, and his familiar face appears as if he's in the room with me, his expression elated. "Emi!" he exclaims. "You did it! We won!"

I manage a smile at him and mutter something back, but Zero's words run through my head.

> **Where are you?**

It's a message from Hideo.

"I'll call you back, Ash," I say, then end the call and type back to Hideo in a fog. If I can just see him in person, he'll be able to explain away what Zero had said. I'll tell him all about it, and he'll know what Zero was referring to.

Barely a half hour later, my door opens, and I look up to see Hideo walk into my room, flanked by his bodyguards. He shakes his head once at them, and they stop immediately in unison, obeying so quickly that it is as if they were programmed to do it. Then they turn and go outside, leaving us alone. I haven't seen Hideo in several days, not in person, and my heart leaps immediately in response to his presence. I hop to my feet. *He can explain what's going on.*

Hideo stops a foot away from me and gives me a strange, solemn frown. "I told you to leave."

Something in his gaze makes me pause. Zero's words come back to me, suspended in the air between us. "Zero was in the game," I say. "He'd rigged the Artifacts with a virus. He said something to me before he disappeared, that he was here to stop *your* plans." I frown. "I don't understand what he means."

Hideo stays silent.

"I mean," I go on, now afraid to stop talking, "I thought his plans were to trigger a destruction of the NeuroLink, maybe hurt everyone connected to it, but I didn't know *why* he wanted that." I stare at Hideo, suddenly dreading his answer. "Do you know?"

Hideo bows his head. His brows are furrowed, and everything about his posture screams of his reluctance to reply.

Zero can't be right, can he? What do I not know?

"What is he talking about?" I say, my voice soft now.

Hideo finally looks at me again. It is a haunted expression, the boy of curiosity and playfulness hidden now beneath a veil. It's the same seriousness I always see on his face, but this is the first time I feel a sense of foreboding from it, like it's more than just the expression of a quiet creator. After a while, he sighs and runs his hand through his hair. A familiar screen appears between us.

### Link with Hideo?

"Let me show you," he says.

I hesitate. Then I tap to accept the invite.

A trickle of Hideo's emotions opens to me as our Link establishes. He's wary, weighed down by something. But he's optimistic, too. Optimistic about what?

"We are always searching for a way to improve our lives with machines," Hideo says. "With data. For a while now, I've been working on developing the perfect artificial intelligence, an algorithm that, when implemented through the NeuroLink, can fix our flaws better than any human police force."

I frown at him. "'Fix our flaws'? What are you talking about?"

Hideo brings up a new screen between us with a subtle wave of his hand. It looks like an oval of colors, greens and blues, yellows and purples, all constantly shifting. "You're looking inside the mind of a NeuroLink user," he explains. Then he swipes again. The oval is replaced with another one, with its own shifting colors. "And another user." He swipes yet again. "And another."

I stare, incredulous. "These are all the minds of your users? You can see into their thoughts? Their *brains*?"

"I can do more than just *see*. The NeuroLink has always interfaced with the human brain," Hideo continues. "That is what makes its virtual reality so efficient and so realistic. That's what made the glasses special. You knew this. Until now, I used that interface as a one-way information system—the code simply created and displayed what your brain wished. You move your arm; the code moves your virtual arm. Your brain is the one in control." He gives me a pointed look. "But information travels both ways."

I struggle to comprehend the truth of what he's saying. *Hideo's invention uses the world's best 3-D effects generator—your own brain—to create for you the most incredible illusion of reality ever.*

The world's best brain–computer interface.

I shake my head, not wanting to believe his words. "What are you trying to say?"

Hideo looks at me for a long moment before he answers. "The end of the game," he says, "activated the NeuroLink's ability to control its users' minds."

The NeuroLink can control its users.

The realization hits me so hard and fast that I can barely breathe. Users are supposed to be able to control the NeuroLink with their minds. But that can also be used the other way—type in a command and use that to tell the brain what to do. Type in enough commands, and the brain can be permanently controlled. And Hideo has created an entire algorithm to do this.

I take a step back, steadying myself against the side table. "You are controlling how people think," I say, ". . . with *code*?"

"Those Warcross lenses were free," Hideo reminds me. "They have been shipped to nearly every person in the world, in almost every corner of the globe."

The news stories of long lines, of shipments of stolen lenses. Now I understand why Hideo wasn't worried about stolen shipments. The more given out, the better.

Hideo brings up another image of the inside of a user's mind. This time, the oval's colors look deep red and purple. "The NeuroLink can tell when a user's emotions shift to anger," he says. "It can tell when they are plotting something violent, and it knows this with incredible accuracy." He shifts our view to the actual person behind this specific mind. It's a person struggling to pull a handgun out of his coat, his forehead matted with sweat as he prepares to hold up a convenience store.

"Is this happening right now?" I manage to say.

Hideo nods once. "Downtown Los Angeles."

Right as the person reaches the convenience store entrance, the dark red oval representing his mind suddenly flares, flashing bright. As I look on, the NeuroLink's new algorithm resets the colors. The deep scarlet turns into a mild mix of blues, greens, and yellow. On the live view, the man freezes. He stops pulling out his gun. There is a strange blankness on his face that sends a shiver through me. Then, as his face calms, he blinks out of it, exits, and moves on down the street, the convenience store forgotten.

Hideo shows me other videos, of events all happening simultaneously around the world. The color maps of billions of minds, all controlled by an algorithm.

"As time goes on," Hideo says, "the code will adapt to each person's mind. It will fine-tune itself, *improve* itself, adding to its automated responses every specific detail about what a person might do. It will turn itself into a perfect security system."

Judging from the footage, people don't even know what had hit them—and even if they had, the code will stop them from thinking about it now. "What if people don't want this? What if they just stop using the NeuroLink and their lenses?"

"Remember what I told you when I first gave you a set of them?"

I recall his words at the same time he says this. *The lenses leave behind a harmless film on the eye's surface that is only one atom thick. This film acts as a conduit between the lenses and your body.*

That lingering film on the eyes will keep someone connected to the NeuroLink, even when they take the lenses out.

I'd understood Zero's plans all wrong. He had wanted to destroy this with the virus in those rigged Artifacts. He had wanted to assassinate Hideo to stop him from moving forward. He had bombed our dorms in an attempt to keep me out of the games and from carrying out Hideo's final goal. And maybe *this* is why Hideo had not stopped the final game when he saw that things were going wrong. He'd wanted me to stop Zero so that I could trigger *his* plans.

*He's doing this because of Sasuke.* He created all of this so that no one would ever have to suffer the same fate as his brother, that no family would ever go through what his did. Our conversation comes back to me in a flash. *You created Warcross for him,* I'd said. And he'd responded, *Everything I do is for him.*

Does Kenn know about this plan? Was everyone always in on it?

"You can't," I finally say, hoarse.

My question doesn't stir him. "Why not?" Hideo asks.

"You can't be serious." I let out a single, desperate, humorless laugh. "You want to be a . . . *dictator*? You want to control everyone in the world?"

"Not me." Hideo gives me the same piercing stare that I remember from our first meeting. "What if the dictator is an algorithm? A code? What if that code can force the world to be a better place, can stop wars with a single breath of text, can save lives with an automated system? The algorithm doesn't have an ego. It doesn't lust after power. It is programmed solely to do right, to be fair. It is the same as the laws that govern our society—except it can also enforce that law immediately, everywhere, all the time."

"But you control the algorithm."

His eyes narrow slightly. "I do."

"No one chose you," I snap.

"And have people been so great at choosing their leaders?" he snaps back.

"But you can't do that! You're taking away something that makes us fundamentally human!"

Hideo steps closer. "And *what* is it that makes us human, exactly? The choice to kill and rape? To war and bomb and destroy? To kidnap children? To gun down the innocent? Is *that* the part of humanity that shouldn't be taken away? Has *democracy* been able to stop any of this? We already try to fight back with laws—but law enforcers cannot be everywhere at once. They cannot see everything. What if *I* can? I could have stopped the person who stole Sasuke—the NeuroLink can stop anyone who might do the same now to another child. I can make ninety percent of the population crime-free, allowing our law enforcement to focus only on the remaining ten percent."

"You mean you'll *control* ninety percent of the population."

"People can still live their lives, pursue their dreams, enjoy their fantasy worlds, do everything they've ever wished to do. I'm not standing in the way of any of that. They can do anything they want, as long as it is not a crime. Nothing in their lives changes except for this. So *why not?*"

Everything about Hideo's words seems contradictory, and

I find myself standing in the middle, not sure what to believe. I think of my own city, how I have a job as a bounty hunter because the police can no longer keep up with the rising crime in New York. I think of how the same has been happening everywhere. *They can do anything they want, as long as it is not a crime. Nothing in their lives changes except for this.*

Except for giving up their freedom. Except the thing that changes everything.

"It's an essential part of everyday life, the NeuroLink," Hideo says. "People work inside it and build businesses on top of it and are engulfed in the entertainment it offers. They *want* to use it."

And I realize that, of course, he's right. Why would anyone give up the perfect fantasy reality just because they have to give up their freedom? What's the point of freedom if you're just living in a miserable reality? It would be like telling everyone to quit using the internet. And even as my skin crawls at the knowledge that I've worn the NeuroLink lenses—*am* still wearing them—I still feel a sharp pang at the thought of never logging back into the Link, a reluctance to abandon them.

Even without the film against the eyes, people would never stop using it. They probably won't even believe that it's doing this to them. And even if they did start arguing with each other about the implications of the NeuroLink's manipulation, their lives now revolve around it. Anyone not logged in to the NeuroLink right now will use it before long, triggering this new algorithm the instant they do. Eventually, everyone will have this installed in their minds. And that will give Hideo control over each of them.

Maybe no one would even care.

"What about protestors?" I press. "What about fighting for what's right or making mistakes or even just respecting people who disagree with you? Is it going to stop people from passing laws that are unjust? What laws is it going to enforce, exactly?" I clench my fists. "How is your artificial intelligence capable of judging everyone in the world, or understanding *why* they do what they do? How do you know you won't go too far? You aren't going to bring about world peace all by yourself."

"Everyone pays lip service to world peace," Hideo says. "They use it as a pretty answer to pointless questions, to make themselves sound good." His eyes sear me to the core. "I'm tired of the horror in the world. So I will *force* it to end."

I think of the times, after my father's death, when I'd picked fights in school or shouted things I later regretted. I think of what I'd done to defend Annie Pattridge. Hideo's code would have stopped me. Would that have been good? Why does it feel like a knife twisting in my chest, to know that *this* is the reason why he flew me to Tokyo? *All those warnings from him for me to leave.*

"You lied to me," I say in a firm voice.

"I was not the one who attacked you." Hideo's eyes are soft and steady. "I was not the one who destroyed what was precious to you. There is real evil in the world, and I am not it."

Zero had destroyed the things that mattered most to me— my pieces of the past, my ornament and my father's painting. *My memories.* Hideo is the one who gave me a way to even store those memories, who saved me from being thrown into the streets, who mourns his brother and loves his family and creates beautiful things.

Zero uses violence to further his cause. Hideo furthers his by preventing violence. Some part of me, some crazy, calm part, sees sense in his plan, even as I recoil in disgust.

Hideo sighs and looks away. "When I first hired you, all I wanted to do was stop a hacker whom I knew was trying to stop *me*. I didn't know that . . ." He hesitates, then abandons the sentence. "I didn't want you to continue working for me without truly understanding the weight of what you were doing."

"Yeah, well, I did keep working for you. And you let me, without telling me why."

The times he had hesitated in my presence, reluctant to take us further. The moment when he'd decided to let me go. My removal from the Phoenix Riders' team. He had been trying, in his own way, to go about his plans alone. The lenses I'm wearing feel cold, as if they were something foreign and hostile. I think about the hacked version of Warcross that I use. Am I safe?

Hideo leans close enough for our lips to touch. The part of me that is made of raw instinct stirs, wanting desperately to close that distance between us. His eyes are so dark now, almost black, his expression haunted. *Every problem has a solution, doesn't it? I want to prove to you the sense in my plans.* His brows furrow. *I can show you the good in this, if you'll let me. Please.*

And through the Link, I can sense his earnestness, his burning ambition to do right, his desire to prove it to me. When I search his gaze, I recognize that curious, passionate, intelligent man I'd first seen in his office, showing me his newest creation. This is the same person. *How* can this be the same person? His expression remains uncertain, unsure.

*Don't leave, Emika,* he says.

I swallow hard. When I respond, I respond with my real voice. It is calm now, even cold. "I can't support you in this."

I can almost feel his heart crack, stabbed right where he had risked opening it up to me, where he had let me see the beating wound inside. He had confided in me, thinking that perhaps I would be the one person who would side with him. Why wouldn't I, he must have thought—I understood his loss, and he had understood mine. We'd understood each other . . . or so we thought. He looks suddenly alone, vulnerable even in his determination.

"Emika," he says, in one last attempt to convince me.

I take a deep breath, then sever the Link between us. The subtle stream of his emotions cuts off abruptly. "I'm going to stop you, Hideo."

His eyes turn distant, those familiar walls going up until he's looking at me in the same way he had during our first meeting. He leans away from me. He studies my face, as if taking it in for the last time. "I don't want to be your enemy," he says quietly. "But I'm going to do this, with or without you."

I can feel my own heart breaking, but I stand firm. He does not give, and neither do I, so we continue to stand on opposite sides of a ravine. "Then you're going to have to do it alone."

# 31

The streets of Tokyo are still emptier than I've ever seen them. I tear down the road on my board, my hair streaming out behind me, the wind making my eyes water.

How complicated everything has become. Not long ago, I had been gliding through the crowded center of New York City, wanting nothing more than to make enough money to keep myself off the streets. Hideo had been a magazine cover then—a glimpse in a news article, a photo in a televised broadcast, a headline in a tabloid. Now he is someone I am struggling to understand, someone with a thousand different versions of himself that I am trying to piece together.

All around me, the only screaming headlines seem to be accusations that the final championship results were unfair, that the game was compromised by illegal power-ups. Fans are calling for a redo of the match. Conspiracy theories have already sprung up all over fan communities, claiming that some employee had planted the power-ups as a joke, or that Henka Games had wanted to raise their ratings, or that the players had somehow stumbled upon secrets hidden in the final world. If the truth were thrown in there, no one would be able to tell the difference.

Everyone else goes about their business without even realizing the subtle, significant shift in the NeuroLink that can now control their lives. And is anything different, really? Haven't we all been plugged in for years now, completely addicted to this world beyond reality? Are we this willing to give up? I force myself to look away as I pass a police car. Can Hideo come after me now, by simply telling the police to arrest me? Would he do that to me? When will his patience run out? When will he turn on me completely?

*I have to find a way to stop him first. Before he stops me.*

I have my old cracked phone out, my hack allowing me to track down the other Phoenix Riders without being subjected to the new NeuroLink algorithm. They have holed up in an apartment that I can only assume belongs to Asher, on the outskirts of the city.

An incoming message appears on my phone. It's from some encrypted, unknown source. Hideo, most likely. I force myself to ignore it, blinking moisture from my eyes as I push my board to its highest speeds along an empty stretch of highway.

As the sun starts to set, washing the city in shades of gold, I pull to a stop at a quiet intersection on the outskirts of Tokyo, where the city gives way to hills and sparse streets. I find myself staring at a gated, three-story townhome, simply decorated in dark and white wood.

Asher greets me at the door. He ushers me quickly inside, then leads me to his living room, where Hammie and Roshan have already gathered. They stand up at the sight of me. Hammie hugs me. A second later, I glimpse others on the couch, too, from some of the other teams. Ziggy Frost. Abeni Lea, from the Cloud Knights. Tremaine is here, as well, sitting noticeably apart from Roshan—but the two are turned toward each other, as if they were talking a moment ago. The tension between them that I'd always felt seems lessened now, if not completely gone.

"What do we do from here?" Hammie asks as we all settle. She's greeted by a long silence.

I sit down, too. "I run a hacked version of Warcross," I reply. "I don't think I'm affected in the same way. Maybe I can figure out a way for you guys to have it, too."

I tell them about what happened from the beginning, of Hideo hiring me after my first glitch, of my frequent meetings with him, of then realizing what had really happened when Zero appeared in the final game. I talk until the streetlamps are lit, and Asher has to turn on the living room's lights.

"I saw him glitch into view," I finish, "during the final moment when we all felt that static shock. It's the first time I've ever seen any data about him."

Tremaine looks at me. "You saw Zero, too? It wasn't just me?"

The others chime in. "I saw him," Asher adds. "He had an opaque helmet on and a [null] name over his head. Black body armor."

Hammie repeats the same, as does Roshan.

Everyone had seen Zero in that instant. That means that he had been exposed outside of my hack, that in that instant, all of his data had been exposed. *All of his data had been exposed.*

Suddenly, I straighten and begin to type. I bring up my Warcross account, then my Memory Worlds. There is one memory in there now, my Memory of the final game. "I need to see something," I mutter as the others gather around. I access the Memory, sharing it with the others so that they can see what I see. The world momentarily vanishes, putting me back into what I had recorded. I see the start of the game, and then the bridges, the robots emerging from their hangars, the battle that ensued. I fast-forward through all of it, all the way until the end. Then I let it play until the instant the electric shock had happened, when Zero suddenly stood in front of me. I pause it.

His data. I've recorded it.

*I can see his actual account.*

"Ems," Asher says beside me as he watches the Memory. "Can you actually find out who he is now?"

With trembling fingers, I scroll through Zero's personal account.

And sure enough, there it is. The trigger had exposed him, if only for a fraction of a second, but it's all the time I needed. I stare numbly at the account info that now displays before us, hovering in the center of the living room.

There is a name, a *real* name, floating alongside a photo of the real-life user who is Zero. I don't even need to read the name to know who it is. Staring back at me is someone who looks like a younger version of Hideo, a boy who resembles how Hideo looked several years ago. A boy my age. My eyes go back to the name, unable to believe what I'm seeing.

### Sasuke Tanaka

● ● ● ● ●

LATER THAT NIGHT, I leave the apartment to stand outside in the front yard. I need some air. The streetlamps outside of Asher's home cast a lattice of light on the sidewalks, and I decide to concentrate on that, forcing myself to clear my mind and find a moment of peace. Then I look up, searching for stars. There are only a few to be seen from here, scattered dots representing the rest of the Milky Way, invisible without a virtual overlay. I don't care. For once, it's comforting to be seeing the real world for what it is, instead of the enhanced version through the NeuroLink.

Sasuke. *Sasuke.*

Endless questions swirl in my mind. There is no way that Hideo knows about this. He would have mentioned it, if he did— he might even have stopped his plans. But how is this possible? Sasuke had vanished so many years ago, taken by a nameless kidnapper. Why has he reappeared as a hacker, trying to stop Hideo? Why hasn't he appeared to Hideo *himself,* to reveal who he really is? Does he even remember his past life—does he know that Hideo is his brother? Who controls him? Who does he work for? And why keep his identity a secret?

Is he even real?

I sit down on the curb and pull my knees up to my chin. What will this do to Hideo, once he finds out? *Would he stop, if he knew?* Do I even want him to stop? What is worse—a world where Hideo fights *against* violence, or a world where Zero fights *using* it?

I wonder what thoughts are going through Hideo's mind right now, and it takes all my willpower not to reach out and Link with him, to feel what he's feeling, to send him a message so that I can hear his voice.

A message. I look back down at my phone, remembering the encrypted note I'd received earlier in the afternoon. A small voice in the back of my head still urges me not to open it, not to indulge whatever it is that Hideo might be trying to convince me of. But my finger still hovers over the message, and after a long moment, I finally decide to open it.

It's not from Hideo. It's from Zero.

> **My offer to you still stands.**

A faint *ding* rings out, alerting me that I've just downloaded something into my account. My hand freezes over the new files.

They're my Memories. *My Memory Worlds.* I let out a small gasp as I see one after another, the Memories of my father that Zero had originally stolen, now blinking back into existence as if they had never gone missing in the first place.

He returned them.

My hand starts to tremble. Then I close my eyes and wrap my arms tightly around my legs, hugging them as if my life had been restored. When I open my eyes again, they are wet.

*My offer to you still stands.*

His offer. Why is he giving me back what he'd originally taken? How dare he pretend he's returning them as a gift, as if he's doing me some kind of favor? I picture his dark figure in that red cavern, his low, quiet voice. I picture the sheets of black armor encasing my arms and body and legs, turning me into someone else.

"Hey."

My thoughts scatter at the greeting. I hurriedly wipe my eyes and turn my head enough to see that Tremaine has come to stand beside me. "Hey," I mutter back, hiding my phone away. Tremaine notices my movement, but even though he casts me a brief, side-long glance, he doesn't comment on it. Enough secrets have been revealed today.

"I was contacted by another bounty hunter," he finally says, stretching his arms over his head. The streetlamps cast their light against his pale skin.

I meet his eyes. "One of Hideo's?"

He nods. "I think I crossed paths with him when I was down under. He was sitting up with the avatars watching the assassination lottery. If we work together, we can probably track our way to him, and he can help us. We're some of the only people in the world who both understand the inner workings of Warcross and also worked for Hideo at the same time."

Zero's message echoes in my thoughts. I turn away again and nod. "Then we'll go into the Dark World. We'll find a way to contact him. We can figure out a solution to this."

"To stop Hideo?" Tremaine asks. "Or Zero?"

I think of Hideo's intense gaze, his single-minded genius. I think of how he'd leaned his head weakly against me and whispered my name. I think of the way he looked up to the stars, searching for a way to move forward from his past. I think of the final words we'd exchanged. Then I think of Zero's surprised voice, his anger as he faced me in the final game, the way he'd stolen my Memories. The way he'd returned them.

*Everyone has a price*, he'd said. *Name yours.*

Tremaine offers me his hand, and after a while, I take it, letting him help me up. Then we continue to stand there, unmoving, looking out at the electric glitter of Tokyo, my boots pointed away from the house and toward the city, my heart suspended somewhere between one choice and another, unsure where to go next.

# Acknowledgments

——

All of my books have a bit of myself in them, but *Warcross* is particularly me-ish. (I mean, one of my corgis makes an appearance in it. That was his fat butt waddling down Hideo's hallway. Love you, Koa.) I could not have written this story, however, without the help of the best minds I know.

To my queen of an agent, Kristin Nelson—thank you for your enthusiasm for *Warcross* from day one, your brilliant outlines, ideas, and feedback, and all of your incredible work championing this book as well as all our past books. I truly don't know what I'd do without you.

To my inimitable, brilliant editors, Jen Besser and Kate Meltzer, for pushing me with every new round of edits and making sure this book was the best it could be. To Anne Heausler, copyediting genius—I just want to marvel at your brain. Thank you for everything.

This is my seventh book with the amazing team at Putnam,

Puffin, and Penguin Young Readers, and every time, I am more amazed and humbled by what you all do: Marisa Russell, Paul Crichton, Theresa Evangelista, Eileen Savage, Katherine Perkins, Rachel Cone-Gorham, Anna Jarzab, Laura Flavin, Carmela Iaria, Venessa Carson, Alexis B. Watts, Chelsea Fought, Eileen Kreit, Dana Leydig, Shanta Newlin, Elyse Marshall, Emily Romero, Erin Berger, Brianna Lockhart, and Kara Brammer. How did I get this lucky to work with you all? I still don't know, but I remain grateful every day. A special note of gratitude to Wes (Cream Design) for the spectacular 3-D *Warcross* cover art.

To Kassie Evashevski, my extraordinary film agent—it means so much to me that this book is with you. I am endlessly grateful. To Addison Duffy: How lovely to meet you in person! Thank you for always being so helpful and awesome.

To my darling, dearest, fiercest Amie Kaufman, Leigh Bardugo, Sabaa Tahir, and Kami Garcia: Thank you for listening to me talk about *Warcross* even in its infancy, for helping me shape this story, for your kind words about the book that always make me smile, and for your friendship and badass hearts.

To my wonderful friends who offered invaluable feedback: JJ (S. Jae-Jones), one of the first to ever read *Warcross*; Tahereh Mafi, for generously answering all of my questions (anything fashionable in this book is inspired by you!); Julie Zhuo, for your deep tech wisdom and insight, and for your friendship (twenty-eight years and counting!); Yulin and Yuki Zhuang, for showing me and Amie around Tokyo and knowing literally *everything* about the city, and for being two of the nicest people I've ever been fortunate enough to know; Mike Sellers, for your endless knowledge of all things and your generous help; Sum-yan Ng and David Baser, for brainstorming with me on late-night streets and offering so much helpful advice; and Adam Silvera, for all of your knowledge of New York City and for being an all-around badass. A special thanks to Ryh-Ming Poon for your industry insight (and love of good food!).

The Think Tank, the eight-intern group that I belonged to as a newbie working in video games, deserves its own callout: Those six months continue to be one of my favorite life memories. Pretty much everything I know about games, I learned from you guys. (Note—that Mario Kart round mentioned in the book, with the epic blue shell thrown right at the finish line? That was a real game we played. Savage.)

To my husband, fellow Think Tank ex-intern, and best human, Primo Gallanosa: Thank you for reading 120,582,015 versions of *Warcross*, for all your fun game ideas, and for always knowing exactly how to make me laugh.

To my mom, who is absolutely nothing like Emika's mom: Emika's resilience, fire, and brain are completely based on you. You are the most capable, selfless, and inspiring person I know. (Hideo's cooking skills are also based on yours. Obviously.)

To the librarians, teachers, booksellers, readers, and champions of books around the world: Thank you, thank you, thank you for all that you do. Sharing stories with you is my deepest honor.

Finally, to all the gamer girls out there. You inspired this.